WORDS IN PRAISE

"All the drama and sensuality expected of an historical romance, plus a sensitivity to the realities of life in a very different time and world . . ."

Ursula Le Guin

"Elisabeth Storrs gives us a complex heroine, grappling with issues of spirituality and culture in ways that are non-cliché and refreshing."

Elizabeth Jane, *Historical Novels Review*

"Storrs should be proud of herself for this gem of a book."

Ben Kane, author of *The Forgotten Legion*

"The fear of death but the zest to live—Elisabeth Storrs skillfully recreates the dilemma of a young woman torn between two of Italy's ancient cultures."

Isolde Martyn, author of *The Maiden and the Unicorn*

Runner-up 2012 Sharp Writ Book Awards for General Fiction

"WOW! I think this is the best book I've read in the SWBA. This book is a combination of a lesson on the life in early Roman and Etruscan society . . . gods and goddesses . . . cults and the impact they can have . . . and enough romance to make any woman's heart flutter without overdoing it so much that men won't want to finish the book."

Smart Writ Book Awards Judge

THE
WEDDING
SHROUD

ALSO BY ELISABETH STORRS

The Golden Dice
Call to Juno (to be published April 2016)

THE
WEDDING
SHROUD

— A Tale of Ancient Rome —

ELISABETH STORRS

LAKE UNION
PUBLISHING

Text copyright © 2015 Elisabeth Storrs
All rights reserved.

Published by Lake Union Publishing, Seattle

www.apub.com

Amazon, the Amazon logo, and Lake Union Publishing are trademarks of Amazon.com, Inc., or its affiliates.

ISBN-13: 9781477828557
ISBN-10: 1477828559

Cover design by Mumtaz Mustafa
Cover image © Elisabeth Storrs
Map © Elisabeth Storrs

Library of Congress Control Number: 2014919196

Printed in the United States of America

To David, Andrew, and Lucas

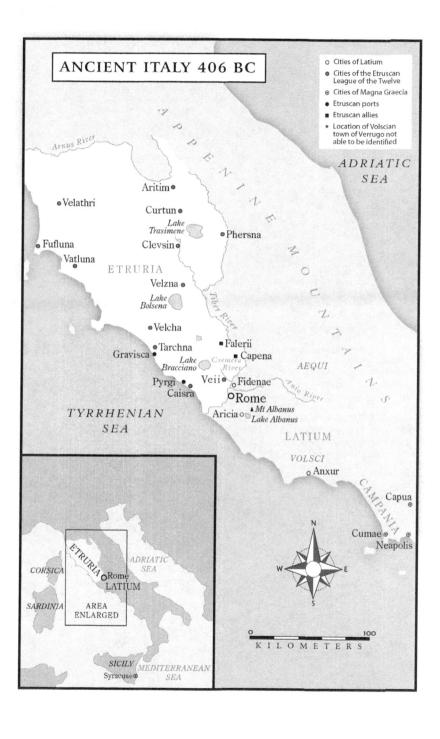

ANCIENT ITALY 406 BC

Cities of Latium
Cities of the Etruscan League of the Twelve
Cities of Magna Graecia
Etruscan ports
Etruscan allies
Location of Volscian town of Verrugo not able to be identified

ADRIATIC SEA

Arnus River

A P P E N I N E

Velathri

Aritim

Curtun

Lake Trasimene

Fufluna

Clevsin

Phersna

Vatluna

ETRURIA

Velzna

Lake Bolsena

M O U N T A I N S

Velcha

Tiber River

Tarchna

Falerii

Gravisca

Lake Bracciano

Capena

Cremera River

AEQUI

Pyrgi

Veii

Caisra

Fidenae

Anio River

Rome

TYRRHENIAN SEA

Aricia

Mt Albanus

Lake Albanus

LATIUM

VOLSCI

Anxur

CAMPANIA

Capua

Cumae

Neapolis

CORSICA

ETRURIA

Rome

LATIUM

ADRIATIC SEA

AREA ENLARGED

SARDINIA

N

W   E

S

SICILY

MEDITERRANEAN SEA

Syracuse

0   100

K I L O M E T E R S

CAST

Rome

Caecilia (Aemilia Caeciliana): A Roman bride (nicknames Cilla and Bellatrix)
Marcus Aemilius Mamercus Junior: Aemilius's son, Caecilia's cousin
Appius Claudius *Drusus:* Friend of Marcus, Caecilia's admirer
Marcus Furius *Camillus:* Roman commander and senator
Marcus *Aemilius* Mamercus: Caecilia's uncle and adopted father
Lucius Caecilius: Caecilia's father
Aurelia: Aemilius's wife
Aemilia: Caecilia's mother, Aemilius's sister

Veii

Vel *Mastarna:* Etruscan nobleman, Caecilia's husband
Artile Mastarna: Soothsayer, Mastarna's brother
Tarchon: Adopted son of Mastarna
Larthia Atelinas: Mastarna's mother
Cytheris: Caecilia's handmaid
Erene: Courtesan, Ulthes's mistress
Arruns: Mastarna's bodyguard
Seianta: Mastarna's first wife
Arnth *Ulthes:* Zilath of Veii, Mastarna's friend

Laris *Tulumnes:* Veientane councillor, Ulthes's opponent

Apercu: Veientane councillor

Vipinas: Veientane councillor

Pesna: Veientane councillor allied to Tulumnes

Aricia: Cytheris's daughter

Velia: Daughter of Mastarna and Seianta

Aule Porsenna: Zilath of Tarchna, Mastarna's father-in-law

Italicized names are used more commonly than full titles.

The Gods

Nortia/Fortuna: Goddess of Fate

Uni/Juno: Goddess of marriage/mothers/children, queen of the gods

Tinia/Jupiter: King of the gods

Turan/Venus/Aphrodite: Goddess of love

Aita: God of the Afterworld (his worshippers follow the Calu Death Cult)

Fufluns/Dionysus: God of wine and regeneration (his worshippers follow the Pacha Cult)

Laran/Mars: God of war

Genius (male)/Juno (female): An individual's guardian spirit (Roman)

Tuchulcha: A demon from the Etruscan Afterworld

Vanth: A demoness who stands guard at the Etruscan Afterworld

Charun/Charon: Demon guardian of the Afterworld/Underworld

Alpan: Angel, handmaiden to Turan

Saturn: God of sowing

Aplu/Apollo: God of the sun, prophecy, healing, music, and poetry

Menerva/Minerva: Goddess of wisdom, arts, war, and commerce

PROLOGUE

Her whole world was orange.

Shifting her head to one side, feeling the weight of the veil, hearing it rustle, her eyes strained to focus through the fine weave.

Orange. The vegetable smell of the dye had been faint when she'd first donned the wedding veil, but now its scent filled her nostrils and mouth, the cloth pressing against her face as she walked to where the guests were waiting.

The atrium was crowded. So many people. Shaking, legs unsteady, Caecilia found she needed to lean against her Aunt Aurelia. Through the haze of the veil she could barely make out the faces of the ten official witnesses or that of the most honored guest, the chief pontiff of Rome.

And she could not see Drusus. Perhaps he could not bear to witness her surrender.

"Stand straight, you're too heavy," hissed her aunt, pinching the girl's arm.

Biting her lip, Caecilia was led forward. The groom stood before the wedding altar, ready to make the nuptial offering. Her Uncle Aemilius smiled broadly beside him.

Aunt Aurelia, acting as presiding matron, deposited her charge with a flourish, then fussed with the bride's tunic. She was reveling in the attention and smiled vacuously at her guests, but the girl was aware that, for so crowded a room, silence dominated.

Drawing back her veil, Caecilia gazed upon the stranger who was to become her husband. To her surprise, his black hair was close-cropped and he was beardless. She was used to the long tresses of the men of Rome—and their odor. This man smelled differently; the scent of bathwater mixed with sandalwood clung to his body.

Head bowed, she tried in vain to blot out his existence no more than a handbreadth from her side, but she need not have bothered. He made no attempt to study either her face or form.

"The auspices were taken at sunrise," declared Aemilius. "The gods confirm the marriage will be blessed."

Bride and groom sat upon chairs covered with sheepskin and waited while the pontiff offered spelt cake to Jupiter.

There was a pause as they stood and circled the altar, then the priest signaled Aurelia to join the couple's hands.

Caecilia wished she could stop shaking. She had to be brave. She had to be dignified. But her body would not obey her. She was still quaking when Aurelia seized her right hand roughly and thrust it into the groom's.

The warmth and strength of his grip surprised her. Her palm was clammy and it occurred to her that her hand would slip from his grasp. Slowly, she turned to face him. He was old; lines of age plowed his forehead and creased his eyes. He must be nearly two score years. What was he like, this man? Her husband?

Aware that she should be making her vows to him in silence, she instead prayed fervently that the gods would take pity and not make her suffer too long or too hard in his keeping.

His hand still encompassed hers. Before releasing her fingers, he squeezed them slightly, the pressure barely perceptible. She held her breath momentarily, amazed that the only mark of comfort she had received all day had been bestowed upon her by a foe.

She scanned his face. His eyes were dark and almond-shaped, like the hard black olives from her aunt's pantry. His skin was dark, too, sun dark. A jagged scar ran down one side of his nose to his mouth.

He was far from handsome.

His toga and tunic were of a rich dark blue, making all stare at him for a difference other than his race. Yet his shoulders were held in a martial pose, no less a man for his gaudiness, it seemed, than the Roman patricians around him in their simple purple-striped robes. And the bridal wreath upon his head could have been a circlet of laurel leaves, a decoration for bravery, not nuptials.

A golden bulla hung around his neck, astounding her. For a man did not wear such amulets once he'd stepped over the threshold to manhood. Only children wore such charms in Rome. He wore many rings, too, but one in particular was striking. Heavy gold set with onyx. No Roman would garland himself with so much jewelry.

There was one other thing that was intriguing, making her wonder if his people found it hard to bid farewell childhood. His arms and his legs seemed hairless, as if they had been shaven completely.

Perfumed, short-cropped hair, no beard. Caecilia truly beheld a savage.

Once again she steeled herself, repeating silently: "I am Aemilia Caeciliana. Today I am Rome. I must endure."

WINTER 407 BC

ONE

All Romans feed on ambition. Like Romulus and Remus nuzzling greedily at the dugs of the she wolf. Lucius Caecilius was no different. Tugging on one teat for personal profit while gorging on another for public gain.

His daughter did not know this.

To Caecilia, her Tata was a champion of the people. One of ten tribunes empowered to veto unjust laws. The highest office a commoner could hold.

In a world riven by a bitter class war, he had succeeded in marrying a patrician. His bride did not welcome the marriage, though, forever after hating her brother, Aemilius, for brokering the union.

Living on her husband's estate, away from the city of Rome, Aemilia bore the shame of her marriage in seclusion by refusing to greet other matrons who sought to visit.

Caecilia's memories of her mother were distant, for the patrician woman cloistered herself within the rambling country house, and when confronted with her child looked disappointed, almost perturbed, that the proof of Aemilius's betrayal still lived and breathed and had taken form as a little girl.

Humiliation formed a canker both within and upon Aemilia's breast, and she lay in a darkened chamber brimming with stuttering coughs, rasping breaths, and resentment. The air was heavy with the bittersweet scent of the hypericum oil she rubbed upon her sores that left a bright-red stain as if to declare she could never be cured. To Caecilia, even the slightest hint of such an odor would forevermore return her to that fetid room, assaulting all her senses. All except for one. All except for touch.

One day, though, Aemilia pressed a fascinum into her daughter's hand, a tiny phallus crafted from bone and tipped in iron. "To keep away the evil eye," she whispered. "You, most of all, will need it."

Such a gesture of concern caused confusion in the child as to whether her mother wished to protect her or thought she was already cursed.

While Aemilia lived, Lucius resided in the city, visiting rarely, always anxious to escape his wife's chilly reserve. And so, knowing nothing else than her mother's disdain and her father's diffidence, the young Caecilia learned to hide in shadowy corners away from the servants. For she soon understood from listening to their gossip that they saw her neither as a patrician nor even a plebeian but only as a brat.

Lonely and silent, she became invisible, only finding happiness when she could slip from dimness into sunlight to trace on foot the limits of her father's land, tying woolen puppets to the boundary stones to remind the spirits to remember and protect her.

• • •

When Aemilia died there was relief. An observation of duty. Nothing more. No tears. Tata hired mourners for that. Ashes caking their faces and hair. Keening.

Freed of the gloom of that oppressive household, the little girl ran wild, dressed in dark-blue mourning clothes but not grieving, using only oil and the scrape of iron strigil to keep clean, hair uncombed, chores left unattended, and wondering now and then whether she should weep.

Seeing Tata's reaction to his wife's death did not help her uncertainty. On the day her mother died, Lucius hesitated before placing his lips over Aemilia's, as though uncomfortable that he should inhale her dying soul with such a kiss.

• • •

Not long after the funeral, Caecilia ran into Tata's study to escape the rain leaking from under the atrium roof covers. Discovering in her father's domain a feast long denied her, the ten-year-old raided its secrets as hungrily as she plundered his beehives for honey, intrigued by scrolls that slithered and curled into rolls when she played with them, or wax tablets upon which words or numbers could be etched.

Summoned by his steward, Lucius was startled to find his wayward daughter guiltily handling his books as though she were a thief caught in his wine cellar.

To her surprise he did not chide her. Instead, father and daughter came to an understanding. Lucius's fingers were crippled by an affliction that made his joints gnarled and his flesh frozen with pain. It had become hard for him to hold a stylus without splattering ink or digging unwanted strokes onto a fresh page. And so he taught Caecilia to read and write, telling her the laws of their people and reciting unwritten customs in long, worn sentences. And in time she wrote his letters and read aloud to him when eyesight and candlelight were both failing.

Amid the tablets and scrolls, bills and invoices, inventories and manuals, Caecilia gained an education that would have been reserved for a son: religion and law, arithmetic, and history.

She gained his love as well.

Each night, after she'd ground a salve of calendula by mortar and pestle, she'd massage his gnarled and tortured knuckles, smoothing the pungent ointment into his skin. And always, while she did so, he'd lace his crippled fingers between hers and murmur: "My honey-eyed child, what would I do without you?"

. . .

Tata was wealthy. Being plebeian did not preclude riches. Riches built upon salt.

When given the chance, Caecilia would hungrily savor the grains sprinkled from the heavy saltcellar upon the table, sometimes pouring the precious particles onto the oak and making finger trails. And a supply was always certain because Tata owned a concession to a salt mine, a treasure trove at the mouth of the Tiber seized from the enemy city of Veii many years ago.

Despite possessing a fortune, Lucius lived humbly and was generous to the people, never forgetting it was they he represented in the Forum. Yet he could not always help them.

On the few occasions when Tata took Caecilia to the village, she would sit safely within the confines of his carriage while he went about his business. For he treated her as a patrician virgin, forbidding her to drink wine and vigilantly guarding her virtue. By thirteen she was old enough to wed, her potential to marry an aristocrat valuable. Tata did not want such a chance threatened by a plebeian suitor. He wanted a grandchild that would be three-quarters patrician. Nobility by degrees.

One day, when peeping through the gap in the carriage curtains, Caecilia saw a man in the square fettered in chains. Filth was spattered across his tunic, remnants of missiles lobbed at him by village urchins. The skin of his face and arms was burned, blisters forming, hair and beard caked with dirt. He looked hungry and thirsty and defeated, his humiliation heavier than his bonds.

A young girl stood beside him. It was not his daughter, wearing as she was the stola overdress of a matron. She carried a baby in her belly and one upon her hip. The little boy was screaming, cheeks red, his mouth so wide with sound it seemed he'd forgotten to take a breath. His mother, face lined and eyes weary, ignored him. She was too busy feeding her husband a watery gruel. He gulped it down, almost choking in his haste to take a mouthful.

Caecilia tugged at Tata's sleeve. "Who is he?"

"A soldier who has fallen into debt. He's been chained there for nearly two months waiting for the magistrate to pass final judgment."

Caecilia stared at the veteran. "He is a citizen?"

Lucius frowned and sighed. "Rome has many enemies, Cilla. Volscians in the south, Aequians in the east, and the sleeping threat of the Veientanes in the north. And so to defend our city our citizens march out to war in spring and only return in winter to plow and sow their land. While they are away their wives and children must see to the harvest, which grows ever meager with each passing year of drought. Debts accrue. Men return to impatient creditors. And so warriors who have not already sacrificed their lives return to forfeit their liberty instead."

"And if he cannot pay his debts?"

Lucius carefully closed the curtains. "He will become a bondsman, Cilla. Or his new master could do as the Laws of the Twelve Tables permit and sell him across the Tiber to become a slave."

"And his wife and children?"

"I will do what I can, but the girl must hope her family will support her."

"And if you were a judge, could you help him?"

She felt him tense. "I'm afraid only patricians can be magistrate, judge, or consul. To take office you need to light a sacred flame. A man must have holy blood to do that. And so, because no plebeian can claim a lineage to the gods, no plebeian will ever sit upon a magistrate's ivory chair or thereafter don the purple-bordered toga of a senator in the Curia."

Caecilia leaned against him so that her cheek was warmed by the soft wool of his cloak, bewildered by such injustice. "So a commoner will never govern Rome?"

Tata gently grasped her fingers. "Cilla, don't you understand? That is why you are the future of this city, my own little patrician, proof that holy and mundane can merge. When there are more born like you all of Rome will feel the trickle of the divine within their veins and then no one can claim greater rights to power than another."

Caecilia smiled, puffed with pride at hearing she had such purpose. Then uncertainty filled her. Just what part of her was godly? Her toes or elbows? Chin or shoulders? Some awkward part, no doubt. Gracefulness did not seem to have been ordained. And if indeed she possessed such blood, how was it that the servants scowled at her and even the cat would not heed what she said? Whatever doubts she had about herself, though, did not stop her believing in her father.

Yet over time, as gossip drifted on city breezes from the Forum, it slowly dawned on her that Tata no longer held office as a tribune of the people, and that his world had shriveled, like his once-strong hands, to the confines of his farm.

• • •

Years later, on a night so cold the wind howled through the atrium's blackened rafters, Caecilia learned of Tata's true ambitions.

On that night, when Marcus Furius Camillus came to call, wearing a thick woolen toga edged in purple, the charcoal and flame flared within the hearth, making her wonder if he would douse the fire or fan it with his fervor.

"What brings you to the country on such a night, Senator," asked Lucius, drawing aside the curtain to the doorway of his study, "when you could be warming yourself in the Curia's heated debate?"

Caecilia followed closely behind Tata and the patrician. She could smell the faint odor of urine and sulfur used to clean his robes. His hands were strong and handsome compared to her father's, and he wore a gold signet ring, a touch of flamboyance for a society used to wearing iron.

Scanning the pile of books that lay scattered on the floor of the study, Camillus turned his attention briefly to her. "Your daughter should be married, Lucius, not straining her eyes on reading."

Tata nodded to Caecilia in dismissal as he led the senator to his study. The gesture was gentle but it was as though she had been slapped, reminding her of what a woman's place should be—would be—if not for his indulgence. She made a show of gathering up the scrolls to delay a moment longer.

"I came here to speak of war," Camillus said.

Lucius seemed puzzled. "Which war? Against the Volscians or the Aequians?"

"Why, against Veii, of course," he said, glaring at Caecilia for still loitering. "The murderers of our kinsmen and the coveters of Rome's salt mines."

Caecilia's eyes widened. The ruthlessness and treachery of the Veientanes could never be forgotten. They had killed Tata's brothers and many other Romans before the present treaty was signed. Knowing this she frowned as she left the study, wondering if the Etruscans planned to steal the salt mines that were prized as though the white stuff were gold.

Pausing behind the bronze safe beside the doorway, she glanced back inside. Camillus was limping slightly as he paced the room, legacy of a Volscian spear thrust in his thigh, proof also of glory gained when very young.

"You talk of war with Veii," said Lucius, "and yet this wretched truce is still on foot."

The senator loomed closer to the door, causing the girl to shrink away. "Wretched truce, indeed. Nearly twenty years have passed with those pampered Veientanes doling out corn to us, while we let go the chance to cross the Tiber and seize their land. And all because peacemakers like your brother-in-law hold power."

The tirade startled her. She was used to Tata teaching his tenets, together with grammar and dictation, with a gentle zeal. This man spoke not just the language of hatred but of passion for Rome.

"I don't disagree," said Tata. "I, too, would see Veii crushed, but our soldiers are already fighting the Volscians at Anxur and Verrugo while the Aequians stalk our borders. Resources are low, as is morale. Aemilius has good cause to counsel caution."

Camillus scraped a chair along the floor to sit close by the plebeian, his body tensed upon the edge of the seat. "Haven't you heard? Martial law has been proclaimed. Rome fights on so many war fronts it needs more generals. While the city is under military rule, four consular generals will be elected instead of two ordained consuls. Do you know what that means, my friend? Commoners will not be precluded from holding such a position. It is possible that a plebeian could lead a legion of Rome."

Caecilia's heart beat faster. How pleased Tata would be that his prayers had been answered and that his counsel was being sought.

Lucius did not reply. The senator's startling news had caused him to cough. It was a racking cough that had persisted all winter, hoarse and painful, deep and wheezy. "Your words bring hope to the people," he eventually said, gaining breath, "but it does not explain how our soldiers will be convinced to fight another war."

The politician leaned forward and gripped the armrests of Tata's chair. "Pay them a wage," he said loudly, as if Lucius needed greater volume to understand him. "Pay them a wage and then their spirits will rise enough to fight ten foes!"

Caecilia thought of the soldier whose valor had been rewarded by bondage. Thought, too, of all those Roman dead who called to be avenged.

And yet instead of approval, Tata fell silent, his hesitation mirrored in the tapping of his cane. "The idea has merit," he finally said. "But why come to me? It's your patrician friends you should be approaching."

"I already have support from those who do not shrink from conflict. But we can do nothing if one of the peoples' tribunes blocks the bill. All I ask is that you speak to your colleagues. Convince them that this would be in all our interests."

Again Tata hesitated. "But will the treasury fund it?"

Camillus shifted in his seat. "No, there would have to be a tax. The people would have to be reasonable and pay their share."

It was Tata's turn to pace, rapping the bookshelves and the table with his cane to punctuate his words. "A tax? Don't waste my time! If you promised booty or land as well it might be different, or if the patricians said they'd pay the lion's share. I can hear the tribunes now, standing in the Forum, faces flushed with fervor. They'd choose some grizzled veteran in the crowd and make him display his scars. They'd shout, 'Tell us, can this soldier afford to shed any more blood? Lose any more flesh? Does he have anything left to meet a tax to pay himself?'"

"Ah, Lucius," said Camillus, smiling. "I've missed your orations."

Tata eased back into his chair, rubbing his knuckles, his voice low. "You know I am no longer welcomed by the Comitium. The people will surely claim I am still a patrician's puppet. There is no way they will listen to me."

"You have more support than you imagine. All you need do is return to Rome and stand up for what you believe." Camillus leaned over and touched the other's sleeve. "You never acted dishonorably, only reasonably, unlike the current tribunes who take every chance to veto a levy of troops. Just one of them can hinder us proclaiming war. It is they who misuse their power, whereas you always exercised good judgment."

Tata continued to massage his crooked fingers. "You mean I never opposed Aemilius and his friends. You mean I was 'reasonable' enough not to veto laws that the patricians wanted passed."

Camillus casually rearranged his robes. "You are too harsh upon yourself," he said. "You've kept your promises to Aemilius, but has he? You funded his elections from your bulging purse yet here you are in this backwater, not one step closer to being consul than when you first met him. Since the censors have been consecrated to light the sacred flame for plebeians, there have been others given the opportunity to step into magisterial shoes. What has Aemilius actually done besides let you lie with his sister and father a half-caste child?"

In her hiding place, Caecilia flinched at hearing such truths, not wanting to believe them.

Her father's chair scraped along the floor. "I think you should leave," he said softly, firmly. "What you say may be true but, for better or worse, I am tied to Aemilius. I will not break my word."

Trembling, the girl chanced one more peek into the room. Camillus stood with open palms.

"Come, Lucius, don't be angry. We are both hawks, my friend, and well suited. And so I offer you this last chance. You can still attain your dreams if you are loyal to me. All I ask is that you campaign for a veteran's salary and war with Veii. In return I'll help you stand beside me as a consular general. Think of it, Lucius Caecilius, imagine! You could be the first plebeian in the city to share supreme office in Rome."

Holding her breath, Caecilia waited for Tata's reply, thinking he would be elated. Instead his voice sounded despairing.

"I am afraid you are too late," he finally said as he stretched out his twisted, feeble hands. "Look at them! Look at them! Do you really think I could command either state or army? I have no more power to sway my people than I have strength to hold a sword."

• • •

Lucius knew his daughter well. After Camillus had gone in a whirl of arrogance and disappointment, Tata called her to him, his words squeezed out in the gaps between his wheezing. "How much did you overhear?"

Caecilia was shaking as much from the betrayal as from summoning courage to confront the man who owned her. "Was I always the residue, not the essence, of your vision, Tata? Am I just the tailings left after you had mined my mother's family for their value?"

Lucius slumped against the doorjamb in another fit of coughing. Despite her anger, Caecilia rushed to lead him to his chair.

"Cilla, you must never think that! Never! My dream was always to unite the classes, but there will never be concord unless the plebeians share power. And so my marriage to your mother served another purpose. It was supposed to help me walk upon the Honored Way—step-by-step up the political ladder to the governorship of Rome."

"Yes," she said, voice trembling at defying him, "through the currency of bronze weights and collusion!"

Tata leaned back, exhausted, face ashen, voice quiet. "There was honor in my dream."

"But you heard Camillus! I am just a half-caste to them. While you see me as half of what could make Rome great, my mother's people see me as half of what would destroy it. The patricians will never let go of their rule."

"I can't believe that. You are the future."

She sank to her knees beside him. "Is that all you see in me?"

Laboring for breath, Lucius put his hand upon her head and stroked her hair. "How can you doubt I love you? Haven't you wondered why you are nearly eighteen and still unwed? I could have given you to a patrician groom by now, but I could not bear to be without you."

Bending down, he swept her plait from her neck to reveal a purplish blemish. "This birthmark is a sign of changing fortune, Cilla, ups and downs. The gods have signaled your life will not be easy. But you must believe me when I say that you and your children will make a difference to Rome, even if I have failed you."

• • •

The cold of that winter's day extended into weeks of ice and months of snow. Tata, lungs choked, hacking and hawking up green phlegm, ribs cracked from coughing, retreated to his bed nursing his humiliation.

Caecilia tended him with devotion, forgiving his corruption and complicity, reluctant to forgo the touch of the only one who'd loved her. And the revelation had some benefit, for she at last understood why Tata hated Aemilius, and why, in turn, her mother hated her.

"Stay with me," rasped Lucius, too weak to grasp his daughter's hand. "Catch my last breath."

When he died, Caecilia placed her mouth upon his still-warm lips, inhaling his soul, proud to possess part of him forever and glad that no brother existed to claim that right instead of her.

There was no need to hire mourners. Abandoned and alone, she grieved and sorrowed.

His bier was plain, adorned by garlands. It bore the insignia of a people's tribune, the highest office he had held. Washed and anointed, he lay within his atrium, feet pointed toward the door. Outside, an evergreen bough was hung to announce to passersby that death had already visited.

He had been cremated at night so that his daughter's farewell, spoken three times, was uttered through the choking taste and smell of burning flesh and cypress. The shock of watching him consumed upon his pyre raised the hairs on Caecilia's skin and summoned a night demon to her dreams. Every time she fell asleep, it sat upon her chest, weighing the same as a small dog, with snakes growing like horns from its head and wings sprouting from its back, its eyes black slits in yellow.

And no matter how loud she screamed, nobody heard her cries.

• • •

It was spring when Caecilia left her home.

At the Liberalia festival people drank from the paltry vintage, singing and praying that the earth's new growth would burgeon instead of wither.

Before she left, the hearth fire was extinguished and not relit. There was no master to perform the rites to reignite it. The flames were quenched with sand, a silent smothering, leaving her with only the memory of a blackened hearthstone in a cheerless room.

It was March, the month of her birthday. The start of a new year.

It was also the month of Mars, the warrior god.

And so, as the girl began her journey, Rome prepared once again to go to war.

SPRING 406 BC

Two

Leaving the vineyards and olive trees of the farm behind her, Caecilia bid farewell to the sights and sounds and smells of the country, the bleating of goats, the wind in the pine trees, and the faint scent of lemons from nearby orchards. Arriving in Rome, the city enveloped her with clamor and stridency and smoke, which seeped through the walls of her uncle's Palatine house together with the stench from the great public drain.

Her Uncle Aemilius greeted her coolly. Even from the grave Lucius had not let the Aemilians forget him. Against custom, he'd appointed Aemilius as his daughter's guardian, a responsibility that would prove a constant reminder to her uncle of his betrayal of his sister Aemilia many years before.

Aunt Aurelia observed her new charge at arm's length as she would a dead rat, declaring that once again Caecilia would wear dark blue for a year.

No more books. No more writing.

No more going barefoot in the summer and building scarecrows in the fields. Instead, baths once a week and combed hair. Spinning and weaving and washing and sewing. Preparing to become a wife. Women's company at last but no companionship. And, apart from her cousin, Marcus, no affection.

In her uncle's house the emptiness did not leave her. Aurelia's chiding and Aemilius's patronizing attempts at compassion did not lift her melancholy either, but Marcus understood her.

He was older than her by two years. A green soldier, unblooded and untested, destined to appear upon the family tree whose branches groaned with the names of magistrates, generals, and consuls. His father expected much of him for there was no other son to bring fame to their line of the clan. Climbing the Honored Way and gaining battle honors was his duty.

Dowdy in mourning clothes, Caecilia clutched at grief as if scared it would be snatched away as swiftly as death had seized her father. Marcus found her pacing the boundary of Aurelia's little garden, hemmed in by wooden houses instead of oak woods, sad that in only a few strides Rome could define and contain her. He snapped a rose from its stem and offered it to her.

"No more weeping, Cilla. Honor his memory with roses, not tears. Ceasing to mourn will not banish him. He will always be with you."

After this shared kindness the cousins became allies, for although Marcus enjoyed his mother's attention, he hated how she beat Caecilia. "You know I won't let her hurt you," he would promise, but Caecilia knew better, glad that her sleeves hid the welts from Aurelia's spiteful pinches. Marcus believed he was her champion, but once he was absent, the matron would continue her mistreatment.

Caecilia concentrated instead on enjoying those fragments of time Marcus could spare. For he trained every day, and every day he railed against the need to wield a wooden sword tipped with a leather button to ensure no accidents befell him. The army did not believe in killing green recruits at practice. There was time enough for the Volscians to do so.

One afternoon he settled beside her before the family shrine—face dirty, tunic torn, forearms and knees grazed—and stoked the cinders of the hearth fire while she took up the mortar and pestle. "Not elder leaves," he said, screwing up his nose. "The house stinks for days after you grind them."

She laughed, then pointed to the bruises on his legs. "Aunt Aurelia thinks the plant is a cure-all. She told me to make an ointment for you."

"Then I better not tell her I think I've sprained my wrist."

She glared at him. "No, otherwise I'll be pulling nettle stings out of my fingers for days after making a compress for you."

"But at least Mother will be happy."

Caecilia laughed again. It was true. The only time Aurelia seemed content was when concocting brews and ointments, salves and plasters, filling the air with smells of calendula and birch bark, or scents of mint or thyme, such plants giving up their bitter or sweet secrets to her.

"As for your aches and pains," she said, "you'll just have to be brave and bear them."

Marcus grew serious, picking at the calluses upon the palm of one hand. "Father spoke to me today," he said. "I am to be posted to Verrugo in Volscian territory this summer."

Caecilia's smile faded. No longer could her cousin whine that his weapon would not draw blood. His sword would be of iron and its tip and blade honed sharply. And with such thoughts came worry, the knowledge that a spear or sword could pierce him and he would be lost to her forever.

"But this is good news," she said, trying to hide her concern. "It is an honor."

Marcus tore a strip of dead skin from his palm, exposing tender pink flesh beneath. Quiet. Voice a murmur. "But what if I lack courage? What if I dishonor our family?"

Caecilia laid the mortar and pestle upon the floor, not sure what to say. There was no reason for Marcus to doubt himself. All his life he'd attained the goals his father had set him. He was, in every way, a golden child: intelligent, diplomatic, athletic—and brave. With his talents he would not fail to climb the ladder of ambition nor would he fail in battle.

Before she could answer, though, he strode over to the ancestor cupboards and flung them open. Caecilia gasped. The death masks of the famous ancestors within were not allowed to be revealed except on special occasions. "Quickly, close it," she hissed, "or we'll be punished."

Ignoring her, Marcus pointed at one image in particular. The firelight flickered upon the waxen face, the eyes blank and staring. "Behold Mamercus Aemilius," he declared. "Liberator of Fidenae! Conqueror of the Veientanes!"

He tapped his chest. "And now behold his great-nephew—the coward."

Caecilia glanced around nervously lest Aurelia emerge. She carefully closed the cupboard. "What are you talking about? You've never backed down from a fight."

Marcus shook his head. "You don't understand, Cilla. The Legion of the Wolf is ancient and esteemed. What if I cannot fight as boldly as my father expects?"

Caecilia took his hands. They were trembling. "Of course you will be brave," she said. "This is just nerves. You'll see, when the time comes you'll face the enemy with courage. You are no coward."

"But I have never killed a man. Perhaps in the heat of battle I will falter." He bowed his head, his voice a whisper. "Cilla, I'm scared of dying."

She was stunned. "All young soldiers must feel the same. What of your friends? I'm sure they have doubts also."

He frowned. "Men do not speak of such fears to one another."

The girl fell silent, sad that her cousin could gain no solace just because manhood had been reached and bravado encouraged. She spoke softly. "Are you sure there is no one?"

His face set into an expression that told her he regretted telling her of his fears. "Cilla, you are a woman. You'll never understand."

• • •

Soon after, Caecilia met a friend of Marcus's who she felt would understand him. His name was Appius Claudius Drusus. He too was a son of a wealthy patrician. He too was expected to walk upon the Honored Way.

Around the time Drusus began to visit, Caecilia found she was no longer oblivious to the physique of the men she was allowed to meet. She was suddenly aware of the height of a man or the width of his shoulders, the strength of his arms or the line of his legs. Aware, too, that she was no beauty. Too tall for a girl—as Aurelia was oft repeating—her nose too straight, her mouth too wide. And, upon her neck, as a constant reminder, the ugly, purple stain.

Cloistered in her uncle's house, she was frustrated that her time with Drusus was always limited to formal visits. He was nervous, always restless in his chair. She could tell Aurelia disliked him: his gruff, halting sentences, his rough social graces. Yet in the minutes it took for her to proffer a dish of almonds to each guest, she could not ignore how his eyes followed her every movement, how he blushed when she caught him watching; how, too, an unexpected shyness welled within her, an eagerness to please that was unsettling.

It was better when the russet-haired youth visited Marcus only, for her cousin would ignore how she'd linger, perching on the edge of the impluvium well, listening to their news and bragging until Aurelia chased her away, scolding her for immodesty.

At such times, Drusus's voice would become louder, his gestures broader, his fervor deeper, his hesitancy gone. He yearned to fight, wanted glory, and hungered for his chance at war.

Caecilia listened to his talk of battle and ambition but did not concentrate on every detail. She would have been content just to observe him. To study how his hands were bony, the knuckles pronounced, how his body, too, was lean and lank with the scaffold of a man's but not yet its core. And how his eyes had a hint of anger, a wildness that made her believe he could be defiant. Defiant enough to consider a half-caste.

One time, to her delight, they had a chance to be alone. A moment after the servant left to fetch her cousin, Drusus took her hand and drew her close, snatching a kiss, light and clumsy, a forbidden kiss which chaperones guard against and for which maidens sigh. Yet, strangely, the touch did not lead to further embrace. They were uneasy at such rashness, at the risk of embracing before the household gods who even now must be muttering with outrage.

To Caecilia's relief the awkwardness did not last. Drusus's kiss may have been askew, but he suddenly gained confidence to speak. "I want to marry you. I want you to be mine."

She was surprised. While she had prayed that this boy might marry her, she had not expected Drusus to dare try. It had been enough for him to notice her, to make her conscious of the swell of her breasts and hips, that her hair was shiny. Now he was speaking of a union that could never be.

Marriage was a matter for family, for the sons yet to be born, for bloodlines and power and wealth. Grandfathers as well as fathers wanted heirs. Love had nothing to do with it. Yet the fact Drusus should speak of his desire for her to be his wife made her smile. And there was admiration, too, for his boldness.

Conscious that they would be disturbed at any moment and aware, too, that both their palms were slippery, her heart beat as fast as when she raced the clouds down the corn rows of her father's farm.

Hearing Marcus approach she pulled away, but Drusus would not let her go.

"I am going to ask my father to speak to Aemilius. Why would either refuse?"

• • •

Caecilia was not skilled at weaving. She always broke the thread upon the spindle and tangled the warp weights on the loom. Yet, hopeful that the elders would come to an agreement, she began spinning fine yarn to weave a flammeum, the veil of Roman brides.

As always, she struggled to start the whorl twirling, aware that Drusus would expect her to be as skillful as his sisters at the task. The prospect of achieving an even weave was also daunting, as was the fear of orange blobs forming when she steeped the gauze in dye of weld.

Yet knowing her labors were for Drusus, the girl settled to the task until she heard Aemilius noisily returning early from the law courts.

Curiosity turned to surprise when he entered the atrium and sat down beside her, bending to remove his dusty boots and slip on indoor sandals.

"I have decided to adopt you," he said abruptly.

Caecilia paused in her work, uncertain what to say. The news was unexpected and intriguing. As her guardian, Aemilius controlled her considerable inheritance. He did not need to claim her nor worry that she was unwed. Yet hearing his words, the possibility of marriage crossed her mind. Perhaps he had brokered a business deal and betrothal in one negotiation. Perhaps with Drusus's father.

"Caecilia, every son is expected to sacrifice himself for our city," he declared. "And such commitment is also expected of a daughter, in a different way. I am going to give you a chance to perform a duty no other Roman woman has ever faced. And in agreeing, you will be lauded, you will be revered."

Unease crept through her and she found herself perspiring as when she sat before a fire too closely and too long. Her voice wavered. "What is it you wish me to do?"

Then he told her of a marriage, but not the one she desired. Hearing this, she dropped the distaff, sending the whorl flying across the room.

"An Etruscan?"

"It is to extend the truce, daughter, so that Veii will not be our foe."

"And if I do not agree?"

Aemilius raised one caterpillar eyebrow. "There is many a maiden who consents to a marriage she does not want."

Caecilia's disquiet flared to panic. She was hot now, as though flames were licking her hands, melting them, melting her. She sank to her knees, knowing that she should not question him. A pater-familias demanded respect, a respect born of an illustrious career and the care of his family. He had the power to kill her. Yet, wasn't what he was proposing worse than death?

She thought of Lucretia, the dutiful Roman wife: epitome of modesty, fidelity, and patience. She'd been compromised, threatened, and raped. By an Etruscan prince. Then venerated for taking her life rather than living with dishonor. "I do not want to be another Lucretia," she choked, tears pricking her eyes.

Aemilius put his hand on her shoulder, a rare contact. "You worry unnecessarily, my dear. Vel Mastarna has shown himself to be honorable in all my dealings with him. And he has held the equivalent position to a consul in the past.

Caecilia swallowed, her throat tight. Being married to an august Veientane nobleman should have granted her comfort yet did not allay her fears. The Etruscan monarchs had been aristocratic tyrants. As far as she was concerned all Etruscans were base.

"Please, Uncle! They say Veientane husbands make their wives lie with other men!"

Startled, Aemilius glared at her. "Who has said such things to you?"

"Please don't ask me to do this," she begged, not wishing to reveal Marcus as her source. "I promise I will obey Aunt Aurelia, I promise I will see to household duties as she bids."

Aemilius pulled her to her feet, face beet red. "Listen to me. Vel Mastarna has assured me that he will not shame you."

There was a silence where she made herself believe him. "Will I ever see Rome again?"

"Of course, of course," he said, avoiding her gaze. "You won't be a prisoner."

Caecilia willed him to look at her but he would not. Frustration welled within her and she found herself remembering Camillus. Over the past months his plans had not succeeded, thwarted as her father predicted by both the people's tribunes and patrician doves.

"Why extend the treaty? Why not declare war?"

His tone was terse with irritation from speaking of such matters to a girl: "Do you think Rome can afford another war front? The city is in the middle of a famine! We are starving because our crops are withering from drought. We need peace. Romans are farmers while Veientanes, although blessed with fertile fields, are traders. Veii supplies us with corn and they, in turn, gain access to the roads that Rome now owns."

"Why a marriage, then, as well as a treaty? Why do both Assembly and Senate want me to wed?"

She felt a bitter satisfaction in seeing his surprise, that she had forced him to wonder at a niece who was enough like her father to argue the point, and enough like her mother to despise him.

"There is no doubting you are Lucius's child," he snapped. "Belligerent and rude."

"Please, Uncle. I need to know."

"It is quite simple. Veii is riven by internal conflicts, as is Rome. Its leaders fear that warmongers like Camillus could gain power. And so, as surety that our state does not change its mind about the truce, Aemilia Caeciliana will marry a Veientane lord."

As he spoke her adopted name, she shivered, finally understanding why she had been chosen. She would now be called by both plebeian and patrician names. "Aemilia Caeciliana" would be a melding of elite and common, a symbol of united Rome.

For a moment she panicked, wanting Tata to be there to stop this, wishing that her father could once again hold her with his deformed, aching hands, knowing that this was not his vision when he married her mother more than eighteen years ago.

She felt scornful, too, because her uncle knew that she was as much a fusion of the classes as oil and water. His cynicism was as breathtaking as it was bold. She was a half-caste. As such he'd not considered adopting her to help her wed Drusus, but he was prepared to claim her for the good of Rome in order to marry her to a foe.

What would Tata have thought? Would he have finally rejoiced that his daughter had been made officially patrician? Or instead been incensed enough to make her another Verginia—whose father slew her rather than let her be shamed?

"And what if old hostilities reignite? Will Rome then be content for me to become a captive?"

Aemilius strode toward the door before turning briefly to her. "Lucius was wrong to spoil you. I am your master now and you must do as you are told. And when I say there will be no war, you will believe me. It is as simple as that, do you understand?"

• • •

Drusus came to her as soon as he heard, body tense with outrage, eyes burning with frustration. And Marcus, as infuriated as his friend at Aemilius's betrayal, ignored his duty to protect Caecilia's reputation and let them be alone.

Fury leveled Drusus's usually halting speech. "Your uncle and the consular generals are pitiless," he ranted, gripping her hand. "It's my father's fault also. He wouldn't let me marry you even though you've been adopted. He said such a union would corrupt our House." He squeezed her fingers, making her wince. "If he were dead it would be different. If I were head of my House you would not be treated so."

Caecilia noticed he had been punished for countering his father. A bruise marred his cheekbone. Drusus must have suffered the blow for her. She was almost giddy with the honor he bestowed on her in risking his father's anger.

She had more sense than Drusus, though. A rebellious child was no match for the Roman state. Her disobedience had been limited, knowing when she was defeated. She could not save herself and neither could Drusus. Understanding this only added to her despair.

Hearing Aurelia's footfall, Caecilia raised her face to his, heartbeat urgent, but Drusus hesitated too long, leaving no time for an embrace, no time for a final kiss.

• • •

"Camillus says that a war will save you," said Marcus after Drusus had left. "He will not let the Veientane have you."

Caecilia shook her head. Aemilius would not like his heir admiring Camillus. Not when the much-feted senator always opposed him.

"War will not save me, Marcus," she said softly. "It will make me a hostage."

"No, don't you see? When Camillus is a consular general he will negotiate your release. The threat of our power will cause Veii to surrender and you will be freed."

She took his hand. "But I am to be married now," she said softly. "Camillus failed to gain office this time and the new elections are not until next winter. Without holding power Camillus cannot protect me."

Caecilia glanced over to the ancestor tree etched so grandly on the atrium's wooden walls. No woman's name appeared upon its branches, the existence of countless invisible Aemilian mothers, sisters, wives, and daughters was only implied.

Caecilia's thoughts turned to her mother, who was also promised in marriage to further political ambitions. A fifteen-year-old patrician girl wedded to an old plebeian man, a union of convenience between her husband and her brother. How powerless she must have felt. How deserted! As a patrician mother she was expected to give birth to a noble son; instead she'd been forced to bear a child that was neither. Now her daughter's fate was to marry a man of another race more baseborn than her own husband.

Yet this glimpse into her mother's world did not give Caecilia any comfort, even though she now understood Aemilia's grief and sense of betrayal. Briefly stroking the ghost's cheek did not compensate a daughter for her mother's failure to touch her when she was alive.

And Aemilius could be right. Her marriage might lead to veneration. Maybe the gods indeed thought she was worthy. For it was not often a woman was given the chance to make a mark. If marriage to an enemy staved off hunger for her people then perhaps she could make a difference after all.

She gently touched a space upon one branch of the ancestor tree where Marcus's name was destined to be written. He and Drusus had both been posted to the garrison at Verrugo to stop the Volscians reclaiming that city. It made her tremble for them nearly as much as she trembled for herself.

As a daughter of Rome she had learned the tales of heroes and battles so that she might teach her sons about sacrifice. She always believed that if she'd been born a man she could have raised a sword, declared war, and saved herself, but today she knew she was too much of a coward to ever do so. Men volunteered to die for the glory of Rome. All she could do was endure what Rome proclaimed. Fortitude was a virtue. The unseen women on the family tree told her so.

SUMMER 406 BC

THREE

"For goodness' sake, stop weeping," commanded Aurelia, face as round and smooth as any of the apples to which she was so partial.

Caecilia wiped her eyes, surprised, as always, that such a large woman could emit such a shrill little voice. Somehow she expected booming vowels, hearty consonants. Had expected sympathy, too, on her wedding eve.

The atrium was dark, the light from the torches barely illuminating the recesses of the room. It was chilly, too, with the tiles cool against her bare legs as she knelt on the floor, but the sacrificial fire from the family hearth was hot against her face.

The gods of Aemilius's house peered at her from the gloom: those of the store cupboard and fire, those that protected the threshold. A few months ago she had ceased sacrificing spelt cake to the spirits of her father's house; now she must say good-bye to those of her uncle's household as well.

Blotting out the sound of her aunt's whining, she dedicated her dolls before the family shrine, weeping as the fire licked at their tiny wooden faces. They'd been some of the few possessions she'd brought to the House of Aemilius. She knew she was too old for such toys, but it was hard to destroy the links with her past when her future seemed so uncertain, so frightening.

Shivering, she removed her childish short dress, then nervously slipped on the long, white wedding tunic, her hands trembling as she fastened her hair into an orange bridal net. Any fear that her attire would be disarrayed by morning was small. She doubted she would sleep that night.

The hardest farewell to childhood was untying her locket from around her neck. The charm had protected her against evil from birth. Tata had placed it upon her. And he should have removed it as she dispensed with her childhood. Instead she dropped it into Aemilius's open palm.

Standing before her aunt the next day, Caecilia kept touching her throat, seeking the comfort and weight of the amulet. Whether maid or matron, she still needed the luck encased within it.

Aurelia tugged at the straight edges of the bridal gown. "Now stand still while I fasten this," she said, tying a woolen cord at Caecilia's waist in a special knot, the knot of Herculeus. "And remember only he can untie it."

"He" was Vel Mastarna, the man she was to wed. The Veientane lord who would take her away from her home, away from her family. The man who would seal the pact between their cities not by wax and stamp but by the stain of virginal blood.

"You are very fortunate, Caecilia," continued her aunt. "You are lucky to finally find a husband. Too old and too much education, that's the trouble. I blame your father for that. What type of wife will you make?"

"One fit for an Etruscan," the girl said under her breath.

Aurelia's slap was hard and sharp. Caecilia chided herself silently, knowing better than to rile her aunt, the matriarch of this House. Once again she told herself she must endure.

Her cheek smarted from the blow, her skin turning pink. If the same damage had been done to the other, it would look like she'd rouged her face to appeal to her groom. A hurt to feign allure.

Once again she thought of Drusus. If she were to wed him today, she would have happily pinched her cheeks to gain such color.

Caecilia ran her hand along the birthmark upon her neck. A mark that would not fade. Tata had said it meant her path would not be smooth. What would Mastarna think of such a blemish? Of such an omen?

She studied her hands. The nails, as usual, were bitten to the quick. No iron betrothal ring adorned them. No such formalities had been observed, such was the haste of politicians to cement a truce. She wished Drusus had given her this token. It was said a nerve ran through the ring finger to the heart.

Drawing up a wooden stool, Caecilia concentrated on admiring her wedding slippers. They were the first pretty shoes she had ever worn. For they, together with her veil, were the color of the sky at dawn.

She fingered the flammeum's weave, the brightest shade she'd ever worn. But the color was reserved for her wedding day. She would never wear such a hue again.

She grimaced as the handmaid started to dress her long, straight hair. The servant's rough, prying fingers jolted her already-frayed nerves as the tresses were carefully divided into six sections by the bent point of a ceremonial spear. Next the woman set about entwining orange ribbons into dark brown plaits. The braids were pulled tight, the strands tugged, the scalp scratched before they were coiled high upon her head.

"Let me stay here," she pleaded. "Etruria is so far away."

Aurelia shook her head as she smoothed the folds of her stola. No amount of preening would help disguise the bulges and the way the cloth ruched around the matron's waist.

"Don't be foolish. This treaty is being arranged because the city of Veii is so close. Twelve miles beyond the Tiber. It is a constant threat."

The girl stretched out to take the matron's hand but Aurelia shied away.

"It is no use crying to me. It has been agreed."

"But they say Etruscans are very wicked. They say their children never truly know who their fathers are."

Face flushed, the matron leaned close, making Caecilia think she would finally offer comfort, tell her the rumors were untrue. "You are distrustful if you think my husband would send you to such a fate. You can teach Veientane wives womanly virtues even if you will never be a Roman matron. Remain pious, modest, and faithful to Rome. Then you will prevail."

Caecilia's shoulders slumped. It was hard not to tremble, hard not to weep.

Aurelia pressed a crown of verbena onto Caecilia's head and carefully arranged the veil over it. The circlet was uncomfortable against the bulkiness of the braids. For a moment, the bride's vision dimmed before the outline of her aunt's face appeared through the mesh. Her breathing shortened.

Standing at the entrance of the atrium, Caecilia prayed for strength, forcing herself to take a deep breath, thinking of Drusus.

Her whole world was orange.

• • •

The wedding breakfast was not as rowdy as was customary. No ribald comments were tossed at the couple, no saucy songs were bellowed. Although most present wished to achieve concord between the cities, they also shared reservations over the marriage of Roman to Veientane.

Caecilia searched the room for Drusus but he was not there. Disappointment filled her so deeply that it outstripped her fear; disappointment that she could have been wrong about him, that it was foolish to think a handful of awkward moments could amount to much. Yet he had proposed. That was real. Even though it was in vain.

Aurelia continued her fussing, but Caecilia had to admit her aunt had done well to present a quantity of food in a city starved for staples, let alone the delicacies demanded of such an occasion. And she did make sure the honored guests wanted for nothing.

The men lay upon the dining couches while the women sat upon chairs. The gathering was large, and so the feast took place in the atrium. It was the first time Caecilia had ever seen the hall decorated with brightly colored ribbons and garlands of flowers, laurel, and myrtle. A fraudulent celebration.

Caecilia thought that being permitted to dine with men other than her family would have made her happy, but the novelty was soured by apprehension. Becoming a wife should also have given her satisfaction at reaching equality with the other matrons. Becoming a patrician, though, had not overcome their prejudice to a half-caste. Caecilia may have represented Rome, but it did not mean she was fit to talk to.

Mastarna was not suffering such a problem. The great men of Rome were in serious discussion with him. Indeed, the Etruscan spoke her people's language without flaw. The Veientane noblemen who'd accompanied her husband proved he was no aberration either. They, too, were garishly dressed. Like robin and wren, it seemed that Etruscan males were the ones to wear vibrant apparel. Or were their wives also brazenly adorned?

After a time she realized the men's cheerful garb was disguise only. With their watchful sloe eyes, she could tell there was little rejoicing among the groom's party either.

Not wishing to accidentally meet her husband's gaze, she studied the ancestor cupboard that had been opened so that the death masks of her forefathers could peer out. Caecilia was sure one or two of them were frowning.

Again she looked for Drusus but there was no sign of him.

"Sweet Cilla," said Marcus, sitting down beside her. "Those lovely eyes of yours look so frightened."

"Where is Drusus?" she said, clutching at the folds of his toga. "Why isn't he here?"

"His father is dying, Cilla. He could not attend."

It took a while to register what he was saying.

"Drusus says not to despair," he continued, patting her gently on the back. "He has vowed to destroy your husband. He has invoked the gods to torment Mastarna's mind and soul."

Caecilia was unsure what to say. Such vehemence on her account! She glanced at the Etruscan, thinking that, although such a fate could not come quickly enough, it would suffice if the gods could make him simply disappear. But cursing her husband's House was not the same as seeing Drusus.

Sure that she should show similar devotion, Caecilia quickly tore a strip from her veil and pressed it into her cousin's hand. "Give this to Drusus. Tell him not to forget me. Tell him I wanted to wear the flammeum for him."

Marcus hesitated before taking it. Overwhelmed, Caecilia covered her face with her hands, desperate to prevent a stricken face being revealed to the world. It was of no use. Tears trickled through her fingers. "I don't want to go, I don't want to go."

"Stop crying, Cilla, and listen," said Marcus, his voice low and urgent. "Mastarna has been granted the right to marry a Roman on the proviso you remain under our father's power. To do this you must return and stay under his roof for three nights by the end of one year and every year thereafter. Do so and your husband will not own you. You will be Mastarna's wife but still belong to Aemilius, the head of our House, and to Rome."

Caecilia stared at him, eyes red-rimmed. "A year? One whole year?"

"Is one year not better when a moment ago you thought it was never?"

"But what if Mastarna does not let me return?"

Marcus pointed to Camillus, who was holding the attention of many in the room. Caecilia studied him, comparing him to Mastarna. Both were of similar age, both nobles. Yet while she'd heard that the Veientane was a soldier, it seemed strange for him to be dressed in vivid robes and bedecked in jewelry. In contrast, Camillus's purple-edged toga hung in precise and even folds. With his hair worn long and beard neatly trimmed he showed what a warrior should be: austere, virtuous, and manly.

If Camillus were elected as a consular general he'd promised to rescue her. But what would become of her in the time between?

Marcus touched her arm. "This will protect you in the meantime." On his wrist was an amulet wrought in iron and engraved with the family horsehead crest. He slipped it over his hand and thence over hers. "Take this. It will keep you safe. And remember, believe in Camillus. Believe in Drusus. Believe in me."

Caecilia smiled sadly. Yesterday she had doted on his every word. Today she knew she had outgrown him. Marcus believed in Rome. Yesterday she had believed in it, too. And deep in her heart she knew that, to survive, she would need to have faith in her city. But as she observed her husband and uncle in conversation, holding her life in their hands with as much care as a cup or plate, she knew there was no certainty. She was only a symbol. And when the other marriage symbols were removed tonight—her wedding robes, her girdle, her veil, her shoes—what would be left of her?

• • •

When Vesper, the evening star, climbed into sight the bridal party entered the streets. Mastarna had left shortly before. It was the custom for the groom to lie in wait and snatch the bride from the presiding matron's care, just as the Sabine women of legend had been seized by the early men of Rome.

Usually a crowd of noisy guests, shouting catcalls and throwing nuts, followed a bridal march, but again the guests were far from bawdy. Instead the procession was sedate, the nuptial hymn somber, the atmosphere more like a funeral than a celebration. Even the drunks who gawked from tavern doors were oddly reticent as the wedding chant was shouted: "Talassius, talassius!"

Then Caecilia turned the corner into the street.

Mastarna stood there waiting.

She stared at him dumbly. "Come, wife, no more weeping," he said abruptly, offering her his arm. His voice was calm, his accent thickly coating her language.

"Caecilia!"

Startled, she turned to see who had called her name. From the crowd of onlookers, Drusus emerged. He held out the patch of orange veil to her before stashing it within his toga. His face pale, his eyes pained, he called her name and struggled toward her, but Marcus restrained him. Caecilia stared at him, astounded, aching to run to him, but he may as well have been standing on the other side of the Tiber; she could never reach him.

Beside her, Mastarna was observing her, observing Drusus. She glanced at him, not knowing how to speak or regard him. When she turned to search for her admirer, it was too late. The youth had gone.

"Come," said Mastarna, still seemingly untroubled by what he'd seen. "There is more to this ceremony."

Catching hold of the hands of one of her three page boys, Caecilia was grateful for the distraction of the procession. It meant she could leave Mastarna's side. Yet she could not help wondering why her husband did not demand to know the name of the youth who'd claimed her veil. Perhaps Drusus didn't warrant his curiosity and, if so, she hoped that it would remain the case.

• • •

Caecilia's fingers were greasy from the pig's fat and oil saturating the strips of wool she wrapped around the doorposts of the house. The ritual was to protect against evil spirits that she might bring from her old home to her husband's, but the doorway she anointed was not Mastarna's. Instead one of the consular generals had kindly offered his hospitality to them for the night.

There was a pause as the need for the ritual was debated. This only emphasized her humiliation. But if he was offended, Mastarna showed no sign.

"What is your name?" His deep voice made the words of the prescribed refrain resonate.

Her throat was dry. Each step of the ceremony signaled another transition into Mastarna's life. She glanced at Marcus, pleading for a rescue that would not occur.

"Go on, Caecilia," said Aurelia loudly, "say the words so we can escape the street."

She raised her eyes to Mastarna. He was facing her but she could tell his eyes were not focused upon her.

Did he have a Drusilla to match her Drusus?

"When you are Gaius, I am Gaia." Her tremulous high-pitched response emphasized their differences.

The married men of the party crowded around her, lifting her over the threshold to ensure she did not invoke bad luck by striking it with her feet. Then before she had even touched the ground, Aurelia was pinching her. "Follow, I must lead you to the bridal couch."

Just as custom prescribed, the nuptial bed had been erected in the atrium. The finest linen had been used and blossoms were strewn across the expanse of sheets. Caecilia did not shake at its sight; instead she froze. If she wept now, her tears would be icicles and she would breathe spiderwebs of frost.

Mastarna did not approach. Instead he took the hawthorn wedding torch from the eldest of the three page boys. All through the procession Caecilia had expected the flame to flicker wildly, an ill omen, but, surprisingly, it had remained smooth and sculpted. Mastarna extinguished the torch, then, blowing on the wood to cool the embers, handed some of the charred remains to each child together with a handful of nuts. "For luck," he said, bestowing a smile upon them only.

Aurelia tugged at Caecilia's gown. "Offer the blessing," she ordered.

Wondering how much more she could suffer, the bride nervously intoned a prayer of thanks to the gods of her old hearth. Next she gave a blessing to all her family. In normal circumstances she would have said a prayer to the god of her new home, but that would be a ritual kept for the house in Veii, the house of tomorrow.

For a time, the wedding guests remained, but soon relief from awkwardness was sought by all. The girl clutched at her aunt's robes when the older woman made ready to go. And perhaps, at last, Aurelia felt some pity, for the matron brusquely straightened Caecilia's girdle and smoothed the edges of her tunic. "You will survive the night, Caecilia. Believe me, going to a man's bed is not as bad as you might imagine. Submit and let him be your master. That is a woman's duty. And pray to the goddess Juno, all-knowing protectress of wives and mothers. She will help you."

Caecilia surveyed the faces around her. They were leaving her to a fate none of them were prepared to meet themselves. She felt utterly alone.

For a moment she tried to conjure her mother's face. A face long erased by death. Caecilia wondered if Aemilia would have guided her, whispering the secrets of the nuptial bed into her ear. But Caecilia doubted her patrician mother would have smoothed her hair or kissed her cheek in encouragement or solace. Her mother did not like to touch others.

Certainly not half-castes.

Not even her own.

It was time to bid good night. Aemilius and the other officials clustered around Mastarna. To her surprise, Camillus did not seek to grasp her husband's arm but instead bowed his head to her. His voice was low, his words reassuring so that gratitude filled her for both his attention and the knowledge that, of all the noblemen here, he pitied her plight.

"I will pray for you, Aemilia Caeciliana," he said, briefly touching her elbow, "as your father would."

Noting this interchange, Aemilius drew his niece, now his daughter, toward him and unexpectedly kissed her on each cheek. "I am proud of you, Caecilia. Remember, I will not abandon you."

Compared to the comfort of Camillus, his words gave no reassurance. Once again, Caecilia wished Tata were there to save her.

The wedding party left. The marriage bed lay ready. The iron hinges of the heavy street doors creaked shut.

Caecilia, at last, was alone with her husband.

• • •

All day she had wished the veil to be gone, but she now longed for its protection as she reluctantly removed it. She clenched her fingers. She was not totally ignorant of the duty that lay ahead of her, the role of a wife.

As a child, it was not just her father's conversations she overheard when she hid in unseen nooks. There were scraps of scandal and gossip from the servants, too. Once, in the dimness of the storeroom, she had chanced upon a furtive, hurried coupling. Although the girl's moaning was alarming and the urgency of the bondsman's thrusts a revelation, it was the picture of grubby hands gripping white fleshy thighs that Caecilia distinctly remembered.

Although confused as to why the handmaid would seek such an encounter, Caecilia told no one of what she had seen. Had nobody to tell. Her mother was dead and the servants shared no confidences with her. Later when she came to Aurelia's there were no intimacies, no secrets passed from woman to woman except instructions as to how to bake bread or spin wool.

And so, lying awake in her narrow maiden's bed, Caecilia would conjure up memories of the rutting servants.

Then images of Drusus would appear. His hands were never grimy.

Why should she be concerned, then, to finally find herself a bride? She was ready for a husband, was overdue for the marital bed, but now, in the drafty atrium, her groom a few paces away, she felt no stirrings of anticipated touch as she would have felt for Drusus.

Would she feel the same if it were a Roman groom who stood before her? A groom other than Drusus? Would she also worry whether he would take her carelessly, perhaps brutally, as she feared this Etruscan would?

Standing before her husband, she couldn't bring herself to speak or raise her eyes. Instead she twisted the cord of her sash, hoping desperately that her uncle, regretting his decision, would return, annul the marriage, and guide her home.

She could not look at Mastarna, yet she could not ignore him. The room seemed to shrink, diminished not only by his presence but by the power he possessed. The ache in her gut tightened, pain that had squeezed her bowels all day and made her anxious to attend the privy.

Mastarna was silent also as he observed her. "Let us go to sleep," he finally said.

She stiffened, eyes meeting his briefly. Perspiration trickled under her arms, the bridal tunic rank from the day's stress and sacraments. He started to unwind his toga. "We need to rise early for the journey home."

She twisted her belt again, confused. Was she to be spared tonight? Or did he speak some code that a wife should understand?

The Veientane sat upon the bed, pulling the garland from his head and rubbing his temples where the stems had dug into his skin. When she remained frozen, he scowled, his accent not thick enough to cover his irritation. "Don't worry," he said, "I don't plan to bed you. I've had enough politics today."

Her relief was not like a long cool drink of water, more like droplets upon a parched tongue. Swaying with tiredness, she remained standing. Being spared a consummation did not remove the need to fulfill her duty. There were rituals to be performed to confirm the marriage. Rites of fire and water. Prayers and blessings. Mastarna may not think there was any more diplomacy to endure but there was a question of piety. It was humiliating enough to be wed to a foe, but she did not want the gods to curse the union.

"There are more rites," she said.

He sighed. "I think I have had enough of rituals, too."

Sweat crept from her pores. She could feel the paleness spread over her face, her lips cold with whiteness. The rumors about Veientane wickedness surfaced again. Iniquity and sacrilege that her uncle had not actually denied.

"So do Veientanes not observe ordained rites?"

Yawning, Mastarna stretched his arms above his head. "Quite the reverse; they are extremely pious."

"But I have heard otherwise. They say your women sell their bodies in the temples and claim it is a sacred act."

His dark eyes narrowed. "Would you speak with such disrespect to your uncle?"

Caecilia blushed and sat down on a chair beside the hearth, wishing once again that she could control her tongue. It was not an auspicious start to the marriage, although he had not cuffed her yet for insolence.

Mastarna swept away the petals that were strewn upon the bed. The damaged blossoms floated to the floor forlornly. "My people have many customs that you will find strange, Caecilia. Just as we find you Romans peculiar. But if it calms you, know that we no longer practice such a custom." His expression was unnerving, his tone one of a teacher to a backward child. "As for any other tales you may have been told, it is best you do not carry the legacy of prejudice to my city. If you do so you will cause offense."

Exhaustion was a burden. By now her ribbons and braids were half-loosened, and she knew she looked tousled and childish in her simple white gown. Her eyelids were swollen from weeping, her fair skin mottled. She wanted to cradle her head between her hands and make him disappear.

To her surprise, Mastarna rose and stood beside her at the fire. So near to her, she once again noticed his scent. His face was shaven but she could already see the soft shading of new beard stippling his skin. It was an ugly face but not an ugly voice. If she had not resolved to hate him, she knew the timbre and cadence of his speech could easily beguile her.

"Do these rituals we need to complete," he asked, "involve this friendly fellow here?" He pointed to the statue of Mutunus Tutunus.

The statue of the ancient fertility god sat beside the Roman girl. The god's phallus was large and bulbous, and Caecilia shivered at the thought that long ago, a bride, helped by her husband, would sit upon the effigy's lap and suffer the cold stone entering her. Thinking so, she glanced at Mastarna, wondering if his penis would be any easier a prospect.

He had placed his hand upon the statue. "Or is this a tradition your people no longer practice?"

Realizing he was teasing, she tensed.

"Do not fear, Caecilia," he continued in a similar tone, "no stone idol will pierce your hymen, although I wager you'll be disappointed with my proportions after pondering the size of a god's."

Her stomach lurching at his lewdness, she quickly turned to watch the fire, letting the heat burn her cheeks to hide her blush. "There are other rituals," she repeated firmly. "And we are surrounded by spirits."

Again he sighed. "Very well."

"You must offer me the fire and water from your hearth."

"This is not my hearth. But I will do so when we are in Veii."

She hesitated, trying not to think about his home, his ways. Not knowing, either, what to do.

Mastarna gently clasped the back of her hand. "Perhaps this will suffice," he said, and guided it over the fire while she prayed silently to Juno, just as her aunt had bid her.

"Now the water."

Handing him a libation dish, Caecilia closed her eyes, finally accepting that the ceremony was complete as the drops splashed upon her. All prayers and imprecations, all offerings and actions to seal the marriage had been made. All actions except one.

• • •

When she knelt to wash his feet, he seemed surprised. Yet was it not right for a wife to do what was expected? After all, she had bathed her father's feet and her uncle's, even Marcus's. It was a role that was not burdensome provided the water was warm and the oil sweet-smelling.

Yet it did cross her mind that, although it may be right for a wife to kneel before a man with ewer and jug, it might be wrong that Rome should bend to Veii.

Fatigue had taken the edge off her fear. It was as if she had been forced to eat bowl after bowl of some noxious brew all day and no longer cared if it killed or cured her.

The intimacy of rubbing his feet free of grime was uncomfortable as her fingers touched the calluses upon his toes and heels. And there was the strange smoothness, too, of the shaven skin of his muscled calves. Soon, however, the familiarity of the routine calmed her, the silence between them the first lull in nerves all day, a quietness that was not strained. Her head was bowed but she glanced up occasionally. He was not regarding her, instead staring at the flames. Dark circles under his eyes. Distant. Far more than a whispered word from her away.

She sat back upon her heels, the movement distracting him. This time he did study her. Instinctively, she covered her birthmark.

"My servants will do this for me in Veii," he said.

Her surprise at the thought of forever being relieved of such a duty increased when he took both her hands. "But you have a pleasant touch, wife, broad-palmed and long-fingered."

She remembered the brief comfort of the pressure of his fingers at the wedding. For a moment she wondered if, as a woman, she should be insulted that he thought lying with her was a matter of state.

"Mannish hands."

He frowned. "No, Caecilia, there is nothing mannish about you."

Rising quickly, she carried the pitcher and basin to the well, unsure why she should be pleased with him, surprised, too, that he would compliment her fleshy fingertips embedded with the sad little semicircles of chewed nail.

• • •

As they stood on opposite sides of the bed, Caecilia turned her back, not wanting to remind him that he'd not yet untied the knot of Herculeus. She clutched a tiny wooden figure of her guardian spirit in her hand. It was a symbol of her essence, her moral guide. A Roman girl called such an effigy her little juno. Caecilia prayed that both her small protector and the mighty goddess would keep her safe tonight.

Tentatively, she lay between the sheets, still fully clothed, her hair braided, only the bridal wreath and her shoes removed. The bed creaked as he slid in beside her. If he thought it strange she had not undressed, he said nothing. Not even jokingly.

"Sleep well, wife," he said softly and, as far as she could tell, promptly fell asleep.

Barely breathing, body rigid, she stared through the atrium's roof opening. No stars tonight. Only clouds. Every nerve within her was conscious of his presence, mere inches away. How was it that she found herself lying beside a stranger who, with one restless move, could embrace her with impunity? How could it be, when yesterday she had been protected from men and distanced from their touch?

Her worries were not lessened by the realization that Mastarna had stripped. When she raised the sheet slightly, the hard contours of his flanks and buttocks boasted no loincloth. His broad muscular back was smooth, the skin dark. He was hairless and beardless but he was no boy. She had never seen a man totally unclad. And though she knew what the masculine form looked like when carved in stone or wood, to see it in the flesh was yet another shock to add to the day's surfeit. Hiding behind her fear, though, was curiosity. Not only could she study his nakedness undetected but, if she dared, she could brush against bare skin.

Sleep would not come. Fear overtaking her once more, she clung to the edge of the bed, ensuring that as deep a channel as possible divided them. But there would never be enough distance to make her safe.

In the shifting shadows and light from the fire, she stared at her husband's back. His breath was sonorous and even.

He had spared her tonight, but tomorrow she would find out.

Tomorrow there would be no more mystery.

Tomorrow she would discover whether the servant girl's moans were those of pain.

FOUR

She never thought she would feel other than despair as she journeyed from the world of always into the land of never before. Yet after last-time looks at the city wall and the Campus Martius, curiosity beckoned her to bid farewell to the confines of the hills of Rome.

Passing through the north gate out onto the Via Salaria and through the farmlands of her people, she found that even the world she used to know had changed. The fields were even more arid and parched, the wheat brittle and stunted, and the cattle lay in dried-up watercourses, dying from thirst.

At the crossroad that led to Tata's farm she felt a dreadful yawning ache to leap from the cart and hide amid the olive groves as she had as a child, but soon the boundary stones and plowed furrow that defined his land receded into the distance as the oxen pulled the two-wheeled cart farther and farther away. Peering around the side of the hooped and fringed covering that shaded her, Caecilia watched her past life disappear.

The sight of children holding out their hands to her distracted her from her own sadness. Horrified, she saw arms and faces crusted with sores, bellies bloated, limbs skeletal. Some were digging in the dirt with bony fingers for husks to give their fathers as paltry offerings to the gods. Seeing such misery made her understand better why Rome needed Veientane corn. Gave her confirmation, too, that her marriage might do some good.

Caecilia asked the driver to stop so that she could offer help, but he did not understand her and Mastarna was sitting astride his horse and could not hear her call. And so the Roman girl was forced to watch the children disappear from sight, saddened that they did not have the energy to chase a line of plodding oxen.

• • •

To avoid the landscape of barren fields and faces, Caecilia closed her eyes, thinking about her morning as she tried to shut out the braying of donkeys amid the chaotic traffic on the road.

There had been turmoil earlier. She'd been woken by Mastarna shaking her and was relieved to see he was clothed. He had been irritable, though, eager to be gone.

"It takes a day to reach my home by bullock train. We are already late to start."

Clambering out of bed, her clothes crumpled from a restless sleep and her hair even more tangled than the night before, she'd expected him to move away. Instead he quickly reached across and untied her girdle. In doing so he cut the knot of Herculeus, not for the purpose of lying with her but to allow her to change her garb.

After this there had been hurried packing and the hectic herding of her dowry cattle as the Etruscan caravan proceeded through the hubbub and stink of the Forum. The Curia Senate House and Temple of Vesta stood grandly above the muddle of stalls and houses while the Mighty Jupiter rode his chariot upon the summit of the Capitoline Hill. To her surprise the people of Rome had lined the narrow streets, somberly nodding to the half-caste bride who was leaving her city for the sake of peace. A lump rose in her throat at their farewell.

Such thoughts were interrupted by the hectoring cries of hawkers calling out to the caravan. Opening her eyes she gasped at the sight of the river Anio flowing to meet its mother, the Tiber. Beyond it towered Fidenae, the ancient hill town that Rome fiercely and possessively cradled like a child, always mindful that her neighbor, Veii, could snatch it from her arms. Indeed she wondered what Mastarna and the other nobles were thinking as they passed through the territory they still coveted as their own.

For it was here on this plain that thousands of Romans had died, their lives taken by the ancestors of the men who were escorting her this day. Men who were neither of valor nor of virtue. Bowing her head, Caecilia murmured a prayer, wishing she could halt and give thanks to fallen heroes, give thanks also to Mamercus Aemilius, her famous great-uncle, for liberating this town. For it was because of him that the fields around her were no longer sown with bones and the world was blue-skied and tranquil.

Today Fidenae, as ever, commanded a view of both rivers, but their waters had long borne away the cries and clamor of past conflicts. As she traveled past the fortress Caecilia could see Rome in the distance. To the northwest another citadel would soon appear upon the horizon. Veii would be the first foreign city she would enter.

Past and future seesawed back and forth within her gaze.

Safety and danger. Known and unknown.

• • •

History lessons were forgotten when they reached the ford. With much splashing and bellowing, the oxen were driven into the water. Riding the ferry to the other side, Caecilia clung to the tilting vessel as the ferryman poled the raft across the narrows.

Finally stepping onto firm ground, she feared that she had crossed more than a river; that she had left civilization behind. Yet the grassy banks and soil looked quite the same as that owned by Rome on the other side.

Soldiers had been patrolling the land around the ford. Their armor was as dull as the look in their eyes. Boredom made them slouch. Caecilia realized that these could be the last of her countrymen she would see for some time. It was disappointing to see such a lack of pride. Embarrassing, too. It was not as she imagined Roman soldiers should be.

They stood to attention, though, when they saw her. News had spread, but whether it was fame or notoriety that made them defer to her she could not tell. It was not often that a political bride would pass their way. She was tempted to speak to them, to cry out that she must return, but such weakness pricked her conscience and reminded her to keep her earlier resolve.

A few paces ahead of her, Mastarna reined in his impatient mount, both man and horse clearly wishing they could be galloping ahead, perhaps already be home, instead of marking time to the steady tread of the carriage oxen.

• • •

The caravan halted at a crossroads inn while Mastarna's steward dealt with the toll master. This time there would be no taxes paid to Rome to pass through the trading routes, thanks to the treaty that was sealed by their marriage.

"Stay close to Arruns," Mastarna ordered as he commandeered a table as far away as possible from the rowdiest patrons. Caecilia did not bridle at such a directive. The men who frequented the tavern were thirsty from their travel and looked as though they did not care if they reached their destinations quickly. Their interest in a noblewoman's presence was obvious. Even when she turned her head from them, their scrutiny tapped her upon the shoulder.

Arruns was Mastarna's man. A protector. Frightening. If she thought Mastarna had strength and muscle enough, Arruns's body was honed and sculpted for brawling. She was sure there was no softness within or without him. Worse, a tattoo covered half his swarthy face, a serpent head with fangs bared, its body coiled around his neck. His shaven head and broken teeth were so unsettling that she avoided his gaze whenever possible. Even though he was short, she imagined him picking up any man, whether taller, heavier, or stronger, and hurling him like Jupiter would a thunderbolt. In this inn full of drunken, unruly men, she wondered if it were preferable to be ogled by them or watched over by Arruns.

Most of Mastarna's wedding party had ridden ahead, their horses so elegant it was as though they were wrought in polished clay, their acclaim as widespread as the infamy of their masters.

Three noblemen remained behind: Apercu, an immense man who held his paunch with the same tenderness as a pregnant woman; Pesna, a lean fellow who looked like he consumed worries instead of meat; and Vipinas, whose face and hands were as though molded from beeswax.

Unable to speak their language or they hers, they were confined to nodding or gesturing, but at least Apercu added smiles to their silent dialogue. She noticed, though, that Pesna treated Mastarna with the same disdain as he did her, making her ponder what welcome awaited her in his city—the glib smiles of Apercu or the sullen glares of his stoop-shouldered colleague?

• • •

In the midafternoon, their journey was again interrupted when an ox fell lame. By this time pastures had changed to ravines through which the Cremera River flowed. Leaving behind the Tiber, the artery that sustained her city, was unnerving. Yet another foothold to her past removed.

Caecilia wandered down to a small clearing near the river. Shadows were lengthening, brightness sifted from the sunlight. The breeze that riffled the beech trees seemed to cause the dappled ground to shift. Throwing wet sand and gravel into the water, she watched the brief splashes, the speed of the current, the color of the shallows and the deep. The walls of the ravine rose above her. On the ridges, cypress cut spear points into the blue. Strangely enough the landscape did not threaten her with its looming cliffs. There was a beauty to the gray-and-yellow tufa stone covered with trailing ilex. For a moment she melted into sweet, yielding sleepiness and tried to rest.

The caravan lay less than fifty yards away. The ox herders' voices were audible as she sat upon the bank. Mastarna and the three aristocratic principes were arguing, no doubt over her. Their anger jarred her, piercing the contentment she felt from standing under a rustic sun far from the clutter of the city house. Their strident tones sharpened the edges of her nerves as well, drawing her again into anxiety and worry and concern.

She sent a handful of wet sand skittering across the water, the splashes spaced mere seconds apart, almost as natural as a ruffle and tremor of wind upon the river. But as she took another handful, a different snatch of sound and motion caught her attention.

A group of men had laced their way through the trees along the riverbank toward the clearing. Their faces and long plaits were smeared with gray loam; their clothes were cobbled strips of animal fur and hide. All carried swords in leather scabbards strapped to their backs, all grasped sturdy pikestaffs.

They seemed as astounded as she was to find her there, but their leader's surprise was short-lived. When one of his men made to grab her he held him back, ordering him in a furious whisper to obey. Even though she did not understand his tongue, his intent was clear. Pointing to the ox train, he commanded them to attack, leaving only one behind to deal with her.

The pit of her stomach was hollow and her heart clawed at her breastbone to let it escape as she tried to find her voice.

He was young. Younger than she. The smear of clay emphasized his pimply skin. He was frowning, his expression that of a junior asked to perform a task too great for him.

His indecision lessened her panic, and although her voice was squeaky it soon found certainty as she yelled for help.

Her screams startled him. He grabbed her wrist but showed his inexperience again when he chose to press a hand over her mouth not a blade across her throat. As he held her, his stench was overpowering, the rancid odor of fat and offal filling her nostrils. His hand was shaking, shaking as much as hers.

A heat surged through her, exploding in her chest, rising in her gorge, coursing through her limbs, and with a fierceness born of desperation she wrenched herself around, raising the river gravel in her hand and grinding it into his eyes, then dug her fingers into his sweating ochre-caked cheeks.

The raider yowled and clutched at his face. She scrambled away and saw Arruns behind him. He slid his arm around the bandit's neck and, almost in an embrace, shoved his sword deftly through the boy so that she could see its point slide out through his belly. Then, mercilessly, mercifully, as the bandit slumped to the ground, Arruns stabbed him through the heart.

As the bodyguard took her arm she flinched, unsure if she was any safer in his hands, but if Arruns noticed he did not care. He pushed her behind him and gruffly ordered her to follow. Again she did not have to know his language to understand, the dialect of action transcending words.

He was silent, though, as he bent down and pulled the sword from the brigand, the blade resisting slightly as it retracted through flesh and muscle.

The boy looked as hesitant in death as in life, his limbs askew as though unsure how best to lie at rest. Blood spilled from him and pooled upon the loam of the riverbank. But, oddly, what struck her most was that the soles of his feet were blackened, his toes chafed, bound only by rope and rags. He must have walked miles to meet his death. How eager he must have been to swap tattered bindings for stolen boots.

Examining him she felt neither pity nor hate. She was numb, as though she were a stranger noticing how Caecilia's heart was pounding and Caecilia's body was quaking.

Arruns growled at her impatiently and she stumbled after him as he strode toward the others. She could hear fighting and cries and shouts, but this suddenly died away as they pushed through the bushes to arrive at the road.

There were more bodies. Two brigands sprawled at Mastarna's feet. Apercu was wiping his weapon clean while Vipinas revealed that, although he looked bloodless, he was prepared to pierce the veins of another. Pesna stood to the side, his arm slashed. The caravan's guards had finished off the other bandits. It struck her that she had thought these perfumed aristocrats effete, but they were warriors after all.

"Are you hurt?" There was relief and concern in Mastarna's voice. He glanced at Arruns to gain confirmation of her answer.

Fresh blood streaked Mastarna's face and clothes. As he wiped his face with his hand, it left a smeary mess. Dark patches were showing under the arms of his tunic and across his back. He reeked of the men he had killed, and as he stepped over the bodies to take her forearm, his palm was hot and his eyes, which before had been reserved, were intense.

She could almost hear his heartbeat.

Her own heart was racing, too, but the fire within her was ebbing. When he touched her she pulled away. She did not want him near her, blaming him for this day, for plunging her into danger.

"You were brave, Caecilia, warning us like that. It gave us time enough to meet them."

She did not look at him, could not stop staring at the slain. One bandit lay with his mouth open in a wide exclamation of surprise or pain, as though frozen at the exact moment when his spirit fled—when his gods, if he had gods, forsook him. There were fine cracks in the clay upon his face as though he had grown wrinkled and old in the space of a swordfight. Yet beneath the lines he looked no more than twenty. The last time she had seen him he was leering at her as does a man starved of his daily meal.

She had seen dead bodies before. Apart from her parents, there had been villagers who'd died of plague or accident or exhaustion. She had even passed, with ghoulish interest, the putrid heads of criminals displayed on spikes at the crossroads, flies tickling their blackened skin, their buzzing a paean to death. Each time she had told herself not to look but was drawn nevertheless to do so.

This was different. She had seen a man killed today. She had viewed crumpled and hacked bodies that only a short time before had a pulse beating within them and who had grappled with needs and wants.

How many times had she watched men go to war? Seen those who returned maimed or bloodied? Mourned others who would not return? But never had she seen the scenes in between. How far blood could splatter, how a weapon was hefted, how empty were sightless eyes.

She found herself crouching, shivering violently, uncontrollably, so that her teeth chattered, her brief surge of courage expelled in a messy porridge of sick. Mastarna bundled his cloak around her, waiting patiently for her to finish. This time she did not fend him off. It was scant comfort upon this awful day.

"I want nothing other than to be far away," she said, wiping her mouth. "Please take me home."

Mastarna put his hands upon her shoulders. "Don't disappoint me, Caecilia. Your nerve didn't fail you against the brigand. Be brave enough to finish the journey to Veii."

She was on the brink of tears. Rome had surrendered her to this savagery. But would it welcome her back on the same day she had said farewell? "Then let us go," she said. "Quickly."

From the corner of her eye she glimpsed the ox herders unloading goatskins from the wagons. Tents for the night.

"We shall camp here," said Mastarna. "It will be twilight soon and too dangerous to travel."

"I just want to lie down," she said. "And never get up."

"Then you may do one, but not the other," he said, smiling briefly, and he led her to her tent.

• • •

Strangely she had not cried. Had not crumbled when facing death. And Mastarna's words had stirred her. No one had ever called her brave. The possibility of a reservoir of courage was absorbing, as was the thought that perhaps the warrior blood of Tata and Mamercus Aemilius flowed within her after all.

In the end she peeled off her stola with its dirt and smell and splatters of blood—his blood, the boy's blood—and took a knife to it, ripping it to pieces, wanting to rid herself of his residue upon her. And then it was anger that fueled her tears: at Aemilius for his betrayal, at her father for dying, and most of all at Drusus for not being there.

It was hard to keep quiet as she wept, to stifle self-pity and hide her weakness. To pretend she was stalwart and stoic as a Roman woman should be. And this failure deepened her misery, as she pressed her face into her palla cloak to muffle her tears, because she knew that they could hear her, that they must be thinking she was no different than any other woman. No different at all.

After her throat had become sore and her weeping painful, she would have fallen into an exhausted sleep but for the clumsy entry of the servant who brought her a basin of warm water and fresh clothes.

Unthreading her six wedding plaits, Caecilia cursed as she roughly tugged at the knots of dust and sweat, but when she began combing her crinkled hair she grew calm, thinking of how Drusus would have been proud of her today.

"You must be hungry." Mastarna had entered the tent without her noticing. She could tell his glance took in the pile of shredded clothes upon the floor, the puffiness of her face, and the redness of her eyes, yet he said nothing.

"I don't want to eat."

He shook his head. "Hunger feeds fretting. You must forget your fears and eat with me beside the fire."

Caecilia scanned his face for mockery but there was only good humor. His shoulders were relaxed, his expression no longer world-weary. How could he speak of food as though nothing had happened that day? As though it was nothing to have killed two men and then forgotten them by washing his hands and changing his clothes? She hoped that killing men was not all that could lighten her husband's mood.

"But that would not be seemly. There are only men. And besides, my hair is undressed."

Taking a tress, Mastarna rubbed it between thumb and forefinger. "Ah, much preferable to those Gorgon locks. I like a woman's hair untied. Especially when it is thick and soft like yours."

Blushing, she eased his fingers away, sweeping her hair around her neck to hide her mark. She was unused to flattery, uncertain if he was being sarcastic, pondering, too, as to how many women he had seen with their hair flowing loosely.

"Come," he continued, "as my wife you are safe to sit beside me."

Her stomach was grumbling but his invitation stirred an altogether different appetite, one that still prevailed after all that had happened that day. He was asking her to sit beside him with his peers. He was treating her as though she were an equal.

. . .

The stars were very bright. Brighter it seemed than those owned by Rome. The fire burned brightly, too, heat and illumination ridding the darkness of ghosts. Arruns had set up a spit and was cooking hare. The aroma teased her hunger after all, and she eyed the roasting dinner expectantly.

Yet at every sound that came from beyond the circle of firelight, her heart quavered, nervous at the thought that more strangers could erupt from the quietness of the evening and kill them. And yet everyone around her was unperturbed.

Apercu, Vipinas, and Pesna did not seem affronted by the presence of a woman. Their indifference was confusing.

"Your cries warned us just in time," said Mastarna. "We are most thankful."

Apercu bowed to her briefly. Vipinas even smiled, and she was surprised to see his front teeth were made of ivory held fast by a band of gold. Pesna, however, with his straight mouth that never smiled, was clearly resentful that he'd risked his life for a Roman and had been wounded for his troubles.

He was not alone in his predicament. She, too, had not expected to be rescued by Etruscans, the very people from whom she wished to be saved.

Fat from the roasting hare spat and sizzled, the flames flaring white with each aberrant drop. Caecilia watched silently as her husband joked with his companions.

Throughout the day she had noticed how the others either ignored or goaded him. She was unsure whether it was because it had always been that way or because of the marriage. Now their hostility had disappeared. They were ready to celebrate an escape from death together.

They played with a set of golden dice that Mastarna shook from a small gilded box. There were strange symbols on the side, not dots. Golden toys. A rich man's playthings. It was a shock, this gambling, this teasing of Fate. Roman men only wagered at the Saturnalia holiday once a year.

After a time Apercu broke off from his betting. Caecilia was relieved to see him take a salver of wine and place an offering of figs and blackberries before the fire. Pesna and Vipinas joined him in prayer and she made her own thanksgiving to the goddess Juno. Unexpectedly, their prayers were long and earnest. Pious, indeed, for a people she doubted even worshipped.

"They thank the god Laran. You know him by the name Mars," said Mastarna. Astonished, she stared at the men as they chanted.

Her husband did not join them.

The perils of the day now translated to an unease. Just as she had the night before, she wondered what kind of man could neglect the rituals of his people.

"Why do you not join in prayer?"

Mastarna scrutinized the three principes. "When I slew those robbers, Caecilia, I gave thanks to Nortia, the blind goddess of chance who is fickle and inconstant." He kissed each golden die in his hand, his face settling for a moment back into the gloomy lines of yesterday. "As usual, she spared me."

Caecilia frowned, her qualms at his impiety growing, puzzled, too, why Mastarna should rue Fate's favor.

"As for a thanksgiving," he continued, watching her tip a libation on the flames, "your piety will suffice for both of us."

Arruns stood before her, offering to pour her a drink from a jug of wine. She hastily covered her cup with her hand. "Patrician women do not drink wine. It is forbidden."

Mastarna snapped at the servant to fill her beaker with water.

"I have never seen such a man," she said, shivering as she recalled how Arruns had sliced through the boy, pulling his blade clear as though sharpening a knife upon a whetstone. "Those markings on his face, is that a Veientane fashion?"

"Arruns was once the Phersu. Phoenicia is his birthplace, although I doubt he would even recognize his mother now, nor she him. He was tattooed by his master and given an Etruscan name."

"Phersu?"

"The masked one. A man who makes sacrifice at funeral games."

"Is he a priest?"

"No, he acted on behalf of the zilath, the chief magistrate and high priest of Veii. Now I retain him to protect me—and my family."

Draining his cup, Mastarna called for another, making it clear he was not interested in telling her more. The principes were drinking steadily too, their laughter raucous and drunken. Their slap-on-the-back joviality made her uncomfortable, even a little frightened, their voices growing louder as they embellished their brave deeds. When Apercu stood up and urinated in front of her, the long, steady stream of piss hit the fire, sending a chimney of smoke billowing into the air. Turning her head, she wished perversely that she could be as she was usually in Rome: unseen and unheard and forgotten.

Mastarna kept steady pace with the others' drinking, but after Apercu's crassness he became pensive, turning his back on the others and attending to her instead.

"Who were those men today?" she asked.

"Gauls. We have traded with them for centuries, but now some want to do more than barter. I have not seen raiders like them so far south before."

"I have never heard of such a race. Perhaps Veii alone fears such marauders."

"Not just Veii, Caecilia, but all the Rasenna. My people. Those you call Etruscans and the Greeks Tyrrhenians. The land of Etruria stretches from the far north where those clay-streaked thieves live to the curves of the western coastline and the borders to the south. My people, Caecilia. Who created an empire long before Rome had even thought to build mud huts. Who ruled your city for centuries and founded its institutions."

"Yes, I know your people," she said icily, remembering her husband's lineage. "We threw out your tyrants long ago."

"Yet there are still patrician families in Rome who are descended from those kings."

"And they have strived for more than a hundred years to overcome their past."

Mastarna sighed. "Yes. Our ancestors have much to fester over. But luckily men like your uncle are wise to extend this treaty instead of letting us spiral once again into revenge and retribution."

Caecilia recalled Tata's hatred for the Veientanes and how his brothers had died at Fidenae. "They have let an enemy put a foot over its threshold without having to force the door."

Mastarna looked her up and down. "You are as warlike as a hoplite, wife—and as single-minded. Rome never lacks enemies. Not when it's so proud of squabbling with its neighbors."

"Rome only wages just wars," she declared, resentful that he should make her question what always was and what always should be. "Our city must be defended and if defense means attack, then so be it."

"So you do not believe in forgiveness, Caecilia?"

"Not if honor is to be denied. Not if we must bury our dead and then forget them."

He paused to throw a log upon the flames, sending a spray of sparks swirling, and she noticed how the fire loved his face, its harsh angles trying to deny the light purchase.

"Look at these men around you," he said presently. "Do you think they haven't lost family too? Apercu and Pesna both lost their brothers, and Vipinas's only son was killed by Romans. Don't you see? Each of us trail a line of dead men in our wake, adding another body each time vengeance is wreaked, dragging us down until we are drowned. And that, wife, is why Veii and Rome must forget old hurts lest the list of both cities' dead grows even longer."

Mastarna spread some ashes across the ground, using a stick to draw a map. "See how Veii sits to the north on one side of the Tiber with Rome on the other. My people must cross at Fidenae to reach the trade route to Campania in the south. But Rome first took the salt beds at the mouth of the Tiber and then, not sated, took Fidenae so it could levy taxes upon our traffic of silver and tin and grain."

"Don't act like you are merely humble traders minding your own business! Veii has tried to conquer Rome more than once."

Excitement and indignation stirred within her, the freedom to dispute a man about war was exhilarating. Her voice rose enough for the three noblemen to look up. Mastarna gestured to her to speak more quietly but he did not silence her.

"Ah, how true," he said. "Veii has long wanted Rome just as much as Rome wants Veii. It is a temptation, is it not? Twelve miles away, our cities lie a god's footstep apart. They are lovers separated by the river in between."

"They are no lovers."

"Of course they are. They long to hold each other, to possess and control. To be as one. Only both vie to be the husband, not the bride; the lover, not the beloved."

"Then you think Veii is now the husband just as you are to me?"

"Things are not so simple. We represent the joining of those contrary lovers for peace."

They were distracted by Arruns pulling the hare from the spit. The aroma was delicious, prompting her appetite. She watched how the Phoenician sliced the meat. He was as dexterous with a carving knife as he was with his sword. Suddenly her brief hunger abated, remembering how the boy's belly had been filled with iron.

"Why did you volunteer to wed me, Mastarna?"

He leaned over and poured more water for her, the action protracted as though he was deciding if he would answer at all or merely tell her what was the best she should hear.

"I agreed," he finally said, "because I was asked to do so by a friend and because I was prepared to take the risk."

"Risk?"

"Yes, Caecilia. My father was killed at the last battle of Fidenae by your ancestor, the great Mamercus Aemilius. I have dishonored my family by marrying an Aemilian. I risk losing the respect of all my tribe."

• • •

Arruns arranged some meat upon her plate and added figs and berries, but she could not eat, stunned as to why her husband did not want to avenge his father. If Tata had been slain by Mastarna's kinsman she would have added vengeance to her duties, no matter how many ghosts would cling to her forever. And who was this friend who could convince Mastarna to deny retribution for his clan?

She tried a mouthful of the greasy meat but found it hard to swallow. In comparison Apercu noisily sucked the bones free of flesh and complained when there was too little to refill his plate.

Nibbling the blackberries, she noticed her palm was scored by dozens of tiny scrapes from gripping the gravel. It was only when she fingered the grazes that she felt the pain, felt, too, that her wrist hurt from where the bandit had held her. There was a bruise form- ing in the shape of his fingers upon the skin, and her body ached from being wrenched and grabbed. Today her hurts had gone unnoticed, but with weariness they were revealed.

The shock of the menace and gore and death of the day returned. If she had not had the gravel in her hand, what would have happened? Her hands began shaking. She clasped them tightly in her lap, taking a deep breath, willing herself not to cry.

Mastarna was watching her, and when he spoke it was almost as though he'd read her thoughts. "I do not regret killing the ban- dits today, Caecilia. Or begrudge Arruns adding your raider to his list."

"Because they were Gauls?"

"No, because they would have made you their bride before me."

She stared at him, unsure what to reply. She was used to being a possession. Her father's, her uncle's, and now his. She did not think of herself as anything other than something to be owned, but when he reminded her of his rights, the heady freedom of talking with these men beside a campfire faded. His words reminded her, too, that the bandit's possession of her would have been brief and shared. The stink of the boy as he grasped her, a stink of fear as great as her own, returned. Would he have been first, or would the others, his elders, have only let him have the scraps?

She stood up, wanting to be alone. The mouthful of hare she'd eaten sat heavily within her, and for a moment surged again into her gullet. She forced it back down, not wanting him to see her vomit twice that day.

As he led her back to her tent she worried briefly that he might wish to claim her, but she was too weary to cope with such nerves. All the other perils of the day had swallowed up any room within her head.

He did not seek to follow her inside, though. "Orion is with us tonight," he said, pointing to the canopy of the sky, "and there is one of the wandering stars that aid sailors to navigate upon the seas."

Caecilia peered into the night but she could only see a mass of stars, little pinpricks that were so dense they formed into a milky spill upon the black. "I can see only stars, not constellations."

"Believe me," he insisted. "In the middle of Orion is a small star, tiny but fierce. It is called Bellatrix in your language."

Despite his guidance, she still could not make out one speck amid a thousand, and so, standing in front of her, he directed her to look along his arm to where he was pointing.

Aware of his nearness, unsure of his motives, Caecilia ignored the heavens and instead considered the strange man she'd married: the groom of yesterday with his reserve and condescension; a husband who talked politics with his wife, her hair pinned loosely before other men; and now a warrior who coldly slew robbers then calmly studied a crowded firmament.

Mastarna turned around to check she was paying attention. "That is you, Caecilia," he said. "Bellatrix, the warrioress. After today you deserve such a name."

· · ·

Caecilia lay restlessly on the rough pallet, her mind grappling with more than the memory of the Gaul's touch and smell. For the sharing of the mysteries of a night sky and two cities' fates was something rare after being denied anything other than the warp and weft of a woman's life. Tonight Mastarna had woven threads of war and history and politics into the fabric, a fabric that usually only clothed a man.

When sleep did come it brought the night demon.

Settling heavily upon her chest it leaned forward with scaly hands, one pressing upon her windpipe, the other clamping firm upon her mouth.

Dreams are messages sent by the gods, and sleep the channel through which omens are revealed. Caecilia lay awake, perspiring and stricken, thinking she would forever be haunted not just by the demon but by the boy, her finger marks still clear in the clay on his unbearded cheek.

FIVE

He was morose the next day, as though waking to a new morning was a disappointment. Apart from asking Caecilia after her welfare, he spoke to no one other than Arruns, and the closer they drew to his home the surlier he became.

With the Cremera still as their companion, the caravan continued its journey. The rocking of the creaky wagon jarred her. The bruises that had bloomed upon her wrists were sore and her joints pained from the bandit's rough handling. Head aching from lack of sleep and worry, Caecilia concentrated on the grooves of the rutted road to focus attention away from concern. And so, constantly sneezing from the dust kicked up by the bullocks' hooves, it took time to notice the wanton scattering of greenness upon the verge, tufts of errant grass that grew carefree from thirst.

Glens of oak had changed to a vista of flowing fields of barley. Dry-stone walls curved along the margins with rows of poplar or pine crowning ridges. Hawthorn trees dotted with bright-red berries crowded together beside the roadside.

All green.

Deep and dark or translucent with light. Thriving on sunshine, not scorched by it—making Caecilia ask why the gods allowed rain to fall upon this side of the river, on Mastarna's people's land; why Rome scavenged for husks while Etruscan silos groaned with grain.

Men were scything grass, skimming the froth of chamomile flowers and setting free their heady scent. They paused briefly in their toil to bow their heads to Mastarna and the noblemen but, realizing who Caecilia was, their glances lengthened into stares. Reminded of the country folk of her village, the Roman girl nodded and smiled but they did not respond. The children, though, ran beside the caravan, squealing and laughing and pointing at the stranger.

Humble wooden shrines dotted the sides of the road before which small votives vied for space as well as for divine favor. Some were fashioned into the shapes of hands or feet engraved with imprecations to soothe crippled fingers or heal a broken toe. The turf altars were adorned with wilted garlands of daisies together with fresh fragrant ones. Caecilia whispered a prayer, knowing she had crossed over the boundaries of their gods while leaving hers behind.

Clinging dizzily to her seat, apprehension and curiosity merged as the cart bumped along the steepening road to reach the Via Veientana. The climb continued until an enormous archway of yellow-and-gray rock appeared on the ridge. Turning in her seat, Caecilia looked back over her shoulder southward. Southward toward Rome. And then she swiveled around again in wonderment. On the tableland opposite her, the square-cut stone wall of the city lay. And around it roads radiated out as though from a hub, extending to all points of the compass. Roads that she had never known existed, heading to places she'd only heard of, all leading to one place, the city of Veii.

"Welcome to your new home, Caecilia."

Mastarna had ridden up beside her and was pointing across the valley to the right of the plateau. There Veii's arx teetered upon a precipitous tufa cliff. At least a hundred feet high, the citadel was crowned with the graceful lines of a temple, its brilliantly black-and-red-painted portico and pediment glinting in the sunlight. Astounded, she felt a kernel of excitement unfurl within her despite her nerves.

The convoy began the descent into the valley, terrifying in its grade, until it reached the juncture where the Cremera met its sister river, one that girded the city to the west.

The final rise to the main city gates commenced. Along the way the caravan fought for space with wagons heading to and from the markets. The acrid stink of molten metal filled the air as Caecilia passed foundries and blacksmiths' shops, hoping plowshares rather than weapons were being forged. It was as though she had kicked the top off an anthill and found another world of industry and intricacy and purpose foreign to her own, exposing herself also to the danger of being bitten.

The hills of Rome boasted characters of their own: the pompous Palatine, pious Capitoline, and plebeian Aventine all teeming with houses and temples and shops that had amazed her when she first saw them. She never thought she'd see anything grander or smellier or noisier, and yet as she passed through Veii's magnificent gates she held her breath, realizing she had crossed the sacred border into another city.

As the oxen trundled into the congested streets, Caecilia needed to adjust to enormity, to immensity, to grandeur, as though she were stepping into the footprints of a giant, reminding her of her smallness.

The main thoroughfare was wide, wide enough for three wagons to pass at once, which was fortunate given the traffic. Here was no simple intersection of main streets running north and south and east to west. Instead two or three broadly paved avenues bisected the road, also extravagant in breadth. Drainage ditches covered by stone slabs running along the streets made the stalwart great drain of Rome seem rustic. Strange people bustled and bumped each other as they hastened down cobblestoned pavements or crossed the street on raised stepping-stones, which were not precaution enough to avoid the stickiness of muck and ordure left by ghost-gray oxen or horses.

Immodesty flourished everywhere as did excess. Caecilia averted her eyes from the many statues of nudes; the skin of males ruddy, the women of pale hue. Concentrating instead on the densely packed wooden houses with their jaunty painted friezes, she soon forgot such indecency, absorbed with the sight of leather workers, carpenters, and potters working in their shops while all around, the catcalls and barking of the vendors bombarded her ears, inveigling her to stop and buy, stop and buy!

Here Caecilia had no idea of each person's status. Most seemed to wear vivid-colored robes with bright borders. In contrast, her world was defined in clothing of white and purple or brown and black. There was certainty in looking across a crowd and knowing exactly who was a senator or knight, citizen or bondsman. Broad or narrow purple stripes on tunics and on togas, and red shoes with ivory buckles denoted who was patrician. All were reassuring. All clearly defined the tiers and limits of society. Strangers were not encouraged. More often than not within the Forum, the only alien faces were those of conquered enemies doing their masters' bidding.

Today she witnessed others as foreign as the Etruscans, with their large cat-shaped eyes and short-cropped hair. There were sun-brown men with pointed beards, their long hair oiled and twisted. Fair-skinned people as well, who made Caecilia think the sun must never shine upon their land. One man with skin as black as onyx stared at her, the whites of his eyes streaked with fine red veins, startling against his darkness. Head swathed in a turban, he bowed when he noticed her scrutiny. She quickly turned away.

Mastarna twisted around on his horse to once again gesture to her to look ahead. "These are the Gates of Uni." Caecilia tilted her head back as she raised her eyes. The portal of the arx stood in front of her, guarded by two ominous stone towers. And beyond, accessed by a wooden bridge and one narrow road, loomed the citadel: her journey's end, and the start of her new life.

• • •

Mastarna's house was made of light. Or so it seemed.

It was clear he did not need the scanty gifts of cattle and gold that comprised her dowry. His residence surpassed any of the homes of Rome. It was of brick, and its entranceway was flanked by two columns with a pediment crowning the roof.

Passing through a monumental bronze door, Caecilia entered the atrium. The high ceiling was supported by enormous rafters decorated in terra-cotta cladding. Incredibly, there were no columns to be seen inside. Sunshine spilled copiously across the floor from the roof opening. To her surprise the ceiling slanted inward, making her wonder what it would be like when sheets of water streamed into the decorated bronze reservoir below when it was raining.

From the doorway, her eyes surveyed a shrine and a hearth fire that was large and fierce and bright. Both sights warmed her, relieved to know the household spirits were also revered in his world.

But it was not this alone that delighted her. Beyond the reception room she could see a garden. Not like the vegetable patch at the back of her uncle's house but a place extravagant with sun and warmth and beauty. An arcade ran along each side of it flanked with shrubs. In the middle was a pool with a fountain. In the face of such artistry Caecilia was forced to wonder what kind of people flaunted water for decoration instead of sustenance or wasted time carving laurel into patterned borders. All within the confines of a house!

"Hail, Aemilia Caeciliana."

A diminutive woman stood before her. Caecilia was not sure what struck her most. Here was a mature matron yet surely not one of any virtue—a noblewoman dressed like a harlot. Her robes were vermilion and were cinched in tightly by a girdle drawn under the bodice. She wore not one but three gold lockets around her neck. Most striking of all was her hair: white as frost and pulled high into the most elaborate hairstyle. Ringlets bobbed over her ears, curls spiraled upon her brow, and the bulk was tied up and covered by a snood.

Mastarna embraced the woman with such force that Caecilia thought the lady's slight bones would crack. "Ati," he said, kissing her as she laughed at his bearish embrace.

"Vel, it is good to see you, son." Then she turned to face the Roman.

"Welcome, Caecilia," she said. "My name is Larthia. I am glad you are safe."

Caecilia hesitated, unused to such effusiveness, surprised, too, that the woman spoke her own tongue, even if clumsily. "Thank you."

Larthia's eyes were as black as her son's but without their harshness. In repose, her face was defined by curved cheekbones and a high forehead, yet when she smiled, the bottom row of her teeth was rotted, forcing her to raise a small napkin to her mouth to wipe away a trickle of saliva. Instinctively, Caecilia ran her tongue inside her own mouth.

Larthia was surveying her also, and Caecilia sensed that, although the Veientane woman was smiling, she must have reservations about welcoming an Aemilian into her home. When the older woman stretched to take her hand, the Roman started. She was a stranger to this woman, and, until today, a foe. Was it customary to be so familiar? She thought briefly of Aurelia, whose hand had only ever brushed her in punishment or bullying.

"Why are you surprised, my dear, that a mother should greet her new daughter so?"

Caecilia did not know how to respond. After a pause, Mastarna touched her elbow. "You might wish to give your present to Ati now," he said softly.

She nodded, thankful for the opportunity to relieve the awkward moment, but as Mastarna signaled to a servant to come forward with her gift, he was interrupted by the entry of a man into the room.

Caecilia's eyes widened as she took in the peculiar costume of the stranger. He wore a tall hat that spiraled to a tip and was tied by straps beneath his chin. His long-sleeved tunic reached to his boots. Heavily beringed fingers played with the fringes of his cloak, which was lined with sheepskin and fastened with a large bronze clasp at his throat. Indeed his hands were striking: long-jointed, in perfect symmetry, the long fingernails painted purple.

The man scrutinized her from head to toe. Unable to break from his examination, she shivered, his gaze hypnotic, the shape of his eyes accentuated by dark lines drawn around them. His face seemed familiar, and then Caecilia realized it was Mastarna she was looking at, only his face had none of the hard edges that war, killing, and pain chipped and scraped from a man's features. She knew, too, that if she touched his milky skin it would be softer than her own and the muscle beneath would give no resistance. But his eyes made her forgive this because, unlike Mastarna's, they were liquid and gleaming and brilliant. They were eyes that had gazed upon the spirits, may even have glimpsed the gods.

"Caecilia, my brother, Artile."

The Roman girl waited for his welcome, but instead Artile spoke abruptly to his brother with a voice identical in timbre and resonance to Mastarna's. Their conversation was brief. And unfriendly.

"Artile requests that the purification rite be performed," said a voice from behind her.

The speaker was a youth who gained her attention not so much due to his perfect Latin but for his perfect physique. He took her hand and bowed. "Aemilia Caeciliana, I am known as Tarchon. May your time here be blessed."

As she struggled to reply she tried not to stare. The youth was as comely as a maid. Dark oval eyes registered amusement and his full lips curved in a bow. His skin was flawless, his teeth even, his body lean and muscular and brown, and if Artile had communed with the gods, the gods themselves surely cherished Tarchon. "You speak the language of my people."

"And Greek and Phoenician and Carthaginian. I won't bore you with the rest of my talents."

"Be quiet," growled Mastarna. "Caecilia does not need to hear your bragging."

But she was sorry her husband had silenced the youth. Despite his boasting, there was sincerity and warmth. "And are you brother to my husband also?"

Mastarna grimaced. "Tarchon is my son, Caecilia."

Of all the strangeness of that day, this was the strangest. Tarchon was of a similar age to her, perhaps no more than twenty. She tried not to glance at Mastarna. She knew he was old, but surely not as old as her father? He must have sired Tarchon when he was only a youth himself.

A son?

And before that there must have been a wife.

"You must miss your mother."

"Yes," said Tarchon, "and my father."

Caecilia looked across to Mastarna in confusion.

"I adopted Tarchon eight years ago." There was an edge to his voice. "His father was my cousin and most honored. Unfortunately my adopted son needs to heed the example of his parents."

Tarchon colored, but Mastarna's rebuff did not stop his teasing. "I am glad to have such a young and gracious mother," he said wryly, and suddenly she was reminded of Marcus who would always try to make her feel at ease.

Artile interrupted, his tone impatient, making Tarchon blush again and fall silent, subservient to the two men. Caecilia was both intrigued and irritated that she could not follow their discourse. Finally Larthia interrupted and the brothers grew quiet.

"Artile will perform the expiation rites," said Mastarna, "to expel any evil spirits you, as a stranger, may bring into this house."

Caecilia glanced at her brother-in-law. It rightly should have been her husband, as head of the house, who performed this ceremony.

"Artile is chief haruspex of the Temple of Uni," said Tarchon, "the goddess you Romans call Juno." There was pride in his voice. "He is a priest skilled in prophecy. Our family is fortunate to have him perform domestic rites."

Artile began his chanting while she stared and stared. This man was a priest? With his outlandish clothes and compelling eyes?

And Juno lived here under another name?

Mastarna distracted her from her scrutiny of Artile. "Perhaps you could give my mother your gift?"

Caecilia hesitated. The palla she offered was simple and uncostly. Larthia was arrayed in rich cloth and bedecked with precious jewelry. The possibility of humiliation threatened as much as criticism. The shawl befitted a Roman matron, not an Etruscan one.

Her fears were unwarranted. The Veientane woman arranged the shawl around her shoulders, stroking the soft white wool and tracing the acanthus leaves decorating its edges.

"It is very fine, and doubly worthy because you have shown that you display wifely skills. I have a gift for you, too."

A delicate mirror of gold was pressed into Caecilia's hand, the valuable metal and the fineness of the engraving emphasizing the paltriness of her gift. The figure of a naked woman was etched upon it, who sat idly gazing at her own reflection. A girl with high arched wings stood behind her, dabbing perfume upon her from a jar.

"This is Turan. Your people call her Venus, goddess of love and beauty. Her handmaiden, Alpan, tends to her."

Caecilia ran her fingers over the looking glass. Even her wealthy father had not lavished such extravagance upon her. However, the mirror's value was not what delighted her most. In her hand a divinity was depicted as real as any woman attending to her grooming. Caecilia had said prayers to Venus many times. Did the Roman goddess truly look this beautiful?

The woman paused, watching Caecilia. "I sense you are a woman of religion, as am I. Know that you are now one of this family. Together we shall appease, placate, and praise the gods that rule us whether they live in Veii or Rome."

Confused, Caecilia glanced at Mastarna, but he was busy talking to his brother. Again she stroked the cold polished surface, raising it to see her reflection, not surprised at all to see puzzlement upon it.

• • •

Aemilius's house had one dining room, as did Tata's. Until now Caecilia thought this was all that was needed.

Mastarna's house had two. The smaller one was startling, with its doorway framed by a heavy wooden lintel and exposed doorjambs. Three lines of red, blue, and black were painted parallel to the floor as gaudily as those upon the colored borders of Tarchon's robes.

Murals covered the walls, where hunters with dark skins, their bows drawn taut, waited for beaters to flush a flock of ducks from the rushes, death as quick as the flick of a bowstring. Indeed, the birds were so plump and real Caecilia wondered if she should seize them from the sky and pluck them for dinner.

Thinking this she glanced back through the doorway to the hearth fire. No kettle or pot or spit or grill hung beside it. Somewhere in this mansion there was a kitchen where servants were cooking. Mastarna's atrium was not the heart of the home—a kitchen, chapel, and workroom, shared by master and servants alike. Instead, the large hearth fire was for worship only, to be tended and ceremoniously rekindled once a year.

Her attention was distracted by servants piling repository tables high with salvers of fruit and meats. This seemed odd. She only needed to slake her thirst after her journey. A humble drink of water or cordial would have sufficed. Instead she realized that a midday meal was to be served.

"We dine formally twice daily here," said Mastarna, leading her to a dining couch.

"Are there no chairs?"

"Women eat with their men here—upon divans."

Hearing him made her realize that the communal meal in the forest had not been due to circumstance but custom, and unlike the single meal she ate with Aurelia in the late afternoon, here she was also to dine with men every day.

After perching gingerly on the edge of the cushioned couch, she finally pulled her legs up and lay upon one side, resting on her elbow. She was uncertain about dining at the same level as the men, but seeing Larthia reclining on her own couch encouraged her to be bold. After a time, though, the novelty wore thin, and her arm soon was numb despite the softness of the pillows. She wondered, too, how men lasted through a banquet without getting indigestion.

The food was too rich—pork liver and quail eggs. Not wanting to seem rude, she ate a little but was content to sip her water quietly, wishing her stomach did not ache so much from having to digest both the food and the surroundings. Her head throbbed, too, when she realized she would encounter this every day, that this was what would become familiar, that this would be her home.

When she was a child she had once eaten an entire bowl of honeyed plums. Coated in a sticky glaze that made the dark skin shiny, she thought there could be nothing more beautiful or delicious. The surfeit gave her a bellyache all afternoon. It also made her cautious of anything that smelled, tasted, or looked too sweet.

She gazed around her at the excess of color and design, the glut of ornaments and utensils, the extravagance of space and the abundance of food and drink, and was reminded of those plums. Was she supposed to embrace all this garishness and luxury? Was she expected to forget frugality, abandon simplicity?

Jittery, uncertain what to do or say, she prayed she would be allowed to retire soon, to find some small corner of silence within this strange new home. There she might remedy the night demon's theft of her sleep and stop her mind racing.

Occasionally stealing glances at Tarchon, she found herself comparing him to Marcus. With his long hair and beard, the Roman was like a scruffy hound to this sleek cat of an Etruscan. There was laziness to the Veientane's beauty, too, an expectation of being admired without the need to woo the admirer. To Caecilia, such good looks were disconcerting, emphasizing her own imperfections and yet awakening a wish for him to consider her worthy of attention.

As though reading her thoughts, Tarchon glanced toward her and smiled, making her wish it was Marcus who was offering her comfort instead of this stranger, that her cousin was there to stretch across and whisper some nonsense in her ear to make her laugh.

Unexpectedly, the notes of a double flute and lyre wound their way through the soft sibilance of the Etruscans' conversation, replacing anxiety with amazement. Was her arrival such a great occasion that it warranted entertainment? Listening to the trills and sweeping chords, Caecilia was calmed. Found, too, that the deep resonant tones of Mastarna's voice lulled her nerves.

"The wedding feast will be held this evening," said Larthia, breaking through Caecilia's reverie. "You will be introduced to the nobility of Veii. But, more importantly, the zilath is attending, so make sure you are well rested and that you wear your finest robes."

Mastarna gestured to a stout servant girl to approach. "Cytheris will tend to you. She speaks your language and is honest enough. Go now and bathe. Rid yourself of the grime of yesterday."

"I am to have my own servant?"

Her husband smiled. "Bellatrix, you command a household of them."

• • •

Perspiration trickled down Caecilia's nose into the hot, deep, blessed water of the bath. She gazed up at the ceiling to survey the mural of a chase. A footrace was depicted. A woman was bending to pick up a golden apple while behind her a man sprinted to overtake her.

The colors were brilliant, the characters almost alive. The billowing robes of the man were so real that she swore she could reach up and grab his hem. How was it that no Roman walls were so adorned? Were the Rasenna the first to learn how to decant beauty into paint?

Relaxing in this marble bath she'd been seduced by the intensity from the light well that flooded over her. She was at peace, letting her mind rest, feeling only sensations, the silence punctuated by the occasional drips from the ceiling or the swishing sound that accompanied tiny movements of her limbs.

Where was the dark, dank cupboard of a room that housed her uncle's bath? The murky, unfiltered water? The cockroaches that scuttled in dim corners? An ordeal she had tried to suffer only once a week.

Next to her, the handmaid named Cytheris stood occasionally sprinkling rose petals and orange blossoms into the water. Caecilia pointed to the naked woman above her, only a swirl of cloth flying around her waist.

"Who is she?"

"Oh, that is Atlenta. Have you not heard of her?"

Caecilia shook her head.

"A woman of great beauty, a huntress as fearless as any warrior. Fleeter, too."

"Why is she stooping to collect an apple?"

"Her suitor tricked her. He dropped three golden apples to distract her and win the race to claim her as his bride."

The water was cooling and yet Caecilia lingered.

"And her father let this happen?"

"It is a sad story, mistress. Her father first abandoned her when she was born, then made her a prize to be claimed by any man who could beat her in a footrace. This was cruel, too, you see, because there was a prophecy that, should she marry, a terrible fate awaited her."

The Roman stared at the painting again, feeling for this Atlenta. "And what was her future?"

Cytheris extended a sheet to dry her mistress, making it clear she wished Caecilia to finish her bath, but the Roman hesitated to step out, naked, in front of the girl, unused to being undressed in front of other women. She quickly wrapped the cloth around her.

"They displeased the goddess of love, I'm afraid, when they wandered into a sacred grove. Their punishment was to be eaten by lions."

Wringing the water from her hair, Caecilia felt uneasy. Atlenta's story had hints of her own. She prayed she would not have so sad a fate.

• • •

The bed was wide.

Large enough for three people to sleep soundly. Large enough, she hoped, for her to avoid touching him by accident. Not wide enough, though, to escape.

The bed was high. It would need a footstool to clamber onto it. There was a linen cover stretched over the deep soft mattress decorated with a strange crisscross pattern of red, blue, and green. Cushions were piled high against a headboard fashioned from beech. If she could use the bed merely for sleep, she would have thought it a divine gift.

A heavy red curtain extended the full length of the bed-chamber, thinly separating it from the loveliness of light, water, and warmth, as well as noise and bustle and intrusion. Looking out, she could view the garden arcade where grapevines with plump, purple grapes were entwined around the columns. Caecilia weighed up the agreeable prospect of greeting the sun while lying in her bed with the discomfort of being seen doing so by all in the household.

On one wall of the room there was yet another mural. A leop-ard rampant, outlined heavily in red and painted yellow, who dis-played black spots numerous and distinctive. He stood in a grove of laurels with a flight of swallows flitting above his head. His gaze was peaceful, his eyes entrancing. She liked him immediately.

How different to her small, gloomy bedroom situated off the atrium in Aemilius's house with the noise of the street piercing its walls. And yet, while it bore no comparison to her new sleeping place, at least she did not need to share it.

Even in this empty chamber Mastarna's existence could not be ignored. His panoply hung upon the wall along with baskets and hooks. Polished, cold, and menacing, the armor revealed not only his wealth but his potential as a foe: the round shield with its bull's head boss, the molded greaves, and the sculpted cuirass. And, most daunting of all, the heavy crested helmet with its hinged cheek pieces stared at her from empty sockets, a warning that, from the time she rubbed slumber from her eyes to when she blew out the lamp, she was a hostage, and that when she lay upon the bed she would be denied any protection.

Drawing the coverlet over herself, she closed her eyes and tried to rest.

• • •

Cytheris's dark hair was like unspun wool. Its abundance made Caecilia's own thickness seem sparse in comparison, especially as the handmaid wore it in one long braid reaching almost to her ankles. When unloosed and brushed it would look like a thicket from which a round and pockmarked face would peer. Pimples still lurked on Cytheris's chin, and although her smile was appealing in its breadth it revealed a missing dogtooth. Caecilia considered she should have been milking cows or mucking out pigsties instead of waiting upon a noblewoman. Yet Cytheris's ability to speak her tongue had made this first afternoon in Veii bearable. The novelty of having a maid to herself was also intriguing. At home, a miserly Aurelia had commandeered the services of the one harried handmaid.

The Greek girl was from Neapolis, a town south of here in Magna Graecia. Just yesterday Caecilia had never met someone from a foreign land; now she was plunged into a world of varied skins and tongues.

Beside the dressing table in the bedroom was a cylindrical bronze casket. Inside the cista were little compartments full of ivory combs, hairpins of bone, and cosmetic jars made of amber.

When Cytheris had opened up the trove, Caecilia laughed at the thought of using such outlandish things. Yet she was delighted at the perfume of lilies the handmaid dabbed upon her skin, amazed that a flower's essence could be distilled and poured into an alabaster flask.

Then she grew wary. Was it really expected she would be so flagrant as to paint her face and redden her lips?

"How shall I arrange your hair, mistress?"

"In a knot."

"That is very plain."

"A knot will suffice."

The maid was bemused but Caecilia was determined to maintain the dignity of a Roman matron. It was thrill enough for her to be free of the demure bun of a maiden but it would be undignified to adopt Larthia's elaborate twisting and pinning.

"How is it that you know Latin?"

Cytheris continued with her task, speaking with a hairpin clenched between her teeth.

"Courtesy of a man from Aricia, a town in Latium. He was kind enough to teach me his language as well as make me with child. The first gift was not particularly useful until your arrival, my lady. As to the second, you can judge." The handmaid nodded toward a small girl who had appeared at the door. She was no more than seven with a solemn air and ringlets of black hair. She handed some clothing to her mother.

"Very well, Aricia," snapped Cytheris. "Off you go."

"I see you called her after her father's city," said Caecilia as she watched the little one leave. "Is your husband also in service here?"

"The Arician was not my husband, mistress," laughed Cytheris. "I was his slave. The gods may remember how many men I've lain with, but I've called none husband."

Again Caecilia felt as though she must be simple. "You're a slave?"

Cytheris's eyes narrowed as though concerned she may have been undergoing some test. "And pleased to be in the care of the House of Mastarna."

"And Aricia?"

"She is also. But does Rome not have such the like?"

"Prisoners of war. And bondsmen. But they are treated as servants and work beside us in the fields."

"The Greek and Rasennan worlds depend on the toil of their slaves," continued the Greek girl. "I would not fuss about it too much. Lord Mastarna is a kind master. Better than some."

"How long? How long have you been enslaved?"

"How long?" Her forehead wrinkled in concentration. "A long time. Father got into debt, you see, and rather than face bondage himself, sold me to a trader. I fetched a good price at auction, too, despite an ugly face. Now shall I finish your hair?"

Caecilia shook her head. "Auction? Were you sold as they do cattle?"

"Most slaves are bought at auction here."

Then she remembered Tata. How he'd said that debtors were sold into slavery across the river. Across the Tiber into Veii. She shivered to think there might be more than one unfortunate Roman citizen enslaved in her husband's house, never able to return home.

She wondered, too, at what kind of people would buy women and children as though bartering sows and piglets.

"Forget my tale, mistress. Look! It is for your wedding feast."

The fabric Aricia had delivered was a robe. Caecilia's mouth dropped open. This was not the simple stola and tunic from her trunk but a gown shimmering with golden thread. Cytheris's manner was reverential as she handed her the dress.

"There's more too, my lady."

A gilded fillet for her hair, a pendant for her neck, gold circlets for her wrists. Her imagination could never have conjured such finery. Caecilia fingered the round pendant—a precious amulet to replace the charm she'd surrendered to her uncle.

Mastarna was both generous and thoughtful.

"This looks like Atlenta," she said, showing the maid the locket.

Cytheris peered at it. "Why, it does, too."

Putting the necklace aside, Caecilia stroked the fine weave of the gown, bringing its softness to her cheek, checking to see if the color suited her complexion. The cloth was light, exquisite. She had never owned so expensive, so elegant a garment. It must have taken magic to spin thread that seemed pure gold. But then she noticed the thinness of the fabric, and how close fitting the garment was. The gown would cling to her, not just defining the curve of her breasts but revealing them.

"Come, my lady, I'll help you dress."

"Get my stola and tunic from my baggage. I am a Roman and will dress as one."

"But this chiton is your wedding gown," the Greek girl stuttered.

Caecilia let the robe drop to the floor. A silence fell between them as Cytheris silently helped her mistress into more sober clothes.

When Mastarna appeared his face creased into a frown. "What's the matter?" he said, scooping up the gown. "Why aren't you dressed?"

He was gruff. Despite his brief pleasure at seeing Larthia, his mood had not improved. She tensed, ready to explain why she must anger him. Yet when she saw him she found herself wordless.

He wore a white kirtle, bare to the waist with a mantle draped across one shoulder. A golden torque around his neck. His brown skin was smooth, but crossing his chest was one long livid scar, a diagonal slash from shoulder to hip as though he wore a living sash of purple. She could not keep her eyes off the wound, wondering who had dealt it, how indeed he had survived it. There were other marks upon his body, too. Less gruesome but nevertheless testament to a whole history of battles and injury: a fine white mark across his collarbone and a longer one above his hip bone and, of course, the cicatrice between his lip and battered nose that she had studied surreptitiously before.

Then she realized that, although he had lain naked beside her that first night, she had no idea of the ugliness lying inches away, an unsightliness that was fascinating. Yet he seemed unperturbed by his disfigurement, equally assured whether bearing himself proudly in elegant society or opening the throat of a bandit in a wood. The sight of his near nakedness was so distracting it took Caecilia some moments to realize he was to remain half clad at the banquet. She dropped her gaze and blushed.

Mastarna ignored her scrutiny, holding out the wedding dress to her. "You must hurry and change. The zilath will be arriving soon."

"I cannot wear this. It would be unseemly. The chiton is too tight, and the linen is too sheer."

He smiled. "Bellatrix, you will look beautiful. There is no need to hide your fair figure under homespun."

Unease flickered at the base of her throat. His flattery was as unnerving as the fact he wanted her to stand near naked in front of others. She shook her head.

Mastarna took a step closer, gently pushing Cytheris aside. "Caecilia, you are in Veii now. You must adjust and act as befitting my wife." His voice was hard. He had not spoken in such a tone before.

Her pulse sharpened, her heartbeat racing as confusion overwhelmed her. After their time together last night she'd found herself trusting this Etruscan, even thinking she might like him. Now he was encouraging wantonness when he had promised Aemilius he would respect her. Stories of Etruscan depravity rushed back into her thoughts. "Yesterday I donned the stola for the first time, the garment of a married woman. I do not think Rome would forgive me for wearing your gown and jewelry."

Shaking his head he offered the robes to her again. "Listen to me, Caecilia. Not all here support the marriage of our two cities. Your refusal to dress this way will be confronting. It will emphasize our differences, not temper them."

"I represent my city. I will not dress like a whore."

He flinched. "Think of it this way. My mother is admired for her grace. The women you will meet tonight will give you a glimpse of something similar, while you"—he hesitated—"while you will look like a peasant."

She bristled at the insult. Was hurt also. It was the first time he had been cruel. "Don't try to shame me into thinking Rome is the lesser for expecting its women to be modest."

He tossed the chiton onto the bed. "Is this how our marriage is to be? Fighting every inch over our differences? I liked you better yesterday when your courage was worthy."

Caecilia lowered her eyes, resenting his words. He'd not been asked to live in Rome, to leave all he knew behind. He'd worn the toga for one day but could slip back into Etruscan robes.

"Very well, I won't force you to wear the dress," he continued. "But you might find that adapting to our ways is easier than resisting them."

Caecilia examined the gown again. He was saying she was wrong to judge his people, but they would be just as severe in judging her. The unfairness stung her.

She glanced at Cytheris, reaching over to draw the Greek girl near, needing an ally even if she was a servant. "Cytheris, you must stay by me all night."

"If the master permits," the maidservant said nervously.

Mastarna observed the exchange but made no comment. "Our guests arrive."

In a slight attempt at placation, she gestured to Cytheris to fasten the Atlenta pendant around her neck.

Mastarna frowned. "Atlenta cannot aid you, Caecilia," he said, offering her his arm, "unless you help yourself."

Bewildered, she lay her fingers gently upon his forearm, trying not to tremble—for if her husband wanted her to dress like a prostitute, what more would he ask of her?

SIX

—

Could the first wedding have only been two days ago?

Once again witnesses surrounded Caecilia as she bound herself to this man, only this time it was under the eyes of his gods. Many of the rites echoed the Roman ceremony, but that simple ritual seemed crude compared to these grand devotions. The offerings were made countless times: salt in gratitude to the gods, honey to placate them, and wine in expiation for the sin of marrying an enemy.

Caecilia glanced at Mastarna. He remained stern as they sat facing each other upon curved backless chairs, each with one hand resting on the other's shoulder. With her other hand, she offered him a pomegranate, a symbol of fertility, a reminder of her purpose as a wife. Once again, when saying her vows to her husband, she strove to hide her nerves.

Artile was presiding. In addition to the sheepskin cloak and strange pointed hat he carried a curved lituus staff, his presence adding solemnity to the proceedings. She did not understand his words but she knew what he was saying as he prayed and exhorted, implored and praised: Surrender to Mastarna. Cross the threshold into his world.

The lustral water was blessed. The priest sprinkled it over her then pointed to the sacred fire. To help her understand his meaning, he guided her hand.

At that moment she noticed two things: that his hand was soft and fleshy, and that he was steering her fingers too close to the flame.

A murmur of concern spread through the guests at her cry. She hoped it was not too dreadful an ill omen. Mastarna was irritable, speaking tersely to his brother to repeat the rite. The men glared at each other but Artile finally sprinkled the water over her again with a flicking, derisory movement. This time only smoke bathed her hand yet uneasiness lingered.

Artile signaled two attendants to hold a large round mantle over the couple, a symbol of shelter and union from those outside. Just like the bridal gown it was light and transparent, a fine thread of gold woven through it. There was space beneath it—a kind of cocoon. Enclosed there, it seemed all sound was blocked out except their breathing, all scents extinguished except lily and sandalwood.

Caecilia beheld her husband and was perplexed. Instead of the aloofness of their first wedding day, misery exuded from him, from sad eyes to defeated shoulders. Their bodies close, Caecilia wrestled whether to offer comfort despite their argument. Tentatively, she touched his arm. "Mastarna?"

The movement made him focus upon her. His face softened. "This is our wedding shroud," he said. "Eventually it will embrace us in death."

She shivered.

As the mantle was lifted from them, a polite smattering of applause filled the room. They were now man and wife under Etruscan law. The second ritual of marriage was complete.

• • •

Arnth Ulthes, Zilath of Veii, smiled. It was not the smile of a politician—no grease was needed—it was oiled by goodwill. It was appealing despite the fact his teeth were chipped and cracked. To her surprise he was wearing a purple-bordered toga, as if warning her that a zilath was as important as any consul.

Caecilia glanced nervously around the atrium as she faced the prospect of meeting Veientane society. Fortunately, its highest citizen was charming. She sensed Ulthes was a listener not afraid to let others be heard above his own voice.

As Aemilius's niece, Caecilia was accustomed to being in the presence of men of high standing. They did not frighten her and being ignored by them was reassuring. This man seemed genuinely pleased to see her and so his interest made her tongue-tied.

"I welcome you because you hold peace in your young hands. I am glad you agreed to marry Vel Mastarna as I wished."

His Latin was rough but intelligible, yet Caecilia wondered at his choice of words. True enough, there had been acquiescence, but she could still feel the pressure of her uncle's palm on her back.

"Lord Ulthes is very popular," whispered Cytheris. "He has been elected zilath three times in a row. It is unheard of. The master is very close to him, although some on the High Council think too close."

She watched Ulthes clap Mastarna on the shoulder. Three fingers were missing from his hand. Her husband's tone was warm, and the zilath, who seemed as old as Tata, grinned at him as boys do when sharing a crude joke. They are friends, she thought, not just fellow citizens. A friendship, it seemed, great enough for Ulthes to convince Mastarna to anger his tribe by marrying her.

"Caecilia, I trust this rogue with my life," said the zilath. "Remember that. The knowledge may stand you in good stead."

"And I think, perhaps, he would trust his life with you, too, lord."

The older man smiled again and ran his hand through his spiky gray hair. Standing closer to him now, she noticed feathery red veins fanned out across his cheeks from his large beaky nose. The creases around his eyes revealed a fondness for laughter, but the deep grooves from nose to mouth hinted of other emotions.

"I hear you fought a band of Gauls. As they are a constant menace I might recruit you."

"My bravery has been exaggerated. I wouldn't want to face the prospect of death every day."

"Oh, but you already do, young one. Tuchulcha awaits all of us in the end."

His tone was sobering, making her see how he had acquired the solemn furrows upon his face. Caecilia would have asked who Tuchulcha was but they were interrupted. The man who addressed the magistrate was as hostile as the zilath was friendly.

The atrium was full of men with scars and stolen limbs. Yet this nobleman appeared unscathed by battle, despite appearing to be the same age as her husband. Broad-shouldered, impressively tall, his thick black hair was swept back, revealing a high forehead. In profile Caecilia thought him handsome, then he turned to face her and she saw that his features were slightly lopsided with one ear lower than the other and his mouth askew. A faint sheen of sweat covered his skin, and when he spoke she knew he cradled this imperfection to him, nurturing the resentment that it caused him.

Voice raised and body tense, he accosted Ulthes in a derogatory tone, then eyed Caecilia up and down in a way that forced her to lower her head. She wished she understood what they were saying, only discerning one word being repeated: "Seianta."

Mastarna bristled and she thought for a moment that he would strike the other, but Ulthes restrained him. The tall man retreated.

"Who was he? What did he say?"

"Take no notice of him. He's a fool," Mastarna said, turning back to Ulthes.

"What did that man say?" Caecilia whispered to her maid.

"Nothing, my lady. He is bad tempered, that one. He doesn't agree with the treaty and wants the city to declare war."

Caecilia scanned the room for the angry man, who stood off to one side, his expression openly contemptuous. He, like Camillus, wanted conflict. Should she admire him as she did the senator?

"But there is more, isn't there?"

The handmaid glanced at Mastarna, making sure he was not listening. Cytheris's reticence annoyed her.

"Tell me!"

"It is nothing, mistress. He was insulting and it does not bear repeating."

"Cytheris is right."

The women were startled at Mastarna's intrusion. The Greek girl bowed her head but Caecilia persisted in her questions.

"Be quiet. You need only know that his father was slain and his corpse mutilated by your people."

She fell silent. How many others here had fathers or brothers killed by Roman hands? Already she had learned that the three principes who'd accompanied her still grieved. Vipinas's and Pesna's dislike of her was evident but had not stopped them defending her. Tonight, they had returned to merely tolerating her. Only Apercu had greeted her with any warmth. It was now clear that while Rome had its qualms, Veii's acrimony had been hidden until revealed in the anguish of this lord. She doubted she would be kindly treated if the compact were to be broken.

But if Mastarna had sympathy for this tall, resentful lord, why were his fists still clenched and his eyes angry?

• • •

The banquet hall was separated from the garden by a curtain drawn aside to allow the guests to move between the two. The area was festooned with soft drapes of silver cloth and there were huge vases of hyacinths everywhere, their fragrance perfuming the air. It was as though Caecilia had been invited to a picnic rather than a dinner, only more sumptuous, more imposing than any basket of tidbits carried to the oak woods on the Caelian Hill.

Inside the hall the ceiling towered above her, checkered with yellow-and-black squares, and a mural extended across an entire wall. A bearded man on a throne was painted upon it. Naked to the waist, wearing a leopard-skin mantle around his shoulders, he sat holding a thyrsus staff while at his feet lay a panther, its tongue lolling from its sharp-toothed mouth. Surrounding him were strange men with tails and ears of horses, guzzling wine and dancing in ecstasy. Caecilia wondered if he was a god or sovereign of some strange land where depravity was lauded—depravity such as she was witnessing tonight.

Her face was burning from the antics of the semi-naked Etruscans. At first she did not know where to look but soon she was gaping at their beauty and wickedness. Tarchon had a face and form that could beguile, but many here tonight were also smooth-skinned and honey-limbed with sculpted hair and kohl-ringed sloe eyes. And just as Mastarna had warned, the women were elegant in their shamelessness, although not all wore beautiful sheer robes.

Unlike the family meal where she'd been allowed her own divan, the women sat on their husbands' couches. These had headboards with deep mattresses piled high with pillows, more bedding than upholstery. The men lay languidly upon them, being fed morsels by their women who sidled up beside them.

She knew they were sniggering at her. At her clumsy garb and drab hair. Indignation welled within her, but at the back of her mind was her failure to heed Mastarna about his gift of the golden gown.

Then there was the feast itself. The dinner was sumptuous: cherry and dormouse, trout's roe, and, as the centerpiece, a roasted stag. Unused to such rich and abundant food, Caecilia ate little, too nervous to do other than pick at the delicacies that were served by naked slave boys no more than nine years old, hair in ringlets down their backs. They must have been chosen for their loveliness.

There were other boys, too, who shared divans with some men as though they were wives. Caecilia supposed they were their sons, too young to warrant their own dining position.

The fathers were affectionate, too, holding them close.

• • •

A woman lay next to Ulthes on the dining couch. One of her breasts was bare. It was full and firm, the nipple pink and plump. Caecilia could not help staring yet the woman seemed to enjoy her scrutiny, glancing occasionally across the room to check if the Roman was still inspecting her. Caecilia reddened every time she was caught.

Was she Ulthes's wife? The zilath absentmindedly stroked the woman's breast, running his fingers along its curves and down her supple white arm while he conversed with others who approached him. Seeing this set Caecilia's heart racing. Taking a deep breath hardly slowed the hammering.

It was not as if the woman was the most beautiful there. Caecilia had spied others in the huge hall who boasted fairer looks. But with her bracelets at the wrist and above her elbows, the creature had allure. Exotic. There was a sensuousness about her. Caecilia had never seen someone with golden hair. Never seen a woman with her hair cut short, the ends brushing against her shoulders, an elegant ribbon wound around her forehead and trailing down her back.

"Her name is Erene," said Cytheris quietly.

Caecilia realized she should stop spying. "Is she wife to Ulthes?"

The maid giggled. "Only in bed."

Caecilia blushed again and pressed her fingers to her forehead where a headache was beginning. "Are you telling me she is a whore?"

"Some would think her so but my people admire her as a hetaera, a companion. Others call her a courtesan. Lord Ulthes is her patron."

Caecilia was bewildered. She had never heard of such a name, but no matter what they called her, the woman was still a harlot.

"If Ulthes brings his mistress, where is his wife?"

"She's not been seen outside their home since their two sons died. Her misery now fills the void their death created in her heart."

Caecilia scanned the garden and hall, studying the women around her.

"And the wives let their husbands bring these hetaerae?"

The maidservant arranged Caecilia's tunic. "I know it is strange for wife and courtesan to sit together. It would not happen in my land. But many men here value Erene for her accomplishments. That is why she is called a companion."

Caecilia frowned, wondering what "accomplishments" meant.

"Mistress Seianta did not like her, though," the maid continued. "She thought Lord Ulthes unwise to pander to her."

At the name "Seianta" Caecilia put up her hand. It was the one the angry nobleman had said repeatedly. "Seianta?"

"Why, the master's first wife. She died nearly four years ago. Did he not tell you?"

The Roman girl shook her head.

First an adopted son and now a wife. Questions swirled in Caecilia's mind. What was this Seianta like? How did she die?

At the other end of the chamber, Mastarna was playing dice, a gaming table balanced between his knees and his opponent's.

The golden tesserae spun and clicked upon the wood. It was clear to her that the betting the night before had been a mere distraction after routing the brigands. Tonight, the gambling was serious. Mastarna's eyes gazed upon the dice as though they were his most precious possessions. His hands caressed them, almost reluctant to let them go, as he made his throw.

Caecilia remembered his distant look under the wedding mantle and realized he must have loved this Seianta just as she loved Drusus. Loved her and honored her enough to be insulted by the mere mention of her name.

They had barely spoken throughout the dinner and she noticed how steadily he consumed the wine. Unlike others, though, he seemed to be unaffected by the vintage. Sitting next to him on the couch, she did not know what to say. About the carousing. The lewdness. The nudity. Yet when he left her to speak to his guests she felt as if he'd abandoned her to the foxes like a lonely hen upon a roost. Reluctantly, she realized his presence had been some comfort, despite their near silence. The night of the bandits had forged a tenuous bond.

• • •

After a while the chattering of conversation and music pushed thoughts of Seianta away. Caecilia called for her goblet to be filled with cordial again, grateful for the drink. It tasted peculiar but was soothing, making her head light, the slight giddiness matching a world spinning out of control.

Larthia lay on a couch by herself, her kerchief pressed to her lips. She ate nothing except a specially prepared gruel. Occasionally, the matron would glance at Caecilia, nodding reassuringly.

Most of the men were drunk. In Rome, the married women had always been shuffled from banquets before the men began their heavy drinking. Even as a maiden, although cloistered in her room, Caecilia knew by the men's voices and raucous laughter when the god of wine had arrived.

Here, the women seemed to be drunk, too. Were they not afraid of punishment? It explained, though, the shocking sight of men and women dancing in the garden, their fingers curved backward, palms opened elegantly. Facing each other, they weaved and circled, swaying and singing to the music of castanets and horns, their lengthening shadows merging and parting in a rhythm of their own.

Tarchon appeared beside her, holding a jug. A faint scent of rose water clung to him, better suited to a woman than a man. He, too, was dressed in only a kirtle, his skin gleaming with a sheen of oil, his dark eyes shining, almost glittering. Her gaze traveled guiltily from his face to the contours of his chest, stomach, and flanks.

"Let me fill your cup again, Caecilia. You will need all your wine for the kottabos game."

"Wine?"

"Yes. Wine."

Her hand trembled as she realized why she felt dizzy and unsteady. Sweat broke out upon her brow, the queasiness in her belly surging into her throat. It did not smell like her uncle's wine. It was spicy, delicate. She remembered Aemilius's routine kiss to check if his wife and niece were sober. Tonight her uncle could easily tell of her crime without a peck upon her lips, and having done so could rightly kill her.

Despite knowing this, Mastarna had still let it be served to her. Once again he'd forgotten his promise to her uncle.

Tarchon was studying her panicked expression. "Caecilia, it is but a little drink. In fact, the finest wine in the known world, or so say Rasennan vintners." When she did not laugh at his joke, he frowned.

"Caecilia has much to learn about us," said Larthia, moving over to them. "She can observe the kottabos if she wishes. You know I have never been fond of the game. It requires no skill, only an ability to drink till you are senseless."

Tarchon laughed, clasping the matriarch's hand. "Maybe you need to try, find forgetfulness for a while."

"Be gone, you are impudence itself," she said, slapping his fingers.

Grinning, he tugged at Caecilia to follow him.

In the garden, men and women were standing around a large bronze stand with two discs balanced above each other. The aim of the game was beyond her but Caecilia could see its effect. The ground was awash with wine as the reeling guests threw what they could not drink in one gulp from their cups into the discs. One woman vomited and then signaled for her goblet to be recharged. It was Lord Pesna's pretty young wife. Finding Caecilia watching, she managed to sneer beneath a smear of sick.

"Try it," Tarchon urged, placing his arm around Caecilia's waist.

She shrugged him away, finding his familiarity as shocking as his suggestion. "No, no!"

"It's not so bad, only some sport, a merriment. No need to be so serious."

"Be off," said Larthia. "The girl is tired. She's had her first taste of wine tonight."

She rested a comforting hand on the girl's shoulder. "No need to feel frightened, no one will punish you here for tasting liquor."

Tarchon looked at her quizzically, filling his goblet. "I'll never understand you Romans."

A shout distracted their attention. A small group was clustered around the gaming table. Putting down the jug, Tarchon roughly pushed through them, pulling Caecilia after him.

Mastarna was still gambling. Opposite him sat the man he had argued with earlier, except this time he was grinning and fingering a bone roundel from a tall heap in front of him. Caecilia preferred his scowl to his smile. Mastarna seemed not to register his wife's presence, but Caecilia was more concerned that Erene was standing behind him, arms encircling his neck.

What was a wife expected to do? Caecilia concentrated on the dice strewn across the table, hoping that ignoring Erene would make her disappear. The courtesan did not do so. At that moment, however, Mastarna prized the woman from him. Unconcerned, she moved across to Ulthes, looping her hand through the crook of his arm while he kissed the top of her head. Caecilia could not forget Cytheris's talk of Erene's many men. Was Mastarna one of them?

Larthia placed her hand on her son's shoulder. "What's the wager?"

"Three wagons of gold and my two breeding stallions," he growled. His pile of roundels was low.

The matron's face whitened. "On a throw of the die? Why not a game of skill?"

"The risk is higher."

"And your opponent, what does he stake?"

"An apology."

"What is the matter with you? There is no need for this."

Exasperated, Larthia again spoke to him, but when he refused to acknowledge her she walked away. It was clear her mother-in-law had resigned herself to the foolish deeds of this son.

Tarchon also leaned across to his father, urging caution amid wine fumes, but Mastarna waved him away. "As if I would heed advice from the likes of you." He nodded at his opponent. "Besides, an apology from him is rare and so is valuable."

Caecilia realized her husband was drunker than she first imagined. What insult could cause a man to act so?

Despite the slight Tarchon did not leave, impressing her with his concern. Until then she had thought him to be enamored of only the frivolous and trivial. Suddenly, even in his drunken state, the youth seemed more sober than Mastarna.

"You tried your best," she murmured.

Tarchon smiled ruefully. "He is impossible when he's in one of his moods."

"You mean this happens often?"

He rubbed his forehead, watching Mastarna. "The tesserae are but one means to satisfy him."

"I don't understand."

Drawing her away from the others, he tried not to slur his words. "The Rasenna like to gamble, to see if the goddess of Fate, the divine Nortia, will grace them with good fortune. But Mastarna does more. He hungers for the thrill of facing risk."

Suddenly Artile was beside Tarchon. He was calm amid the charged atmosphere of the gaming, his tone kindly as he smoothed his fingers along the youth's arm. Tarchon hesitated whether to go, like a child deciding if he needed the comfort of his father. After a pause, though, he shook off the priest's hand. Artile frowned but retreated to a place where he could reserve his scrutiny for the youth alone.

A cheer went up. Both turned back to the game. The nobleman's face had reclaimed its scowl while Mastarna was leaning back, smiling. The angry man sent the table crashing to the ground, scattering the roundels and tesserae across the floor, then pointed at Caecilia. His remark must have been worse than the first insult because all those around her gasped.

Mastarna wrenched his chair away to stand. A tense silence presided. Ulthes pressed himself between the rivals, his wide smile deserting him.

"It is an offense against the gods to spill blood at a wedding. Mastarna will collect the debt when next you meet."

The nobleman hurled abuse at the two men then twisted his way through the throng, his body full of swagger.

"He will have to face Mastarna's sword if he refuses to apologize," said Tarchon.

Caecilia's eyes widened. "What did he say?"

He did not reply, instead slumped into a chair.

Aware that all around her people were staring, her stomach churned. The hatred of these men for each other filled the room. There was a menace also. For it was clear the man's spite was not just directed at her people but was reserved especially for her.

. . .

The long summer evening was drawing to a close, the rosy glow from the setting sun that had touched the golden goblets, salvers, and lamps now settled into twilight, subduing the day with shadows and silhouettes.

She expected to see the servants clearing away, for the guests to begin leaving as darkness bid them to bed, but instead the slaves were setting up candelabras which teetered with candles three levels high.

A servant boy, holding a tall reed screen, addressed her. Not understanding him, she waved him away. Then she noticed that slaves were erecting these partitions around many of the feasting couches. Noticed, too, why the people had asked for them.

The women were entwining their arms around men's necks and kissing them as though drinking in nectar. Their caresses deepened into guttural moans, limbs entangled, as the couples sank into the generous cushioning of the divans, barely waiting for the fragile shields of reed.

The servants continued to surround the couches with panels and then throw flimsy covers over the top. Lurid seclusion on display.

And those comely boys she'd thought were sons were embraced by men who drew them behind the screens and into the boundaries of Caecilia's limited and shocked imagination. She closed her eyes, resisting the urge to hide her face, knowing that her fingers would be seared by the burn of her blush.

Did he expect her to lie openly beside him?

She wiped her hands along the sides of her tunic, palms clammy. Her mouth was dry. It hurt to swallow.

She felt like the mouse she'd found in her uncle's rain well, scrabbling at the brick sides of its prison, sinking momentarily beneath the water before scraping at the sides again until she was finally able to fish it out.

Around her, those who did not lie beneath the reeds looked slyly at her.

Endure, she thought, endure, but when she tried to breathe deeply she found herself choking on air.

"Caecilia, come and stand by me." Mastarna had finally removed himself from his betting.

At first she did not respond, too engrossed in dreadfulness.

He extended his arm. "It is time for us to retire."

The guests erupted with hoots and catcalls, the ribaldry that had been missing from their Roman nuptials.

She stared at him and knew that only he could rescue her. It took all her strength not to fall to her knees before him. "Please, please, don't make me do this."

He frowned. "It is just the way of my people."

This time, Caecilia truly thought she would suffocate. Clutching a fold of his kirtle, prepared to tear the cloth, she tugged at him to come closer. "Please, Mastarna."

"Take a deep breath," he said, prizing her fingers away. "It is time to go."

He was going to spare her. It was hard not to cry. It was hard not to be grateful until she realized he might not spare her greater shame in private.

Eyes downcast, she let him guide her away to bid the zilath good night. She barely had energy to speak.

"Your wife is tired," said Ulthes kindly. "You should put her to bed."

Mastarna did not reply, exhaustion tracing lines upon his face as well.

Erene smugly clutched Ulthes's arm, making Caecilia doubt the concubine would ever be weary. And here was more disgrace. Caecilia tried but could not keep from thinking this woman may have acted as wife to her husband.

"I look forward to talking with you again, Caecilia," continued Ulthes.

Meeting his eyes, Caecilia bowed briefly to the zilath, straightening her shoulders to summon dignity, trying not to lean upon Mastarna's arm for balance, desperately wishing that Drusus could be here to save her.

• • •

The long curtain to their chamber had been drawn against the prying eyes of those guests drinking by the fountain. The garden, which had seemed beyond delight that afternoon, was now invaded and sullied in the moonlight. Caecilia only hoped that the ripple of double pipe and click of castanets would drown any cries she made. It was enough for her to be scared, but it would be humiliating if these degenerates were to know her fear and laugh at it.

Mastarna drew back the curtain and ushered her inside. He did not follow, though.

"Make ready," he said. "I must speak further to Ulthes."

Caecilia sank to the ground unable to take one more step.

When Larthia entered and saw her, she hurried across the room, signaling Cytheris to fetch a cloth and pitcher of water. "What's the matter?"

"Please, I can't do this."

"Nonsense. Nothing terrible is going to happen to you. The gods made man and woman to fit together. And soon there will be children to tumble upon the bed that once had only borne the weight of two."

The Roman girl closed her eyes, embarrassed that this woman should speak to her thus. "How could you let such things happen in your home?"

The matron laid her hand upon the girl's forearm. "Children and fools only see half the whole. One day you will not just glimpse our people's joy but want to possess it, too."

Caecilia shook her hand away.

"Come," said the older woman, ignoring the rebuff. "You will feel better once you are bathed."

"Would you have let him shame me in front of them?"

Her mother-in-law faced her calmly. "That was not my decision to make, Caecilia. It was yours."

Cytheris placed a pot of warm water on the table while the girl climbed the footstool to sit upon the bed. Caecilia clutched her stola to her chest, once again conscious of being naked in front of others. Yet with Cytheris's kindly reassurances she eventually relented, the fabric eased from between her fingers.

The handmaid's ministrations were gentle but did little to soothe Caecilia's tension. She did not want anyone to touch her. She had lived without such comfort since her father died and did not want such intimacy now. Not even when the Greek girl wiped Caecilia's body with the warm cloth, pressing softly along her back, did the Roman's muscles ease.

"Lift your arms," said Larthia, and slipped a nightrobe over Caecilia's head, so soft it was as though weaved from gossamer. She did not refuse it. There was no excuse to resist wearing sheerness in her husband's bed.

As Cytheris untied and brushed her hair, Caecilia recited her prayers, tightening her grip around the little wooden juno, her guardian angel. And all the while Larthia persuaded her to trust her assurances about the unknown.

Aurelia's words came back to her. "Going to a man's bed is not as bad as you might imagine." She had never heeded her aunt before, but this time she hoped she was right.

For, despite Aurelia's bullying, Caecilia had more faith in the Roman matron than Larthia. After all, she had just seen how disgraceful Veientane noblewomen could be.

• • •

Larthia embraced her son when he entered the room, kissing him tenderly upon the forehead. Caecilia sensed his mother's words were of solace more than encouragement, and the same feeling Caecilia had experienced under the wedding shroud returned— that this man was in mourning, that it was another wife he wished to lie with that night.

Larthia and Cytheris said their good nights to Caecilia, who lay down, turning onto her side away from him. On the wall in front of her the leopard spied upon her from the laurel grove, eyes dark and oval against his spotted skin—she would have an audience after all.

The sheets tugged across her as he climbed in beside her. There was a pause and then his fingers gently pressed her shoulder. "It is what is expected of us."

When she rolled over to face him she was surprised. His body seemed to be sighing. Perhaps, she thought, her husband did not relish what lay ahead either. He hesitated again, then leaned over and kissed her eyelids closed, but light still crept in around the rims. She squeezed them shut, wanting darkness, wanting to feel nothing. Instead, sound and smell, touch and taste, remained.

The scent of wine clung to him. She moved her head away sharply when his mouth brushed hers.

"It will hurt a little at first," he said softly, hands moving over the filmy nightrobe, caressing her breasts, belly, and thighs. Then, pulling up the garment to her waist, he gently pushed her onto her side again, his hands firm upon her hips.

The hurt lasted more than a little as he thrust within and against her dryness. She buried her face in the pillow, the bitter odor of the cloth filling her mouth and nostrils. Rigid and silent, she concentrated wholly on obliterating the existence of this man, his body slick with sweat, lying against her, inside her. Then despair settled deep within her like a cold hand rhythmically kneading as steadily as the rocking of his body.

Finally it was over. He pulled away from her. At once the coolness of the evening air rushed over her where only seconds before were muscle and heat. She was wet with his perspiration, her thighs slippery from her blood, his seed.

She opened her eyes and again saw the leopard. He had not averted his gaze.

She heard the beating of her heart but not her breath, her body forgetting to exhale. She was alive, though. She noticed the music drifting in from the garden, the sweet haunting notes of the double flute in a reflective key.

Mastarna also seemed barely to breathe, and when his still silence continued she turned.

He lay on his back, eyes closed but not asleep, not even in repose. A deep groove creased his brow. After a time he raised himself on one elbow, surveying her solemnly. His fingers traced what should have been a line of teardrops from eye to nose and then to her lips. "It is good there are no tears." She flinched and he jerked his hand away as though scalded.

Her nightgown was still around her waist. She was aware of her bareness, of his also, yet the rawness of this exposure didn't bother her. She was beyond embarrassment. Even so, she held her breath anxiously when his hand moved downward, relieved when he merely folded the nightgown over her then rested his hand carefully on her thigh. She could feel the pressure of each finger.

The pendant of Atlenta lay between her breasts. He reached over and traced the embossed figure. "Atlenta was a strong woman. You are like her, Bellatrix. Much is expected of you by many people."

Caecilia snatched the ornament away. "I know Atlenta's tale. She was abandoned, tricked, and sacrificed. And you," she snapped, "are vile and so are your people."

Mastarna sighed. "You are very young and it is hard to understand our ways. Time will solve both predicaments."

Angry he should dismiss her, she sat up. "Time will not erase the insult you inflicted. To serve me wine! To expose me to immorality! To make me dine with a whore."

Narrowing his eyes, he sat up, too. "You need to calm yourself."

"Were we expected to provide a spectacle or did I prove to be a disappointment when I did not prostitute myself before your friends?"

Shaking his head impatiently, he pointed to the mural. "See the leopard? He is the guardian of the dead and minion of Fufluns. Did you not see that god watching over us as we dined in the banquet hall? My people follow his ways and celebrate life knowing all too well that death stalks us, that in time it will deny us wine to drink, food to eat, lips to kiss."

She stared at him in disbelief. Was she expected to forgive impiety because the Rasenna were afraid of death?

"And what of your dead wife? Did she worship Fufluns on her wedding night?"

The sight of him pressing his nails into the palms of his tightened fists made her regret her words. Despite all he had exposed her to this night, she knew he did not deserve her cruelty.

"You need not worry about Seianta," he said coldly. "You need not mention her again."

"I'm sorry," she said quietly. The words were not easy. She wanted to hear them from him, too.

He did not speak nor try to touch her again. When he snuffed out the candles and at last blanketed them in thankful darkness, her husband turned his back to her. She sensed he, too, wished to define the channel between them and lie as closely to his edge as she to hers.

SEVEN

"Your teeth are chattering, mistress."

Caecilia did not answer. The painted Atlenta stared down at her. She had done so for hours.

"Perhaps it would be best you get out of the bath."

Caecilia noticed goose bumps were prickling her arms, and her fingers and palms were wrinkled. Had he infected her? Was this a disease caused by last night?

"Look how long you've been there," said Cytheris, pointing to Caecilia's hands. "You'll end up a prune."

"I am not sick then?"

"Of course not, mistress," said the maid as though talking to a child. "The water causes it."

Caecilia had never refilled a bath, nor for that matter bathed two days in a row, but today she needed to wash. Needed to rid herself of him.

Had she slept? She didn't think so, but she must have found dreamlessness because she woke from it to a vacant bed. Relief had filled her. Then emptiness. Salt had dried on her eyelashes, her tears leaving traces. Crusts of melancholy.

His smell permeated the bed; his sweat and scent pervaded her, too. She rose, pulling off the sheets and stripping herself of her nightrobe, unconcerned with Cytheris's scrutiny. Such modesty seemed pathetic after he had lain against her, closer than anyone had before, body meeting body, limb against limb, skin rubbing skin, and within her, as hard and thick as the stone phallus of the bridal chamber's god, he had scraped her womb.

Nothing was the same. And yet she looked no different. In the mirror she saw the same Caecilia: large, round, anxious eyes set in a solemn face. She ran her hands over her body, wondering if there should be some permanent mark upon her, some tattoo like Arruns bore, to remind her every day of what it meant to be a wife. She found evidence. His seed, powdery upon her thighs, and a patch of blood—residue that could be washed away.

Inside her, though, it was not the same. He remained. No water would remove him.

What had she expected? Why did she feel this loss? As though he had robbed her of that part she wanted safe and hidden. Safe for Drusus. Would it have been different with the Roman because she sought his caresses and ached for his touch? Or was this how all brides were taken? She could not believe that Drusus would hurt her. She was certain he would not have shamed her.

Sinking beneath the water, she stared through ripples to the distorted face of the painted Atlenta. She knew now how Lucretia must have felt—her womb sore, her spirit dirtied. The legendary matron would surely scorn Caecilia for failing to take her life.

Water streamed from her as she finally surfaced. The bath had lost its heat but she still lingered.

"It is not always easy the first time, mistress," said the Greek girl, holding the drying cloth ready.

Caecilia glared at her. "Cytheris!"

The handmaid's mouth set into a hard line and her eyes failed to mask impatience. Immediately, Caecilia was sorry she'd spoken so curtly. This girl knew things, things that Aurelia had not or would not mention.

An image of the Roman servant girl and the bondsman came to her. Caecilia realized now that the maid's groans were not of hurt. She'd felt pain last night but had remained silent. And then it occurred to her that perhaps she was not like other women. That even Aurelia had assured her that there were worse things than going to a man's bed. Aurelia had said to submit. And she had. Aurelia had said she would not make a good wife. Perhaps that did not only mean she was inept with household obligations. Perhaps her aunt had meant more.

"The women last night who lay beneath the reeds—were they wives?"

Cytheris sniffed. "A few. Courtesans, too. Slaves are brought in also."

The Roman wondered how she was supposed to tell the difference. She had thought Erene to be a wife at first. It was hard to know which were nobles and which were base, hard to tell if it was their own husbands with whom they laid.

"Don't worry, mistress. I was shocked when I first saw such a scene. Greek wives do not even eat in the same room with men. Nor drink wine at all. That is what courtesans are for. Although I turn a blind eye to most Tyrrhenian ways, such wantonness still troubles me."

Caecilia finally stepped out of the bath and the maidservant wrapped the sheet around her. "So, are all wives expected to act so?"

"Only if they wish. When the Festival of Fufluns is held, though, no restraint is shown."

"The god in the banquet hall mural?"

"Yes. My people call him Dionysus. He is worshipped by those in the Pacha Cult."

The emptiness inside Caecilia seemed to grow, spreading its hand from the pain in her belly and gripping fast her bowels. Mastarna had shown her the leopard last night and told her he believed in his master. What lay in store for her if he forced her to worship this god?

"And the boys? The youths?"

The Greek girl rubbed Caecilia's hair dry. "The Veientanes are particularly fond of beautiful boys, just like Greek men. And Romans."

Caecilia wanted to protest but she couldn't disagree. The servants often gossiped about Aemilius's infatuation for stable boys. It was not until last night, however, that she understood why their laughter was so loud when comparing his riding of grooms to geldings.

"Did she lie beneath the reed?"

The handmaid combed Caecilia's hair with her fingers. "You mean Mistress Seianta?"

"Yes, Seianta."

Cytheris continued her ministrations, causing Caecilia to frown as she teased loose a knot. "Yes, my lady. The master and she sometimes lay beneath the reed, but they wanted no others."

Caecilia began chewing her fingernail, uncomfortable at hearing of Mastarna's intimacy with his first wife. Would he also expect her to prove some sort of marital devotion after a banquet's fruit had been eaten, and with only the rind of darkness left, shadows merged behind an unsteady, flimsy screen?

Cytheris drew the sheet tightly around her shivering mistress, briskly massaging Caecilia's back and arms. The Roman closed her eyes and let the maid comfort her like a little girl.

"It is time for the evening meal. Mistress Larthia will wonder where you are."

"What about the master?"

"Oh, he has gone to the country. Some problem with his tenants, I think."

Caecilia's relief at the news was brief. He would return and the same routine would be repeated. If not tomorrow, then the next day or the next.

What had she expected of him on their wedding night? She could not exactly say. He had caused her loss, though. And hurt. Something else, too, which she could not understand.

Disappointment.

• • •

Nothing was the same.

Last night the people at the feast had shocked her, but the little things about Veii were unsettling, too. The air was rich with aromas, so thick with scent she parted it like a curtain. Even the water tasted different, as though she was drinking the smell of stone.

Waiting for Larthia in the dining room, Caecilia yearned for familiarity, wanted just one thing to be the same as what she had grown up with. But most of all she wanted to be home.

As Larthia approached she noticed the older woman was once again dressed gracefully, her hair immaculate, yet her face was drawn and a spasm of pain shadowed her features as she dabbed her mouth with her kerchief.

As both women lay upon dining couches, Caecilia wished she could return to her room and be spared the effort of civility.

"Cytheris says you have not been well. I hope it was not some piece of food that upset you."

Caecilia shook her head and tried to get comfortable on the deep-cushioned divan.

"No doubt you found the banquet a little overwhelming."

She hesitated as to whether to offend the matron. "When Roman wives dine with guests they do not share feasts as you do."

Larthia raised her eyebrows and suddenly Caecilia remembered how Aurelia's slaps could sting. Now she wondered if an elegant blow would smart.

"You think Veientane wives unvirtuous, Caecilia?"

"Rome would not call what I saw last night worthy of a wife—nor of a husband either."

A tremor of pain crossed Larthia's face, chased by one of irritation. "You are far too prickly, my dear. Roman rectitude seems to prevent you gaining pleasure. The Rasenna think differently. We like to celebrate even as we weep at the prospect of death."

Caecilia frowned at this echo of Mastarna's excuse for dissipation. "I only know I will never act that way, no matter what you ask of me."

"We shall see," said Larthia, slowly patting her mouth with her napkin. "No one here will compel you to enjoy yourself."

The sarcasm was unsettling.

The matron beckoned to a servant to bring her meal. "Let's forget about yesterday, shall we? Tomorrow is so much more important."

Larthia took a spoonful of the unappetizing pap, grimacing as she did so. As she finished her painful swallowing, she nodded to the girl. "I can tell you are wondering about my mouth."

"You often seem to be in pain."

"I have ulcers that never seem to heal."

Caecilia forgot her vow to remain aloof. "Have you tried oil of clove and salt? Although it may help, it will sting and is unpleasant to the taste."

The Veientane smiled, and this time Caecilia did not feel her condescension. "I'm afraid such a remedy has failed in the past. But how is it you know such things? I would not have thought you interested in the healing arts."

"I know very little really. Aurelia, my uncle's wife, is experienced in such skills and knows those plants that cure and those that harm. I would help her sometimes."

"You do not like this Aurelia?"

The girl frowned. "Why do you ask?"

"You say her name as though spitting out a lemon pip."

Caecilia coughed to hide her own smile, remembering how Aurelia's gnawing discontent would disappear for a time when brewing chamomile tea for stomachaches or eyebright for spring fever.

"Perhaps she talks too often of virtues and too little of life," said Larthia.

Caecilia looked away. She did not want to like this woman, a matriarch who presided over dissoluteness, but it was not so easy. How could she resent Larthia for trying to understand her? Resenting graciousness was like beating fists uselessly against the air.

"Tomorrow you will commence your duties," said the matron.

Caecilia sighed. At last she would be revealed for what she truly was. Her inadequacies exposed. Her misery compounded by the drudgery of household chores. "I must confess I do not know how to weave garments such as yours."

Larthia swung her feet to the ground and extended her hand. Caecilia hesitated before taking it. As she did so the matron spied the legacy of the bandit's bruises still darkening upon the girl's wrists. Leaning closer, she traced the contusions gently with her fingers. Caecilia winced in surprise as much as pain.

"Poor thing. Please know that, unlike the robber, none of us means you harm. You are one of our family now. I understand your mother died when you were very young. I hope in time you will come to call me Ati, as do my sons."

Unfamiliar with the shape and sound of a matriarch's kindness, Caecilia did not know what to reply.

"It's no small thing to travel from your father's house to that of your husband's," continued the Veientane. "To leave the certainty of your world to go to a man's bed and his dominion. I remember it well when I came from Tarchna to marry my Mastarna."

My Mastarna? Caecilia doubted she would ever claim such possession.

"I, too, was terrified, but I grew to love my husband. I know few are as lucky, but at least you should understand that my son will not dishonor you."

The older woman ignored Caecilia's silence. "If you wish, I will teach you the rituals that guide our lives. We, too, piously honor the gods, even though it does not seem so to you. And remember, you are a strange new thing for us also. If we both learn a little of each other's ways, perhaps our lives will both be richer."

Shame filled Caecilia at her churlishness, remembering that Larthia's Mastarna had been killed by an Aemilian yet was prepared to welcome one into her home.

"Thank you. I look forward to learning of your gods, but please remember I won't ever forget I'm Roman."

Larthia laughed. "I don't see that happening, do you? Now come with me, I have something to show you."

Leading Caecilia to the book-lined reception chamber, Larthia pointed to two high-backed wicker chairs and a marble table. "Tomorrow we greet our family's tenants. They will see you and know that you are now Mastarna's wife and must be respected."

Caecilia surveyed the bench. What nonsense was this? A woman acting as if she were a patron? "I think you are mocking me."

"No, it will be your first lesson in Veii. A wife is partner with her husband in both family and business."

"But isn't Tarchon the head of the house while Mastarna is away?"

Larthia nodded. "Of course, but my son expects me to deal with all matters. I am afraid that Vel considers Tarchon too feckless to rely upon. I wish it were not so."

"But I would not know what to do, what to say."

"You will over time. But first you must learn our language. Tarchon is useful in that respect and is a good teacher."

The girl needed to sit down. "Will I also do this when Mastarna returns?"

"Of course. I always sat beside my husband, even when I was heavy with child."

Caecilia looked down, fiddling at the quick of her fingernail, reminded again of her other wifely duty.

"You are no longer a maiden," said Larthia, sitting beside her. "Don't be afraid to leave childhood behind and learn the role of wife and mother."

Caecilia stiffened. "I understand my duties."

"You must learn to manage the household, too. Supervising slaves can be demanding. You must only beat them when they deserve it, not as your temper dictates."

Caecilia glanced at Cytheris, who seemed unperturbed at being spoken about in such a way.

"And when you are settled I will show you my workshop."

"Workshop?"

The matron nodded as she pointed to one of the vases on the table. It was made of thin-walled black clay decorated with lines and dots. "Why yes. I employ artisans to manufacture kraters and rhytons, which I export to Carthage and Phoenicia. Humble bucchero ware like this bowl."

Caecilia did not know what was more scandalous—the fact that Larthia was given such authority or that nobility was dealing in trade. "Do you really speak the truth?"

"Of course."

Caecilia reached for the modest earthenware vessel. It was coarse to the touch—plain. She recognized the pattern upon it. It was the same as one she'd seen in Rome—the vase Aurelia used to fill with anemones: blooms with red sore hearts like the scarlet stains upon Aemilia's skin.

"There is good here, too, Caecilia," said Larthia.

The girl gave a small smile, overwhelmed.

"Ah," said the matron, hiding her rotten teeth behind her hand as she also smiled. "That is much better than the melancholy and misery that greeted me at dinner."

Once her mother-in-law had retired, Caecilia lingered. Sitting on one of the wicker chairs she leaned forward to trace the veins within the marble table. The stone was smooth and cool. She laid her cheek against it, arms outstretched. Exhausted.

What had she expected? Not this. Not independence.

He was her husband. She could tolerate his world, withstand his touch—as long as the price of lying with him was the right to sit beside him at this bench.

• • •

"Aricia! Hand it to the mistress!"

The little girl started at her mother's command, then dutifully presented Caecilia with a brush. It was yet another of the many presents Mastarna had given her.

Caecilia smiled, crouching down beside the child and pointing to the engraving on its back. "Who is this?"

There was a huntress carrying a bow. Beside her a youth was holding aloft a boar's head. Aricia shook her head.

"She doesn't understand you, mistress," said Cytheris. "She might bear the name of a Latin town but she speaks none of its language."

"Then you tell me. What is the name of this beautiful maiden?"

"Lenta," said the little one very quietly after all. Cytheris cuffed her. "Go and see if Cook needs help!"

Caecilia frowned as the child slave left the room. "Why were you so short with her?"

The handmaid took up the brush and started to rapidly stroke Caecilia's hair. "It is best to teach them young not to expect kind words."

"Oh, and is that what it was like for you? Did your mother scold you for no reason?"

"Of course, mistress. For as long as I lived with her. Didn't yours?"

Caecilia smiled, acknowledging that Greek and Roman mothers shared the same temperaments and tempers. "Who was Lenta?"

"Atlenta. It's the same girl that adorns your pendant."

"So the man is the suitor from the race?"

"No, it's Meleager, whose love for the huntress led to his doom."

Caecilia touched the engraving, amazed this woman had more than one lover.

"The Tyrrhenians love myths as much as Greeks do," continued Cytheris. "They tell stories of immortals and heroes, and call them names similar to those of my people. They have gods of their own, though, powerful and unseen."

Amazed, Caecilia studied the burnished metal. Larthia had shown her Turan and her handmaid; now she beheld two ill-fated human lovers. How could she have been so ignorant of the legends of the gods, not known what they looked like, been so unaware of their joys and woes? Somehow the histories of Roman ancestors and heroes seemed stilted and stolid compared to this fantastic glimpse into the heavens, this revelation of the emotions of the Divine.

"What, then, is Atlenta's other story?"

"It's the tale of the Calydonian boar, a favorite of my people. Meleager killed the beast to prove his love for her, then angered his family by giving it to her as a trophy. When the youth killed his uncles to stop them claiming it, he was cursed by his own mother and doomed to die."

Her words made Caecilia shiver. The brave, reckless youth reminded her of Drusus. He had been prepared to spurn his family to marry her, and his father would have been entitled to kill him for dishonoring their family.

"You see, mistress, even before these two lovers joined in that hunt," continued Cytheris, "the inexorable Nortia had already decided their fate. She had already raised her hammer to drive a nail to mark the end of Meleager's time."

Suddenly Caecilia wanted no more of the story. Wanted no more gloom. Nortia and the Roman Fortuna were one and the same, and could be capricious and spiteful. The deity had already cut short her time with Drusus. Caecilia did not want to think what else the goddess might have in store.

Cytheris sniffed and continued brushing Caecilia's hair. "So you are glad, mistress, to sit with Lady Larthia tomorrow?"

"Indeed."

"It has taken away the sadness of this morning?"

Caecilia thought of Mastarna again. No, not entirely.

"Of course, many women are envious of you, mistress. I don't think you realize that. Most of the maidens in Veii have had their eye on the master. And some of the matrons as well." Cytheris chortled at her own wit.

Caecilia stood up. "I think you can stop brushing now."

The servant helped her to disrobe but Cytheris was not finished talking. "They say he is as fair in bed as he is ugly in face. You are very fortunate to have such a husband."

Caecilia pushed the girl's hands away, tears pricking her eyes. "If he is the best in this city, then I pity all Veientane women. Drusus would have been a better husband—" Checking herself from revealing her heart to a servant, she broke off into sobs.

Cytheris briefly raised her eyebrows then busied herself working Caecilia's hair into a loose plait. "It is time to cease crying, mistress," she said softly.

Surprised at the maidservant's boldness, Caecilia glared at her.

"I don't know what happened last night," continued the maid, undeterred, "but the master is not a cruel man, just a troubled one. In the end, you know," she said, bending close, "all men are the same. You just need to use that to your benefit. And in doing so, you can find pleasure."

Intrigued, Caecilia wiped her tears. "What do you mean?"

The handmaid grinned. "Men are ruled by only one thing, my lady. It lives between their thighs like a rudder beneath a boat." She held her hand between her legs as though grasping a pole.

Caecilia blushed, suddenly unsure if she should be sharing confidences with this servant but wanting to hear more. "And why should that be worth knowing?"

"Because a tiller needs a helmsman," said Cytheris, laughing. "And if you are clever, mistress, you can play that role."

Caecilia stopped the maid fussing over her as she climbed into bed. "I still do not know what you mean."

"It is very simple. When I am with a man, for that brief moment, he is the slave, not me. He wants me to govern his rudder, so to speak. And in pleasing him, sometimes a woman can steer a man both with and without the bedchamber."

"Like Seianta?"

The maidservant nodded.

"Like Erene?"

"Ah, that one can captain more than one ship."

Caecilia leaned closer. "And did she lead Mastarna?"

Smoothing the bed's cover, Cytheris mumbled, "That's gossip, mistress."

Irritated that the maid had suddenly grown circumspect, Caecilia pressed her, wanting to discover why Seianta and Erene sought out Mastarna's caresses. Why they savored what she found sour. "Are you saying women can enjoy lying with men?"

"Of course," said the handmaid, putting away the brush and mirror. "I love men. I love their smell and taste and feel, their strength, their deep voices, the hugeness of their embrace and, if I am lucky, their—"

Caecilia cut her short. "And was it always so? Was the first time easy for you?"

Cytheris lowered her eyes. "No, mistress."

"But you still— You still like lying with men?"

"Yes, mistress, when I choose the man."

"That is a choice I do not have."

The maid began filling a lamp with oil rather than face her. "I am sure the master will not let you hate the marriage bed," she said quickly.

Caecilia shook her head slightly, disbelieving but still wanting to comprehend, thinking that perhaps Cytheris had not suffered so badly at the hands of her lover if she'd found the pleasure of which she spoke. "What happened your first time?"

The slave girl placed the light on the table, subdued, no more chattering, no more gossip. "It is a long story and not worth the telling."

"Please, I want to know."

The handmaid fidgeted, avoiding Caecilia's gaze, but when her mistress was insistent, she reluctantly began to speak. "When I was ten years old my father sold me to a fat innkeeper to repay his debts. This innkeeper had tits as large as a woman's and his farts smelled of cabbage and his breath of fish. He liked young girls whose breasts were not yet budding and whose mounds were smooth and hairless. For two years I suffered him bruising my womb and crushing me, my face buried in his thick belly hair. Then I began to bleed each month and I was spared."

Caecilia listened, wide-eyed, remembering how at ten she'd played with her dolls and walked in the woods looking for birds' nests.

"The fat pig would have sold me but he needed a housekeeper. He kept me to tend his home and bought another little girl to warm his bed. And another, and another after that. All of them sold when they became women. Only I remained."

Caecilia watched her, digesting the maid's story, reflecting on her own.

"Yet you lay with other men after that?"

"Yes, mistress. I was lucky. A trader from Latium taught me that not all men are like the innkeeper. He was kind and gentle. It was then that I discovered I could choose men. And there was a lot of choice. All those travelers: Latin, Greek, Tyrrhenian, even a few Romans. They mainly liked my big, soft breasts. Some used them as pillows, others cried between them, but all of them liked to squeeze them. And then I fell with child. The innkeeper was delighted. It was so much cheaper to breed slaves than to buy them."

"But the baby could not have been Aricia."

"No, she was my fourth."

"Fourth! Where are the others?"

Cytheris paused, taking a breath, using it again to sigh. "Gone, mistress. All except Aricia."

"And the first?"

"The little girl died after a few days. I was fourteen."

"And the father?"

"I do not know who her father was," the maidservant said impatiently.

"And the others?"

Cytheris suddenly smiled, as if blowing on the embers of a sweet memory. "I bore twin sons, healthy and bawling."

"And why are they not with you?"

Even as she spoke, Caecilia knew she had erred in asking. The Greek girl turned away, touching her face, but if it was to wipe away tears Caecilia could not say.

"You don't have to tell me."

"No, I will, my lady, but then you must ask me no more about it, for it is too painful to keep repeating. Although, strangely enough, it began with contentment. The trader from Latium started to frequent the tavern again. I chose him. And even though my face was coarse, my hair unruly, my body ungainly, he cherished me. Then, when his wife bore him a son, he saw the chance to bring me to his home in Aricia. He bought me to suckle his newborn and, because he loved me, he was prepared to pay a high price to buy my children from the innkeeper so that they could come with me."

"And what of his wife? Did she know of this?"

"She learned soon enough. Wet nurses must not sleep with men in case it curdles the milk. But my trader did not mind his child taking a sour mouthful. All that year, we made love in the cellar with an armful of straw keeping the chill from our backs. But then it ended."

Caecilia could guess why.

The handmaid stared at the floor. "It is said that a woman who still cups a babe to her breast cannot fall pregnant with another. And we believed that until my flux did not come and my belly grew larger. His wife must have suspected his infidelity when he refused to whip me for my crime."

"And the child was Aricia."

"Yes. She, with her father's black curls, is a daily living and breathing reminder."

Caecilia wanted to stretch over to take the maid's hand but knew she must maintain decorum. The handmaid knew the rules, too. She stood up rather than gain comfort from her mistress.

"He went away soon afterward to trade his goods in my homeland, Magna Graecia. His wife acted swiftly. The beating was so severe I thought I would lose my child, but Aricia was stubborn, clinging inside me."

"And the twins?"

Her already ruddy complexion was highlighted with spots of color.

"I did not lose my unborn child but I did lose my little boys. You see, I had taken the wife's dearest. And so she took what was dearest to me. I alone was sold to a slaver the next day. I have never seen my sons again. Nor their father."

The Greek girl busied herself, folding Caecilia's tunic and crossing the room to open the heavy wooden linen chest. The room was silent, the only sound that of the slave's long braid swishing across the tiled floor when she bent to a task. Caecilia could not see her face but she was sure there were no tears; the sorrow was stored in her heavy tread, slumped shoulders, and bowed head.

"But at least you have Aricia."

Cytheris turned to face her, voice quivering and strained, deference banished. "You have already made me prod an unhealed wound, do not ask me to speak of one that is yet to be inflicted."

"What are you saying?"

Tears finally welled in Cytheris's eyes. "It has already been decided that Aricia will be sold. When she turns eight she will become a lady's maid in another household. Her birthday is next summer. I have little under a year to be with her."

"Why sold?"

"She is not needed, mistress. And she will bring a good sum."

"Why, then, are you so stern with the child? You have so little time to hold her close."

Cytheris brushed away her tears and once again spoke more like the mistress than the slave, the wise one than the fool.

"I still dream of my sons, even though they would be fierce slayers of monsters by now with dirty faces, sturdy limbs, and wielding wooden swords. Now that I know Aricia is leaving, it is better that my memories of her are less tender."

Caecilia could not meet the Greek girl's gaze.

"I am lucky, though," said the servant, gathering up some slippers and dropping them into one of the baskets on the wall.

"How can that be?"

"There is always good fortune to be found, especially if you are not seeking it."

"And why would you possibly think Fortuna has blessed you?"

"At least the master has let me keep my girl all this time. It could have been different. I could have been alone with someone like the innkeeper. Instead, two weeks after Aricia was born, the slaver brought me to Tyrrhenia and the master bid highest to buy me to be wet nurse to his daughter."

Caecilia straightened her back, stunned. "Daughter?"

"Yes, but the sweet girl passed away. Only a year old, the poor mite. And that is why the master is a troubled man, losing a wife and daughter so closely in time."

Words failed Caecilia. There had been no babes born within her family to cherish. She tried to imagine losing a child but was not yet able to compare all shapes of distress with these women—with Cytheris, with Seianta—nor the double loss felt by Mastarna.

Cytheris picked up the oil lamp before retiring. "Time for sleep, mistress. And remember, no more weeping. Not over a man. Crying should be kept for our children until the tears run out."

The girl caught the servant's hand, no longer reluctant for contact. "Cytheris. What am I to do? I don't want to lie with him."

The handmaid hesitated but did not break from Caecilia's grasp. "Listen to me. The master was upset that night. Lady Seianta still wraps her arms around him. But he will be kinder when he forgets her."

"When will that happen?"

"You must make him need you. Make him want only what you can give him. Then you can have what you desire."

"But I don't want him to love me. Nor I to love him."

Cytheris patted the girl's hand. "This has nothing to do with love, mistress."

"Then what could I possibly give him that is alone in my power?"

"That is easy, mistress, very easy," said the slave. "Give him living children. Give him a son."

• • •

Caecilia tried to calm her mind and think through all that had happened that day—and, in particular, in this last hour—wondering again about family secrets and whether she would ever learn all of the House of Mastarna's. Another piece of the puzzle that was Seianta had been revealed, the same piece of the puzzle that explained Mastarna's pain.

She did not fully understand what Cytheris had told her about men, though. She was ignorant of their world, their needs, their wants.

When she finally blew out her lamp, her thoughts played with sleep like a kitten with a ball of string as she realized she shared something with her mother after all. A dilemma that Aemilius had caused both of them to face.

What would happen to a half-blood son or daughter?

Could she love an unchosen child?

EIGHT

Dust motes danced, captured by the sun. Standing on her toes, Caecilia swiped at the particles, sending them swirling in a flurry as pretty and fanciful as first snowflakes.

"It is good that you can find delight here, even in so small a miracle," said Tarchon, watching her childish play. "But try and concentrate. Guess how many acorns I hold in my hand."

Caecilia laughed and held up five fingers while saying the number's name in Rasennan.

"Wrong."

Prying open his hand she counted five. "What is the word for 'cheat'?"

Tarchon grinned. "There are five but you said four."

Caecilia put her hands on her hips.

"It is not my fault you don't like losing," he laughed.

"Another game then," she said, greedy for nonsense.

Tarchon put a large vase a few steps away and drew a line on the ground. "Stand here and see how many nuts you can toss into the jar."

Her acorn banged the lip and spun off to the side.

"Let me show you." He lobbed a kernel into the neck. It clicked as it hit its brothers within. "Superior aim," he said smugly.

She tried unsuccessfully, once again, to hit the mark.

"Now count aloud the number of nuts in Rasennan. And don't forget all the ones strewn across the ground."

Caecilia hummed to herself as she counted the acorns. Weeks had passed and, unlike Rome where sunlight was for utility not ornament, each day the sun's rays revealed beauty, beauty that somehow diluted her shock into disquiet, and her disquiet into a discomfort that she could mostly abide.

One such beauty was Tarchon. Having always felt plain, it made her uneasy, at first, to compare herself to his face with its perfect symmetry, his body with its taut contours made smooth after the hair had been stripped away by pitch—pain in return for comeliness. His smile promised whomever was with him that they were his dearest, but she soon realized that, although he was the tutor, she was much older than he in common sense. He was an exotic creature, first admired but later taken for granted.

When he irritated her, though, she could not be stern with him because, after all, he and Larthia had freed her. Even so it was disconcerting to cope with his familiarity, how he would take her hand or, worse, put his arm around her waist, touch her hair or kiss her cheek. Even Marcus, who at times afforded her affection as a first cousin, would not have dared to do other than hold her hand. It was shocking how this stranger had so quickly secured her affections; shocking, too, that she should let him.

He had become a friend who gossiped and teased and shared confidences and laughter as though he were another woman. Marcus had always made it clear that he was a man offering kindness and protection. Marcus and Tarchon were as unalike as earth and water, and yet there was something about them that made her think there was not so great a divide. In the end she concluded it was Tarchon's eyes that summoned comparison. Not the shape or color, eyebrows or lashes, but rather the hint of an emotion that haunted them both—the need for approval, the dread of failing expectations.

"Why don't you ever wear anything pretty?"

"There's nothing wrong with my stola and tunic." She continued to search for the acorns in the far corners of the atrium.

"How can you resist the elegance of pleated skirts and vivid hues?"

It was not easy, she thought, when each day she saw Larthia wear more wondrous chitons and even more dazzling jewelry. She fingered the simple amulet on her wrist then touched the fine artistry of the Atlenta pendant. Both sheltered her from evil, through Roman and Rasennan means.

"I have my wedding slippers on today," she said, stretching out her feet to display the orange shoes.

"A sad sight," he scoffed. "I will buy you some shoes that are worth displaying. With fine laces and soft leather. Just wait."

Caecilia sighed. Each day she asked herself what danger was there in relenting to temptation. What did it matter if she curled her hair or wore elegant robes? But old rules were hard to break. She knew she must remain resolute because there was a peril. One change would lead to another, then another, and one day she wouldn't be Roman at all.

"You are so lazy, Tarchon. Help me find them."

Her tutor resumed his seat beside the hearth. Irritated by his idleness, Caecilia stopped searching and instead studied the ceramic plaques on one wall that chronicled the deeds of family ancestors, their surfaces shiny, the figures upon them finely drawn and colored.

"The sons of the House of Mastarna are prestigious, Caecilia," said Tarchon, noticing her studying the medallions. "Even the zilath defers to Artile in matters of ritual and prophecy. He is a haruspex above all others, a seer of immense talent. The gods often whisper in his ear."

"Haruspex?"

"Yes. A priest who reads the livers of animals to foretell the fate of cities and men."

"A type of augur?"

"Yes, but far more skilled than your Roman priests who only ask the gods to answer yes or no to their questions."

"And Mastarna? You said both sons of the House of Mastarna were esteemed. Exactly how wealthy is my husband?"

"Most of the pasture that you passed through is owned by him. Why do you think he has been away so long? Because his estate is vast and his tenants many."

Caecilia shook her head when she realized that the green, watered fields she had compared to the parched land of her people belonged to her bridegroom.

"Why do you think he can marry you, a Roman? Do you think his friendship with Ulthes alone shelters him from the disapproval of many in this city?"

Annoyed at his condescension, Caecilia picked up the vase and resumed her task. The kernels rattled as she dropped them inside. "The leaders of Rome told me very little, Tarchon. If they had, I would have begged my uncle to either kill or spare me."

Tarchon took her hand and kissed it. "So dramatic! Would you really have wanted to miss the chance to have these lessons with me?"

Caecilia chewed her thumbnail, trying not to smile. "Why does Mastarna dislike Artile?"

Tarchon hesitated. "What do you mean?"

"They circle each other like cocks spoiling for a fight," she said in broken Rasennan.

Tarchon took the urn from her, emptied its contents onto the table, and studiously began counting. "I dread what you will be like when you speak our language fluently."

"You have not answered my question."

"Artile hates Mastarna and Mastarna has always been jealous of Artile. Larthia's pride could not be hidden when it was determined her younger son would be ordained a priest, not just an ordinary cepen but one with the Gift of Sight."

"So why does Artile hate Mastarna if he is so favored?"

"Because Artile, in turn, could not abide his father favoring his firstborn or the fact that Mastarna is the youngest man to have ever been elected zilath."

She thought of the warmth of Mastarna for his mother. "Larthia seems to be proud of him also."

"Ati loves both equally, but Mastarna thinks Artile gained too much favor when he left to sail upon the Tyrrhenian Sea."

Caecilia remembered the night Mastarna had shown her the stars. "Mastarna was a sailor?"

"More a soldier who loves the sea. He still keeps a fleet of trading ships that sail with copper and tin from his mines to Carthage and Athens and Rhodes."

"Why did he first go to sea?"

"Ati told me he was always restless when he was young. His father died when he was fifteen. War lust soon overcame him. And so, when he turned eighteen Larthia and Mastarna's grandfather encouraged Ulthes to teach him the art of war. They sailed with the Tarchnan navy, coming home rarely and always eager to return to sea."

Caecilia paused, remembering how Marcus had told her of Etruscan pirates, but she doubted Mastarna could be a brigand.

"Yet a man has no duty to fight another city's battles."

"But it is the duty of a man to learn to fight. My mother and Larthia were cousins. Our family lived in Tarchna where the Syracusan Greeks have cut off our sea lanes and hindered Rasennan trade for years. Mastarna gained battle hardness for the honor of Ati's people."

"And so he gave service to that city's zilath?"

"Yes, and that is where he met his wife."

Noticing he squeezed an acorn between thumb and forefinger as he spoke, Caecilia reached over and gently took it from him. "You mean Seianta."

"Daughter of Aule Porsenna, Zilath of Tarchna."

"So it was a political marriage? A pact between two cities?"

"No, it was a marriage arranged as any other, but Mastarna courted her before he made the contract."

"Courted her?"

"Yes, because he had fallen in love with the little girl who'd grown up before his eyes."

Love? Caecilia thought of Drusus.

"What was she like?"

"Tiny, a little plump. Mastarna called her 'his plum.'"

"I see." She could not stop herself making a comparison.

"She had a wicked tongue that made me laugh and was generous with her own mirth, too, not like some who dole out humor as though its supply were scarce. I miss her even now."

"And did Mastarna laugh with her?"

Tarchon nodded.

"And yet he will not speak her name. Why?"

Suddenly Tarchon scooped up the nuts and poured them back into the vase. "The lesson is over."

"Tell me," she said, tugging at his sleeve.

He shook his head. "One's still missing. There should be fourteen."

In the awkward silence that followed, Caecilia resumed her search, wishing the game had not been spoiled by her curiosity.

"Here it is." She retrieved the errant nut from beside the well. As she straightened she noticed the wellhead had two images sculpted upon it. On one side was a pretty winged woman while on the reverse of the terra-cotta was a monster.

The monster that had long haunted her dreams.

All sense of sunlight disappeared, her chest constricting. It was as if her fingers, like the mouse's claws, were scrabbling upon the moss of dank slippery walls.

It was the night demon. Only ghastlier. Donkey's ears, vulture's beak, face the pale gray-blue of rotting flesh, its knife-shaped feathers were alternately colored red and white, and coiled around its arms ready to slither toward her were two spotted snakes.

"Caecilia, what's the matter?"

"Who is that?"

"The demon Tuchulcha. He waits to torment us on our journey to Acheron after death."

Caecilia studied the gruesome face and shuddered. Would she always suffer from fright and suffocation as the night demon followed her from mortal to eternal sleep? "What is this journey?"

"To the Beyond," said Tarchon. "Each of us is greeted at the gate of Acheron by demons that either guard or terrify us. They are servants of Aita, god of the dead."

"Lord Ulthes mentioned this Tuchulcha."

Tarchon pointed to the carved figure on the other side of the wellhead. "And this is Vanth, the winged demoness who keeps a scroll of names to announce your fate."

Caecilia surveyed the carved demon with fair face and lovely form, dressed shamelessly with a tiny pleated skirt, short hunting boots, and a baldric crossing bare breasts. An eye painted upon each arch of her wings, she carried a key to open the gate to the Beyond and a torch to guide the dead through the dark. Only the two snakes twisting around her arms like bracelets hinted at her menace.

Caecilia said a quick prayer, hoping that her fate lay with the Roman world of the dead, that milling group of Shades, instead of with these demons.

"Is our destiny damnation?"

"If you are devout enough the gods may admit you to be one of the Blessed."

"The Blessed?"

"The Blessed are as important as the gods who guard your house, your storeroom, and your larder."

Caecilia had to sit down. The prospect of being raised to the level of a household god was enthralling. "You mean you will be immortal? How?"

"The rituals of prayer and sacrifice must be followed exactly and we must show devotion to the ancestors."

"Exactly?"

"Every word as prescribed and as often as is decreed."

Caecilia thought about such strictures. Everything here was elaborate, complex. An honest bowl of beans became steaming and fragrant, and giving thanks for such a dish bordered on ritual. At home a brief prayer sufficed with a daily offering of spelt cakes to the hearth fire. In Veii, when a rite was performed, the food could grow cold if prayers were not precise in movement and word. If any mistakes were made they were repeated and repeated. And so, after only a short time in Veii, Caecilia was aware of just how many errors she could make.

Now, sitting on the edge of the well in front of these demons, she was conscious of the burden of such beliefs, of her inadequacy. Aware that the prospect of reaching a chance of immortality was slim. "How do you know if the prayers are the right ones?"

"The Book of the Acheron, the Book of the Beyond, describes what must be believed and followed and recited."

Caecilia prided herself on being clever, her arrogance a goad to the dull-witted Aurelia. Now Tarchon was teasing her for being slow with the same conceit. For he spoke of a book of rituals, sacred knowledge written in ink just as the law was laid down in Rome in the Twelve Tables. Her ignorance seemed bottomless.

She glanced once again at Tuchulcha. "There is a book? May I see it?"

The youth ushered her away from the well, seeming to gain comfort as he grew further distant from the demons. Caecilia picked up the vase, absently dropping the last kernel into its depths.

"You may have married the richest man in Veii, Caecilia, but that does not mean that all mysteries can be revealed to you. Only the principes, the nobility of Veii, may read the sacred texts. In time, though, Artile may instruct you in the Book of Acheron, if you wish to follow our religion and if he deigns to teach a Roman."

They were distracted by the outer door opening. A small cloud of dust swept in through the passageway from the street. Startled, she saw Mastarna entering the atrium, Arruns behind him.

Many times since his departure, Caecilia had imagined their reunion. She would be remote, disdainful. Now that he was here she'd had no time to collect herself.

Servants hastened to take the master's cloak. Caecilia had forgotten how muscular and broad he was, how his shoulders strained the fabric of his tunic.

Again, she felt as though she were suffocating, her breath becoming short and frantic. She thought she had managed to forget, yet here he was, no more than ten strides away, and the memory of the wedding night welled up in her mind. As he neared her, she dropped the vase, acorns and shattered pottery skittering across the floor.

Mastarna, face bruised and a cut above his eye, glared at Tarchon, speaking in Latin. "You are supposed to be teaching her, not playing games."

Caecilia put up her hand. "Husband, Tarchon is a very good teacher," she said in perfect Rasennan.

Mastarna surveyed her, mouth slightly ajar, but continued to use her language. "Is that so, wife? Or perhaps he has a very good pupil."

She blushed, nonplussed at his compliment.

Tarchon gestured to Mastarna's face. "How did you hurt yourself?"

"It's nothing—a boar hunt." He gingerly touched his cheek.

"You look more like prey than hunter, or didn't you use a net at the kill?" Tarchon shot a glance at Arruns, who nodded behind his master's back.

He has hurt his arm as well, thought Caecilia. Did he crave new scars?

"It was a hunt, no different than any other," Mastarna growled. "We feasted for days. There is nothing more to say."

He gestured to the stone bench from where she'd received clients that morning. "Word came to me that you've been greeting the city tenants with Ati."

"Yes," she said, pausing to find the correct words. "It is wonderful to do so."

"Good," he said, still unsmiling. "Then tomorrow we will meet our obligations together."

She nodded, trying to imagine what it would be like conversing in daylight after a night lying soundlessly beneath him.

He stooped and picked up a nut. "I am curious. Just what do you learn by throwing acorns?"

"To count."

Mastarna examined Tarchon. "Perhaps you are not such a bad teacher after all. But now I must change. I am due to dine with the zilath."

Tarchon stepped toward him. "Did the coward agree to fight?"

Mastarna glared at his adopted son, speaking rapidly so that Caecilia could not follow. Tarchon reddened.

Her husband turned on his heel, leaving them standing among scattered nuts and potsherds.

Caecilia put her arm around the youth. "He is curt with you. What have you done to displease your father?"

"I've told you before. He is not my father. My father was a mighty princip, a nobleman who fought bravely for Tarchna. I will never forget him, nor my mother."

"Don't lie, Tarchon. You long to please Mastarna, don't you?"

The youth sighed. "What son does not want respect?"

"You will gain it. I am sure of it."

They knelt and picked up the pieces of vase. "I know you were asking him about the angry man at the banquet. Who was he?"

Tarchon concentrated on clearing up the mess. "His name is Laris Tulumnes and he is no friend to either Ulthes or Mastarna."

Caecilia blinked in surprise. All Romans knew the name of Laris Tulumnes—the king who started the last Fidenate war. Her great-uncle, Mamercus Aemilius, had ordered his execution. This man must be his son. It was no wonder he hated her and her people.

"You are right to call him a coward. His father was as untrustworthy and cruel as any Etruscan can be."

Tarchon sat back on his heels, eyes narrowing. "No crueler than you Romans. What Mamercus did was barbaric! Besides, it was the Fidenates who caused the trouble. It was all a misunderstanding."

Caecilia glared at him. Tata had often told her Tulumnes's story. How Fidenae appealed to the Veientane king to assist them when it rebelled against the Roman yoke twenty years ago. And how four Roman envoys visited the monarch to demand an explanation and found him playing dice. Tulumnes barely gave them greeting other than to say that his next throw would give them his answer. It was a signal. As the tesserae spun upon the table the Fidenates butchered the innocent messengers. "Laris Tulumnes deserved his fate."

"Do you truly think so, Caecilia?" Tarchon's voice rose in indignation. "What man deserves to be wrenched from his horse, pinned to the ground, and bludgeoned to death by the edge of his shield? What warrior should suffer being stripped of his armor and his head spiked on a lance so that his soul is forever paraded as a trophy on a phantom battlefield?"

"One who can end four men's lives on the throw of a die."

"And did Mastarna's father deserve to be killed by Mamercus Aemilius, too?"

His words checked her anger. Both Mastarna and Tulumnes had reason to hate the Romans. Her great-uncle was responsible for the death of both their fathers, yet one was prepared to forgive the Aemilians while the other would never do so.

The scene at the wedding returned. Words spoken but not understood. Emotions spiking, tempers sharpened.

"What did Mastarna tell you today?"

"Nothing."

"Please."

"Tulumnes refused to apologize, claiming he was justified in what he said at the wedding."

"So the enmity increases."

"Yes, Tulumnes should have defended his honor. Now he is humiliated because he is considered a coward."

Caecilia sat down cross-legged beside him, no longer wanting to argue. "What did he say that night to make my husband so angry?"

"You do not need to know other than it was offensive."

"Tell me."

"He said Mastarna had disgraced the city by marrying a Roman."

"I understood that without knowing a word of your tongue," she said impatiently. "What else did he say? Please, I will not hate you for another's words."

Tarchon looked disconcerted, but she could see she had finally worn him down. "Very well. Tulumnes claimed Mastarna had insulted Seianta's memory." He paused. "By fucking a Roman whore in her bed."

It was as though she had been slapped. The vulgarity of the words struck her as much as their meaning.

"I'm sorry, but you wanted to know."

"Such pain and anger."

"Yes, Tulumnes will not release the past."

"No, I mean Mastarna."

She remembered his cold fury when she had said Seianta's name. Cold fury after a cold consummation.

Tarchon brushed her cheek with his fingers. "You are a strange one."

"No stranger than you." Her smile was bittersweet.

The youth took her hand and Caecilia could tell he was summing up whether to disclose more. This was turning out to be far more than a language lesson.

"Mastarna was inconsolable when Seianta died," he finally said, knowing the questions she wished to ask.

"Is inconsolable," she added.

He nodded. "They had lost their little daughter the year before. Seianta was bereft."

Caecilia thought of her own grief for Tata. Sympathy for Mastarna filled her. "How did Seianta die?"

Tarchon hesitated, then said almost too quickly, "Of a broken heart. She could not bear to see little Velia die."

She sensed he would talk of Seianta no further, and she wondered why Mastarna's first wife caused all who knew her to maintain such silence.

"He wears anger and grief like a mantle," he continued, "warming himself with them, reluctant to shrug them from his shoulders."

"Since she died."

"Yes, holding hurt close instead of her."

"Why won't he let the pain go?"

Tarchon ran the fingers of one hand through his hair. "Because it is hard to lose an excuse for shouting at Fate and seeing if she will smite him down."

The afternoon sun had left the atrium. No more dust motes, only shadows lurking around the haunted face of Tuchulcha.

"Does he often hunt death?"

"Yes. Chariot races, duels, tournaments, boar hunts. And yet he survives. Perhaps deep down he clings to life as a punishment. Or Nortia is mocking him."

"But doesn't he fear the demons?"

Tarchon frowned. "Mastarna does not believe in the Book of Acheron."

Caecilia remembered the leopard, Fufluns's guide to the Beyond.

"But what concerns me now," continued Tarchon, "is that he has raised the stakes in his plunge to destruction."

"Because he scorns Tulumnes?"

"Yes," he said, "and so puts you at risk as well as this family."

Caecilia lightly squeezed his hand. "And do you also hate the Aemilians?"

He smiled, making her glad the afternoon was not entirely destroyed by their argument. "We have been at peace for twenty years," he said. "Like you, I have been taught prejudice but not by Mastarna. He believes it is fruitless to continue teaching such lessons."

His admiration for his adopted father once again bled through his words.

He reached over and picked a sliver of pottery from one orange slipper. "Besides, we are the same, Caecilia. Both orphaned and adopted. We should be friends, even if you are a Roman."

"I agree," she laughed. "Even if you are an Etruscan."

• • •

The fibula was of gold. Small, intricate. A mother wolf was embossed upon it, suckling the twins, Romulus and Remus.

"I had it made for you," said Mastarna.

A keepsake to remind her of her home. Caecilia traced the figures. "It's beautiful."

"I am glad it pleases you."

Caecilia said nothing, merely stared at the trinket, turning it over and over in her hand. She had been hopeful that he would not return from his dinner with the zilath, but it was not to be.

Mastarna looked weary. The scar from nose to mouth was purple in relief against wan skin. The bruises from the hunt competed in their shadows with the dark circles beneath his eyes. Perhaps he will want only to sleep, she thought.

"Wear the brooch on a new cloak. It is time to shed Roman drabness. It does not suit a comely woman like yourself."

Immediately, she put her hand to her neck, wondering if he was mocking her.

He stepped closer and traced the outline of the birthmark with one finger. A pulse beat spasmodically beneath her skin. "This is considered a sign of a fortuitous marriage by my people."

Caecilia raised her eyebrows. "Now there is an irony."

He smiled briefly. "Time will tell. And soon, perhaps, you'll find our ways aren't so terrible. After all, you seem to be happy with your role as matron of a Veientane house."

"Taking audience is much different to the sins I have observed."

It was his turn to raise his eyebrows. "I am afraid it is not so easy to pick and choose, Bellatrix. The pleasures you saw at our wedding are freedoms and can be as tantalizing as your newfound authority. I wager that soon you will be seduced by us. Our world is hard to resist."

She pointed at his bruised face. "And must I seek out hurt while I enjoy life to the fullest?"

He touched the swelling. "No, risking death is my choice alone," he said quietly.

His patient mood, despite tiredness, was disarming. As she took in the warmth of his fingers' touch, her thoughts returned again to the night at Fidenae when he'd given her the name of a star and talked to her as though she were a man.

"Here," he said, searching in the folds of his cloak. "Hold this." He placed the tiny golden box with its gilded dice into her hand. The hard skin on his palm scraped against her, evidence that he still trained with the sword even if high office threatened to make him soft. His vices, it seemed, did not weaken him either.

She dropped the tesserae onto the sheets as though they were embers, her thoughts returning to the wicked Veientane king, suspicious of Mastarna's motives. "I don't want anything to do with your gambling. Men should only play dice at the Saturnalia."

He laughed. "Sometimes it seems you know as little about Rome as you do of Veii. Men drink and wager and embrace prostitutes in your esteemed city just as keenly as they do here. Only they manage to exclude their wives from observing such pursuits."

He gathered up the dice again. "Besides, what is there to fear over two tiny tesserae? You will have to get used to wagering, Bellatrix. Our people only survived because of it."

Again she wondered at his mood. Had he been drinking? What had the zilath said to release him from irritability?

Thinking any delay was welcome, she asked him what he meant.

Mastarna dropped the dice into the box. "Long ago the Rasenna lived in a country whose harvest could no longer fill the bellies of all. So the king cast half his subjects, led by his son Tyrrhenus, adrift upon the Tyrrhenian Sea to find another realm or perish. The prince landed safely in the land of Etruria, but until crops could be sown and reaped and eaten the first survivors had to scrounge for food and shiver through the winter. Yet not one person died."

The tesserae clicked together in the container. Caecilia wanted to pretend she was not interested, but Mastarna, knowing better, continued.

"So Tyrrhenus commanded that half the people take it in turns to eat while the other half gambled." He smiled. "Behold, hunger pains were staved off with the roll of the dice."

He offered the golden box to her again. "Sometimes my people place lots or dice in tiny canisters like this, then ask the gods to answer yes or no to their queries."

Mastarna curled her fingers around it. "Perhaps you would like to ask the gods a question?"

"What would I ask?"

"Whether they wish you to lie with your husband tonight."

She tried to pull her hand away but he held it fast. "Your jest is cruel."

"I don't mock you, Caecilia. I want you to desire our couplings, not endure them."

She stared at the little golden box and thought of Cytheris and choosing men. Mastarna was making Fortuna choose for her, but she did not understand why this would make her desire him. Winning the throw would merely give her a chance to avoid misery for one night.

"Also, I am embarrassed," he continued, "for acting like a Roman on our wedding night."

This time she managed to pull her hand from his grasp. "How dare you!"

Mastarna twisted his gold and onyx ring around his finger. "Do you think your Drusus would be a good lover?"

The girl was astounded. He'd never mentioned the youth who'd called her name in the twilight on their wedding day. "How do you know who he is?"

"I made it my business to discover who covets my wife."

"Then know that Claudius Drusus would never treat me as a harlot!"

"I have already explained these things to you," Mastarna said evenly.

"Or his harlot as his wife!"

Mastarna's eyes narrowed. "I see Cytheris has been more than your interpreter. She should be whipped for her gossiping."

"That is your right as her owner, I suppose. Is whipping a woman another freedom I've gained? Would you have Erene whipped, too, if she was insolent?"

"I would not dare," he snorted.

Caecilia scowled, infuriated that he was treating her concerns so lightly, but when she heard him suddenly sigh she knew that he, too, was frustrated. They may be conversing in Latin but they spoke the language of very different worlds.

"Forget about Erene. She is not my mistress but Ulthes's. She is not a slave but a freedwoman. I have no say in what she does. Do you understand?"

She nodded, but wished she knew whose version she was to trust. His or her maid's.

After a time the silence grew awkward between them. He rubbed his brow, wincing when he brushed the cut above his eye. He gestured for her to sit beside him. "When I said I acted more like a Roman I meant that I denied you pleasure."

He cupped her chin with his fingers, the gesture of a man certain of possession, unconcerned that she had been unfaithful in thought. She brushed his hand away, annoyed that he was dismissing Drusus as a rival. One thing was certain, Mastarna had not pleased her on their wedding night and she doubted he could remedy his failing.

Pleasure. Cytheris had spoken of it. Would there be different versions of this, too?

Once again Mastarna held out the dice. "If you throw a number higher than mine, it will be a sign that the gods wish you to do other than sleep in our bed tonight."

She gasped, astounded at such a proposition. What would he do if she refused to honor the wager? Would he then force her to perform her wifely duty and do so every time he wished to claim the right of a husband? Surely the chance of avoiding his embrace, on the throw of the dice each night, was better than such a future?

And so, holding her breath, praying to Fortuna to be kind, she summoned up courage to scatter them on the sheets.

"Now, we will test how well you learned your numbers," said Mastarna as she peered at the symbols written on the sides, adding the values, then waited anxiously to see what numbers he would throw as he rolled the dice between his palms.

Her brief flare of hope was doused immediately.

Mastarna did not gloat; instead he drew a glass alabastron from his robes and swallowed some of its contents. "Drink this."

"What is it?"

"It is called Alpan after Turan's handmaiden. Both act as love's helpers."

Caecilia swallowed nervously. What had the goddess of love got to do with them?

"What will it do? Make me drunk? Make me sick?"

"The potion is safe. A love philter only. I'm not sure what is in it exactly. A little mandragora I am told."

Caecilia sniffed the top of the vial. She knew of the herb. Aurelia grew it. If her aunt understood it could be used to awaken passion, though, it was unlikely she would have used it for that purpose. All Caecilia knew was that it soothed aches and made you sleep.

It could also be a poison.

Mastarna held out his hand to draw her to the bed. "See I have taken it already," he said, reading her mind. "It will take you far outside this room to pleasure and then to sweet sleep. And"—he stretched and touched her mark again—"it will leaven the flickering here and in your breast from fear to wanting."

Caecilia stared at the deep blue of the glass. She doubted anything could conjure a longing for him, but she'd seen how wine had unchained the women at the banquet and suspected this potion was as potent a brew. If she could not flee the room, was it not better to relent and choose the elixir with its promise of escape?

"And you, what will it do for you?"

"It will make me forget," he said quietly and bent to kiss her.

She put her hand across his mouth. "We Romans kiss the dead to catch their souls. You cannot have mine."

He frowned. "You are far from dying."

She did not reply.

The taste of the elixir was cloying with a hint of bitterness for caution. He stripped and she saw there were more injuries from the hunt, scars and bruises within and without. Then he made her stand as he unfastened her robes so that she stood naked beside him. Small-breasted and boyish, she was tall enough to meet his eyes, but she could not.

Then a droplet of elixir hurtled through her, and another, shepherding her cares to the tips of her fingers where she could shake them away with a flick of her wrist.

She was lying beside him, eyes closed, letting the warmth ripple through her until languor immersed her and he disappeared. She floated upon waters, wavelets buffeting at her gently. Sound was banished except for her breathing. If she moved her head slightly her hair writhed, touching her as though alive. The water's skin adhered to her own. She would have to peel it away when she rose. And all the while the current bore her along, letting color and light glide by her, pulling her toward calm, toward stillness, toward peace.

Drusus spoke to her and she smiled. She could see his long reddish hair, his fierce eyes, and the beard framing dark-pink lips. He turned her on her side, his finger and thumb squeezing her neck lightly, sometimes playing with the soft short wisps of hair at the base of her skull.

Drusus's hands were warm, dry, and broad. They encircled her buttocks. Then his fingers moved up and down her spine, circling and pressing each ridge, releasing pockets of tension in brief exquisite bursts of pain.

She licked her lips, hoping to eke out some small remnant of the philter as the current drew her onward.

Drusus leaned closer, his breath a whisper. His hand slid along her belly to touch between her thighs, to the wet soft fleshiness and secret hardness, his fingers discovering what she had never explored.

She clutched his wrist, eyes flying open. Mastarna beheld her, his dark, almond-shaped eyes promising her.

The current eddied around them, its pull unyielding. She closed her eyes. She drifted. She let his wrist slip from her grasp.

• • •

It was late when she woke. Sunlight was lapping beneath the bottom of the curtains and peeking around the edges.

He was not beside her.

A different type of relief filled her. The apprehension that they would share the bed banished. Stretching her arms above her head, she delayed rising, enjoying her nakedness, the feel of the linen's softness against her skin.

There was an aftertaste in her mouth. Glancing over to the tiny vial, she smiled.

The color of the alabastron was appealing. Deep blue with swirls of yellow trapped within it. The visions she'd seen under its

spell had freed her. For Drusus had been with her while Mastarna
held her. She hoped that they would share the potion again soon.

Then she remembered Mastarna's reason for also drinking it.
He'd wanted to forget his loss for Seianta.

Realizing her husband also dreamed of being in the arms of
another made Caecilia worry again that Mastarna was comparing
his wives. Was she less of a woman because he'd not lingered to
greet her in the morning?

Sunlight streamed in from the garden as the maidservant
swept back the curtains. "Get up, mistress. The master is waiting
for you to take audience with him."

"When did he leave this morning?"

"The master? Oh, he always rises at dawn to train with Arruns."

Caecilia sat up, rubbing sleep from her eyes and yawning,
strangely pleased to learn Mastarna's escape was not entirely
because of her lack of skill.

As she stepped down onto the bed's footstool, she noticed the
leopard. "Ssh," she whispered. "Don't tell Aurelia."

Eager to meet the tenants, she bade Cytheris to help her dress
quickly, ignoring the knowing look upon the maid's face. There
would be time later to speak of what happened, but she was uncertain whether to share the secret of the Alpan.

Hurrying into the garden, she found Mastarna there, talking
to the steward before entering the reception chamber. As usual his
manner was intense, preoccupied with business, authority emanating from him.

The deepness of his voice made Caecilia pause. Memories of
the first morning after their wedding night returned. The night in
Rome also. How she had feared his power, his nearness. Today that
sensation was gone but she was still acutely aware of his presence.

Shyness overcame her. After she had lain with a man in such a
way, what was she supposed to say? To do? To feel?

His face relaxed when he saw her. "Did you sleep well, Bellatrix?"

She nodded.

"Then let's hope there are more nights when you can find such rest."

It was a simple statement yet she blushed.

Offering her his arm, he led her from the garden. "There is an artisan I wish you to meet," he said. "He crafts the most beautiful bronzes and seeks a patron. Do you think you would like to act as his?"

She stopped walking, mouth agape. "You want me to be his patron?"

Mastarna smiled. "Why are you so surprised? Ati sponsors many craftsmen. Potters mostly from her workshop. It will gain you favor with my clan if they see you value artwork."

She smiled broadly, nodding fiercely.

Mastarna laughed, bending to whisper in her ear so that the steward could not overhear him. His words were unexpected.

"You should smile more often, Bellatrix," he said. "When you do, your serious face becomes as beautiful as one of Turan's angels."

NINE

Caecilia gasped. "Did your people truly create this?"

Tarchon nodded.

Before them the river was being swallowed into the belly of a gray-and-yellow tufa rock. The tunnel was monumental. Wide enough for a boat to pass through, and with a vaulted ceiling as tall as that of a vast temple. And, at the end of its great length, she saw an archway bright with sunlight through which the water escaped. She gazed upward, spying two apertures hewn into the roof above. Caecilia gazed at it, questions rattling inside her head. "What are the holes for?"

"The slaves used them to remove debris as they bored the passage through the rock. See the grooves made by their picks scarring the surface? The roof forms a stone bridge over the river leading from the city gates to the forest beyond."

The coolness of the cave beckoned to her, a respite from the heat. They had traveled for most of the afternoon through crowded traffic to the northern gateway with its high towers to see this marvel.

"Are there other tunnels like this?"

"Yes, many caves lead under Veii. Not as grand as this, though. And my people have dug canals under their farmland. They draw water through them to feed dry soil or use them to drain swampy land. One day I'll show them to you, as well as the drains and cisterns carved into the cliffs beneath the city."

Caecilia stared at him. As much as she condemned these people for their wickedness, she could not but be amazed at their ingenuity to divert a river. The mystery of a checkerboard of fields remaining verdant in a sunburned world had been answered.

The water running through the cave gallery looked quite shallow. More stream than river. The lure of exploring was too great for her.

She sat down and unlaced her new red boots. A small temptation. She'd only hesitated briefly before accepting them. Since then she'd reveled in their soft leather, delighting in how small they made her feet look, smiling each time she pointed her toes so she could better admire them.

The sin of wearing such luxury was compounded by her removal of another layer of decorum. She no longer wore a stola overdress, willingly shedding its ugly woolen weight once Mastarna told her it was a barrier to gaining the trust of his tenants. She felt guilty in peeling off the Roman robes, but she could not deny that the gaze of his clients was less chary as she sat in audience.

Ignoring Tarchon's concern, she carefully laid aside the boots, not wanting them ruined.

"What are you doing!"

"I'm going to look inside."

"Don't be silly," said Tarchon crankily, grabbing her arm. "You'll slip. The river banks are steep and mossy."

Scooping up the edges of her tunic, she scrambled down and splashed into the river. "Come on, Tarchon! Join me."

The youth pouted, irritated that she would not heed him. "Don't think I'll rescue you if you fall in."

She laughed. The water was warm at the edges, the silt ooz-ing between her toes. As she waded into the depths of the cavern, the rush of river was amplified, the sound of her laughter echoing around the damp lichen-covered walls. However, the pull of the current soon pushed against her, making it difficult to progress, the pebbles slippery beneath her feet. When she found herself hitching her dress up to her thighs she reluctantly ceased her exploration.

Tarchon sat on the bank, glowering at her. "Don't ever do that again! Mastarna would kill me if you were hurt."

Giggling, Caecilia lay upon the palla shawl strewn across the grass.

Tarchon granted her a begrudging smile. "I like your laugh," he said. "It has a hint of childhood in it."

"I feel like I did when I ran barefoot on my father's farm."

The youth stretched out beside her, closing his eyes. "I forget you're half plebeian."

Caecilia ignored his haughtiness. "Why don't you want to go wading?"

"Because I don't like the feel of sand beneath my feet."

She studied his beauty as he lay dozing beside her. He wore one turquoise earring, claiming it was a male fashion in Carthage. Another instance of his foreignness and effeteness. She tried unsuccessfully to imagine Marcus or Drusus wearing such an adornment.

Observing Tarchon, Caecilia knew that, despite her friendship with the Veientane, he could never replace Marcus in her heart. Her cousin and she were of the same clay, formed from the same mold, their Romanness ingrained.

Yet she'd heard no word from him. The letters she'd sent with official correspondence to Rome were unanswered. Had he for-gotten her already? Or had something happened? Surely Aemilius would send word if the garrison at Verrugo had been attacked.

Her attention returned to Tarchon. From his pallor it was plain he'd been out drinking and had not slept the night before—a common occurrence despite bleary eyes and an aching head the next day upon wakening. Not that Tarchon thought he'd missed half the day by the time they began their journey. The Veientanes saw midday as the official start of their day. To them midnight was only halfway through waking hours.

"I think you must drink more than any Veientane I've met," she scolded.

"Then you haven't met many," he grumbled.

Basking in the sun in the ripe, lethargic afternoon, Caecilia ignored his bad mood. Around her crickets sawed the air with song. Staring upward she gazed at the lazy billowing clouds and wished that summer was not ending.

Today there was no sense of foreboding as she lay next to the Cremera, the same river beside which she had fought the bandit. Instead she felt secure. For together with the river on the opposite side of the city, the two streams formed a perimeter that embraced Veii and kept its territory safe from invaders.

Close to Tarchon, she noticed a bruise shadowed his jawline. He often had such marks upon him. She never asked him how he came by them, assuming they were legacies from drunken fist-fights, although the thought of the soft-living Tarchon provoking violence seemed unlikely. "You should be training to be a soldier, not getting into brawls," she said, pointing to his chin. "Marcus used to practice on the Campus Martius every morning."

The youth did not comment.

"It must be time for you to join the army soon," she said, prodding him. "Marcus is your age. He's fighting the Volscians."

Tarchon opened one bloodshot eye. "I'm sick of hearing about your cousin," he snapped. "Besides, except for Rome, Veii doesn't fight its neighbors."

"I don't believe you," she said, sitting up.

Tarchon yawned, touching his bruised jaw tentatively as he also sat up. "It's true. All the cities in Etruria have formed a brotherhood that has lived in peace for centuries. The twelve greatest form a league to ensure concord continues. Tarchna is one of them. So, too, is Veii. Each year they meet north of here at the sacred spring at Velzna to elect a leader from among the twelve. Seianta's father, Aule Porsenna, has been voted in as head zilath this year. As long as Rome keeps the treaty there is no opportunity for me to fight."

"Then go to sea. Fight the Syracusan raiders. Make Mastarna proud of you."

To her surprise the youth gave a bitter laugh. "Do you really think Artile would let me be a soldier?"

"What has he got to do with it?"

"The priest has been more of a guardian to me than Mastarna. He looked after me when I first came to this household. He wanted to train me to become a priest."

"So why didn't he?"

Tarchon suddenly became preoccupied with rearranging his necklaces and adjusting the buckle on his embroidered belt.

"Tarchon?"

"Mastarna was against it," he finally said. "And now he thinks Artile has made me soft. He wants me to marry and father children, enter politics, fulfill my duty to my city."

"As is fitting."

He patted her as though she were a child. "I belong to Artile, Caecilia. I am not destined to be any of those things while I am his beloved. It is but another splinter under Mastarna's skin."

For a moment, Caecilia wondered if she'd heard correctly, then an ache returned to her head and belly. Here was another tier of rot revealed, the beautiful veneer stripped away. Only this time it was Tarchon who was wanting. No Roman citizen would submit to being the bride of another. A father would be justified to kill his son for such a disgrace. If he were in the army he could be executed.

"How can he be your lover when you are both freeborn?" She could hardly bear to say the words.

"Caecilia, I wish you could understand. I am Artile's beloved but he is more than my lover. I was eleven when my father died and the youngest of seven sons. My mother could not afford to keep me. I was sent to live with Larthia Atelinas, her wealthy cousin. I bid farewell to the arx of Tarchna and welcomed that of Veii's; said good-bye to sea breezes and greeted woodland and streams. Seianta and I traveled here together. Mastarna claimed and agreed to raise me."

His mention of Seianta's name made Caecilia turn to him, her hunger to know about the woman overcoming the discomfort of listening to his unnerving story. "You arrived here at the same time as Seianta?"

"Yes. They were just married. Mastarna took little notice of me other than to grasp my shoulder and declare his home was mine. It was as though nothing else existed for him. Seianta was like a sun that warmed his stony soul or drained it if she denied him smiles."

The youth picked at a loose thread on his embroidered belt. "I yearned for her to notice me also, enjoying her flirting cleverness, grinning at her antics and ploys. She rarely acknowledged me, though, feeding me tidbits of attention. Enough to take the edge off loneliness but not enough to fill the hole. She was fourteen and could captivate adults and cajole men. Why would she waste her time speaking to an eleven-year-old boy?"

"But Artile did?"

"Yes, he took notice of me, recognizing my loneliness and abandonment with those eyes that both terrified and seduced me. He was not yet chief haruspex but his fame as a seer was growing. I was overwhelmed that this agent of the gods cared about me.

"At that age my body was much the same as a girl's: the hint of breasts, sloped shoulders, straight waist, and legs that had yet to decide how tall they should grow. I felt clumsy and ugly but Artile made me feel wanted. When we were alone together, he'd let me parade around his chamber dressed in his fringed shawl and hat. If I was good, he'd allow me to bisect a liver, my fingers sticky with blood, slimy with membrane. 'It's good practice,' he'd say, 'for when you become a priest.'

"He told me once that he'd been sent away to the Sacred College at ten to learn about the Holy Books. There was pride at being chosen, but I could hear the timbre of loneliness and home-sickness within his voice.

"I had other schoolmasters, of course—a whining Greek whose birch rod stung my knuckles, but Artile soon sent him off and became my teacher, wrongly taking it upon himself to be my lover as well with no intention of teaching me the ways of man-hood and citizenry and war."

Caecilia stared at him. His blood was tainted—even though it had been the priest who was the corrupter. "What do you mean wrongly? When is it ever honorable for a nobleman to lie with a princip's son?"

Tarchon shook his head. "Poor Caecilia. How confusing it is for you. You see, if another lord had offered to teach me there would have been no problem. In Veii, noblemen act as mentors to aristocratic youths; they become lovers and beloveds. It is only when their pupils fail to grow into soldiers, husbands, and fathers that the boys are shunned as soft ones, what you Romans call 'molles.' My dilemma, you see, is that Mastarna wishes me to be a man while Artile does not."

Caecilia covered her face, her cheeks flushed. These people condoned debasing children. It was even worse than she thought.

Tarchon reached over to pull her hands away from her face. Instinctively, she shrank from his touch. He dropped his hand to his side as though used to disappointment.

Unable to look at him, she fingered Marcus's amulet, praying its charm would protect her. If she could just concentrate on it she could continue listening. Concentrate on it and not think too deeply about what Tarchon said.

Despite her rebuff, Tarchon plowed on with his tale. "At first Artile asked nothing of me. He would beckon me to his bed as innocently as would my mother. I'd lie against his chest as he stroked my hair and face. I felt safe. But as my body grew lean, waist narrow, shoulders broad, and chest and belly muscled, his embraces grew more ardent. He would spend himself between my legs. 'Your sweet thighs,' he would say. 'My sweet, sweet boy.'"

It was as if Caecilia had plunged her face into an ice bath. The fact she'd braced herself for the painful burning cold did not stop it from being excruciating. The thought of the priest touching her at the wedding made her skin crawl, and she was repulsed by the idea that he could hold such sway over Tarchon—that a kinsman could defile an innocent boy.

Slowly she faced him, realizing just how different his childhood had been to hers. Tata had protected her, but who had protected Tarchon? Where was Mastarna when this happened? Suddenly she needed to hear the rest of her friend's story. It was the time for him to tell it and for someone other than Artile to listen. This time she touched his hand. "Go on."

Tarchon smiled briefly at her encouragement. "Don't look so sad. Even though Artile broke the code I don't regret what he did for me. I was scared at first; bewildered that he had changed from father to lover. He told me not to tell Mastarna. Not to tell anyone. I did not want to anyway. Artile was my world."

"How could Mastarna not have seen it?"

The youth's face hardened. "Because he chose to be blind. Because, by the time I turned fourteen, his daughter had died and Seianta was sick with grieving. I was invisible to him, but I did not care. I was happy with Artile.

"But one day he must have decided to take notice. He berated his brother, his bellows informing the neighbors of the scandal. He forbade Artile from seeing me and then adopted me so that I became officially nephew to my lover, yet another barrier between us. Finally, although I begged to be a cepen, he forbade me taking any further instruction. 'There is already one too many priests in this house.'"

"But you are still with Artile. How can that be?"

Tarchon bowed his head and Caecilia saw that he'd picked clean the pattern upon his belt, threads tattered. "Because Seianta died. In his hurt and misery, Mastarna did not care what we did. I was able to return to Artile. But four years have passed and he cannot afford to ignore us any longer. He has said he will shun me if I do not leave Artile."

Anger rose in her. Not at Tarchon but at her husband. He should have stopped his son's corruption when the boy had first come into his care. Again the specter of Seianta emerged. It seemed that she'd controlled Mastarna when she was alive as much as she haunted him in death. Distracting him first with her desire and then with her despair. But at least Mastarna was finally recognizing his duty. And if Tarchon heeded him, he could yet avert disaster.

At home, she would not need to meet with a man such as Tarchon. The servants would have whispered his name, smacking their lips at rumor, and, in turn, her guardians would have pursed their mouths and forbidden mention of him, even though in the Forum his name would be on everybody's tongue. It would have been easy to maintain contempt for a man known only to her through gossip. But in Veii, she had gladly spent each day with him. She knew she should spurn him, hating her people for expecting her to do so. But she could not do it. For he seemed no different from the Tarchon she knew before. It was not easy to despise a Veientane who wanted a Roman as a friend.

She put her hand on his shoulder. "Do you remember how you said we were the same? Well I think that is so in more ways than one. There are echoes of my life in your tale. Both of us are controlled by powerful men. You've been stained by another, while many in Rome would see me as tainted for wedding a foe. But it is not too late for you. Reject Artile and you won't be shunned. You can have other lovers. Slaves. Freedmen. Anyone but another freeborn."

Tarchon frowned. "This isn't Rome, Caecilia. We aren't tainted and Mastarna will not kill me."

"Are you foolish? If Mastarna shuns you, so will Veii!"

"I don't care. Artile will protect me."

"You're mad," she shouted. "You'll think differently when people turn their back upon you. I thought you wanted to please Mastarna."

Arrogance and stubbornness surfaced upon Tarchon's face. She recognized them from looking in the mirror.

"It's not that simple. Even if I broke off with Artile, Mastarna won't respect me. I'm not meant to be a warrior. Besides, I will never leave him."

As he strode away, Caecilia stared back into the tunnel, at the darkness within its vaulted arch. What had been delightful now seemed ominous, the Veientanes's artistry sullying nature. It was as though she'd bitten into an apple and found a worm. The sweetness of the afternoon was spoiled, her world, once again, turned upside down.

• • •

Arruns was shaving Mastarna when she returned. Because of his heavy beard her husband often liked to do so in the evening. Both men's chests were bare, the air redolent with masculinity and perfume.

Musicians were playing in the garden. Normally she would pause to listen, always grateful that such artists were employed for mundane purpose, not just for ceremonies; the burden of their slavery relieved by plucking strings, beating drums, or trilling pipes. And it seemed the Veientanes captured the lilt of melody in their limbs even when no lyre or horn could be heard.

Mastarna's barbers made smooth his body by pitch, but he trusted only Arruns to shave him. The servant was careful in his ministrations, using the razor skillfully, scraping the bristles from Mastarna's chin with a precision that ensured no nicks were made.

Despite spending nearly all their waking hours together, the freedman and his master were not friends, not even companions. There was a bond between them, though. Arruns was Mastarna's shadow. It was clear he would die without hesitation for the princip.

Caecilia felt no such affinity toward the Phoenician. And yet there was a connection between them that stemmed from him having saved her life. The blue tattooed snake that writhed around his torso and bit into his face did not frighten her. She felt no menace, but she was wary. His strength was awesome, the danger he posed to Mastarna's enemies ever present. Yet, strangely, Arruns was more like a Roman than all the other Veientane men she'd met. There was no sense of excess about him, his reserve had dignity, a sense of duty was instilled within him.

Mastarna frowned when he saw her. "What have you been doing? You look bedraggled."

"I want to talk to you about Tarchon."

"Why? What has he done now?"

Aware that their conversation should be held in private, Caecilia turned to Cytheris, who was busy choosing a change of clothes for her mistress. "Go and get me some hot water to wash my feet."

As the handmaid reluctantly left the chamber Caecilia stared pointedly at Arruns. She hoped that Mastarna would give a similar command, but he gestured to his servant to continue with his task.

The constant attendance of the two servants in Caecilia's life was unsettling. Cytheris and Arruns seemed to share all intimacies except the time spent lying or asleep with her husband. Shared secrets also. Sometimes she longed for solitude instead of being crowded by people who tended to her every comfort.

"Tarchon has told me about Artile."

"What do you mean?"

"Your son is a freeborn man submitting to being a bride."

Mastarna's eyes widened in surprise. "And where did a Roman maiden learn to speak in such a way?"

She thought of the servants' gossip about Aemilius. How she had snatched and squirreled their words inside her head, not understanding them until now. Realized, too, why such eavesdropping was of value.

"I've learned more than how to count in my life. How could you let it happen?"

At her words Mastarna turned and dismissed Arruns after all. Suddenly Caecilia was nervous, realizing she had blundered. They'd not quarreled since she'd defied him about the golden gown. Even so, she had to hear his side of the story.

As before with her, his contempt was cold and deliberate. "I don't know what Tarchon has told you, but I can assure you I am not at fault here. I did not condone Artile taking a boy who was not eligible or of an age to be his beloved. And when I discovered his deception I forbade him to continue. But both my brother and my son have continued to defy me. It is Artile you should accost, Caecilia. He is the one who denies Tarchon the right to be a man now that my son has grown a full beard."

"What has that to do with it? A Roman boy becomes a man at fourteen. Tarchon was that old when Artile stained him."

"Growing a full beard marks the time when a mentor must release his pupil to enter public life."

Caecilia could not believe Mastarna was excusing such a despicable practice. She pointed to the bronze shaving basin and pedestal. "How can you tell if a youth has grown hair upon his chin? All you Veientane men have smooth cheeks like children."

Mastarna slowly stood up. Wiping away remnants of lather from his face, he crossed the room. "Do you think I'm not a man, Caecilia?"

She glanced away, embarrassed. He had shown her more than once that he was virile as they lay beneath the Alpan's spell. The scent upon his skin and the gentle music to which he listened in no way detracted from his maleness. "Of course not," she said, her voice trailing away.

Mastarna drew her close and she sensed he was no longer angry. "Bellatrix, I can understand how bewildered you must be, but there is no dishonor in a nobleman teaching a boy to be a man. Artile abused the rules and won't admit he is condemning Tarchon to humiliation. Tarchon is being foolish, too. I have no choice other than to shun him if he doesn't break with my brother. But you might be able to persuade him. He just might listen to you."

Glad that there was one instance where Veii's rules were the same as Rome's, Caecilia nodded. "I'll try."

"Good," he said, kissing her on the cheek before breaking away to take his cloak off a wall hook.

"Where are you going?"

"To meet with Ulthes then dine with the other high councillors."

"Again? I thought you'd already met with them today."

"Tulumnes is being difficult."

Caecilia weighed up whether she should question him about such politics, but she could see he was in a hurry. His role as one of the elders of the city often called him away at night. The Etruscan government intrigued her. It was not a republic. The common man did not have a voice. Discovering this shocked the plebeian in her. Instead of their six tribes electing consuls or generals together with a body of senators to advise them, the principes chose magistrates from their own ranks to sit in an electoral college. The clan chieftains, who formed a high council, then elected the zilath. Mastarna was one of these leaders together with Vipinas, Pesna, and Apercu. Tulumnes also.

She sighed. It was rare that her husband returned from such meetings in a good mood. The councillors argued over every proposal, and Tulumnes and Pesna were constant thorns in Ulthes's side.

Mastarna cupped her chin with his fingers as he bade her good night.

"As for my shaving," he said, all traces of their argument gone, "I've never known a woman who wanted her skin scratched by her lover's beard."

When he'd gone, Cytheris returned. As the handmaid knelt to wash her mistress's feet, Caecilia wanted to tell her all that had happened but she was too tired. Instead, staring into space, she was at last free to lose herself in thought. The task of convincing Tarchon would not be easy. For if he could challenge the authority of his father, why would he heed the counsel of a young Roman girl?

AUTUMN 406 BC

TEN

A bright-yellow sun beat down upon them; a sun more suited for summer than for the blue sharpness of autumn. Caecilia gazed out to a sky streaked with clouds, giddy at the heights upon which she stood. For the citadel of Veii clung to a hurtling cliff of red and gray, and, impregnable, brooded over dark valleys of carpeted russet and gold.

The gentle undulations of the Roman hills were humble compared to such gaudy geography. Vulnerable, too, although that was a word she had never before applied to her city, a city that lay so tantalizingly close.

The Temple of Uni lay near to the precipice, allowing the goddess to preside over her dominion without having to edge closer to its rim. To Caecilia, it seemed that the giant citadel wall was the only thing that prevented the sanctuary from toppling to the landscape below. The immense terra-cotta goddess stared balefully at the ministrations of her servants, her gaze encompassing the vast crowd that murmured and jostled beyond the steps of her temple. Below her, priests fussed with paterae and axes, knives and draining bowls. An aulos was being played, the graceful notes of the double oboe twisting through the air like ribbons of smoke. Crafted in clay, head and shoulders covered in goatskin, studded with jewels, and brandishing a lightning bolt, Uni stood ensconced in glory within her own chamber, triumphant that the gods, Aplu and Menerva, had been relegated to the two temple cells on either side.

Uni.

Roman Juno.

It was a comfort that she lived in Veii. Here was a deity who was more than Mother Goddess. She was also a fearsome warrior-ess, a liberator.

"Tonight," Mastarna had informed her earlier, "we will sacrifice a bull in thanksgiving for a bountiful harvest."

Hearing this, Caecilia had been too excited to sleep. Unwed Roman girls were not permitted to witness a state ceremony. Instead she'd only observed her uncle taking the auspices over domestic concerns and familial decisions. And so she was grateful to stand on the temple porch among the high-ranking principes, the chief haruspex, and the zilath, and survey the round stone altar that stood in the forecourt below.

The unseasonable heat made the air suffocating, stifling. The temperature had been rising all day, but proximity to the sacred table made the overpowering warmth bearable, her exhilaration defying the heat, suppressing discomfort.

Solemnity had not yet settled on the people at the prospect of sacred rites. The sanctuary was crowded with Veientanes enjoying themselves. Used to the worship of the ritual phallus, Caecilia nevertheless found her cheeks burning at the startling number of steles and womblike stones adorning the temple and its precincts, proof of the people's belief in the sacredness of fertility and rebirth. Many took long drafts of wine, dancing to the music of double flutes and lyres as they pressed their bodies together, arms draped around necks, singing. Both men and women urinated openly while some vomited noisily where they stood, their neighbors taking care to avoid the mess. The god Fufluns was making his presence known, encouraging drunkenness.

Screwing up her nose, Caecilia thought it was no wonder the cat-eyed Rasenna treasured their religion; daily expiation was surely needed to counter such sacrilege.

She wished Larthia was with her. Her mouth and gums ulcerated, the pain painting her face gray and making her weary, the matron attended fewer and fewer public events. Mastarna was not by her side either. Tonight he stood with the other councillors, playing the role of politician. She had been left to stand with the wives, homespun among finery.

Scanning the temple precincts she finally saw Tarchon, the scarlet and black of his tebenna cloak noticeable across the throng. He was talking to a youth, one arm slung across the other's shoulders. Both were shaking with laughter.

Seeing them amused by each other, hands and bodies brushing together affectionately, she had to turn away, wondering if his companion was freeborn, too, and whether Tarchon had added infidelity to his wickedness. He would have to take care. Artile seemed possessive. Or perhaps jealousy had no currency among male lovers.

It was not Tarchon, though, who was being shunned today. The councillors' wives gathered apart from Caecilia in careless conversation and careful exclusion. To ignore them Caecilia gazed upward to the heavy wooden beams of the ceiling, sheathed in painted terra-cotta as brilliant as Tarchon's cloak. Brightness matched by the colorful robes of the statues of many deities balanced perilously upon the temple roof, keeping watch upon her.

Someone else was observing her, too. The zilath's mistress stood separate from the others on the edge of the portico. The whore moved closer.

"It seems they like Romans even less than a hetaera."

Caecilia turned away slightly, exercising her own form of ostracism, but it was impossible to pretend the Cretan woman was not there—although, granted, Erene's perfume this time was subdued, and the carmine and albumen on her lips and face subtle. Far from indecent by Rasennan norms, her sleeveless cream chiton nevertheless seemed shocking to Caecilia, exposing as it did her firm and supple arms and hints of her shapely legs through the skirt's long side slits. Fine chains ringed her neck, bust, and waist, gold bracelets coiled up her arms, and ivory rings embraced her long, slim fingers. Caecilia wondered why the woman didn't jangle when she walked; at least it would give warning of her approach.

The courtesan nodded toward the cluster of women. "I agree. We should ignore them."

Caecilia suppressed a smile.

"I see you have decided to dress like a woman," observed the Cretan. "Or at least like half a woman."

The Roman girl instinctively put her hand to her hair. Cytheris had dressed it in the Etruscan way. A small lapse, surely. The curls were disconcerting. She thought the maidservant was about to brand her when she produced the curling tongs. The scorched smell of hair was also unnerving, yet the brutal instrument had forged sinuous ringlets that even now tickled her cheeks. A band of bright blue was threaded through her locks. A blue that matched the fine eastern boots upon her feet.

The courtesan was not pointing to her hair, though. Caecilia was suddenly conscious of her golden whorl earrings, Atlenta pendant, and the five amber bangles that challenged Marcus's simple horsehead amulet on her wrist.

They had been hard to resist. More small trinkets. More little temptations.

Despite her resolve to remain aloof, Caecilia felt the need to defend herself. After all, she still wore a sober Roman tunic.

"In respect to my Rasennan family," she said, "I choose to bow to some of their customs. It does not mean that dressing modestly makes me any less a woman."

"I see," said the hetaera. "So you wish to please the Rasenna? Or perhaps you wish to please your husband?" The woman leaned closer. "Or half please him at least."

The girl wished she could squeeze the smugness from the other's voice or deny outright that there was any truth to her jest.

That morning Mastarna had given her another present. A palla dyed from pure saffron, not the juice of cheap marigolds or humble weld. "The color suits those hazel eyes of yours," he said. "You should wear more of it."

She was getting used to his compliments. He was never reluctant to tell her she was clever or appealing. At first she'd been embarrassed at such unfamiliar flattery, sparks of doubt always flaring to melt his praise. Over time, repetition softened her suspicions. Sometimes she even dared to accept that, possibly, she was as he described.

"I think you have gained some curves," continued Erene when there was no reply.

"Mastarna will like that. You are too tall and thin." The Cretan companion spiked any of Caecilia's delusions that she'd suddenly grown winsome. "After all, he frowns on women visiting the gymnasium."

Caecilia was surprised Mastarna had never mentioned this. "I thought only men used such places."

"That is the custom in Athens, but the Rasenna are much more liberal. They allow women to exercise their limbs," she paused, "beyond the bedroom."

"You are mocking me."

Erene shook her head. "No, as I said, Mastarna likes soft contours to counter his hard lines."

Caecilia remembered Tarchon's words, how Mastarna had called Seianta his plum: firm, round, and sweet. She glanced down at herself. The courtesan was right. She had gained weight. The midday and evening fare had rounded her shape and increased her appetite. Not just for food either. Suddenly she was hungry for beautiful things. And knowledge.

Erene took her wrist. "You bite your nails. All this Roman disdain is merely show."

The girl twisted away, but not before noticing the softness of the other's skin, her sensual touch. How many men had she delighted?

The wives' murmuring had grown louder. Erene gave them an acid smile. "Of course, half measures will never win him."

"What makes you think I want to?"

"Oh, you want to. I can tell. You no longer have that timid virginal look. In fact I think you want to do more than half please him with your kiss curls and blue boots."

Caecilia willed the ceremony to begin. Their conversation was beginning to assume a familiarity that did not exist. She wished Mastarna would gesture her to take her seat; instead he remained intent on his conversation.

The trouble, of course, was there was some truth in what the courtesan said. Erene was no longer speaking of jewelry or ribbons. Caecilia had become greedy for something else. Greedy for the pleasure granted by her husband and the contents of a tiny flask.

Her appetite had increased, a hunger emerging for the Alpan and the delight felt under its sway.

There was a routine. When he produced the little blue vial she understood that he wanted her. Cytheris would be dismissed. He would undress her and they would lie naked together. There was no need for the dice game.

But one night Cytheris brought in a tray of peaches, steeped in syrup. She also placed the usual jug of wine onto the table. His wine.

"Have one," he said, offering Caecilia a slice of fruit.

Beneath the sweetness of the syrup there was a strange flavor. If heat had a taste then this was it. Headiness spread through her as it had on the night of the wedding banquet.

"The fruit is soaked in Sardinian wine. You can taste the grapes, sun-drenched, near bursting with nectar."

"You know I cannot drink wine."

Reaching for the jug, he poured some into the two goblets.

"Come, Bellatrix, don't be foolish. You no longer need to abide by Aemilius's rules."

"It will make me wayward, wanton."

He laughed. "Wayward? You are already wayward!" He gestured for Cytheris to leave. The Greek girl smiled as she left the room. "You have become wanton, too."

Her heartbeat quickened. He had broken the routine. "Where is the Alpan?"

"You trust me, don't you?"

"I do not fear your touch."

"Then there is no need for it anymore," he said evenly. "I gave it to you to quell the nerves of a bride, not for it to become a habit."

Caecilia frowned. "I want it. It brings peace."

"It was a mistake. I did not think you would grow to crave it." He held out his hand to her. She did not take it. "Don't you understand, Bellatrix? The elixir will possess you. Your visions will grow shorter, your dreams less vivid. Your need for it will be stronger than the draft can assuage."

His tone was earnest, almost imploring. Caecilia pondered whether he had suffered such symptoms. She scanned his face, remembering that he, too, had a reason for taking the philter.

He was a man escaping grief. Was he saying that he could forget Seianta?

"It will make you sick, too. It is not wise to keep supping on mandragora, no matter how small the dose."

His words made her pause. Caecilia had not dared to brew some of the potion because she was ignorant of how much of the herb was in it. Aurelia had always been careful not to add too much to her medicines.

"There is always good and bad to everything," he continued. "Alpan is a guardian angel but she also anoints the dead with unguents from her alabastron. Keep her as your protector, Caecilia, but don't let her tend to your corpse just yet."

She hesitated. How many times had his lips touched her skin? With the Alpan they had left the emptiness of the wedding night behind, the cold embrace and sadness. And she could not deny that, even within the reverie, she knew that it was Mastarna's arms around her, that it was he who was leading her into a world of senses and sensuousness and sensation; that it was not just the potency of the draft but also the warmth of his hands that pleased her.

And she recognized some truth in his warning. It was getting harder to imagine Drusus. The light seemed to brush his face away, how he smiled, how he frowned. There were only fragments of memory now. Yet she wanted to remain true to her Roman. Under the Alpan she could be flagrant in her unfaithfulness to Mastarna, careless of her vows.

She pointed to his scarred face, battered knuckles, and the bruises upon his arms. "How can you preach? You hunt the drug of danger. Tell me you are not in thrall to risk."

Ignoring her, he moved closer, tipping over the serving table as he did so. Peaches slithered across the floor, the dark syrup staining the tiles.

She stared at the splattering of segments of fruit. "Please, Mastarna," she said, confused. "I want the Alpan."

"Don't you understand? The elixir douses passion."

He meant lust. And lust was what lay beneath the reed.

"If you lie with me without it you will become a lover, Caecilia, not just a beloved." When she would not reply, he drew her to him. "Believe me, Caecilia. If you keep taking the Alpan you will end up its slave."

She raised her eyes to him. "You are already my master."

Bringing her hand to his lips, he kissed the inside of her wrist, her palm, then each fingertip before placing it against his cheek. His skin was taut, freshly shaven.

"No, I am your husband."

Kissing her throat, he cupped one breast in his hand, smoothing the small of her back with his other. A heat coursed through her, rising, fiercer than the burn of the peach's liquor. She raised her face to his, seeking the taste of the syrup on his tongue.

• • •

The bellowing of the bull broke through the haze of noise and heat. The crowd quieted. The ceremony would soon begin.

"I hope Ulthes is well," said Erene. "He gets so nervous on these occasions."

Her tone was affectionate, that of a wife who can easily read the moods and manners of her husband. But she was not Ulthes's wife. Ulthes's wife lay at home in a darkened room smothered by dark thoughts.

"Do you love him?"

The courtesan kept her gaze on Ulthes, smiling. "You are naïve, Roman. Besides, what is it to you?"

Caecilia reddened, wishing she'd remained silent. She turned to join the gaggle of wives, realizing it was simple of her to think there would be love between an expensive whore and a man. Why, there was not even such an expectation between a husband and a wife.

"Wait," said the hetaera. "It is rare for one such as me to love, but there can be loyalty. There can be devotion."

Erene's gaze moved to Mastarna. "And there can be pleasure, too. Even a Veientane wife can expect that, despite her husband's dead wife still calling to him."

Caecilia felt the scorch of embarrassment. Intimacy was being forced upon her. A sharing of secrets that she had not hoped for and was uncertain she wanted. Before Veii she'd not stood naked before another person. Now she was being exposed in public by a courtesan. Yet there seemed a kindness to Erene. No spite tinged her teasing. Perhaps the hetaera hoped for solace even as she confirmed what had been hinted—that she had lain with Mastarna and with Seianta's ghost.

Forgoing the Alpan had made a difference. Yet the discovery that she wanted to be bedded by her husband without it was complicated. For she'd also found that Mastarna could not forget Seianta.

The spirit of Mastarna's dead wife was persistent, always present, so real that she'd often wake to find the dent in the bed where the ghost had slept between them and feel the remnants of warmth as she smoothed the sheet with her hand. When she lay with him, it was confusing to think that he was imagining his first wife's legs wrapped around him. Yet she did not need to wrest him from Seianta.

They had become lovers. Without loving.

Held in his potent embrace, Mastarna made her believe that he wanted her, that while in his bed she was beautiful, not plain. He spoke tender words, not hoarding his smiles as he did outside. And she, in turn, no longer doled out hers.

She did not want his love but she did want his desire. And she knew it was wiser not to compare Drusus's gaze to her husband's. The Roman's had merely traced her curves, the Veientane's stripped her.

Mastarna had shown her why the maids in her uncle's house bedded men and why the women at the wedding feast climbed onto their partners' dining couches. She had learned to relish lust enough to seek Mastarna readily in the rectangle of their rumpled bed.

She liked to cling to him in the surge, to hold on to him as they climbed. The distant abandonment granted by the elixir was no match for the explosion of tangled limbs and grinding bodies, of moaning and sighs, and the taste and smell of seed and sweat and musk, or the exquisite sensations wrought by fingers and tongue.

"So take heed." Erene touched the girl's arm, making Caecilia concentrate upon her again. "You may please him but do not try to possess him. Nor hope to truly be the mistress of his house. For, you see, in the ebb of your lovemaking she will sidle up beside him and lay her head upon his shoulder, enjoying how his body heat merges with hers until he falls asleep."

Caecilia avoided the hetaera's gaze, recalling how after lying with Mastarna he would hold her for only a short time as though counting a beat in his head. Then they would break apart, a gap between them. He was always gone when she awoke.

Should she expect more, even if she didn't love him? Would it be different if Seianta did not claim him? Wasn't it enough that he made her feel desirable while teaching her what Roman men cosseted and guarded from the ears and eyes of maids and matrons? Allowing her to digest politics with honeyed venison, savor knowledge with roasted peacock, or drink in secrets that were scooped up and spilled across her pillow from one conspirator to another.

"I do not want to possess him," she said, instantly regretting her disclosure. She wanted to know what the concubine felt, not to tell the other of her thoughts.

Erene's eyes narrowed. "That is fortunate," she said, although her doubt was evident. "Besides, you may yet please him more than Seianta could."

"You mean children."

"Yes. Give him a child."

"Why didn't you?"

The Cretan laughed. "Bearing children is a wife's job. Men want heirs, not bastards. No, it is only Veientane noblewomen who can play both whore and matron within and without the bedroom."

Caecilia scanned the woman's smooth fair skin. For the first time she noticed tiny lines cracking the white makeup at the corners of her eyes and around her mouth. Erene's laugh had been sour, making Caecilia wonder if this hetaera had broken the rules about falling in love.

A horn sounded. The ceremony was about to commence. Caecilia frowned, not wanting to be interrupted after all, not when Erene was garrulous with advice and secrets.

The courtesan touched Caecilia's arm again. "Remember my advice. Give him a son who is whole and he will never let you go."

"Whole?"

She nodded. "Not like Seianta's."

Caecilia glanced over to her husband. Mastarna had a son?

"What do you mean 'whole'?"

Lord Apercu's wife, stout as her husband but without his smile, approached, cutting short their conversation. Her polite exterior rankled but Caecilia rivaled it. Following behind, she was led to one of the seats set between the two lines of tall black-and-red columns. As the procession of the nobles and priests commenced, Caecilia looked down the row to see if Erene sat with the other wives. She wasn't there. The mistress had been invited but not included. She had returned to stand with the crowd. A concubine.

. . .

Hamstrung, the white bull staggered up the ramp of the altar's podium, the bells on its long, cruel horns tinkling. How could such a beast be reduced to bright ribbons and jingling? Its coat brushed to a shiny brilliance, the animal should have been meek, made docile by potions. With the crush and smell of men and the staggering wall of heat assaulting it, the beast swung its head back and forth in agitation, its horn bells drowned out by bellows of distress.

Caecilia suddenly felt uncertain whether she wanted to witness its demise. She may have helped to cure a side of pork or prepare a ram to be butchered but, holy or mundane, gouts of blood made her queasy.

When the sacrificial victim had first appeared, an expectant hush had fallen over the eager crowd, but now their silence dropped an octave from anticipation to apprehension as the bull was dragged to the stone killing table. What would the gods think when a proffered sacrifice showed such fear?

Caecilia felt a cool breeze playfully squeeze her neck, making her shiver. It was followed by a gentle wind that made even the goddess Uni sigh with relief. For a moment the cries of the white bull were forgotten as the flames of the great altar fire and the charcoal braziers flickered and wavered with the freshness.

Caecilia closed her eyes, enjoying the respite. When she opened them, the zilath stood at the altar.

To her surprise, Ulthes bore the trappings of a triumphing general: face painted with vermilion in honor of Jupiter, a crown upon his head, and dressed in a toga of splendid purple embroidered with gold, his black-clad lictors flanked him, rods and axes bristling. The Etruscan kings of Rome had also worn this costume, evidence of the power they once held over her people.

The zilath hailed the throng, calling for utter silence. His face was impassive despite the increased bawling of the bull. How different Ulthes seemed. The friendly politician changed to an awesome statesman. Yet Erene had not been wrong to worry at his nerves. Caecilia soon noticed how he tapped his thigh persistently with his three-fingered hand.

Artile was no less impressive in his fringed shawl and strange hat. Here, too, was a different man. No longer hemmed in by domestic rivalries, he radiated serenity. He was calm despite the anxious fretting of his priests and the seesawing temperatures. Despite her disgust for the haruspex, she could not keep her eyes from him, hearing only the deep bass of his chanting. The whites of his eyes were mere rims around dark vision as he observed the souls swirling about him, breathing upon his cheeks and lips, drawing him into their world, granting him power. The people gazed upon Artile, too, heaping their hopes upon his shoulders, their fears into his palms.

The chanting ceased. The haruspex washed his fingers in a deep, bronze salver, then signaled to the sacrificing priest and his helpers. One slender acolyte had delicately tapered hands. A woman's hands, and mouth, and brow. A priestess. Wondrous. It would seem that Rasennan gods allowed females to do blood sacrifice alongside men.

The animal struggled as wine was poured on its head and flour sprinkled on its horns. The priest backed gingerly away from the dangerous swing of the points. Flour was sprinkled on the knife and handed to Artile for consecration. With the beast trussed tightly, even the priestess gained courage to approach the bull with the others. Between them they turned its head to the sky and then to the earth.

Still the beast roared as the crowd stood silent, doubts rippling across the Veientanes as they shifted their feet from side to side and craned their necks to watch.

Above the distress, Artile raised his curved lituus staff above his head. "O Great and Mighty Veiled Ones, we pray and beseech you to be well-disposed to us. We offer this bull. We have worshipped you and still worship you. Accept it in thanksgiving." Then, pointing to the acolytes, he called in a voice that rivaled the bellow of the bull, "Am I to strike?"

The wind was rising, whipping Caecilia's robes. She glanced across to Mastarna, who was also concentrating on the bull's writhing. His frown commanded his features, a deep furrow upon his brow. Her scrutiny moved to his hands, knowing, like Erene, what his tell would be. Fingers clenched at his side where the golden dice box was secreted in his robes.

Observing her husband, Caecilia did not see the first lightning streak, but she jumped at the crash of thunder. Turning to the skyline, she searched for the next flash. The mass of people all turned, too.

And then the whistling began. The sound increased, in varying pitch and duration, discordant and increasingly frenetic as more thunderbolts exploded in the darkening skies, illuminating the city below in freakish displays.

Ulthes stood, eyes scanning the horizon for the next strike. He commanded the crowd to cease their eerie whistling. "Be silent. You do not ward off the evil ones," he shouted. "Instead you harry the gods. Let them speak," he shouted. "Let us hear what they say!"

The sound faded with only a few stray notes wheezing into whispers. Artile motioned the priests to cease preparing the bull for killing. Two cepens labored to hold the beast still as it strained at its bonds.

As the haruspex hastened up the stairs of the temple to better behold the horizon, a bewildered Caecilia mimicked the other wives and crowded to the edge of the portico. Enrapt, they waited for Artile to speak. Caecilia searched the crowd for Erene. The hetaera was staring at Ulthes, anxiety wreathing her face.

Watching the storm, Caecilia did not notice at first that Arruns was now standing behind her. Mastarna must have sent him to keep guard. She turned to the Phoenician. "Should I be afraid?"

Arruns bowed but did not reply as yet another flash struck and thunder boomed.

Faced with this violent storm, Caecilia knew what the people must be feeling. Hysterical, fervent, afraid. She knew she would think the same if such a violent portent occurred in Rome: that disaster was about to strike. Or that a travesty should be righted.

Perhaps the travesty of continuing a treaty with a foe.

Did Jupiter wish such a pact to be broken? Was he demanding expiation by sacrificing her for bringing divine wrath upon this city? Panic tore through her nerves to the top of her head, leaving her arms weak and tingling. Turning her back on the brilliance and clamor about her, she left Arruns and ran to Uni's chamber, sinking to her knees.

The goddess sat in darkness, the torches about her buffeted by the wind and casting little light. Caecilia hoped that she was indeed the Roman Juno, the great savior and sky goddess. "If you spare me, O Great and Just One, I will make sacrifice to you every day. I will bring you offerings of riches. I will be your servant always." Frantically pulling off her earrings, she laid them at the goddess's feet, the amber bangles and the golden wolf fibula clattering beside them, gifts to show that she would keep the bargain.

Not the Atlenta pendant, though. It surprised her that she hesitated to add Mastarna's other gift to the pile. Such a good luck charm would be needed in a tomb where Tuchulcha and Vanth might lurk. Nor could she part with the iron amulet. She must be buried with Roman luck as well.

The girl prostrated herself upon the cold temple floor, praying her offerings would be enough. That a contract had been sealed.

"Caecilia?" Tarchon's eyes were bright, his pupils pinpoints. As he dragged her to her feet, he smiled broadly and spoke a little too loudly. His breath was sour and his teeth stained with the juice of something he was chewing. He seemed not to realize she was trembling, his lack of concern strange.

It was not the first time that she wondered whether Tarchon supped on an elixir more powerful than Alpan or wine. Or was the manic glitter in his eyes pure elation from watching the lightning?

Relieved he had come for her, she gripped his hand as he led her to the portico again, tracing an arc in front of him. The temple commanded a view southward to Rome. It was as though the whole world was spread before them as they studied the lightning coming closer.

"Watch carefully, Caecilia, at how the gods' knuckles whiten as they clench their darts and spear them through the thin autumn air."

"Why do you speak of gods? Only Jupiter hurls thunderbolts."

"Jupiter? No, these thunderbolts are not from his domain. Artile will tell us which god throws them."

"But I don't understand."

He shook his head impatiently. "You are such a child."

The gods must have agreed because there was a flash so intense that Caecilia felt as though she had looked into the sun. The thunderclap that followed reverberated around the sanctuary, jolting her senses, setting her nerves thrumming.

Artile held his arms to the darkened skies, chanting loudly. The yearning to commune with the Divine was burning among the crowd with as much heat as the day had bestowed upon them only hours before. Many were shrieking, their dancing frenzied. Others were standing as though entranced, eyes rolling back in their heads. Many stamped the ground and howled, their prayers ecstatic.

Tarchon screeched hysterically, shouting praise, too, his eyes transfixed on Artile. His gaze was of adoration; naked, vulnerable, devoted. Caecilia backed away from him, wanting the Tarchon she knew to return, realizing with nauseating clarity that the youth did, indeed, adore this man, this priest, this freeborn.

Every scream of the throng grated. Once again she turned toward Juno's chamber, thinking that if she could cling tightly enough to the goddess's terra-cotta feet, the crowd would not be able to take her.

"Do not be afraid, mistress," said Arruns, subtly barring her way. She had forgotten the protector and the safety he afforded. Moving as near to him as was proper, she watched Tarchon and the crowd crying and surging together to the deafening thunderclaps.

The wind was fierce, yanking at the canopies on buildings and snatching up handfuls of dust. It shepherded the clouds, massing them together to hang over the city like tightened fists. Soon another cloud would collide and a bolt would be thrown. Caecilia waited. She was not disappointed. There was a searing flash and, simultaneously, a deafening crack. A drop of rain smashed onto her cheek. A driving needle.

Caecilia peered through the curtain of water, trying to see what the lightning had hit. She could not see but she heard. The word was spreading.

The palace had been struck.

• • •

The thunderbolts ceased with the rain.

Ulthes shouted over the din of the crowd. "Go home. Wait there until the will of the gods can be announced."

The people trudged away, pushing dripping hair from their eyes, bowing their heads, their shoulders hunched, their ecstasy drowned.

The sanctuary's braziers had been doused, the flames extinguished, although remnants of smoke still threaded their way through the air. The temple steps were smooth and slick, puddles forming in the hollows between the river stones of the forecourt.

Tarchon had left her, moving to Artile's side like a dog to its master. He stood in adulation, waiting for a command. She wondered at such attachment. And still Arruns stood faithfully by her, a different type of hound.

Erene remained alone, watching Ulthes prepare to lead the procession from the temple.

The atmosphere was of anxiety and uncertainty, and as the other women joined their husbands, all pushed Caecilia away with fretful glances.

Mastarna moved to her, taking her hand. Searching around in irritation for his adopted son, he frowned when she told him that Tarchon had gone with Artile. "Come," he said, leading her toward the entourage of principes leaving the precincts.

"Please, Mastarna, I'm afraid." She grabbed his sleeve, not trying to hide how her voice quavered or her fingers fumbled with courage.

He squeezed her hand briefly. "Keep calm. Until Artile tells us what this means there is no use in worrying."

But he did not let her hand drop from his as he led her past the stone table; instead he clasped it tightly as though shielding a quaking child from ghosts. And for a moment she wondered if he were gaining strength from her grip, too, that he also had something to fear from the fierce lances of light, that he might suffer punishment also if the thunder strike pointed to her city, pointed to her, as some kind of scourge.

The bull lay on its side, exhausted and silent, the jaunty but bedraggled ribbons trailing in the wet, the bells silent. Its distress had been an omen in itself. A beast resisting sacrifice did not bode well. It was all so complicated—communing with the gods, witnessing how divine secrets were revealed.

She shivered. Wanting desperately to be home.

ELEVEN

The god who hurled the thunderbolt meant men to take notice.

At the palace the principes inspected the damage, taking turns to file past the site where the lightning had gouged a scorched furrow into the fired-brick wall of the building. The rain pelted all, the women's flimsy parasols no protection as everyone stared at the puddles surrounding the rut left by the fiery spear. Some gasped at the wound, others paled. Many murmured a prayer.

Mastarna was impassive, no longer holding Caecilia's hand. The register of her voice was low and hoarse as she asked him what it meant, but he could give no comfort. "Pray the gods remember they blessed the treaty. Pray they are not fickle."

After that he followed Ulthes into his inner chamber through bronze doors that extended as high as the ceiling. Only six were allowed to hold counsel with the zilath. Five high councillors and Artile, chief haruspex of Veii. The doors swung heavily on their hinges when they closed. Two slaves were needed on each to move them. They shut with a clang to signal the secrecy that was to begin.

Tarchon took off the scarlet cloak, his good mood also discarded. Instead he seemed drained, the high emotion siphoned from him, first by the excitement of the storm and then by the anxiety trapped within the antechamber.

At first Caecilia was amazed that women were allowed to remain, but she was soon aware that the other wives were used to waiting upon their husbands' deliberations. Their voices were muted as they probed and examined every aspect of the evening's drama. Occasionally they would glance at her, as they had at the temple. Caecilia wondered why they bothered to be surreptitious. They might as well stare.

Erene was nowhere to be seen. Caecilia almost felt disappointed at the absence of an unlikely ally.

The members of the College of Principes waited also. All those who had gathered at the temple to observe the signs now gathered in the hall to hear the verdict. Dripping, steam rose from their robes along with the smell of fine wet wool. Sodden fabric clung fast, revealing here a skinny calf, there a plump arm. The nobility plucked at the soaked cloth, pulling it away from their skin, pushing clinging hair from their eyes. The marble hall resounded with squelching footsteps from sopping shoes.

The chamber was enormous but not large enough to comfortably house all. Crammed together, the elderly were offered seats on claw-foot couches. The remainder pressed together in groups, then parted, gossip hovering between one person's lips and another's ears, whispers fraught with argument and conjecture, and all laughter banished.

Curtains of golden thread billowed from checkered ceilings. Cramped, people leaned against immense murals depicting the stories of the Divine: Turan and Laran, love wedded to war; Fufluns and his satyrs; and Tinia and Uni, king and queen of the gods.

Examining the paintings, Caecilia marveled how Rasennan children were fed on ethereal chronicles, myths, and fables, while Roman heirs had to make do with the history of mortals like Romulus and Aeneas. Why was it that in Rome her gods had only purpose and a name, and yet across the Tiber they revealed their lives? Why had the Divine chosen to expose their thoughts, deeds, and emotions here? Why were these people so blessed when they were so depraved?

Tarchon touched her forearm, startling her. She clasped his hand. "Please stay with me."

"Don't worry," he said, gesturing to the crowd. "All of us are afraid."

His words were brave but she could tell he was nervous. It was clear, though, he was prepared to take responsibility for her. She was family now and he would not let her stand forlorn as he had done at the temple. Arruns had not left her side either. She was growing used to his presence, no longer drawn to study his tattoo instead of his eyes.

"We lived here for a year when Mastarna was zilath," Tarchon said. "It's still called the palace even though there is no king. Beautiful, isn't it?"

Caecilia nodded, trying to imagine Mastarna residing in this splendor with his Tarchnan bride, honored and revered. His new wife brought a different type of standing.

Tarchon pulled a pouch from his tunic. Drawing some fresh green leaves from it, he rolled them into a plug. When he began to chew them Caecilia frowned in distaste, understanding why his teeth were stained and his breath stank.

"We could be waiting for a long time," he said, offering her some. "This Catha will help quell your fears."

His pretty lips curved into a conceited smile knowing she would be wrestling with curiosity.

"Catha is named after our sun god. It will liberate you from space and time. It will make you exultant, elated."

Here was another plant of which Aurelia had never spoken. She thought of the Alpan. This Catha must be like river rapids compared to the gentle buffeting current of her elixir. It held no allure, though, with its pungent sour smell. She guessed its taste would be no better. "I have never heard of it."

"It is from the land called Aegyptus. Their traders bring it here."

The Roman girl shook her head, wary of chewing the leaves of an herb seeded in even more foreign soil than Veii's.

Tarchon shrugged his shoulders, then gestured to the principes around them. "See how they bicker about the portent, confident in their own interpretation? A vain pastime. Only Artile will know exactly what the lightning bolt foretells. He is as great a fulgurator as he is a haruspex."

"Fulgurator?"

"A priest skilled in interpreting the will of the gods from lightning and thunder. Artile will be able to read the signs contained in the Book of Thunderbolts."

"Another holy text?"

Previously, Tarchon had been reluctant to tell her about the Book of Acheron, but today, perhaps unnerved by the lightning, he was prepared to talk about this other sacred tome. How it revealed that the deities held domain in sixteen different sectors in the sky. How those that lived in the northwest were to be dreaded and those in the northeast were to be beseeched to show their favor.

Caecilia thought of how many times she'd pointed at the stars, unaware that she might be touching the smile of Uni or Turan's brow. With all the Etruscan gods, angels, and demons, the heavens must indeed be crowded. "And these gods, can all of them throw thunderbolts?"

"No. Only nine can throw the splinters of sound and light. It is the task of the haruspex to interpret the meaning of their source and destination. There is an almanac that lists the import of thunder heard on certain days to which all principes can refer, a calendar detailing omens including warnings about war, governments, and conflicts."

"And what does the almanac predict for today?"

"That is what everyone is arguing about and why people frown and fret. For if thunder is heard on the fourth day of this month, the bolt signifies the downfall of a powerful man."

The rapid beating of her heart had subsided slightly while waiting, but now it stirred again. The downfall of a powerful man? Could it be her husband? Or Ulthes? If so, her demise would follow theirs.

Tarchon leaned closer. "Don't worry. The calendar is not such a simple thing to read. As chief fulgurator Artile will decipher the portent."

Caecilia tried to push her fright away. The anticipation of hearing bad news was exhausting. She wished the doors would open and her fate be declared. Still, it was hard not to marvel at Tarchon's lesson. Her people relied on custom and memory for their rites. Books held knowledge and the law, not divine words. Roman deities had not allowed their magic to be recorded in ink and paper.

How splendid these Rasennan books of worship must be! Did they creak as they were unfurled, the scrolls thick and heavy with wisdom? Did men's skin burn as they touched such mysteries or their eyes moisten when reading holy terms?

"Whatever the omen," continued Tarchon, "Artile will conduct the rites to bury the lightning."

"Bury lightning? How can you do that?"

"The bricks that were scorched will be broken up and buried. All prodigies must be destroyed after they have revealed their portent in case any evil also exists within them. That part of the palace will never be used again."

As Tarchon returned the Catha to its pouch, Caecilia thought of Artile, who could grapple with a lightning bolt, break it asunder, and decipher its spark. It was no wonder the youth believed in his lover.

• • •

Weariness overwhelmed her as worries circled within her head. Body aching from staying in one position, her neck sore from tension, Caecilia leaned back against a mural, her head resting upon that of a painted centaur. Its scrutiny was permanently fixed upon the middle of the room while hers traversed the entire chamber.

As time passed into the dead hours of the night, more chairs were brought and all sat, heads nodding, voices muted except in pockets of disagreement, their murmurs an accompaniment to the melodies of the court musicians.

And then the bronze doors opened.

The zilath entered wearing his crown, the vermilion dye upon his face still immaculate, his shoulders straight. Fear had not eked its way into his face to cloud his eyes, furrow his brow, or tighten his mouth, yet Caecilia knew he was struggling to harness calm. His deformed hand tapped nervously against his thigh.

Through the doors, Caecilia could see a huge table clad in bronze upon which lay folded linen books laced with lettering. Wisdom wrapped in cloth? Could this be the Book of Thunderbolts? Such plainness was disappointing after visions of scrolls sheathed in gold.

Artile followed Ulthes, arranging his fringed shawl with precision. With one finger, the nail painted black, he smoothed the arch of his eyebrows slowly, savoring the anticipation of the waiting principes, making it apparent he enjoyed his position as both interpreter for the deities and mediator between men.

Mastarna and the other high councillors entered the hall. All five of them had been zilaths at one time. All understood the pressure that Ulthes must withstand. Fat Apercu plucked at his bullfrog chins while even the waxen-faced Vipinas, whose veins bled vinegar, seemed perturbed. Lanky Pesna loitered behind the others, watching Laris Tulumnes like a slave anxious to avoid a beating.

Tulumnes, with his crooked face, was smiling. Not his usual pinched and poverty-stricken look but broadly, gladly; and his body, usually tensed into the rigid lines that defined his own type of hunger, was oddly relaxed as though replete from a hearty meal.

Her husband's face was covered in stubble, his eyes ringed with shadows, the muscles of his neck strained. He searched the room for her and nodded curtly when he saw her.

Caecilia sat forward, anxious to hear whether the gods sought war, that her role was to change from a symbol of goodwill to that of hostage—worse still, of an evil prodigy needing to be slain or burned and buried, like the lightning.

The zilath called for silence, nodding to Artile.

"The warning bolt flashed red," declared the chief priest, "and was thrown from the southeast where Laran, the god of war, resides. It also struck the palace. The Holy Book says such an event portends the rule of the zilath is in danger."

The brief silence in the hall evaporated as the principes fought to be heard all at once. Before Ulthes could address them, Tulumnes stepped forward, careless of offending the zilath. His words instantly proved Artile had foretold the truth. "Heed me, my noble friends," he called. "The gods are calling for the return of a king."

Caecilia struggled to understand his talk of monarchy. She'd believed that all kings were long buried by both Romans and the Rasenna. She'd also thought the ambitions of the descendants of Veientane royalty had been watered down or washed away.

Mastarna broke away from the other councillors and strode over to Tulumnes. "You are deluded if you think Veii will ever crown another lucumo. I will never let this city return to oppression, no matter what Artile may claim the gods might say."

Caecilia watched Artile tense at his brother's criticism. No one else in this room would dare to question the priest's authority and interpretation. Ulthes frowned at his friend's rashness, and for the first time Caecilia noticed how old he was. Till now she'd always marveled at his youthfulness compared to her Uncle Aemilius, but deliberation over the future of his city had stripped him of that vigor. The red dye upon his face failed to hide the lines of age, his tenseness, and his weary expression. "The fulgurator is not to be challenged."

Artile smoothed one eyebrow again and nodded to Ulthes in acknowledgment. "Thank you, my lord. I have declared the meaning after consulting the Holy Book. I can do no more."

The humility in Artile's voice must have goaded his brother for Mastarna turned his back on him. The insult caused the assembly to mutter and shuffle in concern, but Caecilia's husband ignored them. His gaze was directed alone at Laris Tulumnes. "You may rejoice in this omen, but no city in the League has installed a sovereign for many decades. The twelve cities will despise us, even spurn us if we do."

"Perhaps it is long ago for the likes of Tarchna," Tulumnes shouted. "But don't forget my father died just twenty years ago." He swiveled around to point at Caecilia. "Killed and mutilated by her people."

The princip's glare was one of sharp, deep hatred. Caecilia could feel his menace being hurled across the room. Tarchon put his hand on her shoulder. Arruns moved quietly to stand beside her.

Mastarna's voice exploded with anger. "Whatever the Romans may have done, Tulumnes, your father was a despot. Veii chose to replace him with a zilath rather than bear the tyranny of another king."

The usual sheen of perspiration on Tulumnes's face had thickened into rivulets of sweat. At Mastarna's taunt he strode toward Caecilia, stabbing his finger in the air at her, his eyes dark, paining for vengeance. "Mastarna and Ulthes have insulted us with this marriage. No one here should forget she is a descendant of

Mamercus Aemilius. Now is the time to use this Roman whore to our advantage. Let us hold her as a hostage. Then Rome must choose to surrender or let her die."

The familiar gnawing in the pit of Caecilia's stomach returned. The destiny she'd feared when Aemilius first told of her marriage could come true. As Tulumnes advanced toward her, she cringed in fear. His great bulk loomed above her, malevolent and gloating. She was shaking, skin clammy beneath her damp clothes.

Mastarna was only a short step behind him. He wrenched Tulumnes away with a cold anger, a serious fury. "Touch her and I'll kill you."

"Be quiet!" Ulthes's voice cut through the tension between the two lords, pushing the men apart as surely as if he'd laid hands upon them. Then, with his lictors shadowing him, he stood between them.

Mastarna took a step toward Caecilia but Ulthes restrained him, motioning her to come to him instead and offering her his arm.

Caecilia could not stop shaking, the terror of the temple returning, her heart pounding.

"Take courage," he whispered. "Stand straight."

Her knees buckled a little but he held her steady, placing his other hand over hers. Caecilia gripped his forearm, grateful for his protection but wishing he were Tata.

"The College of Principes agreed to extend the treaty with Rome through this marriage. We will not dishonor that pact while I govern for we have nothing to fear. Rome is weak from starvation, it poses no threat." As he spoke he hooked his calloused thumb around Caecilia's as a warning not to bridle before a company of frightened people.

Both Mastarna and Tulumnes tried to speak at once but Vipinas, cool amid rising tempers, interrupted them. "Be quiet, both of you, and let the zilath speak."

Caecilia noted his respectful tone with surprise. Mastarna had told her before that the colorless man did not approve of the treaty.

"Today," said Ulthes, "the god of war warned us that my rule is in danger. Laran has spoken to us and we cannot ignore his message. For centuries the Rasenna have chosen lucumo or zilath, king or magistrate. Veii must choose again how it should be ruled. I do not want the destruction of our city from within—Veientane brother fighting brother. He gives us a chance to choose concord or conflict—a zilath and peace or a lucumo and war."

The nobles who had whispered and gossiped as they waited now muttered in querulous murmurs at his words.

"And so I propose that Tulumnes and I will be the only candidates at the upcoming election. In spring the College of Principes will determine the city's destiny. In the meantime each tribe must make its choice."

The chamber erupted into protest and quarrels. Apercu, his fat cheeks puffed like a wind god, fended off questions from his clansmen while the pallid Vipinas grew paler.

Tulumnes, the regal candidate, suddenly seemed to tower over those around him, his eyes radiant, his lopsided face somehow gaining symmetry from the chaos. Pesna crowded close to him, mimicking his crony's responses to those who sought a hundred answers.

Strangely serene, Artile took his place behind the bronze table in the inner council room. As he neatly folded the linen pages of the holy text, Caecilia thought he seemed strangely satisfied at having let one of its secrets escape and cause pandemonium.

The zilath smiled grimly as he released Caecilia into the care of her husband.

Mastarna put his arm around her waist. "Are you very shaken?"

She shook her head in a lie.

"Best you sit down. This could take some time."

As Mastarna dealt with his angry tribesmen, Caecilia listened to the arguing, frightened people, praying that this palace would never again house a king.

Finally the zilath's voice boomed over the crowd: "There will be no more discussion. The heavens have delivered their message. Go home."

• • •

All had been dismissed. All except Mastarna. And Aemilia Caeciliana.

The Roman sensed the grudging looks and resentful thoughts of the others at such favoritism. With a worried look, Tarchon reluctantly turned to continue his wait for them outside. Only Arruns remained inscrutable as he prepared to stand sentinel outside the door with the other lictors.

Ulthes sat, wiping the red paint impatiently from his face with a cloth, his fingers stained as he drew them through his spiky hair.

Watching her husband pacing before his friend, Caecilia was struck at how close they were. Like older and younger brothers. It was no wonder her husband despised Artile when blood ties were like milk compared to such a friendship.

Mastarna did not break his stride. "Why do you give him a chance to take power?"

The zilath was calm. "I have placed my faith in our equals. They voted for the treaty and I do not think they will fail us now, Vel. No one wants to return to oppression."

"It will not happen because I will order my men against him."

"No!" The hard edge to the older man's voice was no longer brotherly but as a father demanding obedience from his child. "I will not let you start a civil war."

"I am my own man, Arnth Ulthes." Mastarna's voice had found an edge, too.

Stunned, Caecilia wished the men would cease their arguing, wanting to point out to them that the gods must be laughing at their cruel joke. How in cautioning men against discord they had awakened it. Wondering, too, why Ulthes believed Mastarna held power enough to combat Tulumnes alone.

"I won't let Veientanes slay each other." Ulthes displayed his reddened palms. "If I do there will be blood instead of paint on my hands."

Mastarna grabbed one of his wrists. "Don't you see, it will be your blood, Arnth, when Tulumnes claims the crown? Why give him a chance to be elected? When the blood of kings courses through other nobles in the college? Through you. Through me."

Ulthes wrenched away. "You forget yourself."

Caecilia could sense Mastarna's embarrassment at showing such disrespect. "Forgive me, my lord," he said, bowing his head.

Ulthes's voice softened. "It is better this way, Vel. Tulumnes's ambition is like a canker. He will never stop in his quest to be king unless the boil is lanced. Let all the principes wield the scalpel, not you."

"But what if he wins? Veii is ill-equipped to fight a war. We have grown fat from twenty years of peace and our weapons are blunt and rusted. Do you expect me to stand by while Tulumnes harms my wife and forces her people to surrender? Do you think I would let Tulumnes kill her?"

Both men looked at her, conscious that she should not be listening to their dispute. Mastarna's words were making real the threat when all she wanted to hear was reassurance.

"Of course not. But we will handle that danger when and if it happens. In the meantime we must see to it that we win the election," said Ulthes, smiling faintly at her. "So Aemilia Caeciliana will be safe."

The zilath bent closer to Mastarna, voice intense. "Promise me you will not start a civil war."

Caecilia was bewildered. "I don't understand," she said. "How is Mastarna able to challenge Tulumnes?"

"Because my tenants owe allegiance to me, Caecilia. They form an army that I pledge to the city. The largest army in Veii."

Caecilia stared at her husband. Tarchon had hinted at the extent of his power, and now she realized there was no exaggeration. Her city's strength came from citizen soldiers whose every sword stroke reserved their right to their piece of soil, their piece of Rome. Here private armies battled for their lords, either together for Veii—or among themselves.

Once again Ulthes pressed his friend for an answer.

Mastarna rubbed his brow, hesitating. "Very well," he finally said. "If Tulumnes is declared lucumo by our peers I won't rise against him. But don't think he'll accept defeat if you are voted zilath. And don't think I'll stand by then and let him rule by force."

"It will not come to that. We know Apercu has no liking for kings. All we need is to persuade Vipinas to favor our cause."

He nodded toward Caecilia. "Your wife is weary. Both of you get some sleep in whatever is left of this night. Tomorrow we begin our campaign. For my election and against war."

Mastarna hesitated, not ready to concede the argument was resolved. Caecilia tugged at his arm. "Let it be," she whispered. In return she weathered a dark look, but finally Mastarna bade the magistrate good night.

As they moved away, Ulthes called after them. "Have faith in our peers, Vel. Have faith in me."

She thought she would faint from exhaustion, feet dragging as she tripped to match Mastarna's stride. He did not lessen his pace. As she stumbled tiredly after him, she considered Arnth Ulthes, who had power to ask the richest man to defer to him.

Who called Mastarna by his first name when she did not.

And Vel Mastarna, her husband, who'd claimed and defended her.

• • •

The storm had passed and the metallic smell of earth mingled with the fragrance of rain. Water dripped off the roof opening's edges, striking the atrium's pool with rhythmic dollops. Vanth's and Tuchulcha's stone cheeks were streaked with tears.

Larthia greeted them dressed in her night robe, her acanthus-embroidered shawl loose about her shoulders, hair untied, elegant in her disquiet.

Mastarna strode forward, Caecilia and Tarchon following upon his heels. No one had spoken since leaving the palace.

"I have been waiting a long time." She bestowed a kiss on her son.

Mastarna put his arm around her briefly. "I'm hungry. I'll tell you everything while we eat."

Larthia kissed Tarchon on the cheek, too, then, turning to Caecilia, opened her arms. "You must be very frightened."

Caecilia was greedy for the hug. It was the first time she had been held so by another woman. She assumed her own mother had once embraced her when she was a child but there was no memory of it, only of the hard band of Aemilia's fingers gripping her own or the formal brush of lips on occasion. She found herself standing stiffly, conscious of breast touching breast, the smooth weave of the acanthus shawl against her arms, the wisps of Larthia's hair straying across her face. "No harm will come to you," her mother-in-law whispered, and Caecilia found herself reluctant to leave the closeness, knowing that this is what a mother would promise— assurances without proof, protection without guarantee.

Caecilia had no appetite to eat the steaming bowl of lentils and onion sauce offered her. After what she had heard, she needed to calm her nerves and so she held out her cup for the servant boy to fill with wine. Having grown used to the sobriety of his foreign mistress, the slave hesitated. Tarchon put his hand upon her wrist, his eyes questioning, but Larthia waved him away. It was not the time to query what now seemed a trifle.

Mastarna observed his wife but said nothing. She swallowed the contents of the cup quickly. It was not like the sweet Sardinian wine that had warmed her belly and her senses so swiftly. This watered-down vintage was disappointing, giving her no mild euphoria, no balm to her spirits. Instead it seemed to summon melancholy. She wondered why she had fretted so about drinking it.

Mastarna concentrated on eating, almost as though it were a duty, wiping away any sauce that splashed upon his chin with the back of his hand. She wondered at such an appetite. How could he feel any mortal need tonight other than a desire for the gods to make things right?

While he ate, Mastarna related the events at the palace. Larthia cupped her cheek, her face ashen with more than the pain of her mouth and her voice tremulous as she asked haltingly about the return of a king.

Caecilia nodded as she listened, perplexed. "Do you really think a lucumo will be elected? I believed Etruscans thought even less of royalty than Romans."

Mastarna fiddled with his goblet, running his finger around the rim, over and over again. There was no fervor left. Nor anger. Exhaustion had put a halter on him. There was bitterness, though, left over like the dregs of wine in his cup. "Because, if bribed richly enough, some nobles choose to forget that kings can become despots and that a monarch, once elected, rules until he dies."

Caecilia pressed her palms against her eyes until flecks of color burst through the blackness, knowing she was on the verge of either tears or collapse, resentful of being helpless, that her fate was reliant on people in an alien world.

"Then we must take Tulumnes by force," said Tarchon, finding courage to speak.

Mastarna glanced at his son and grimaced. The stained red fingers of the zilath came to Caecilia's mind and Mastarna's covenant with him.

"Enough talk of deposing tyrants," said Larthia, standing. "Let us thank the gods for their warning and that Artile can read the signs."

To Caecilia's surprise, Mastarna rounded on his mother, knocking his empty cup over as he leaned forward. It clattered onto its side and spun slowly to a stop. "Don't talk to me of Artile's fortune-telling."

The silence that fell was short-lived. Tarchon's chair scraped across the tiles as he stormed from the room with footfalls, no doubt, that would soon echo in the chamber of his priestly lover.

"You are sacrilegious, my son. Artile is chief fulgurator. It's dangerous for you to speak so."

"You would say that. You who are always so quick to defend him."

Caecilia saw the tiny woman brace herself against the table as though too fragile to bear such accusations. She also saw where Mastarna must have obtained at least half his courage, for after only a few seconds Larthia met his gaze steadily and her voice was firm. "I defend both of you. I love both of you. I am proud of both of you."

"You say that, but each day you reek of his incense and linger at his side for crumbs of sacred comfort."

Caecilia gasped but Larthia did not even flinch.

"I gain counsel from him as a priest, not a son, just as I look to you to be master of this house."

"Then suggest to your priest that he prorogue this prediction. After all, he claims to be an expert at deferring fate."

Larthia glanced at Caecilia, and the girl sensed that the conversation had left behind lightning strikes and monarchs and had fled back in time to some other premonition, some other dread.

"Don't worry, Ati, Caecilia can listen. She can learn that Nortia can be implored to postpone her intentions."

"You are being unwise." Larthia's tone was firm, but it did not stop her son.

"Do you think this threat serious enough to defer Veii's fate for thirty years?"

"That is not for me to decide. Only the College of Principes has authority to seek such a prorogation."

Caecilia held her breath. Defer fate? The thought of such a possibility was astounding.

Further words died upon Mastarna's lips as he slumped back in his seat. Standing behind him, Larthia put her hands on either shoulder, kissing the top of her son's head as though there had been no stones thrown. "Seianta knew that Nortia could not always be swayed."

Mastarna leaned back against her and closed his eyes. Caecilia felt as she had when, as a child, she'd eavesdropped behind storage chests or doors only to hear the speakers complaining about her. Tonight she felt the same discomfort, knowing she should not have heard their words, witnessed this scene.

"I am going to bed," said Larthia. "Let's ponder this further tomorrow. Tiredness is no companion to reason."

The matron bestowed a kiss upon Caecilia who responded in kind, tempted to lay her own cheek gently against the softness of the other's and linger. To ask the matron to answer her questions: How was it that destiny could be postponed? And what did Seianta ask the goddess to defer?

• • •

Shoulders stooped, Caecilia sat upon the bed and stared at the fine blue boots that had so delighted her earlier but were now ruined. The blue ribbon had been lost, her hair tangled. Not wishing to be fussed over, she'd dismissed Cytheris but soon wished she hadn't, finding it an effort to even remove her tunic.

Exhaustion did not seem to hinder Mastarna. Just as he had diligently eaten the supper of lentils, he did not vary from his nightly practice. Pouring hot water from bronze pitcher to ewer, he meticulously wiped his arms, feet, legs and face, a ritual that he'd insisted she adopt, too. She could not do so tonight. Too tired to even seek what she knew would be pleasant.

Next he removed his heavy gold wristbands, then placed them and the little dice box into a cista. Seianta's signet ring with its onyx stone remained. Also the gold bulla placed around his neck by his mother upon his birth. It was a good luck charm that would be needed more than ever.

Saying nothing, he stripped and slid into the bed, rolling onto his side and closing his eyes, making Caecilia wonder when, with all that had happened between them, they had fallen into domesticity.

When she continued to stare at her boots, he grumbled, "Douse the lamp and go to sleep."

"I am too tired to sleep," she said, aware of her childishness.

"Before a battle you need to eat and rest when you get a chance."

"But what if Tulumnes wins the battle? What if he holds me hostage? Rome will never surrender. Nor could I expect it to."

"It will not come to that. I've told you already. He won't win. Apercu and his clan are likely to support the zilath, but we'll need to convince Vipinas to be on our side."

"But Vipinas hates Romans! They killed his only son. He already disapproves of the treaty."

"Stop worrying, Caecilia. You will wear yourself out. In the end Nortia will decide. Now go to sleep."

"Can your people really convince Fortuna to defer a city's fate?"

For once he gave into her badgering. He sat up, the scar on his chest a dark slash in the dimness. "Some of the Rasenna believe that both a city and a person's fate can be deferred, but they are deluded. Lady Nortia must laugh at such entreaties."

"So your people are wrong to think they can control her?"

Mastarna rubbed his brow and sighed. "Nortia fixes a nail to end our lives at the time and place she alone has chosen. She may let us roll our dice and make small choices, but our destiny cannot be changed. She alone holds the rudder that guides our lives."

"Yet you taunt her to reveal your own."

"You do not need to know why I bait her," he said brusquely. "Just remember not to let Artile convince you he is Destiny's agent."

Caecilia wanted desperately to ask him about Seianta's desire to delay Fate, but his face was seared by weariness, pale beneath the tan, expression closed. Whatever his first wife sought from the gods would not be disclosed by him tonight, if ever.

"Go to sleep," he growled and slid back under the covers.

Her emotions stirred even higher. She tapped his shoulder. "How can I rest when my people are threatened?"

"Bellatrix, you'll go mad fighting battles in your mind. Tulumnes will need the support of the League of the Twelve to fight Rome. No easy thing when that congress balks at raising arms for brother cities."

"Then Rome is safe?" The question was a wish.

"Only the gods know that for sure."

"Gods you do not trust."

He grunted and reached for the lamp. "Come. Lay your head on the pillow. The sun will soon rise."

As he leaned over to blow out the flame, she stayed his hand, not wanting the suffocation of darkness. He was, after all, her protector while she was in Veii, the head of his House, obligated to ensure her safety from Tulumnes and from his people. And yet today his world had been threatened, too. If destroyed, he could no longer help her. Or himself. If Mastarna had no influence, what was she to do?

"Please take me home."

In the wavering light of the lamp, he shifted to face her. "I expect more of you, Caecilia. If I returned you now your city would be insulted. We might start the war we want to avoid."

She seized his hand, slightly knocking the lantern so hot oil spat upon his skin. He flinched more from irritation than hurt. "Tell me you will honor your promise!"

His surprise was genuine. "What promise?"

"To return me within the year. To let me sleep three days under my uncle's roof so that I may continue under his authority. To remain a Roman."

Mastarna frowned. "Who told you of such a promise?"

"My cousin, Marcus." Tears welled and she rubbed her eyes, fists staving off weariness and weakness.

"Then he misinformed you. You have married me under Veientane as well as Roman law. I only agreed to divorce you if the treaty failed."

Caecilia felt she was falling backward as she had once done before, after losing balance upon the narrow, uneven stone wall that divided her father's fields. She had merely been winded then but the terror of falling through space, unable to grasp safety, not knowing when she would strike the ground, returned to her.

Aemilius had truly betrayed her. Yet again she had become a misfit as well as a symbol. Neither patrician nor plebeian, neither Roman nor Rasennan.

"Are you telling me I will never again see my city?"

"Only if Camillus triumphs over Rome's peacemakers and the truce is broken."

"But if Tulumnes wins the election he'll be the one to declare war and I will die!"

"That won't happen," said Mastarna impatiently. "Ulthes will be successful."

Caecilia clenched her fingers. He was acting like Aemilius, expecting her to believe there was nothing to fear just because he said so. "Are you saying there is no chance you will return with me if peace continues?"

Mastarna examined the skin of his hand where the oil had scalded him. "It's my hope that soon you'll no longer want to be a Roman daughter, Bellatrix." He raised his eyes to hers. "I hope instead you'll welcome being a Veientane mother. And I'm afraid if that happens, I can't let you return at all."

Her head thudded against the earth, her fall ended, her limbs broken.

"I don't understand. When did conceiving a child become a barrier to passing through the wall of Rome?"

"Because I can't risk you taking my son. Once returned to Rome, you might persuade your uncle to reclaim you and our child."

"But children belong to their father. I would have no case. Aemilius knows this."

He shook his head. "A mother's pleas might sway him. And I would be on foreign soil and at a disadvantage. I don't want to lose any more children."

His words reminded her of the question she'd asked of Erene. Here was a chance to gamble on an answer. "The loss of your son must have been dreadful."

The dice box was not in his hand to reveal his tell, and in the dimness of the chamber she could not read his face. But he hesitated for the smallest moment.

Not even the length of a breath.

Long enough to cause her to doubt him.

"I think you mean my little daughter." His voice had the tone heard whenever she trespassed onto any mention of Seianta. "I only have one son, Caecilia, who doesn't listen to me. Am I to have a wife who does the same?"

This time he blew out the lamp so that blackness engulfed them, the smell of the extinguished flame lingering in the darkness. "Go to sleep," he said sharply. "There is no more to be said. Veii is your home now."

Caecilia silently undressed. Creeping beneath the covers, she drew her knees to her chest, facing away from her husband. Was it he or the hetaera who was lying?

When she closed her eyes they watered and ached. She felt numb, too tired to be angry, too exhausted to be scared. It was as though she had gone back in time and was being told by Aemilius about her marriage. She had no say in that either.

Mastarna was wrong to dismiss her fears. Wrong to take hope away. She was trapped. If she bore his child he would never let her leave, and when she bore a half-blood, Rome would never welcome her home.

Their longings were balanced. Hers for Rome, his for a son.

She thought of Cytheris and Erene. They both claimed she had power but it was one that could only be exercised in captivity. Mastarna might do anything for her if she gave him a child, anything but fulfill her desire to see Rome.

TWELVE

Mastarna's hesitation weighed on Caecilia's mind as much as any of the threats that assailed her.

The next day she tried to concentrate on her lessons instead. But practicing the exercises Tarchon had given her was not easy. Although she was mastering the Rasennan language, she found it difficult to read. Their alphabet was different—strange marks upon the page that were read from right to left. After yesterday Caecilia knew that her life, too, was going in the wrong direction.

Cytheris was helping Aricia to card wool, dragging the fiber through the sharp teeth of the paddles to tease out the threads, her frizzy hair oddly similar to the fleece. Knowing the handmaid knew all the household gossip, Caecilia could not resist trying once more. "Did Seianta and Mastarna have a son?"

Cytheris paused before looking up. "Why yes, mistress, but he lived less time than his mother labored."

The betrayal stunned her. Learning that Mastarna had lied was more than hurtful. She felt like she was a little girl again just after her mother died and before Tata loved her—alone and forlorn and bewildered.

Why had he denied the little boy? Why had no one told her? Did a few scant breaths not amount to a mention? Not enough to be entitled to a name? Not long enough to form a soul?

"Why didn't you tell me?"

Again Cytheris hesitated. Just like Mastarna. It was catching. "The master doesn't like us to talk about the baby. Mistress Seianta died giving birth to him."

"Why? Wasn't he whole?"

There was no break in the maid responding this time.

"Who told you that?"

"Erene."

The handmaid frowned. "You should not be talking to one such as her."

"At least she was prepared to tell me the truth. What about Mastarna's daughter? Was she whole?"

"Yes, but Velia's heart was weak and she struggled breathing. She never took a step or even learned to crawl."

"And what was the matter with their son?"

"I did not see him, mistress. I was sick that night with fever, but the midwife told me that a curse still hovered over the mistress."

"Curse?"

"There was more than one dead child who slid from the Tarchnan's womb too early."

Pity filled Caecilia for Mastarna and his wife. Yet there was no compassion in Cytheris's voice. "You sound as if you hate her."

Cytheris's expression became closed and grim. "She was jealous that Aricia lived while Velia did not. It amused her to whip me to the beat of castanets and flute. And always when her husband and Mistress Larthia were absent."

Here was a different version of Seianta. So far all who'd mentioned her did so with affection. The cruelty of the dead girl and her sinister use for music was disturbing.

Caecilia studied the maidservant with her pockmarked skin, the bright-pink tips of her ears jutting from her bundle of hair, and fully comprehended her power over her. It was one she had not known before. Her uncle's servants only did as she bade after they had first seen to Aemilius, to Marcus, to Aurelia. Cytheris was hers to do with as she wished. To neglect or pamper or torment, whatever a mistress wanted.

Yet the Greek girl had become more than just a slave. She was the cipher to open the mysteries of being a woman. Caecilia had grown used to the servant, her gossip and wisdom, the smell of aniseed upon her breath. Grown used to another woman's touch, to comfort, to being half-dressed or naked without the urge to quickly draw her robes around her, her mother's legacy and Aurelia's coldness dispelled. Tarchon might teach her about customs and history and culture but the maid gave her lessons in life.

"Oh, Cytheris, I am so sorry."

The servant was startled. "There is no need for you to be sorry, mistress."

An awkward silence fell between them and Caecilia once more thought about Mastarna. It was inevitable she would fall with child soon if the marital bed was to be used as constantly as it had been. Unless she was barren.

Suddenly it struck her that Cytheris had not borne a child since Aricia. And given the handmaid's liking for men, she doubted it was because the Greek girl was chaste. "How is it you have not given birth to any other children?"

Cytheris frowned. "Why do you ask?"

"Because I don't wish to bear a child that could be deformed."

The maid opened her gap-toothed mouth in surprise. "Mistress, you should not speak that way. I told you it was not the master's fault. A mother is to blame if there is any disfigurement."

Caecilia was impatient. "Listen to me. I will be the mother of a half-blood child. The gods might curse me for bearing a son of two cities. So tell me how you remain as though a maiden."

"Hardly like a maiden, mistress."

"Tell me!"

"There are ways. But you could not use them. Master would be very angry."

"I don't care."

The handmaid shook her head. "There is only one certain way to stop a seed being planted, mistress, and that is to stop lying with the man. And yet to do so is to fail as a wife." Cytheris looked at Caecilia slyly. "And when a woman has a liking for pleasure it can be difficult to steer such a course."

Caecilia blushed. What would Mastarna think when his eager student suddenly showed reluctance? To refuse him would only bring suspicion. She had to admit, too, that having been deprived of love she did not want to surrender desire.

She shook her head. "That's not a choice. In any case, are you telling me you no longer lie with men? Or perhaps you have some secret that keeps you free of children, like Erene?"

Caecilia frowned. "No, mistress. I haven't scraped my womb by rod or potion."

Here was another thing to learn and, as usual, Cytheris spoke as though it were common knowledge. Did Roman women ever have to deal with such?

"I have lain with very few men since my daughter was born," continued the maid. "It is enough to have three living children sold, don't you think?"

Caecilia was surprised at her defiance.

"I am careful not to give the master the chance to harvest me for more slaves. Aricia will be the last child my owners take from me."

Caecilia's gaze traveled to the small girl who was listening, wide-eyed, to their conversation. The knowledge that she was to be sold often troubled Caecilia. She had grown fond of the little servant. Denied the friendship of other children herself, she found it amusing to watch Aricia's mischief when Cytheris's back was turned. Better still to be rewarded with a timid smile when granting the slave a surreptitious kindness.

"Don't think your plight hasn't touched me. I asked Lady Larthia and Lord Mastarna if they would keep Aricia, but I'm afraid they refused me."

The handmaid's expression was first of bewilderment then of gratitude so intense Caecilia had to look away, uncomfortable with such devotion.

Her lack of success at trying to save Aricia still rankled. Larthia had flatly refused to show mercy. Her mother-in-law could be fierce as well as gentle. Her illness did not preclude her running her house and business with authority. No sympathy was shown. Aricia was goods already purchased. The matriarch had given her word.

Mastarna had been similarly disinterested. "It's Ati's decision, not mine. Slaves are merely assets to be bought or sold. You should not grow too attached to them. It makes you reluctant to discipline them."

"And yet you never rebuke your servant."

"Because Arruns is obedient. He is also a freedman."

"Free Cytheris then. She is loyal. Free her daughter."

Unlike her father, Mastarna was rarely worn down by pleading. He did not change his mind. And, in truth, his answer was not surprising, not when charity was looked upon with suspicion and human bondage was a business. Yet she did not regret asking. After all, she was unable to forget what it was to be small and powerless, humbled and humiliated, or how it felt when her ownership had passed from dead father to adopted one.

As she watched Cytheris scold her daughter to return to the carding, Caecilia was suddenly aware that, although she'd failed to help the handmaid, the bond between them was stronger.

"Now, tell me," she said. "How do I stop falling with child?"

Cytheris spoke of the moon. How powerful it was to bewitch the tides of the sea and the ebb and flow of a woman's blood. How women could tell, from its waxing and waning, when they were fertile so that a seed will either flourish or languish in the womb.

"But you cannot rely on this, mistress, for your flux does not always follow the moon's cycle."

"And is there no other way?"

"Yes, but it would be dangerous."

Caecilia was not ready to concede so easily. She needed to have hope when he caressed her and his seed flowed into her.

"Please, I'll try again to get him to free both of you."

Cytheris's reluctance was still obvious as she answered. "There are certain plants that can help stop a child from growing. One is called silphion, imported from the distant city of Cyrene. It is very potent and used by most of the women here."

"Procure it for me."

The maid was trembling. "Mistress, it could be hard to keep such a purchase secret. If the apothecary told the master we could both be thrashed."

Caecilia sank into a chair. "Are there no other ways then?"

Cytheris took a deep breath. "The skin and pips of some fruits are useful. The pomegranate may be a symbol of fertility but its seeds and rind can protect a woman from falling pregnant. I have used both combined with rue. But, mistress," she said, her voice imploring, "Nortia ignores such puny measures if a child is destined to be born."

"And Erene's way? She seems to have survived. Is it not the best choice?"

"A bloody mess in a pail? It is the last choice you would make. Mother and child often die. Leave that to those who cannot choose."

• • •

She would never eat pomegranates again. The sharp, pungent smell of the coarse red fruit would linger upon her fingers for some time.

Pulp discarded, Cytheris smeared a paste of its juicy seeds, rind, rue, and oil upon a scrap of fleece and held it ready. Caecilia's blank look turned to horror when the girl moved to assist her. "Leave me alone," she said, knowing it would take time to find courage, that she would not suffer such intimacy easily.

It was not just the dislike of the red fruit that made her queasy. The scent brought to mind an odor of long-ago admonishment. And a taste of guilt.

At eight years of age, her mother had discovered Caecilia trying to look at her nakedness in a mirror, each part reflected in the small burnished oval of bronze. There was a crash as Aemilia had cuffed the mirror from her daughter's hand. A harder slap across her face. "Cover yourself!"

Aemilia did not often visit her daughter's room because she was too ill, confined most days to her putrid bed in her dank chamber. The absence suited the little girl. Meetings brought rebukes and humiliation. And always that same smell. Faint and clinging, it pervaded even the distance of two paces that Aemilia demanded be kept between them. This time the girl's crime had closed the gap. The daughter gagged at her mother's stench. The blow was sharp. The welt would be angry and swollen. "Decent women do not expose their bodies," said the patrician, retreating after the assault. "Roman women are modest."

Caecilia believed in the virtues taught her by her mother. Understood modesty most of all. But at eight, her timid exploration of limbs and torso when she bathed in the cloudy, secondhand water of the bath was unsatisfactory. She wanted to know exactly how she looked, why it was that people stared when they saw her mark. She needed to know that her body was whole and that it did not bear any other spot, any signs of sickness.

Because her mother had made her afraid. Had shown her what could lie ahead. What caused the smell.

Aemilia wore many layers. Layers of the finest weave of linen and wool, soft and textured. Layers that she rarely changed: undergown, two tunics, a stola, and a cloak. Even in summer. But steeped perspiration was not the only smell that turned Caecilia's stomach. It was the stink of ooze from the creamy fibrous growth encrusting her mother's breast, a canker the girl had seen by accident when she'd spied the maid smoothing hypericum upon it. That Aemilia allowed herself any relief from pain surprised Caecilia. Even as a little girl she could tell her mother yearned for death and did not mind joining the Shades. As though gladly enduring penance for a sin imposed upon her by her family.

Fortitude was a virtue.

$$\cdot \; \cdot \; \cdot$$

Tentatively, Caecilia pushed the fleece inside her, intrigued by the soft, satiny warmth of the fleshy cushioning of her womb.

How could she be so ignorant? A stranger to her body?

How could it be that he had learned more about her than she? For this is what he desired. Where all men came from.

She let her hand linger. There was pleasure here for her as well. He'd taught her that, too.

Hoping that she had placed the soaked pad correctly, she withdrew her fingers, noticing a trace of her own scent fleetingly, realizing that what she was doing was not wifely.

Imagining, too, how a child would feel, pushing his way along the narrow, slippery passage. Defiant. Covered in pomegranates and rue.

• • •

That night she felt guilty, even though he also had deceived her. Then she forgot for a time because Mastarna sought all her attention. She did not mind all of his.

Later, instead of holding her even briefly, he broke from her, turned on his side, and blew out the lamp. The gap resumed between them, a handbreadth apart as always. When he did not bid her good night, did not speak at all, she grew anxious. His silence seemed a reproach but she could not be certain.

In the darkness she so loathed she wondered whether next time her deceit would be easier or if he would let there be a chance for trickery at all.

In the morning he was still there, dressed and sitting beside her on the bed. For a brief moment she found herself pleased. Smiling, she pushed herself to sitting, rubbing sleep from her eyes.

His somberness made her nervous, his words so measured they were frightening. "I do not like the taste of pomegranates."

Caecilia felt the burn along her cheeks as she put one hand to her face.

He did not raise his voice or fists. "You are lucky I don't believe in beating wives. Why did you do this?"

She clutched at the edge of his tunic. "I'm sorry. Please don't be angry! I just wanted the chance to see Rome."

Mastarna prized her hands from his sleeve and held them, the pressure of his fingers firm but gentle. "I thought we'd come to care for each other. Would it be so terrible to bear our child?"

Throat dry, Caecilia swallowed painfully. "But what if he is like Seianta's?"

He dropped her hands, eyes widening. "What did you say?"

"When were you going to tell me about your son?"

He turned away so she couldn't see his face. "I told you there were things I needed to forget. Did you know my wife died giving birth?"

"Why won't you say it? I know the boy was cursed."

For a moment she thought he would break his rule, his eyes like charcoal. "Did Cytheris tell you that? I should have her whipped."

"No! Punish me only. It was Erene who first told me."

His eyes flickered in surprise, then his voice hardened, anger flattening its cadence. "I don't know what lies the hetaera has spoken but my son's only fault was to be born too early and die too soon." He stood up abruptly. There was no hint of forgiveness in the stiffening of his shoulders and his rigid stance.

"If you truly care for your servant's freedom, Caecilia, you'll do well to believe me rather than Ulthes's mistress. Because if you try to do this again, I'll sell Cytheris at auction."

When she began crying, he backed toward the curtain wall, his tone tinged with hurt and frustration. "Bellatrix, you have been very foolish. I told you that you can't cheat Fate. Believe me, I have tried."

• • •

The room was large, piled high with clay amphorae. One had cracked slightly, a trickle of linseed oil oozing along the tiles, leaving a trail like that of a snail on its evening parade. The air was thick with the aromas of the various contents of the pots: perfumes, oils, preserves.

Servants were bringing the summer furniture into one of the many storerooms. The task should have been done some time ago, for autumn had the world in its grip. Hardier furniture, bronze and timber, was now required. Wicker chairs and outdoor tables were sent to hibernate.

Caecilia hastened to find Cytheris amid the bustle, leading her to the corner of the room. "He said he did not like the taste of pomegranates."

Cytheris's face paled. "Did he hurt you?"

She shook her head.

"Will I be whipped then?"

"No, but I have made it worse for you. I am sure he will never free you or Aricia."

The maidservant shook her head. "Don't worry, mistress, I never expected to be freed."

"Oh, Cytheris, he was so angry! What am I to do?"

"There is not much you can do. At least he did not beat you for trying to stop the quickening of a child."

"He denied his son was disfigured. Why won't he tell me the truth?"

The handmaid lowered her voice in reply, nodding her head toward the other servants as they scraped the furniture along the floor, edging them into spaces. "You must forget about Seianta's baby, mistress. You can't trust the gossip of a courtesan. And besides, there is many a mother who cradles a child who will never hold children of their own."

Caecilia glanced at Aricia. There were other factors that would prevent Cytheris from embracing a grandchild. As usual the Greek girl did not linger on her own sadness but turned to practicality. "Maybe you should just be happy you have a husband who uses his tongue for more than talking. If it was your Roman boy you could have used the fleece without detection."

Caecilia flushed crimson. "But I am not in Rome! And if I had a Roman husband I wouldn't be worrying about falling with child."

"Maybe so, but it seems to me you are not so miserable when it comes to sharing the master's bed. I'll wager your Drusus would not make you as content. Romans do not think about a woman's needs. It is all cut and thrust as though they are on the battlefield."

Caecilia was sorry she'd ever confided in her about Drusus.

"Thinking only of themselves and always doing so in the dark," continued Cytheris, garrulous with relief at avoiding a whipping.

Caecilia closed her eyes, wishing the slave did not always throw her off balance. Were Roman men such terrible lovers? She had assumed that all men made love like Mastarna. Would Drusus hide from her in darkness and be shocked that she would want the light of wax?

"You'd think they didn't like to look at their women," said Cytheris, interrupting Caecilia's thoughts. "Although with my face there is reason enough for a man to blow out the candle," she chuckled. "But Veientanes always make a woman, even an ugly one, feel beautiful."

Caecilia touched her neck. She, too, had a reason to snuff out the flame, but Mastarna had taught her to forget this.

"Or perhaps it is not a woman's face they are wanting."

"That's enough," she said, embarrassed by the maid's crudeness.

Cytheris's silence was only brief.

Amid the various nightstands and stools was a high-backed wooden chair with the family insignia of a bull's head on the headrest. Made from oak it looked very old, the sallow wood richly polished.

"This is the family birthing chair, mistress. For centuries each child of the house has been born through the hole of the crested chair. Trust in the gods and forget your fears. It will be an honor to bear the heir of the House of Mastarna. There are worse things than mothering the child of the richest man in Veii." To her surprise, Cytheris then bowed her head. "And I will also find joy in caring for your baby."

Caecilia stared at the chair with its high seat and padded armrests, touched by the servant's words but feeling suffocated, hemmed in by other people's hopes.

If she were married to Drusus there would be none of this torment, only a happy anticipation. A fulfillment.

It would be simple.

She would be safe.

• • •

Mastarna did not speak of her deception again, arrogant in his settling of the matter, but his chilly anger matched that of autumn's red and orange raining down.

His rage over Tulumnes led him once again to vie with peril, this time betting a cargo of silver lying in a distant harbor on winning a chariot race—and losing.

She could not forget the screams of six steeds colliding head-on with Mastarna's rig in a circuit with no center rail. Or how the horses' brushed, glossy chests and heads thudded and cracked together. And then the heaving cruelty of watching their dispatch.

Mastarna's chariot had exploded into fragments of bronze and wood, hubs and spokes. And he, thrown clear by the mercy of the gods for which he seemed so ungrateful, lay unconscious with several broken ribs and a shower of large splinters embedded in his arms and back.

Soon after, he made good his losses after betting on how speedily his hounds could run down a hind, making Caecilia wonder if it was more than recklessness that fueled his gambling, whether it was also a kind of sickness.

Politics consumed him. He and Ulthes kept jealous counsel, unsure of whom to trust. They were often away garnering support. They needed to be. Her safety and the peace within the city were resting with them.

She wondered if she'd ever been in control at all in her brief life. Her one puny attempt had led her to being even more under her husband's thrall. What right had he to play the aggrieved when he was holding her captive to his wants? When he had deceived her, too?

Both shared the same space in bed but retreated more than ever to the farthest confines. But she knew it would not be long before his desire to have a child would overcome his anger.

Fortitude was a curse. Railing against Fate had become a daily prayer.

• • •

The bowl shattered against the wall, shards clattering onto the tiles, but the mixture of beans and fish remained glued until it slowly smeared its way down to the floor. Caecilia glanced at the mess, then leaned forward over the dining table and laid her head upon her arms and wept. Her mood swung from remorse to anger and back again. Melancholy consumed her, entwined with frustration.

Her gown was grubby and her hair unwashed, finding comfort in childish dishevelment. Cytheris had begged to dress her hair and tend to her clothes but Caecilia refused. Had done so for some weeks.

And every time she sought respite in sleep the night demon would visit.

Lack of rest made her body thrum with nerves and she had taken to chewing her nails again, tearing at the quicks till satisfied she had drawn blood.

She had lost her appetite for food also. In Veii nothing was plain. Cheese was not cheese without being covered in fragrant ashes and olive oil. Instead of tempting her, the smell of cooking assaulted her. She had taken to picking at simple meals like lentil porridge, but no matter how often she instructed the cook to add no spice, the dish was not the same as at home; the repast was aromatic with rosemary and garlic.

Her curiosity and awe over the grandeur of Veii and its people had waned. The opulence was like a cloying aftertaste from gorging on sweets for too long. She wanted a long drink of water from a Roman well.

She wanted, once again, to walk the boundaries of Tata's farm and its corn rows, praying that, if she returned, Aemilius would let her live there safely instead of with him; a humble shrine containing small statues of the household spirits declaring it was, once again, her home.

Most of all she wanted to see Marcus. To talk to him and gain his comfort. But such thoughts only led to more worries. How was he? And what of Drusus? Both had boasted of being posted to Verrugo but her cousin had still not sent word of how they were faring. Although hurt by such neglect she excused him, blaming youthful thoughtlessness or the onus of fighting, but in the back of her mind she always wondered if she was resenting a dead man for not putting pen to scroll. Had the garrison the two young soldiers were protecting fallen and Aemilius not told her? How terrible if they had died and she did not know. The twelve miles between them was a chasm.

Taking off Marcus's wristlet, she weighed it in her hand. What would he make of her now? She already knew the answer and was ashamed. She was lying to herself, too. She talked of austerity but was still tempted, unable to remove the new gold rings upon her fingers. Letting amber and silver bracelets complement Marcus's amulet upon her arm.

"You were not at the morning audience, Caecilia. You are making it a habit." Larthia stood at the doorway, leaning upon the jamb for support.

Respect for her mother-in-law made Caecilia stop chewing her thumbnail and take notice. "There is no point."

The older woman directed a slave to bring a chair. "I don't understand," she said. "You seemed to welcome such responsibility before. Why do you wish to shirk it now?"

"No one is going to heed the counsel of a Roman."

"Not if she acts like a drab and fails in her obligations."

The girl lowered her head, but before she could respond, Larthia pointed at the food smeared across the wall. "Is this what Roman women do when they lose their tempers? Why not pull out your hair and stamp your feet as well?"

The rebuke had none of Aurelia's venom, but its effect was just as severe as a cuff across the ear. And more deserved.

"Come," said Larthia, her tone matter of fact. "I can tell Vel has done something to annoy you. This tantrum smacks of domestic drama, but it is no excuse to act this way. You should be more concerned with supporting him than with throwing food and refusing to bathe. And you will do that by managing his affairs while he is absent from the city. I expect you to take audience with Tarchon tomorrow."

"I'm sorry," said Caecilia solemnly. "You're right. No Roman matron should act so."

To the girl's surprise the Veientane smiled. "Don't worry, Caecilia. I would never accuse you of not knowing your duty—or of lacking courage."

Caecilia raised her head. Words of praise were always savored. Memories of those spoken by her father and Marcus were treasured. They would be worn thin if they were clothes. Mastarna had praised her, too. Each word a surprise and a gift. She was thirsty for admiration. Hungry for approval. Yet she doubted Larthia's words. "I merely try to endure what the gods have decided."

The widow raised her eyebrows. "Do you truly think so? If you sought only to endure you would have hidden from us after your wedding night and refused to tolerate our ways. No, there is a difference between enduring and surviving, of choosing to persist instead of suffering. And despite the terror of leaving your world I think that secretly you were proud to be selected. And relieved to escape, too. For here you are neither patrician or of the people."

The grim contours of her mother's face returned to Caecilia. Aemilia had chosen misery, locking herself in her room, dry-eyed and dried up inside, merely existing.

But would she have been proud of her daughter? Would that sad woman have felt Caecilia's sacrifice was for a good purpose?

Deep down Caecilia knew her mother would have wanted her to go. Not for peace but for the honor. And despite her shock and sense of betrayal, the girl knew Larthia was right, that she was strangely pleased that Tata's dream had come true when both classes of Rome had finally joined together, if only briefly, to see her wed.

"I believe you will survive our world. A vine flourishes because it can climb and weave and explore. It survives even though its roots may be planted in earth far from where it roams. In time I think you will be content. For here you can be more than mother, wife, or daughter. You can foster your own ambitions at the same time as supporting your husband's."

Caecilia looked away, watching a kitchen maid mopping up her mess. It was difficult to meet her mother-in-law's gaze, to believe that what she said was true. She knew she'd unexpectedly found bravery in a glade beside a river, but what Larthia spoke of was different—a courage that must be sustained through every moment of every day, whether dealing with tedious tasks or momentous crises.

"Now what has my son done to upset you? You can tell me."

Caecilia shook her head, not wanting to divulge what had occurred.

Larthia leaned down from her chair to pick up a shard of bowl. "It must be of some import if it has come to breaking pottery," she said, smiling. "Luckily the House of Mastarna is wealthy."

Caecilia blinked, nonplussed at the jest. It was odd to hear such words when all she could see before her was the wan, drawn face that did not hide Larthia's pain but implored her not to notice it. The older woman's voice was raspy and soft, each word frayed and tattered. Caecilia saw how it pained her to swallow. The suppurating ulcers meant she could eat little, yet Larthia had not retired from her life. Her bones were of metal, not soft ornamental bronze but iron, the ore of weapons and warriors. She was a survivor even as she suffered.

"I am sorry about the mess."

The matron pointed to the wall. "Well, your aim is true. You hit Vel in the face."

The mural the servants were cleaning extended the full length of the chamber. Caecilia had studied the picture of the parents and children dining together many times; the intimacy depicted in the tincture and pigment seemed somehow shocking. Until now she thought it to be a scene from another age, but as she looked closer she saw that the wife dining in the garden was indeed Larthia. A Larthia with dark hair instead of white, with sensual lips instead of blistered mouth. The woman extended her hand across the table to tenderly clasp that of her husband's. Here was the Mastarna of whom her mother-in-law so often spoke.

Larthia held a little boy upon her lap. Rolls of fat evident, he held a half-eaten orange in his plump grip while another boy, legs sturdy, was showing how he could throw a bone to a handsome dog that crouched beneath the table. It was this child to whom Larthia was pointing. Could it truly be Mastarna, lord of the house?

There was no doubting the bloodline. Both sons had inherited their father's dark features. Caecilia thought it odd to look upon someone who was father to her husband but younger in appearance. Vel Mastarna senior did not even look to be thirty in the paint that formed him.

The matron sat down again, wiping her mouth with her kerchief, frail, face pale. "You know, Caecilia, you remind me of myself. I, too, was an old bride. Married at seventeen after an earlier betrothal come to naught. Like you I came from a different city. My father wished an alliance with the wealthy House of Mastarna. Vel's grandfather was also happy for the partnership, gaining sailing ships for his cargoes.

"I also trembled on my wedding night and prayed to Uni that my groom would spare me hurt. I was determined not to like him, not to feel the lesser for coming from a family that could not boast such wealth as his. I need not have worried. My Mastarna was no more than twenty and resentful of being married before he'd proven himself in battle. At first both of us were prickly and proud, but common nervousness led to affection. He became friend as well as lover, the one who could both calm as well as stir me."

Caecilia concentrated again on the sight of the young Vel, uncomfortable with Larthia's open declaration of her love. The matron seemed not to notice.

"I fell with child easily and bore my two sons without trouble. And I thought the gods would bless us with many more, but it was not to be. After many peaceful years the truce with Rome was broken. Fidenae rebelled against the Roman yoke and Veii came to its aid." Larthia's voice faltered slightly. "And my Mastarna marched to war." She quickly patted her mouth to grant an excuse for letting her mask slip.

"After that it seemed as though there was no time when I did not fear the Romans would break through the Fidenate lines, cross the Tiber, and march upon Veii. No time when I did not dream of them butchering my sons and raping me."

Caecilia fiddled with a bean on the table that had escaped the flight of its brothers, anything but face her mother-in-law. It was strange to hear the enemy's side of the story, how they lived in the shadow of death cast by her people. Her city was always at war, taking its battles to the gates of its foes so that its women and children did not have to always live in terror. For Rome did not sit astride a cliff like Veii. Rome besieged other cities because it could not itself withstand a siege.

"Every day I waited to hear news that my Mastarna was dead," continued the widow. "It was a torment beyond torment—not knowing, waiting."

Caecilia squashed the bean into the table, gluey beneath her fingertip. She knew the end of the story. Larthia's Mastarna had died. At Mamercus Aemilius's hand.

Larthia gestured to the maid to fetch a beaker of water.

"After I buried him, Caecilia, sorrow would soothe me to sleep and then greet me when I woke. After that I learned what it meant to survive, that a woman must do whatever it takes to get through each day, to conquer grief and grow stronger inside. Guided by Vel's grandfather, I ran this household. I supervised tenants and sat in audience with clients. And then I started my workshop so that I would not have time to remember what I'd lost or indeed forget what I had to live for, why I had to survive."

Caecilia did not need to ask what that was. Two sons, both jealous for her attention. Two sons growing into men.

"You must hate me," she said, biting her lip. "How could you watch your son marry an Aemilian?"

Larthia took a sip of water from her cup. And then another. "There is no denying I found it hard at first, but if welcoming the daughter of an enemy into my family prevents other sons being killed, then I will gladly do so."

"But didn't Mastarna want to avenge his father's death?"

"Of course he did. When Fidenae fell he was fifteen, desperate to fight but of course too young. Just like Tulumnes he was impatient for vengeance, but the enemy they wanted to defeat was no longer a foe. The twenty-year truce had been signed. After the lucumo was slain, the Veientanes argued among themselves whether to elect another king, but chose not to bow once again to a potential tyrant. Tulumnes felt the loss of his father keenly and wanted retribution. He was and is still tortured, too, by the thought that his father's ghost wanders in eternal shame."

For a brief moment, Caecilia understood the depth of the princip's hatred, realizing that Rome had only told her the bones of his father's story. This woman was adding flesh to fact and emotion to legend.

"Why did Mastarna change his mind?"

"Because of Arnth Ulthes, of course. He believed there was no point in avenging endlessly."

"A lesson taught when Mastarna went with him to sea?"

Larthia shook her head. "No, before that. Vel's grandfather expected him to learn to be the head of this House. While civil unrest continued, Ulthes helped him in this regard. He had long been my husband's friend."

"And then they went to Tarchna?"

"Vel was eighteen by then. Old enough to experience battle, not just pretend to do so at training. Neither I nor his grandfather could stop him. With Vipinas at last installed as zilath and peace agreed with Rome, he was keen to go with Ulthes."

"And Artile. Did he not want to avenge his father?"

"Artile was a strange child never born to wield a sword. I don't think he cares whether there is peace or war provided he can converse with the gods."

"So there is no reason for Mastarna to be jealous?"

Larthia tightened an ivory hairpin that had come loose, sighing as she did so. Her white hair was thinning in places now and had lost its sheen. "It is difficult not to grow fond of a son who helps me stay in communion with the dead. Vel mistakes this for preference."

"So Artile is a comfort to you even now while Mastarna stirs concerns."

"As I said before, I love my sons equally. Both have achieved greatness and did so at an early age. Artile showed exceptional talent as a seer when only ten years old. I thought my heart would burst from pride when he was chosen to study at the Sacred College, although it was painful to leave him with the priests. He trembled greatly as I peeled his fingers from my own, even though I wanted never to let them go."

"And Mastarna, were you sad to see him go?"

"Why, of course, but it was different. He was a man by then. And when he returned after his grandfather had died, he was elected zilath when only thirty years of age, achieving fame and standing greater than his father."

Larthia rubbed her brow in weariness. "Despite growing up, though," she said, "men are still little boys. Mastarna and Artile are just as they were when this mural was painted, both arguing as to who may claim me first."

The frail woman lifted the beaker to her lips, gripping the cup as though even the weight of so small a thing was a burden, but Caecilia recognized Larthia's might. This woman knew there was power in doling out favors. Her sons gravitated to her for advice just as Caecilia had seen Marcus rely upon Aemilius.

The Veientane matron claimed to have no favorite and yet Caecilia had seen how her assurances seemed to stoke the brothers' envy and their ambitions, Larthia's ambitions. It did not shock her. In fact it gave her reassurance. Rome looked to its women to be the mothers of brave and powerful sons. Beside Larthia, Caecilia felt insipid. It was unnerving to be given a lesson in being a Roman from a foe.

For a moment stillness rushed in to fill the gap in conversation, and as it did so Caecilia felt that in learning this woman's story she'd discovered she could never be as strong, could only exist, did not think she could survive. "I am so very afraid," she whispered, "I don't want to be held hostage."

Larthia leaned over and took her hand. "Hush, you have a right to be scared, but we are all destined to die. Fate is unyielding. You say you must endure. But fortitude is only one part of virtue. Celebrating life noisily can be as great a quality as suffering hardship. Enjoying life even as you fear its ending is a strength."

"It's not so simple."

"Maybe, but if you truly wish some comfort about your future, Caecilia, Artile can help you. He will seek to divine your fate."

The pulse in Caecilia's temple was fast and painful. Since traveling here, she'd witnessed Artile's powers. Still, it was a dangerous game to ask the gods to reveal her future.

"Why would Artile do this when he has shown me only disdain?"

"That is just his way. He resents his brother for marrying an Aemilian but does not oppose the treaty."

"Did he divine Seianta's fate, too?"

The older woman dabbed at a strand of spittle that had fallen to her robe. Over and over, her face distorted with a stab of pain. Her breath was rank, the smell of death inspired and expired. It reminded Caecilia of her mother. Only with this woman the odor evoked sadness.

"You told Mastarna that Lady Fate could not always be swayed," she prompted. "Can destiny really be deferred?"

Her mother-in-law put her hand up to silence her. "Forget Seianta. Her obsession to prorogue destiny caused her and others to suffer. Fate is unyielding; even those who try to postpone it know this to be true."

The girl had never heard rancor in Larthia's voice before. Even when she spoke of her husband being killed by Roman hands, her tone had been measured. Larthia's contempt for her daughter-in-law was startling. Her impatience at the dead woman's failure to survive was clear.

The matron stood, swaying with exhaustion. "Come, let's not speak of Vel's dead wife. It was because of her that the rivalry between my two sons increased to hatred." She paused. "And Vel has never been the same since she died."

Caecilia hastened to steady the woman. "Aren't you afraid to die?"

"Of course, that is why I strive each day to become one of the Blessed. I pray the gods will grant immortality to my Mastarna, too." The widow halted, dark oval eyes studying Caecilia. "I'm tired. It is best you speak to Artile about these things. You are young and should be thinking of bearing a child. Perhaps you would miss your home less if you had an infant of your own. A child would help you become a Veientane, just as it did for me."

The girl was silent. Larthia was a Rasennan whether she lived in Tarchna or Veii. For Caecilia to forget she was a Roman was not the same. Nevertheless, she did not want to shrink from the matron's touch. She wanted to tell this woman all her fears, every single one of them, but she did not dare.

She glanced at the mural, at Larthia's two little sons, and briefly hoped that if she bore a healthy child she would be different than Aemilia, able to spoil an infant with caresses, able to both want and be wanted.

The older woman's voice was soft and husky, creeping through Caecilia's thoughts. "Every woman wants a child," she said. "And it would be a sweet thing to hold a grandson in my arms before Vanth leads me to Acheron. It would please Mastarna, too, Caecilia, please him greatly." Reaching over to kiss the girl on the cheek, she whispered, "And then you can truly call me Ati."

THIRTEEN

She heard the cackle of hens first, the whirr of wings. Then Tarchon's voice, loud, his accusations heated. The youth's anger seemed sacrilegious in such a hallowed place and the jarring tone did nothing to settle Caecilia's uneasiness as she stood before a temple within the City of the Dead.

Imposing votive statues were scattered throughout the sacred precinct, safe behind stone walls and an ornamental wooden gate. Chimera and Bellerophon wrestled, frozen in bronze, while winged horses and griffins stood with dedications inscribed upon them, silent reminders of the piety and gratitude of the rich and mighty. The tombs were grand secret reservoirs for riches—sepulchres that declared the greatness of clan heroes. Compared to these, the crypts of Roman nobility were insignificant, mere cupboards to house urns of ashes. More amazing was the fact the graves lay within a sanctuary owned by the Mastarna family alone. Holiness procured through wealth.

Following the sound of Tarchon's shouts, Caecilia and Cytheris stole into the dimness of the priests' quarters, blinking away the glare of the day. The chamber was crowded with cages of squawking doves and pigeons, the air filled with their stink, their wing beats spreading dander and lice that made Caecilia's eyes and nostrils itch.

Their presence was reassuring. She understood how birds could herald a god's whim. In her city, the subtle flight or varied calls of owl or crow, eagle or raven, determined the favor of the gods. Today, though, there would be a different type of divination, her future read in blood and gore.

The hatred in Tarchon's voice was startling, more so because it was directed toward Artile. What had happened to the Tarchon who stood in awe and adoration of the haruspex? Finding the bickering of the lovers repellent, Caecilia swallowed nervously, her saliva metallic, as though disgust had found a taste. Usually she could pretend these men were not like wife and husband, but the screech of a domestic squabble could not be ignored.

Artile's responses were quiet and deliberate. So quiet that the women could not catch his words, only their sound. But they invoked fury in Tarchon as he denied Artile the right to possession of him, chiding the priest for his jealousy. The women would have turned to escape but a young cepen appeared. He seemed oblivious to the argument. Such frays must have been familiar. He nodded to them and courteously ushered them to the lovers.

The smell of the birds was overridden by a pall of myrrh and thyme, wood smoke and stifling heat. A fierce fire burned in a brazier, reminding Caecilia that while the autumn sun shined brightly outside its warmth did not permeate indoors. A great mahogany table stood in the center of the room. Cluttered upon it were tiny votives of bronze and stone and clay, little gods jostling for space, waiting to be dedicated to their mighty counterparts in the sky.

After a while the men noticed Caecilia, but not before she had studied them, once again struck by Artile's calm. Compared to the fury of the other, he seemed like a patient father waiting for a young child to finish his tantrum. Nevertheless, Caecilia noticed his discomfort when he realized he had an audience. He turned away, clearly embarrassed that she was privy to their quarrel.

Tarchon was glaring at her. Tension had replaced his litheness, a grimace spoiled his lovely mouth. She did not wish to see him that way, ugly in his petulance. She was used to his selfish charm, so easily disarmed by it. Today he was disdainful of her judging him and his freeborn lover. Unable to check his anger, he strode out into the sanctuary and sunlight, but not before she noticed a red weal upon his cheek.

Artile greeted her as though Tarchon had been a phantom and his invective no more harmful than the protests of the temple birds. His friendliness was also an unspoken request not to inquire further about this discord. Embarrassment silenced her anyway, suspecting the older man had struck Tarchon. Chancing upon their indiscretion was as awkward as finding her father's servants furtively rutting among the stout amphorae of olive oil all those years ago.

What type of man was this Artile to keep a young nobleman from fulfilling his manly duties? To expose himself to ridicule as he clung to the hemline of a beauty who was unfaithful? For either failing, she knew she must choose whether to condone his conduct or shun him.

But her brother-in-law had something to offer. A soothsayer's gift. And so she would don a blindfold once again to Rasennan behavior. Indeed she was getting used to the feel of the band tied tightly behind her head, crushing her hair, pressing against her eyes.

"So, Sister, Ati tells me you seek to know something of your fate."

He was speaking Latin. Caecilia stared, surprised at how well he spoke her tongue, as though born to its rhetoric and syntax. Until now he had chosen to quarantine her by his rapid use of

Rasennan. "Why do you only now greet me in my language when before you would not converse?"

The priest passed his palm over his hair slowly. It was longer than most Veientane men. The hint of curls in Mastarna's short crop was unchecked here. The gesture showed his irritation at her bluntness. Unlike her husband, this man would not tolerate a woman's questions. "I speak Latin, dear Sister, because I want you to understand exactly what I tell you. Misunderstandings can be dangerous when dealing with the gods. Besides, it is pleasant, is it not, to hear the words of your people when you are so far from home? To recall the autumn shivering of yellow poplars or the fragrance of a garden of rosemary and thyme."

She wondered if this man had been to Rome, glad that he had let her revisit it briefly, surprised, too, that he should know what her homesickness should feel like, look like, smell like.

His eyes were similar to her husband's in shape and color and size. But that was the extent of the resemblance. Mastarna's were of stone; Artile's gleamed. Mastarna's were flinty enough to strike an angry flame; Artile's soft enough to reflect a sliver of what could be. Her husband, as a warrior, looked at men to size up strengths and shortcomings. Artile, as a priest, saw only their possibilities.

Near to him, she noticed his breath smelled of bay leaves: strong, aromatic. When he talked it was as though her people's language was flavored with herbs. A smell of cleanness also. Of rose water. He must have bathed recently, as befitted a priest who would perform the rites. His belly would be empty, too, from his ritual fast. There was effort involved in his preparation, even when telling the future of a Roman.

Was this the man who'd guided her hand too close to the nuptial flame? Perhaps it had been an accident after all? Perhaps Mastarna was too ready to blame? When Artile had touched her at the wedding his skin and flesh had been soft, vaguely abhorrent. But in this room, with its clutter of offering bowls, candles, and votives, it seemed right that they should be so. A warrior would be out of place. Hard hands and harsh voice would unsettle the birds that clucked and scrabbled within their wicker cages, cooped up until allowed to spread their wings. And how would the clumsy hands of a soldier skillfully incise the liver of a sacrificial victim when used to hacking flesh from limb?

She had to be cautious, careful. The power of a man who could catch a thunderbolt could not be ignored.

• • •

The haruspex led her outside to a podium with a stone altar scored with deep grooves to collect libations. There was blood upon it. Fresh. Its smell mingled with that of candle wax and sanctity. A lamb was tethered next to it. It was not bleating; instead it kneeled, quietly waiting, its beady yellow eyes dull. Caecilia examined it. It was for her alone—a mere woman. The private augury made her skin prickle.

The lamb's ears flicked lazily as Artile bent and tickled its head. "I usually find that when someone asks me to look into their future it is because they are not prepared for death. Is this so with you, Sister?"

"Tulumnes's threats frighten me."

"I think your visions of Tuchulcha should terrify you more."

Butterflies stirred in Caecilia's belly. How did he know her secret? Mastarna and Cytheris knew she had nightmares, but she'd told no one of the night demon. It was both the guardian and author of her fears. "How do you know of my dreams?"

He made her wait for his response as he donned his sheepskin cloak and pointed hat. "Because you have the look of one haunted by a demon. I know the signs and I fear for you, Sister. And for your parents. All of us must face Aita, king of the Beyond, but salvation is possible by discipline and devotion. Follow the Book of Acheron and you may become a lesser god."

Scared to face him, Caecilia watched the young cepen cleanse the stained altar. Was it always to be her fate for the weight of Tuchulcha to lie upon her? If Tata lived in Acheron, was he trapped in agony now that she could no longer leave food and wine and honey at his tomb? Resentment stirred, not wanting her religion criticized, not wanting to believe his truth. "I pray to my gods and pay my parents due honors."

"I am sure you are most pious, Sister, but are you sure they are not hungering in winter or thirsting in summer while you are absent?"

Caecilia shivered.

"Because it is sobering," he continued, "to think what lies ahead if you are not one of the Blessed." He pointed to a frieze of beaten bronze that decorated the altar. "Here is the passage to the Beyond, a journey that extends across both land and sea, strewn with pitfalls and monsters. Where Vanth lists the names upon her scroll of only those who have gained salvation."

Caecilia studied the carving. A demoness, holding a ball of thread in one hand and scissors in the other, beckoned to a dead man from behind a half-open gate. Next to her, Vanth, wings arched high above her head, held a torch and scroll while six horses with stamping feet and snorting breath pulled a chariot toward the sea. There, as though marooned in air, a dreadful sea serpent coiled toward a ship and a dolphin scythed through water. Beyond this Tuchulcha lay in wait to trap the journeyer. Finally, another decomposing fiend with his hammer and tongs guarded a door behind which the dead man's ancestors were seated at a banquet.

Caecilia closed her eyes. The journey seemed both perilous and arduous, an ordeal that would need courage to face and the assistance of the mighty to complete. To avoid the dangers of the journey to the Beyond, however, required her to forsake Roman beliefs.

Did she really want his afterlife, his people's sadness and terror? Their quest for pleasure could not hide the fact that the reverse side to ecstasy was despair. Yet could she disregard this priest and his library of divine books? How was she to refuse the greatest of all temptations—to be immortal?

"How then do I become one of the Blessed?"

Behind her Cytheris murmured a prayer, but Artile ignored her as he instructed a novice to light the candles.

"By adherence to the Calu Death Cult. Sacrifice and prayers and libations. Every day we must placate Aita and praise him. Placate his demons also. And we must expiate our sins, give penance for any failure in our worship. He must be implored to protect us from allowing the dead to rise up and harass the living. And then, when your life is ended, your family must make glorious sacrifice at your funeral. A very special offering. For if Aita and his minions deem you are worthy, you may claim the soul of the bull as it rises from its body and thereafter attain everlasting life."

The lamb bleated unexpectedly, startling her, betraying her nerves. Artile stroked its head. "Let's talk no more of death, Sister. It is time to ask the gods to reveal your future."

Caecilia nodded, glad that the haruspex had decided to end the discussion, not ready to consider fully how Veii was not only changing her life but also trying to define her death.

Cytheris moved to her side but Caecilia did not acknowledge her. The servant had not wanted her to come here, and she guessed there were fears and doubts in her reluctance that led back to Seianta.

The novice came forward and scooped up the drowsy sheep and laid it on the altar. The animal knelt obediently again, uttering a fragile bleat, the drug restraining any struggle to remain alive.

"Sister, before I begin I must ask if your husband knows of your desire to peek at your destiny?"

The butterflies were in a frenzy, bumping against her rib cage. Mastarna was unaware of this meeting. They'd spent little time together, his coldness and absences making her feel lost as well as angry; his lies about his son and insistence that she could not return home pushing her to discover her fate.

She told herself that her subterfuge did not matter, convincing herself that Mastarna would not begrudge her a glimpse of her future. After all, prophecy was a gift given to the Rasenna. The only problem was that the priest giving the prediction was Artile.

The haruspex moved closer. She could feel warmth emanating from him as she shook her head.

"Sister, I do not think your husband would look kindly on you seeking revelation. Do you wish to continue?"

His voice was the same as Mastarna's. No different. Mellifluous, compelling, seductive.

Caecilia raised her eyes to his as he beheld her. She could not look away. "I wish to know," she said, covering her head with her shawl in a sign of piety.

Artile smiled.

· · ·

There was drama to his ministry. When he marked the sacred boundaries with his lituus, and carried the patera of water around the altar, she could almost see the lines that divided holy from profane appear.

Water was offered as a libation to the gods as the priest dipped his hands into an offering bowl to cleanse them, the wetness glistening upon his flesh. No chance of blood lingering in the whorls of his fingertips, although his black-painted nails may well have hidden half-moon crusts beneath them.

Both animal and long ritual knife were blessed with wine and flour. The lamb's head was turned from sky to earth. Then the haruspex calmly called to the Veiled Ones in a clear voice, his foot planted firmly on a ceremonial stone, keeping contact with the earth as he beseeched the heavens for an omen.

After being granted permission to strike, the young cepen delivered a hammer blow to the melancholic strains of the aulos. One blow then another. Music could not muffle the thuds. Unlike the white bull of the temple, though, this victim surrendered silently under a noonday sun that had banished shadows.

After the knife was used with practiced hand, the carcass of the lamb lay slackly upon the altar, its silence belying the eloquence that its viscera had produced.

The sun pressed upon Caecilia's head, inching through the weave of her palla, giving her a headache. The heat made the smell of the offal and blood loiter, the stink of the stained fleece adding to the stench. Flies buzzed lazily over the remains.

The liver lay dissected before Artile, juicy with promises, revealing an unwanted future.

Caecilia sank to the ground, face white. Cytheris harried the novice to fetch a stool. "It is good news, mistress. It will please him."

The high priest washed his hands carefully in a bowl held for him by his acolyte. "You are an unusual woman, Sister, to bemoan the role of the mother of a healthy heir."

Bemoan the news indeed. She was a hypocrite to hail herself as virtuous. What daughter of Rome would rail against being a true wife: devoted, subservient, passive—and fecund?

"Are you sure I am to have a child? I did not hear you ask that question."

He frowned. "A haruspex does not interrogate the god by asking for a yes or a no. He merely proclaims what is revealed by the cosmos. Your magistrates act as your augurs. Wise men, perhaps, but not skilled in divination."

Caecilia thought of her wedding. The whimsy of an eagle had determined the auspices for her marriage. At that moment she could gladly lace her fingers through the pinions of that bird and fly to Rome.

The cepen placed the liver in a salver, so darkly red as to make Caecilia think it was composed only of blood. A fly landed on it then flitted onto her cheek. She flicked it away in disgust.

"You see, Sister, there is science to prophecy." His voice was as gentle as a lullaby. "For the liver is a templum divided into quadrants like those in the heavens."

Caecilia peered at the satiny organ, wondering which god she might offend or even harm by touching it.

"Today, Uni the liberator, goddess of childbirth and the sky, revealed herself within the lamb's organ. Her sign was clear and came from the northeast sector, the zone of greatest good fortune. You should be joyful."

It was true. She should be pleased to learn that her son would beget children of his own. Still, it was hard to thank Artile for swapping one kind of concern for another. His forecast had imprisoned her, confirming that she would never again see her home.

When Caecilia remained silent, Artile lost his patience.

"Would you rather the organ be disfigured, Sister? Would you rather see blood clots in the northwest where the demons dwell?"

Behind her, Cytheris started to speak, but Artile snapped at her. "Be gone! You hover over your mistress like Vanth."

The Greek girl bowed her head but did not budge.

"Come, let us sit in the shade," he said, removing his hat to wipe his brow. Its brim was grimy with perspiration; his kohl-rimmed eyes were bloodshot with exhaustion. Communing with the deities had taken its toll.

• • •

A cooling breeze played upon her cheeks as Caecilia rested within the precinct of the sanctuary. It was peaceful there with ivy growing profusely along its walls. Ivy. One of Fufluns's plants. A plenitude of phallic steles also decorated the landscape. Engraved upon them were other symbols of the god: double axe and two-handled cantharus, goat and panther. The clan of Mastarna must also revere the lord of fertility, rebirth, and wine.

Her husband believed that Fufluns, not Aita, was Lord of Acheron. Mastarna would not be pleased that she was listening to his brother's beliefs.

Artile settled on a stool beside her, placing his hat at his feet. "I can understand your dismay, Sister. It would not be easy to bear a child of two cities and so bind yourself to Veii forever."

Caecilia gasped. He could read minds as well as omens. He understood her plight.

His voice was kind as he continued. "It will not be easy either to risk bearing monsters like your husband's."

"Monsters?" Her question was barely a murmur.

"Yes, fiends born too early, and a son with no eyes and its mouth cleaved in two."

"No eyes?" Her stomach was churning, sick that Mastarna was hiding the enormity of what he could plant within her.

"Didn't my brother tell you?"

She shook her head, concentrating on studying the soft fleece of his cloak, the supple leather of his boots, rather than face him.

"It was lucky, I suppose, that it died within a few hours of its birth, otherwise my brother would have been obliged to kill it under the law."

A tear trickled down her cheek, imagining Mastarna's grief.

"At least you will bear a healthy son," he said, smoothing one eyebrow, "but you should also pray to avoid Mastarna's curse."

The butterflies rose to her throat. It was thick with them, her voice nearly smothered. "You mean Seianta's."

His attempt to hide surprise failed him. "I see that someone has been teaching you our family history, but you should understand that the gods did not only punish Seianta. Although it is foretold Mastarna will sire a son who will also bear a son, it will only happen after great anguish."

Caecilia frowned. "Has he not suffered that already?"

"Perhaps, perhaps," he said, eyes narrowing. "But how many monsters will you bear before bringing forth an heir?"

Artile watched her calmly as she struggled to take even small gasps of air. He bent near to her. His face was close-shaven, not stippled by the shadow that touched Mastarna's jaw by afternoon. She closed her eyes, thinking of her husband. Caught between the image and the presence of these two men.

"Sister," he said, his deep voice enticing. "Would you like to defer such a fate?"

Caecilia slowly opened her eyes. "Mastarna says you cannot cheat Nortia."

He laughed. "For once I must agree with my impious brother. I cannot alter destiny nor indeed would I wish to. But, Sister, the gods do not just control the space around us. If we supplicate ourselves, we sometimes succeed in persuading them to speed up or slow down time."

Caecilia stared at him, finally comprehending. "Do you mean the Rasenna can postpone death?"

"If the rituals of the Book of Fate are devoutly followed."

"The Book of Fate?"

He nodded. "And if you follow my guidance piously I can call down lightning as proof that Nortia has answered your prayers."

Thunderbolts again. Dangerous and beautiful.

Caecilia felt as if they had risen far above the world, far away from the odor of the liver boiling in a pot of bubbling water near the altar, the sound of the novice scraping dried blood off stone.

Suspended in space. Time slowing.

When Cytheris knelt beside her, Caecilia jumped in fright. The handmaid tugged her arm, whispering urgently not to listen to him.

Grabbing the Greek girl's plait, Artile yanked it to make her stand. Cytheris whimpered as strands of her hair came away in his hand, her mouth with its missing dogtooth agape in pain.

"Go," he growled. "Wait for your mistress outside."

The servant did not wait for a countermand but ran from them, weeping, while Caecilia anxiously called after her.

The spell was broken. Cytheris's fright engulfed her. It was as though she had waded into a river and too late found herself struggling for a foothold in sudden depths.

And yet she did not drown. Artile's calm was as forceful as drawing a deep breath. It made Caecilia think that she could breathe even if the waters rose over her.

"Forget your slave and listen to me," he said firmly. "Your people think Rome will exist forever provided they act like soldier ants: single-minded and joyless, building and protecting their nest. Know instead that every person, every city—indeed, even the Rasenna nation itself—has a limited life span. Ten sacred saecula is all the time our race has been allotted and it is no different for people."

"So what is the length of a postponement?"

"Seven years of life may be prorogued at a time until a man reaches three score and ten."

"And you claim Nortia might delay other parts of your destiny?"

"Yes, you may pray to delay any element of your fate or indeed of another person's. Don't forget, though, that destiny cannot be canceled or averted."

The haruspex leaned nearer, mere inches away. She could smell lanolin and sweat seeping from his sheepskin cloak from the heat of the day. "Do you want me to call down lightning?"

Caecilia knew now why Cytheris had implored her not to listen. The handmaid knew the temptation would be overwhelming.

Mastarna had taken hope from her. Artile could return it. Mastarna warned her not to cheat the gods. Artile would procure their favor.

The butterflies spiraled within her belly again. Better butterflies than a baby. "Yes, I wish to delay conceiving a child."

The haruspex smoothed his eyebrow once, twice, three times. "If I help you, Sister, it must be our secret."

She hesitated, knowing that as soon as she spoke she was committing herself to his power. She remembered, too, that the Tarchnan girl had not convinced Fortuna. "What about Seianta? Why did she fail?"

For a moment Artile's face gained some of the edges of Mastarna's. "Forget about her. She lacked piety and so failed to defer the death of her daughter. A tragedy but also a lesson. To succeed in the rituals of the Book of Fate you must be dedicated. And so I'll ask you again—will you keep this secret?"

Doubts rose at placing trust in the brother Mastarna so hated. But it was not the priest she was choosing. It was his magic, his heavenly persuasion.

Noticing her trembling, the priest took her hands to quell her nerves. This time the softness of his touch did not repel her. Instead comfort flowed through her.

She nodded, one conspirator to another.

The seer replaced his hat upon his head, tightening the chin-strap, then barked an order to the acolyte who was setting up a spit to roast the sheep. The cepen scurried to the temple, returning with clean salvers and kraters.

"As the Veiled Ones have not granted Nortia the power to throw lightning, we must call down the one thunderbolt Uni is entitled to hurl. Pray and sacrifice to both goddesses. Uni will then reveal if Nortia has granted your wish."

Uni, Mother Goddess. Juno Lucina. Bringer of light and life to both nature and humans. Would she not think it strange that Caecilia prayed that the conception of a child be slowed instead of encouraged?

"How long can I delay conceiving his son?"

The haruspex drew a wad of Catha leaves from his robes and began chewing them. Clearly it was not only the gods that liberated Artile from space and time.

"No more than seven years."

Seven years: a lengthy guarantee. Seven years of living with guilt.

Once again she thought of Mastarna's eyeless son. "How long will it be before Uni grants me a sign?"

The priest led her to the altar and directed the novice to light fresh candles. "Only when Nortia is satisfied you have been pious and devoted and committed. You will do that by always obeying me, for I am a divine mediator. Seianta did not understand this and therefore tasted failure. Do you understand?"

Caecilia knelt before him. She was different than Seianta. She was pious, devout, committed. She would not fail.

When he extended his hand over her head, the gap between palm and crown might not have existed. Her skin prickled, charged. If he touched her, the spark would make him flinch.

"Sister, will you obey me?"

She met his gaze. His pupils were wide in his dark eyes. Promising her.

. . .

She was exhausted. Her instruction was detailed and had taken a long time: lustration, placation, and thanksgiving, all performed to the music of the aulos and the chanting of Artile.

She realized she had not eaten for hours, but her stomach rumbled quietly enough not to attract attention. The lazy hues and shadows of afternoon spread around her. The autumn warmth of the midday sun had been subdued, cold now easing its way from the earth, numbing her legs as she knelt upon stone. Her throat was hoarse from praying, but the pain was worth it. Surely such pleas could not go unheard. The aroma of roasted meat wafted to her. The lamb was ready to be consumed. She would feast gratefully, in celebration and thanks.

In her hand lay an unexpected boon. Artile's gift. A tiny alabastron. Its contents would help her converse with the god and give her joy. It was not Alpan. A love philter would serve no purpose in her quest. Artile called it Zeri. It was made from poppies called the joyplant. "Obey me and this will be your reward," Artile had said. "Obey me and I will bring you happiness."

Tomorrow her devotions would continue by making offerings every day, offerings containing life: spelt or fruit, honey or milk.

And blood. The goddesses would be thirsty.

WINTER 406 BC

FOURTEEN

Larthia was dying.

It was cruel to see the older woman constantly drooling, the faint scent of urine dwelling in the folds of her gown as she took the sacraments of the Calu Death Cult. Seeing her this way made Caecilia consider whether Larthia's decline was from attending too often to her nourishment in the afterlife instead of struggling to eat in her own world.

Exhausted, the widow would lie while Caecilia stroked the inside of her wrist, the skin translucent, blue veins like rivulets snaking beneath. The girl's hands were firm and smooth and steady. She would compare them to Larthia's skeletal fingers, rings swiveling upon them and bangles clattering upon emaciated arms, while thinking of her own death, the abyss that yawned before her. Would she disintegrate as Larthia? Would she die like her mother, suffering from a loathsome canker? The fear of death was ever present, and the dismay of worrying that her parents were indeed suffering in Acheron was constant.

There was an urgency to Larthia's worship, too, that infused the girl with panic. "You must begin your prayers early, Caecilia," the matron rasped, anxious to gain immortality for both her husband and herself, "lest you run out of time."

And so, although at first resistant to abandoning Roman beliefs, Caecilia finally heeded Artile's promise of becoming a lesser god. The solace the priest offered to his mother was both powerful and poignant. He could smooth the pain from Ati's face with both his words and his caresses. Finding the priest could give her comfort, too, Caecilia chose to kneel before Aita.

Every day Ati would grip the edges of the litter on her way to the family sanctuary with Caecilia at her side. Mastarna saw her accompanying his mother but did not stop her. How could he criticize her for providing the devotion of a daughter? Indeed Caecilia was slowly taking over Larthia's role in all household matters: organizing the house, managing the slaves, telling the steward how to deal with land agents and merchants.

But Mastarna did not like his wife following the Calu Cult. "I thought you'd never worship any gods but Rome's."

"And I thought you'd be pleased I was following your religion."

"I meant believing in Fuflun's Pacha Cult and his rebirth, not the torments of Acheron. Ever since the Syracusans gained control of our sea, the Rasenna worry that the end of our civilization is drawing closer. Priests like Artile take advantage of this, peddling death and spreading fear. You should not listen to them."

Caecilia did not follow his advice, instead remained intent on following the haruspex. She was careful nonetheless to finish her devotions by the time Mastarna returned from training.

There was a bigger secret, though. One she kept from Larthia, Tarchon, and her husband. On the eighth day of the Etruscan week she would draw her cloak over her head and visit Artile in secret to perform the rituals, coaxing Nortia to defer fate and imploring Uni to hurl her thunderbolt to show that no child would quicken within her.

Procuring a deferral was arduous. There were so many prayers, so many hymns, so many rites. All prescribed in the Book of Fate, all scheduled precisely in the Holy Calendar. Hard to remember, hard to recite correctly every time. Artile made her kneel until her knees and back were aching and she had recited without error. He made her weep with tiredness and cruelty. He chided her. He mocked her for mistakes. He taunted her with failure. And, when she thought she had learned the words, he required a different liturgy to be sung to ensure balance within the cosmos.

He could be inspiring, too. Sometimes when her voice was hoarse and her body paining she would look at him and see hope. He would touch her with those soft, sure hands, stroke her hair, wipe sweat from her brow, and she knew that this man, and this man alone, had the knowledge to save her. To lead her home and to reward her with a prize for which she had become too eager.

• • •

Artile's Zeri made the grueling rites bearable. Far more potent than the potion from Mastarna's blue vial, a few drops could summon paradise. And so she needed to deceive Mastarna for another purpose: so she could sip ambrosia.

Soon she was neglecting the household, using Mastarna's absence with Ulthes in the afternoons to make her escape, her reveries limited between the time taken for shadows to progress around the sundial from zenith to mealtime.

As Caecilia journeyed into the world of visions and freedom, Cytheris would stand guard over her, a mortal angel, making excuses should anyone come near. Upon awakening, though, her mistress noticed the maid's mouth was rigid with disapproval and her eyes full of concern, warning her that Artile had also given the Zeri to Seianta.

Caecilia chose to ignore her, believing that she would not fail like her predecessor, that she would not waver from kneeling an extra hour every day, then another. She had survived the journey to an alien land, been subjected to debauchery, and endured. She would be stronger than Seianta.

• • •

One afternoon Caecilia had retired to her chamber to drink the potion when Mastarna unexpectedly appeared in the doorway. Arruns was not at his side.

For a moment she panicked, glancing at the little cista in which she hid the elixir. Had he found out about her deception? She glanced over to Cytheris guiltily. There would be no escaping punishment this time.

Mastarna's aloofness toward her had vanished. "Bellatrix, why are you here? Are you ill?"

"No, it's nothing. I'm just a little tired."

As he stepped forward he signaled Cytheris to leave. "I have missed you," he said, touching her cheek. "I no longer want us to be apart."

Any desire for the Zeri disappeared. She encircled his neck with her arms. "I've missed you, too."

He began untying the knot of her belt.

"But it's daytime!"

"It's not forbidden, you know," he said, laughing.

Caecilia glanced out into the garden through the open drapes of the chamber, thinking it was a luxury to steal working hours for this type of pleasure, such theft a scandal.

The day was fine and fresh and sharp. Winter nipping at the heels of autumn. Anyone passing along the garden arcade would see them if they looked into the bedroom. "Wait," she said, running to draw the curtain. The room was suffused with soft, clear light.

Mastarna sat on the bed, pulling off his tunic. "Maybe one day I'll convince you to lie with me in bright sunshine." He stood and deftly loosened the ties of her gown, slipping it from her shoulders. "Let's make a child from light."

He must have sensed her hesitation. "Please, Caecilia, forget about little Vel. I'm sorry I didn't tell you I had a son, but you mustn't worry. I've been told I'm destined to sire a healthy heir." He kissed her throat. "And you will be the mother of that son."

She waited for him to say the rest of the prediction, the sting in the tail, the anguish. It did not come.

Yet disappointment did not stop her wanting to see his face and body defined by daylight instead of candle shadow. "Is that the only reason you have sought me?"

He frowned. "I'll show you why I want you," he said, lifting her to straddle him. "Stop talking, let's not waste time."

Needing to believe him, Caecilia smiled, raising her hands to her head, unpinning her hair.

• • •

Afterward, she watched him dressing from the warmth of bedclothes, wistful that he did not wish to linger. If he'd not come to her, it would have been a different type of languor, a different reason for robbing time. She did not begrudge him, though, for preventing her drinking the Zeri.

"Won't Ulthes wonder why you aren't at council?"

"No, it was he who chided me for neglecting you."

Afternoon chill was encroaching into the chamber and she drew the coverlet close around her. She had missed more than his being in their bed. It had been hard to forgo his company on the divan, excluded from conversations with Ulthes and other nobles, resenting not being able to share politics and intrigue.

"You know, you wouldn't have to deal with Tulumnes's threat if Veii was a republic. No Roman citizen would vote for a king. The power of our consuls is checked by the people and the Senate."

Mastarna adjusted the fibula that fastened his cloak. "You know best of all that the elections are weighted toward the nobles. After all, your father was prevented from being a senator by the so-called founding fathers."

"Are you saying I am not patrician enough to be your wife?"

"Believe me," he said, bending to kiss her good-bye, "being Roman is more than enough."

After he'd gone, Caecilia lay in the room that was darkening with shadows, a kernel of happiness growing within her, pushing through the layers of anxiety, homesickness, and fear, reminding her, too, that if she were in Rome, such conversations would be denied her and that, strangely enough, it was Drusus who had made this clear.

Young men long to be blooded. They are impatient. Once she'd listened to the eagerness of her cousin and Drusus for battle, thinking them brave and fierce for seeking war against Veii, sharing their hope that Camillus would be successful in gaining support to pay the troops.

Sitting in her usual place beside the atrium well, she'd been wide-eyed to hear of such things, thinking that for the first time she would be included in their talk about the Assembly and the Senate, elated not merely to listen but also to be able to speak of such matters. She had been nervous but found courage enough to speak. "Tell me, does Camillus still demand a tax to raise funds to pay the soldiers?"

Marcus frowned, silently chiding her, but Drusus reddened. "I am thirsty, Caecilia," he'd said very slowly, very coldly. "Fetch me some water."

She'd not been sure whether he was chastening her or merely cautioning her not to forget her position, yet his words were as hurtful as any rap from Aurelia's hand.

There was a dipper on the edge of the well. She'd shakily scooped the liquid into a cup and then hastened away, thinking he would never speak to her again, wishing that the curiosity that dwelt within her could, once and for all, be quelled. For if every day women were content to brush the hearth and bake spelt cakes to make offerings to the household gods, why couldn't she?

Drusus's admonishment seemed long ago and yet only two seasons had passed since then. How strange it was that she'd been contrite at upsetting him, regretting that she'd spoken, that she'd even dared to question him. Now she realized she should have been angry at his rebuke, should not have been concerned at offending him, that instead it had been he who had insulted her.

For Mastarna may have scolded her, been exasperated and annoyed by her, but he never dismissed her for being a mere woman, never forbade her denouncing his aristocratic beliefs. There was no longer the need to perch on the edge of a well and let men tell her what to think and bid her not to speak. In Veii, she owned her opinions and her arguments. In Veii, she did not need permission, either, to share them with men.

• • •

The next evening Ulthes held a banquet. With the end of their estrangement, the dull worry returned that Mastarna might ask her to lie with him when the reed screens were arrayed.

But, as usual, her husband did not compromise her. Instead, by way of perversely honoring his promise to her uncle, they indulged in a lesser vice.

At the gaming tables he heaped those strange gold coins before her, so different to the bronze weights Romans used. And then she joined him in throwing the tesserae or knucklebones, intent on good fortune, ignoring the moans and cries and laughter from those reclining on the feasting couches behind them.

Her betting was timid, but Mastarna's wagers, of course, were reckless. At other banquets he would play until dawn or until the host politely told them to leave, proving that his gambling was indeed a sickness.

That night he was quiet, concentrating, calculating loss and gain, making the stakes higher and higher so that she wondered if he thought there was anything too valuable to lose.

In the light of the candelabras, hemmed in by guests craning to see the result of the throw, she found herself sharing the expectation and excitement. But just when she thought she understood his thrill at winning and his obstinacy to recoup a loss, he took her hand before throwing the dice. "Did you know, Bellatrix? The thought that ruin hovers above the twist of a wrist is as heady as when two people fall in love."

She stared blankly at him as he resumed his gambling, remembering the vague stirring she'd felt when she first spied Drusus, certain it was nothing like the startling pulse Veientane wickedness engendered. No longer able to deny she'd feel this way if her husband told her that he loved her.

• • •

Mastarna was hosting a tournament for the Winter Feast, an entertainment of lavish proportions with only the best Greek and Etruscan boxers and wrestlers. A private affair for those principes he knew were loyal and those he hoped to persuade to the zilath's cause.

Arnth Ulthes would be present, too, not as magistrate but as candidate, vulnerable despite currently being entitled to wield the eagle scepter and wear purple robes.

Traveling to the country posed a problem. Continued devotion to the Calu Cult and the rituals of the Book of Fate would not
be easy.

There was also the ever-present knowledge that, unless Uni
sent her sign, she was playing a different type of dice game—the
risk that a child could be planted within her, maybe had already
begun growing. A child Mastarna alone had chosen to conceive.

Caecilia knew there was also a price to be paid if Artile thought
she was wanting. When the priest refused her the potion, he let her
understand that the pounding in her head, pains in her stomach,
and trembling of her hands were the result of her failure, of disappointing him.

She was disappointing him even now. He did not want her to
travel to the family estate. He was as jealous as a Roman husband,
jealous of her faithlessness in neglecting her devotions, possessive
of each prayer she uttered, each chant made, each offering she laid
before the altar.

Every vow she spoke, every drop of Zeri she drank bound her
to him. Yet she wished to follow Mastarna to the country. To act
as hostess and dutiful wife. He would wonder at her reluctance if
she did not. And so, cursing the haruspex for refusing to supply
her, she would have to eke out her reserves of Zeri a little each day,
staving off wretchedness and thirst.

The elixir did not keep Tuchulcha from her dreams, though.
On the eve of the tournament, the night demon, as always, settled
heavily upon her chest. She struggled in her sleep to cry out, the
sound strangled, muted, until emerging to wakening she pushed
the monster from her breast, her scream escaping as does water
surging forth from a breached dam wall.

Eyes open, darkness smothered her. In the chillness of the
dead hours of the winter morning she shivered beneath the bedclothes and hoped that dawn was not far away.

Startled from his sleep, Mastarna called to her. "Caecilia? Why
do you cry out?"

"Tuchulcha," she whispered.

He was quiet for a moment and she expected him to turn over,
dismissing this fear as he had done with all her others. Instead he
reached over and drew her to him. "Why, you are like ice." Then he
did what he'd never done before except in lovemaking. He wrapped
his arms around her. "You have been spending too much time with
Ati and her gloomy religion. Think instead about the leopard, the
guide to Fufluns's realm. Remember the leopard when Tuchulcha
visits you. He and I will guard you."

The heat of his flesh against hers was like a balm, spreading
through her lazily, making her legs unfurl and body cease hud-
dling. Head upon his chest, she heard the heartbeat beneath. His
breath ruffled her hair gently. She pressed her body along his and
tentatively stretched her arm across his belly, brushing the soft
ridge of scar. He covered her hand with his. In the darkness, seeing
nothing, she lay cocooned, surrounded by the scent of his freshly
washed skin, listening to her own breathing, feeling the soft wool
of the covers against her face, hooking her leg over his.

After a time she realized he was asleep. Listening to the rise
and fall of his breath, traces of the nightmare disappeared.

Held close by him, she understood what Erene meant. Knew,
too, why Seianta would not let him go. Understood that passion
was not enough. Wanted this every night. Was filled with envy.

• • •

Winter had stripped the grapevines, reefing their dense green-
and-red foliage from them, only a few stubborn yellow leaves left
fluttering upon their branches. Sinewy, gnarled arms wrapped
around each other's hunched shoulders, surefooted within dark
soil, wooden hoplites.

Caecilia traveled through field after field of vines. And field after field of plowed earth, dormant with barley and rye, guarded at a distance by low, brooding gray hills. She was venturing past the looming, impregnable arx of Veii to travel to an estate vast and fertile, belonging to Mastarna, richest man in Veii.

The city mansion paled beside the villa. With so many rooms it was almost a maze. Arches of tufa stone revealed hidden courtyards with enormous urns holding fruit trees, almonds and pears, denuded but aching to bud and bloom, their scent imprisoned until spring. Carved hedges of yew lined the garden walls and stepping-stones led outside to a grove of exotic date palms. Fountains still flowed, defying the cold, and in sunny alcoves birds chirped and hopped within wicker cages.

Ulthes had traveled to Mastarna's estate for the tournament, bringing good weather with him even if his heart was in turmoil, the early winter sun spreading a soft light upon them and the icy wind that hinted at snowfall dropping away.

On the morning after their arrival, Caecilia discovered a courtyard with a mosaic floor brimming with the denizens of the ocean: octopus, squid, and dolphin. Her soft calfskin boots trod on tiny turquoise-and-red fish while a monster with a snake's body, dragon's head, and fish scales threatened her. Caecilia, who had never seen or smelled or touched the sea, wondered if such a creature was real or merely a tale conjured from the lips of sailors. Crouching to stroke the small tiles that formed the creature, she realized Ulthes was watching her, two of his lictors standing to the side.

"Careful, it bites."

She straightened, brushing dust from her skirt.

"You look as though you were collecting shells," he said.

"Shells?"

Ulthes pointed to another part of the mosaic. "Small sea creatures live in them. The shells are their armor."

The shapes were intriguing, the creams and pinks pretty. "I have never seen the sea."

"No, I suppose you haven't."

"Until Veii, I had never passed beyond the seven hills."

It was not difficult to like him. He reminded her of her father, even though there was no physical resemblance. Perhaps instead it was his trust of her, the daughter of his enemy, and the way he saw her as more than a symbol of tenuous peace.

"Then I must make sure that Mastarna takes you to the coast one day. No one should die without striding the wharves of a port or watching slackened yellow sails swell and strain with the wind."

She stared at him. Veii was not his only passion.

Ulthes laughed. "I am sorry for my zeal. I miss the sea. My youth is entwined with it. As is Mastarna's."

"When you went to find war?" Her tone was a little eager, realizing there was a chance she might learn something of her husband.

Ulthes studied her for a time and she sensed he was weighing whether to reveal what Mastarna may not want known. But it was Ulthes's history, too. It was his story to tell.

As he spoke he was unable to hide what he thought of his friend, his voice warm, his memories affectionate. "After his father died Mastarna was young and eager to become a warrior. And so I took him to Tarchna where Larthia's people dwelt. There we helped protect its ships against pirates and fought its wars by serving Tarchna's zilath, Aule Porsenna. We did so for many years, sailing to Sardinia and Phoenicia and many places in between."

"I hear that it is the Rasenna who are the pirates," she said, forgetting to whom she was speaking.

"And I hear that Romans eat their babies," countered Ulthes with a laugh. "Come, Aemilia Caeciliana, why are you so ready to condemn us?"

She smiled. "Then did you catch many brigands?"

"I profess to thousands, but your husband is more modest. We both agree, though, that only one ship we protected lost its cargo—and that left its mark on both of us." He held up his mutilated hand.

Caecilia had often studied Mastarna's scar. Whenever she touched it she found it smoothly irresistible, a ridge of softness traversing muscle. Yet as tempting as it was to explore its contours, it was doubly so to find out how it came to be there, how the once-smooth flesh was slashed and then puckered into a cicatrice and memory.

"It was the last voyage we made. Mastarna had become an equal instead of a pupil. It was a bad way, too, to end what had been our adventure."

The story was simple when he told it. None of Tarchon's drama in the telling. No emotion other than concern that Mastarna had nearly died. No sense of the terror of the fight or the screams of the slain. They had woken to the sound of the Syracusan pirates boarding the ship in the dark. In the confusion, Mastarna hauled himself onto the deck without wearing even a linen corselet. The thieves meant to flay him but Ulthes denied them.

Afterward, he insisted his former pupil's wound be tended to first, ordering the cut to be bathed in seawater before salving it with honey, relieved to see it was not deep enough to pierce Mastarna's insides.

"Mastarna says it is the sting of salt on the gash that remains with him, not the slice of the sword, but I think he makes little of what looks much."

"And you? You must have suffered."

In response, the zilath straightened out his hand, examining his injury, then shrugged. "We gained a few more scars when we got back to Port Gravisca. Too much wine, I'm afraid. Mastarna did not stop gambling for days, so relieved was he to see dry land. The only trouble was that he was too lucky with the dice. A disgruntled loser slashed open the skin above his lip while I cracked my teeth in a brawl. Luckily Aule Porsenna dragged us to his house before we could suffer further harm."

"Seianta's father?"

He nodded. "When Mastarna saw her there was no question of returning to sea. He courted her at the same time as seeking Porsenna's approval. A prior betrothal was broken. It is not often a father is persuaded to consent to such a match. Vel's wealth was no obstacle either, especially when news came that his grandfather had died."

"And you, did you remain?"

"No, I returned to Veii as well. To my family."

The conversation ended. Caecilia sensed that Seianta's name evoked a sadness in Ulthes not related to her death. Mastarna's marriage meant the end of the zilath's time on the sea, the end of his time with his friend. It meant returning to his wife whom he had married for duty, as was proper.

Caecilia scanned the walls of this newly found courtyard. Until then she'd thought it was Larthia who'd decorated it. After all, Ati came from near the coast. But she was wrong. The floors and the hallway were all adorned with living things from the sea, all created for her, for Seianta, the Tarchnan, to remind her of her home.

Ulthes was surveying the room also, and for a moment Caecilia wanted him to know she understood that Mastarna's first wife had changed his world as surely as she now haunted hers.

• • •

Ulthes's retinue was small but he had not forgotten to bring his mistress. Many of the other nobles had also left their wives behind in snug city dwellings, instead bringing their own comfort in the form of courtesans and slave boys.

Erene wore winter clothes, but this protection from the cold made her no less provocative. She wore a tebenna—a man's cloak.

She did so with an easy stylishness that banished any hint of masculinity, instead emphasizing how awkwardly Caecilia stood and how plain and tall she was.

The tebenna was a deep blue. For a moment Caecilia thought of her uncle, struggling with his senatorial toga, always rumpled in appearance. In Rome, prostitutes wore men's mantles also. She was certain her uncle would be disgusted at his niece for admiring the elegance of a courtesan wearing male robes.

Caecilia had not spoken to Erene since the temple, even though she'd acknowledged her at the many banquets to which Mastarna was invited. Once again she was torn whether to indulge in conversation when their last one had caused such trouble.

"I see you have progressed to being at least three-quarters a woman," said the Cretan, pointing at Caecilia's clothes.

Having discarded, layer by layer, her dreary tunic, stola, and palla, Caecilia had thought her fall complete. Her homespun clothing was crammed at the bottom of a large chest under tiers of colored robes—proof of her steady seduction by the Veientanes. In fact it was a little frightening how quickly she let the luxury of fine linen and soft wool slide over her body, cinched in by bright sashes and girdles. Today she wore a pale-yellow chiton embroidered with hundreds of white flowers, such needlework a whimsy after using thread only for straight seams and mending. She had succumbed to more than a pretty wardrobe, though. One thing after another she had compromised: wine and jewels, potions and pleasure.

Each time she gave in to temptation another dimension was added to her guilt.

There was a levy on falling from grace, irking her that she could not truly enjoy all that might otherwise delight her. There was always an aftertaste. A confusion. There was always a voice that whispered, "You have forgotten Rome."

Around Erene, though, Caecilia sensed her Roman reserve: shoulders held a little too straight, her neck too tense, her walk too brisk.

The Cretan's smile retained the condescension of their prior meeting. "Stop playing at being a Veientane and start being one," she said. "Halfheartedness can be painful."

Caecilia rubbed her hands along the sides of her chiton nervously, uncertain whether to walk away, irritated also that Erene was right. For in not totally abandoning seemliness she'd placed herself where she could neither argue its merits nor denigrate its counterpart. She was, as the courtesan said, not quite Rasennan and no longer completely Roman.

Perhaps the Cretan woman thought that teasing Caecilia was far too easy a sport because, to the girl's relief, Erene turned to leave. At that moment, however, the servants of the team of Greek wrestlers and boxers arrived. Both women watched the slaves carry their masters' belongings through to their rooms. These athletes were aristocrats, not common actors or acrobats to be sent to the servants' quarters for lodging.

"I see that the champions of Olympia are arriving," said Erene.

"Olympia?"

"All the states of my country compete at that city's games, declaring peace for such time as the contest runs. To attain the victor's wreath is to become a hero and win a fortune. There is rumor that Amyntor will be fighting here. An honor indeed. I have never seen a champion of the pankration."

Caecilia held her tongue, not wishing to weather scorn for her ignorance, but Erene was prepared to be gracious.

"Pankration is the contest of all contests. A test of all powers, cruel and valiant, where men fight each other by whatever means, through boxing, wrestling, and kicking."

"You sound as though you have seen such a challenge."

"Not at Olympia. Unlike the Veientanes no Greek woman attends the games. But my patron held a competition like this at a symposium once. I saw the bout along with the other hetaerae."

Caecilia turned to the woman, no longer intrigued about a wrestling match but about Erene herself. The courtesan met her gaze.

"Come," she said, "I will tell you my story. It is only fair, I suppose, since I know so much of yours."

"You know nothing of me!"

Erene laughed. "All matrons of Athens and Rome have the same lives, dull and dutiful. It is only what you might become here in Veii that will make you interesting."

Suddenly Caecilia wished Cytheris were beside her rather than assisting others to prepare for the feast. She was sure that her maidservant would have bundled her away with some excuse. But, as usual, Caecilia felt a terrible attraction toward Erene and her life. And so, instead of upbraiding Ulthes's mistress for insolence, she gestured her toward the warmth of an inner chamber away from the bustle and chill air.

• • •

"I am no whore, as you may think, but I am the daughter of one. My mother, Euterpe, was a flute girl who delighted men by standing naked before them with only a thigh band and necklace adorning her. But being fair of face and able to play a double flute as sweetly as Pan did not save her from poverty. She lost her living when I, still tiny within her womb, thwarted the potion she drank to purge me from her. Men, you see, do not want to see stretched bellies and breasts at their symposiums.

"Our master was prepared to keep her to entertain men in his brothel where no music was needed to gain their attention. He was kind enough also to let Euterpe keep me, keen for me to grow to learn the skills of the porne who lifted their skirts and spread their legs for his profit.

"My mother had a higher aim for me. I was a pretty child. Customers clamored to be the first to taste my loveliness and youth, but Euterpe shielded me, wanting me to become a rich man's mistress, telling the master that it would be to his benefit to auction the firm breasts and tight loins of a virgin to the highest bidder. And having watched my mother suffer the tedious rhythm of men's rutting, then wipe their smeared seed from her thighs before taking another, I, too, prayed I would never live through such soulless drudgery nor have to bathe and salve the cuts and bruises of flesh and spirit."

Stunned, Caecilia stared at the woman. She was fluent now in Rasennan but the courtesan was speaking the language of degradation, her words not only hard to understand because of her accent but because, to Caecilia, she was describing the indescribable. Caecilia rubbed her hands along the sides of her robes yet again, discomfort prickling her scalp. Still leaning in slightly to listen, though. Unable to leave.

"To my good fortune an Athenian named Telamon visited our town in Crete. He succeeded in purchasing the right to hear my melodies in bed for a hefty price. My mother did not cry when he took me away, telling me as she painted my lips and cheeks to make them rosier, 'He's agreed to make you a hetaera, a companion, not a mere slave. Here is your chance to never be porne or flute girl. Do not fail me.'"

Erene took a deep breath, then primped her short, shiny golden hair, and played with the tips of the scarf that was tied across her brow and flowed down her back in a streak of blue. "Telamon brought me to a house off the Agora replete with soft beds and a full larder. A woman who had once been a hetaera lived there who bore the residue of loveliness and poise in the tilt of her head and the upturned corners of her mouth. She taught me what my mother could not—grace in movements and elegance in dress that denied the robust nudity of the flute girl.

"And there I became a companion, groomed to be witty and artistic and educated, to keep men amused discussing politics and philosophy at their symposiums, to entertain with song and flute and lyre, and be a symbol of a man's status, a symbol of the beauty and talent he could hire. I also acquired those skills that madden men with wanting, just as sweet sounds are teased from a lyre."

The Roman girl raised her eyebrows. "So you don't deny it was not just music, art, and oration with which you amused men. You just said so yourself."

The hetaera's reply was spiced with irritation. "You think I'm just a costly whore, but I am more than that. You have only recently learned a language other than your own, yet I know many and was taught to craft the Athenian tongue into the language of persuasion."

Caecilia tensed, not ready for her own accomplishments to be questioned. "I would not be prepared to pay the price for such instruction."

Erene shrugged her shoulders. "Telamon was proud of me, showering gifts upon me, giving me rooms that were proof to his peers that he valued me as a jewel to be marveled at and admired. When I lived with Euterpe, men's gazes fell heavy upon me, their stares like fingerprints upon my skin, but in Athens the lusts of men were tempered. They could desire my beauty or cleverness but their hunger had to be requited by flute girls instead—or their own companions. Telamon alone enjoyed my favors.

"My house became a place to meet and talk and be entertained. Not a brothel, as I can see you are thinking. There were gifts, though. In exchange for my company, men would show appreciation, be it rings upon my fingers or priceless art in my home."

Caecilia shook her head in confusion, making Erene laugh.

"Don't you see that I enjoy the same freedoms as a Veientane wife? And I wouldn't want to be a good Athenian woman anyway, shut away in women's quarters and only expected to breed fine citizens."

The companion did not wait for the Roman to comment.

"Of course, bearing a child is something a hetaera would be foolish to covet. My mother taught me that lesson. Besides, I no longer need worry about making such a choice. I'm barren from too often scouring my womb of children." The Cretan sounded sanguine about such sorrowful acts, but there was a hint of sadness in the way she spoke in a rush of sentences.

Caecilia, uncomfortable in discussing the choice of whether to curtail an infant's life or avoid bearing one, quickly changed the subject. "How did you come to Veii?"

"Telamon was a collector who possessed a trove of fine wine from Carthage as well as Tyrrhenian terra-cottas. He admired the pottery of the Veientanes most of all and, wishing to visit the craftsmen here, brought me with him."

Caecilia found herself edging forward on her chair as Erene's tale crept closer to her own. "And it is here you met Ulthes?"

The Cretan woman nodded. "And your husband."

Caecilia felt the familiar tug at her sleeve, the inward reminder that her nosiness would take her to uncomfortable depths if she did not heed such a warning. There was queasiness, too, that she had so often known when as a child she crammed her mouth full of honeycomb, tempted even though it would make her sick. This courtesan was about to tell her what she did not want to hear but wished to know.

Erene did not appear to be concerned that Caecilia would suffer embarrassment at being told that her husband sought companionship. Even Romans were known to go whoring or keep servant girls as concubines, but a clandestine visit to a brothel was one thing; parading a courtesan at a drinking party or giving her a house was quite another.

"Ulthes was gripped with grief. From two sons dead from plague, two heirs taken from him before he could reacquaint himself with other than their names and forms. When he left they were still clambering upon his knee or clinging to his footsteps like early morning shadows. On his return he expected to find gawky, pimple-faced youths whom he could teach to be the kind of men he wanted them to be. Instead, he arrived to find them sick with fever. They died before he could show them how to heft a sword or draw a bowstring.

"They say his wife cradled their cold, stiff bodies for two days as time made them supple and the smell of decay oozed from their skin. Then she retreated into the inner rooms of her house, shunning even other women and cursing Ulthes as though his return had brought the disease. As secluded as an Athenian wife, even though her husband did not bid her to be so.

"My patron let me entertain the grieving princip. I made Ulthes cry as I played the lyre and recited sweet poetry. I made him smile, too, as I mimicked the antics of his fellow nobles in their cups: Apercu with his bulbous nose and throaty giggle, Tulumnes's brooding barbs, and Mastarna's gruffness, which could be cajoled into laughter."

Caecilia was disbelieving. "I have never seen my husband drunk with mirth."

The hetaera smoothed her hair, releasing the fragrance of the soft wax with which she had dressed it. "And perhaps you never will."

Caecilia glanced away. The tale was edging closer to Seianta also.

"When Telamon finally decided to return home, he granted me my freedom with his farewell."

"Why didn't you return to Athens?"

"It would have been hard to reestablish rooms," she said, frowning. "I needed to find another benefactor. But luckily Fate was kind. Ulthes, a man with a wife but no wife, took pity on me. He gave me a house and I tended to him in his loneliness, a loneliness that came as much from the loss of his family as from the theft of Mastarna."

Theft was a harsh word to use.

"What was Seianta like?"

The companion paused as if deciding which version of the Tarchnan she should disclose. "When I met her they'd been married for a year, but Mastarna doted on her as if she were still his bride. There was a dimpled prettiness about her, but I thought she was like one of those fruits whose tartness either appeals to one or doesn't. She pleased Mastarna with her jokes and stories, making light of his brusqueness. She pleased the principes and their wives, too. In truth, Seianta would have made a fine hetaera with a little training, for she had wit and style and an ability to charm." The Cretan smiled wickedly. "Although no doubt Mastarna was teaching her some skills. He was not a man to be satisfied with the talents of a girl of fifteen."

Caecilia quickly glanced away. What then did he think of an eighteen-year-old?

The courtesan fiddled with the peculiar gold half-circles of her necklace. "Don't worry, you may be an old bride but you are still young enough. And I am sure you are as apt a student as Seianta, or has Mastarna finished your lessons?"

Caecilia faced Erene again. She was becoming accustomed to the Cretan. The companion might be prepared to reveal her life, but she was not about to share her own secrets. "Tell me more," she said curtly.

The sin in the courtesan's smile was undiminished. "Very well. When Seianta lost her daughter she became a wraith, consumed with bearing Mastarna a healthy child. For it seemed she'd acquired another trait of my kind—no living children. But whereas I chose such a course by use of silphion or rod the poor girl railed against her fate. How weary she became, how desperate, as unformed babes one after another slid from her womb or, like her tiny son, died within hours of his arrival."

"Her deformed son," said Caecilia softly.

"Yes, Seianta's curse."

"And Mastarna's."

Erene seemed surprised. "The father's? No, it is always the mother's weakness, the mother's failure."

For a brief moment, Caecilia felt some hope that any child she was destined to bear with Mastarna would be whole. Glimpsed also the possibility of sharing his joy. Yet Artile had made it clear who would be to blame for planting the seed of a monster. The judgment of a haruspex must hold more weight than a whore's.

"And then she died."

"Yes, and Mastarna fell into drunkenness, bellicose and gloomy. There were few times when he was sober. It would have been better for him to take poison, but he considered that to be cowardly. Instead, more and more he would stake his life in dangerous pursuits, mad and frenzied, so that he might join his dead wife and children in the Beyond. After a time his wildness turned to bedding his friends' wives until he erred in choosing those whose husbands did not turn a blind eye.

"Ulthes calmed him, understanding his grief. My rooms became a place where we could grant comfort to Mastarna. Ulthes was generous, too, offering my companionship to his friend when he alone was entitled to my services."

The Roman girl flinched. "As much as his dead wife would let you."

The deliberate way Erene adjusted her robes revealed that the comparison was uncomfortable. When she spoke, the Roman recognized the hetaera's tell just as easily as she could identify

Ulthes's. Erene's hand did not tap against her thigh, though; instead, the companion, who was normally so composed, let her refined voice momentarily lapse into the coarseness of the Cretan gutter.

"You are right. In my language the name Erene means peace, but I could not bestow peace upon Mastarna. He wanted something I could not provide. He wanted me to be Seianta, but I could not replace her in his bed because she still lay upon it." She was defiant. "And nor will you."

It was strange to hear the anger in the courtesan's voice, to understand she was envious of a dead girl. A lifetime ago Caecilia had never seen a hetaera, nor spoken to one, nor wished to. Now she was listening to one who'd shared her husband.

She had grown used to strange things, but she never thought she would envy Seianta as Erene did. Yet after last night she realized she was just like the courtesan—hurt to think Mastarna did not want her enough to bid his dead wife farewell.

This morning, the fit of their bodies had been broken by slumber. He'd not tried to mend it. Seianta must have chided him for his lapse, tightening her grip around him. His retreat was upsetting and confusing.

The Tarchnan would be twenty-two had she lived. Old. Would she, like Erene, have to wear more white lead to hide the lines, wear more clothes to hide her flesh, smile less to hide stained or missing teeth?

Would Mastarna still love her?

"At least I have Ulthes," continued Erene. "I've found contentment with him, almost as though we were man and wife. I do not think he will abandon me for someone younger. He assures me I will be provided for when he dies." Smoothness had returned to the plain vowels of her voice but it could not hide her apprehension as to her future.

Humiliating as it was, Caecilia could not help being drawn to this woman. The Rasennan wives still kept her at a distance and only Cytheris and Larthia showed her any fondness. The two women, Roman and Cretan, foreigners in an exotic world, had found a brittle liking for each other.

"I must go," said Erene. "I wish to bathe before the contest. My story is not remarkable, Aemilia Caeciliana. No more remarkable than your own."

Caecilia stayed for a while, picking at the quick of a fingernail, wincing when it tore, confused, always confused. Would it be different if Mastarna exorcised the ghost and wanted only her? Would she be brave enough to cease begging Nortia to reset time? Be prepared to risk a monster if Mastarna stood by her through their loss? Her head was throbbing as though forced to sit too near a drum, the beat becoming a pulse inside her telling her she was a fool.

Rising to make ready for her guests, Caecilia told herself she need not worry. She doubted Mastarna would ever love her or that Seianta's spirit would ever let him go.

FIFTEEN

Since the night of her wedding feast Caecilia had only been close to Laris Tulumnes once. At the palace. At other times he kept his distance, turning his back and speaking to others as though she was a child unworthy of address.

Today, barging his way into the villa's atrium, boots muddy and tebenna damp from the rain, he could not ignore her. Steam rising from his robes, his face flushed, he was unable to hide how his chest swelled and fell sharply. As always, his face gleamed with a faint sheen of perspiration. He stank, too, of wet wool and onions. Throwing off his cloak, he waited for his two young slaves to gather it up and begin drying his arms and legs.

The boys were tiny, blond, and blue-eyed. As she studied them Caecilia marveled at what it would be like to possess a piece of sky within her. Then she remembered Tarchon's gossip that Tulumnes imported the slaves from a snowcapped country far to the north, and that the princip only used them for a short time because they aged so quickly after being mastered. She felt nauseous at the thought.

His liking for youth was not limited to boys either. He'd been married twice to maidens so young that they died bearing his daughters. There was another betrothed to him with instructions that they be wed as soon as she ripened. She was chosen, they said, not just for her wide hips and placid nature but for the prediction that she'd give him sons. The princip would not take any more chances with delicate bones, narrow waists, and nerves.

Despite facing Caecilia in her own home, Tulumnes still tried to be dismissive, demanding that her steward summon Mastarna without even bestowing a greeting. Caecilia refused to be intimidated by this interloper, although, in truth, she felt like running and hiding behind a grown-up like a child. She signaled the majordomo to heave the massive outer doors shut.

She was buoyed by the memory that this man did not fight the duel with Mastarna. She suspected that, despite claiming to be from a dynasty of warriors, Tulumnes would be at his most adept when piercing a man's back.

The nobleman ran his fingers through his hair, smoothing it back upon his high brow. A drop of water flicked upon her cheek as he did so, reminding her she was standing far too close, but the Roman in her made her wait for him to move first.

At the wedding he'd spat an insult she'd half understood without the need for translation. Now she had learned his language and its invective. She was no longer a frightened girl in a room full of strangers. Today she was not prepared to be bullied by his height and words or concede to the type of man who would cast a slur upon another's wife and then slink away when honor was demanded.

"You act as though you are mistress of this house when you can never be more than a trespasser in any Veientane home," he growled.

"Remember that here," she replied calmly, "it is not I who am uninvited."

Nonetheless, when Tarchon appeared suddenly, Caecilia was relieved to step aside. Her brief defiance had been exhausting, her knees unsteady, trembling with the simple act of standing. She was also touched that her tutor was seeking to protect her. She did not expect such bravery from Mastarna's son.

Tarchon had arrived late to the villa, clearly unhappy that his father would not permit him to join the men in their discussions. The youth tried to ignore this rebuff by loitering around the wrestlers and their trainers, even sparring with a few. Such pursuits would normally have made him garrulous with arrogance. Instead he slouched as he sat amid the hubbub, disheartened, speaking with politeness rather than fervor.

For Mastarna had slowly exchanged disapproval with blatant exclusion. Tarchon was not acting as expected or as bidden. By remaining nestled within Artile's arms, acting as a boy even though he could grow a beard, his actions could no longer be overlooked as those of one still on the cusp of manhood.

She found it hard to watch her tutor's plight, even though she knew he deserved it. Yet knowing that a child should feel the sting of a birch rod made it no less easy to strike. And so when she'd heard Mastarna berating him she'd asked that he wait a little longer before cutting ties with his son.

Mastarna had turned upon her, astounded. "Since when has a Roman defended one such as Tarchon?"

She'd faltered then, confused at facing the difference between emotion and reason. "It's so painful to watch."

Mastarna touched her wrist gently. "My answer is the same as when you keep pestering me to free Cytheris and her daughter. These things have already been decided. Tell Artile instead to free Tarchon. It is he who is making my son an outcast."

Today, though, she thought Tarchon as brave as any soldier as he spoke firmly to the intruder, but when Tulumnes drew himself to full height, pushing his face to within an inch of the youth's, she could see his courage flag. Instead of trying to eject the princip, Tarchon gestured to him to sit while his father was informed.

The aristocrat made it clear he did not want to wait. "Hasten and call him. I don't want to linger with Artile's bride and a Roman."

For a moment Caecilia thought Tarchon would object, but daring failed him, turning away like a chastised child, recognizing that the insult was too close, too true.

• • •

Inside the meeting chamber Ulthes held counsel with the clan leaders. Caecilia knew how he could finesse an argument by stroking his opponents' conceit until they purred, but when she and Tarchon led Tulumnes to where the principes were assembled, she wondered if flattery would be enough.

The zilath needed the support of Vipinas as leader of his tribe. Apercu had already pledged his allegiance, but the thin man was coy, weighing up the gilded promises of Tulumnes against the principles of Ulthes, lapping up the attention of the two candidates as does a child enjoying the favors of doting grandparents. Pesna had not been invited as Ulthes did not want to waste his time on a lost cause. Tulumnes had long ago become his master.

When Mastarna saw Caecilia and his son enter, he frowned and beckoned to them, but before they could speak Laris Tulumnes burst into the room with the eagerness of one ready to share bad news.

The zilath's lictors scrambled to form a shield around him, rods and axes at the ready, but Ulthes, as ever, was composed. He ordered his men to fall back and for the principes, who had sprung to their feet, to be seated. Caecilia could see the fury beneath his calm by the sharpening of his speech and the tapping of his hand upon his thigh.

Caecilia hesitated whether to leave but Mastarna took her arm. "Stay," he said. "This will involve you."

She edged behind her husband's enormous high-backed chair, instinctively wishing to hide, aware that the other men might consider her an interloper.

"You are not welcome here," said Mastarna, glaring at Tulumnes and directing Arruns to eject him.

Although the guard was shorter than him by more than a head, Caecilia could see the nobleman hesitate to oppose him. "Wait!" he said, warily eyeing the Phoenician. "Tell your man to withdraw. He touches royalty."

"You are not king yet," said Ulthes, the feathery veins on his nose flushing red.

"Then you defy the gods to say so. I've come to tell you a lamb has been born on my estate with purple fleece. A prodigy. A sure sign that I am to be the gods' anointed king." He was almost breathless with excitement. "The omen is listed as one of the miracles in the Book of Fate. Crimson fleece signifies the owner of such offspring will be granted the greatest good fortune. It is clear the gods wish to grant me the divine right to rule."

The color rapidly drained from every man's face even as they slowly digested the announcement, but no man was paler than Ulthes. The zilath was a pious man, devoutly worshipping the Calu Death Cult. Although he counted Mastarna as his friend he did not share his disregard of portents. He was not taking the reported miracle lightly if it was, indeed, a sign that the gods were weary of rule by the electoral college.

Apercu rubbed his neck with chubby fingers, chewing on the import of the miracle like a cow on its cud. As the Maru, head of the college of the Pacha Cult of Fufluns, he was also known for his piety. He could not ignore the portent either.

"Let us dispense with your ridiculous election," continued Tulumnes, "for there is no doubting the miracle's meaning."

A furrow creased Vipinas's smooth waxen brow. Caecilia knew little about him other than he valued keeping a distance from those around him. He was silent as he grappled with the sanctity of the news, only the clicking of his gold and ivory teeth as his tongue worked against them revealed his disquiet. Being a religious man, he laid his hand upon her husband's arm in caution, but Mastarna shrugged him away.

"Where is this fleece? Or have you only just now been able to rid yourself of the purple dye upon your fingers?"

All in the room were quiet. Caecilia scanned the faces of the principes who were looking anywhere other than at Ulthes. Apercu kept rearranging the folds of his robes and Vipinas rubbed his hand repeatedly along the bronze armrests of his chair as though intent on wearing them away.

Tulumnes bristled. "Are you saying you're not prepared to take the word of a lord of Veii?"

Mastarna snorted. "And has my brother, the Great and Holy Haruspex and Fulgurator, seen this prodigy? Has he interpreted this so-called wonder?"

The assembled men gasped. Caecilia wished Ulthes would say something to rein in her husband. Once again his ridicule of Artile was dangerous.

His words, however, seemed to make Tulumnes uncertain. "Artile did not inspect it but when I described it to him he said there was no doubt it was one of the listed omens."

Tulumnes's response turned Mastarna's sliver of skepticism into a wedge. Doubt crept into the chamber.

"Where is this fleece now?"

The nobleman was not about to be cowed. Having traveled into his opponent's territory to prove his case, he did not falter. "It was burned, as all prodigies are required to be destroyed under sacred law."

The silence that fell was different than before—a pause signaling that all in the room shared the same questions rather than the same fears. Mastarna's possible sacrilege was of less concern now that Tulumnes was unable to provide evidence to verify his claim.

"Then did someone else other than you witness this?"

A sheen of sweat covered the princip's face like a cold frost on a metal goblet. He used his wrist to wipe it away. "You should not doubt the word of a lord," he said again.

"You are wasting our time," said Ulthes.

"Lord Pesna also saw it!"

Caecilia recalled the stoop-shouldered nobleman. He'd suffered a wound defending her on the road to Veii. The cut had healed but his contempt for her had not.

"And what did you promise Pesna to bear false witness for you?" spat Mastarna. "The right to rape the people with taxes and tribute once you are king?"

Apercu and Vipinas rose in their seats. Even if the fleece had been destroyed, two of their peers were saying they had seen a marvel. It was no small thing to accuse them of collusion.

"Forfeit your candidature, Arnth Ulthes," said Tulumnes, ignoring Mastarna, "and let me lead Veii to glory while we have the chance. For it is not only this prodigy that heralds change. Word has come that the Roman garrison at Verrugo has fallen. The Volscians have slaughtered any Roman soldier they could find."

Caecilia uttered a cry. All had forgotten her presence except Mastarna, who pulled her to his side.

Verrugo had fallen. Rome could be next.

Throughout her marriage she'd feared never returning home, but never that there might be nothing left if she did. Her city was meant to be invincible.

Had Marcus and Drusus been slain? Since leaving home both their lives could only be conjured from memory, but she always convinced herself she would see them again. She always told herself they were alive.

Falling to her knees, Caecilia put her hands to her face, tears hot against her skin, willing herself not to sob, feeling as forlorn as the morning she'd found Tata lying dead. Her cousin had later consoled her. Who then would soothe her over the death of Marcus?

Mastarna helped her to sit down, squeezing her shoulder gently as he stood beside her. "Don't believe him. The defeat might not be as bad as he claims."

Ulthes waved dismissively at Tulumnes. "Veii has no need to start a war and Rome is not yet conquered."

"It is best to strike when a foe is weak," countered the princip. "We may not have such an opportunity again."

"We have been through this all before," replied the zilath wearily. "Let the college decide these matters in the spring."

Not waiting to be ejected, Tulumnes turned to go. "Know then, Arnth Ulthes, that you and Mastarna offend the gods by offending me. Remember that when I have defeated you."

· · ·

The zilath sighed, closing his eyes as if he hoped life would look better when he opened them. Vipinas and Apercu sat with heads downcast.

There was nothing more Ulthes could ask of his peers other than faith. No small matter when it involved disbelieving one of their own. For when word got out of the purple fleece many would think that Fate had shown its hand and rumor would outstrip proof.

The enormity of Tulumnes's news affected Caecilia also. Before today she had come to believe Ulthes and Mastarna to be stronger than their rival. Now it was not altogether clear. The promise Ulthes had extracted from Mastarna not to start a civil war took on greater meaning. She understood her husband's frustration. If Tulumnes succeeded she would want Mastarna to fight, to stop the threat to her city and to his.

Slumped upon the chair, Caecilia pressed her fingers to her temples, trying to hold back the headache that encircled her skull and hammered the back of her eyelids. She murmured a prayer that the two Roman youths had somehow survived, conscious also that the consequences of being made hostage were more frightening than ever.

A voice inside her told her to endure, told her that Rome must endure also, but it was drowned out. Instead of a Roman hymn to fortitude, all she could hear was Artile's liturgy urging her to sup on fear and revere dread.

· · ·

In the stillness that followed Tulumnes's departure, the sounds of servants bustling about in preparation for the tournament filled the hush, the abrasive voice of the steward rising above the din.

The tension within the room was broken when Arruns returned from escorting Tulumnes to the door. The servant hovered cautiously beside his master, wishing to speak but unsure how to deal with Mastarna's mood. "Our chosen wrestler is ill, master," he said finally, "with stricken bowels and a rebellious stomach."

In the drama all had forgotten the entertainment. Mastarna scowled and swore as though nothing would be right that day. "Then tell the Greeks I will fight instead."

Ulthes growled impatiently. "Let another man fight. Greater things concern us than indulging in a pankration."

Arruns scratched his chin. "Their champion is much younger than you, master."

The comment merely goaded Mastarna. He roared at the Phoenician to tell the Greeks of the change.

Caecilia hoped Ulthes would compel her husband to see sense, but she knew it would be unlikely he'd succeed. Both had heard the familiar note in Mastarna's voice. Her husband was being given the chance to combat frustration by wrestling flesh and pummeling bone. It was easier than grappling with Tulumnes's miracle and his quest to be the king.

. . .

As the guests waited for the bout to begin, Caecilia sought comfort by Tarchon's side. He was bright-eyed and jittery, his encounter with the princip pushing him to chew Catha leaves. "Here, take some," he urged. Caecilia shook her head and once again cursed Artile for depriving her of enough Zeri.

The room was crowded and hot, everyone jostling for position around the small circle. The guests did not touch her, but whether it was because she was Mastarna's wife or a Roman she could not tell. She felt oddly disconnected, events moving too fast.

Word of Tulumnes's claim had not yet leaked to the various clansmen assembled there. The mood was buoyant and boisterous, somberness restricted to those few who'd met with Ulthes. Instead of his normal cheeriness Apercu looked as though he was suffering from indigestion. Vipinas's face bore the impatience of a school-master, disdainful of Mastarna's stunt as one is with a tiresome child. Ulthes was pensive, irritated by the rashness of his friend.

Caecilia tugged at Tarchon's sleeve. "Why doesn't Mastarna make Arruns fight the Athenian?"

"Pankration is for freeborn warriors to train them for war. Mastarna would insult Amyntor and the other Greeks if he offered a freedman as an opponent."

. . .

The Greek's hair hung in ringlets to his shoulder blades. Caecilia thought it odd on such a man, this vanity, so used was she to unkempt Romans or short-cropped Etruscans. Picturing how his lovers would plait the long curls into their own after lovemaking, she knew from gossip and Tarchon's admiration that it was not only women who could coil the tendrils around their fingers.

His hair was fair, not the brassy dye of Erene or the blond of the slave boys from the north, but the light brown of leaves when tired of their vividness. His eyes were a strange gray above a nose broken so often it had forgotten it was ever straight. As he twisted his hair into a knot, she noticed how his hands were bruised and cut in places. He did not smile, concentrating on what lay ahead as his trainer bound swollen knuckles, calloused palms, and scratched wrists with leather thongs, a meager protection.

But it was his soft, full-lipped mouth that made her wonder. Just as all who watched him were wondering, imagining, as he stripped and called for the oil, smoothing the sleekness across his sturdy thighs, arms, and calves, the triangle of his shoulders, chest, and waist, across the fine fair hair of his body, untouched by pitch or tweezers.

He enjoyed their scrutiny, expected it, did not acknowledge it. There was time enough later to make his choice. Liquid in his movements, Amyntor, champion of Olympia, rolled his shoulders, stretching his neck from side to side. Ready for the greatest contest of all. Brutal and bone cracking. A fight without limits, without rules, without mercy.

Pankration.

· · ·

Larthia had introduced Caecilia to Attic vases with their tiny red-lined figures jumping and fighting, singing and dancing, upon shiny black surfaces, captured forever in static movement.

Wearing only corselets of flesh, Mastarna and Amyntor looked as though they had leaped from such glazing into the ring, but unlike the painted figures they could struggle and tumble and kick their way through to victory or defeat, feet upon sawdust not within clay, explosive in motion.

The Greek was taller and younger than Mastarna, but the bulk of the Veientane's shoulders revealed how battles fought and men slain can build sinews and thews. There was knowledge and cunning within him, too. Caecilia prayed the wiliness that had helped him live as long as he had would see him victorious today.

The boxing ring was small, guaranteed to keep the fighters confined. Erene stood beside Ulthes, shrugging her shoulders as if to say she had seen too much of Mastarna's impetuosity to feel concern, or perhaps giving an assurance of sorts to the Roman.

A burly man from Thrace was the referee. He wielded a stout switch with which he could beat the competitors should they infringe the rules. Likewise, any spectator who edged too close would also receive a rap.

"Some fighters prefer to cheat and receive a thrashing from the referee rather than succumb to serious injury from their opponent," said Tarchon. "It could be a dirty fight."

• • •

Amyntor was sweating. The moisture beaded upon his oiled skin. Caecilia could feel his heat as he circled past her, eyes never leaving Mastarna's, as though besotted, wanting to enjoy violent embrace.

The Athenian was known to break his rival's fingers if given a chance. Mastarna did not wait for the younger man to strike, punching him with short hooking blows to his head. Blood erupted from the champion's nose, but the Greek only paused briefly to wipe it away and spit out a tooth.

Caecilia instinctively retreated, but the Veientanes jeered at Amyntor, who was leveling kicks at Mastarna's thighs and groin, which her husband dodged deftly. Each time the wrestlers shook their heads to clear their eyes of sweat or blood, droplets were flung in an arc across the crowd. And each time the people roared, seemingly oblivious to the spray, others licking it from their fingers. No matter how often it happened, Caecilia flinched.

Soon her neighbors forgot any reserve, shoving Caecilia aside to get a better view. Strangely, she found herself standing her ground by elbowing them in return. Her face was hot from the closeness of the room, smoke from the braziers looming above her. The stink of her neighbors assaulted her as they exhaled the remnants of their last meals: fish or pork mingled with wine. The reek of hair wax, perfume, and grease-streaked robes was nauseating, but most overpowering of all was the smell of sweat and excitement trickling from their pores. She was perspiring, too, realizing what was at stake: that Mastarna could be thrashed before her eyes, or maimed and crippled and beaten.

More than an hour passed. Neither wrestler seemed to be tiring. Both men tried to grapple the other to the ground, the oil upon their skin making it hard for either to gain an advantage.

Caecilia shifted from foot to foot to ease the soreness in her legs and back. She was grateful that Tarchon stood beside her, one hand holding her arm, guarding her from being shoved into the ring. "He could win," he said, "if he'd just get him in a choke hold."

Mastarna's right eye was bruised and his face cut. Every time he was pinned down or struck Caecilia felt a fist within her chest squeeze tight and then ease when he recovered. When the Greek grabbed her husband's hair, pulling his head down and hitting his throat and face, she found herself yelling with the others for Mastarna to break loose, urging him to do the same to his rival. Although repulsed by the sound of fists and feet thudding against muscle and bone, the stench of fighting, the viciousness of punching, and the twisting of limbs, she could not stop watching. She wanted Mastarna to win even if this meant Amyntor must suffer pain. There was only one other time she had felt close to such a feeling—when the bandit attacked her and then was killed.

Mastarna gained the advantage, grabbing Amyntor's leg when the Greek kicked out at him. The younger man twisted desperately in the joint lock. "Break his knee! Break his knee!" Tarchon was shrieking as fiercely as the others. Caecilia closed her eyes but only for an instant.

Amyntor, though, was champion of Olympia for a reason. Suddenly he arched backward and, placing his hands and the top of his head upon the ground, spun himself from the Veientane's hold. Mastarna was stunned and took too much time to gain composure. Jumping onto his back as though riding a horse, the Greek scissored his legs around Mastarna's abdomen while holding his arm across his windpipe.

The Greek supporters yelled, urging their man to finish him, to force him to yield. Mastarna staggered under the other's weight, trying to throw him, but Amyntor locked his legs behind his opponent's thighs, one arm squeezing his neck.

At first the Veientanes frantically urged Mastarna to resist, but as they watched him being strangled, his face scarlet, the veins on his neck bulging, their calls changed to "Yield! Yield!" The referee hovered, waiting to declare the winner.

After a few minutes all in the room realized Mastarna was not going to concede. The only sound in what had previously been clamor was his gasping as Amyntor kept pressure on his throat. Even the Athenian seemed confused, wondering why the challenger wanted to die, that he would have to be his killer.

When Caecilia's voice had become hoarse from calling to him, she glanced across at Erene. The hetaera's face was ashen. Caecilia knew then that her husband was mad, that not even the companion had seen him act so. Beating her way through the spectators to Ulthes, Caecilia clutched at the zilath's robes. "Make him yield!"

"I can't," he said, wincing as he listened to his friend's choking. "It's his choice."

Arruns had followed her. "Do something," she croaked. "Please, do something."

The Phoenician nodded toward the ring.

It happened rapidly, so rapidly that Caecilia was not quite certain how her husband managed to break free. Despite gaining a choke hold, Amyntor failed to push Mastarna to the ground. Unable to break the Greek's grip around his throat, Mastarna grabbed hold of Amyntor's thighs instead and began to rock until, losing balance, both men toppled to the side.

As the wrestlers hit the ground, Mastarna slammed all his weight onto Amyntor's ankle, snapping it as easily as a diner breaks a wishbone. The referee waited for the Greek to yield. The champion did not stop screaming as he raised his hand.

The Veientanes's roars were deafening. Mastarna had won.

The spectators crowded around him, hooting and yelling. There was little chance of Caecilia reaching him.

Still on his side in the ring, the champion of Olympia lay with chest heaving, his beautiful body streaked with sawdust and sweat, blood still streaming from his broken nose, red marks ready to bloom into bruises upon his flesh, cuts covering his face, his bones cracked and his eyes soft with pain.

There would be no lover for him tonight to comb his curling hair and kiss his torn and swollen lips. The night ahead was one of suffering and restlessness and ignominy.

He would never again know glory—his future that of a cripple.

• • •

Throwing a cloak around him, his admirers led Mastarna to a bench where he sat, hands resting lightly upon his thighs, shoulders relaxed, fatigue momentarily held at bay by triumph.

As people crowded about him, the Phoenician tried to bathe his master's wounds with vinegar, making Mastarna wince with each sting. His eye was swollen shut and blood from a cut on his cheek had only partially dried. Worst of all was the bruise upon his throat. The morning would no doubt reveal more injuries to add to old scars.

He was grinning despite this. Caecilia had never seen his mouth stretched in such delight before. She found herself smiling, too, the tension of watching him fighting replaced by the elation of all around her. But she did not try to break through the tight band of supporters around him, unsure of what to do.

Ulthes slapped him on the back. "As ever you are a fool, Vel."

His friend grinned even wider, and she sensed what it would have been like between these men when they fought side by side for Porsenna. Knowing Mastarna better than anyone, Ulthes had been right not to interfere. She doubted she would ever match his understanding.

Erene bent to Mastarna, her fingers trailing across the crushed redness on his throat. "One day you won't escape."

He kissed her hand with a flourish. "If so, make sure I die in a pankration, then I will know that death worked hard to take me."

Caecilia stiffened at their intimacy, resenting the fact that all around her seemed to know what to do and say. The Rasenna had gained energy from watching the possibility of him dying. This was what life was about—squeezing it dry.

Ulthes's good humor was short-lived. Knowing Mastarna was safe meant he could return to other worries. "We must talk before the Winter Feast starts. See to your hurts quickly."

Mastarna nodded, then waved everyone away. The supporters slowly drifted into groups, already beginning the task of exaggerating what they had witnessed. He turned to Arruns. "Where is Lady Caecilia?"

As she approached his smile flattered her, as did the way he stretched out his hand even though the bindings around his knuckles were wet with sweat and blood. "I am sorry if I frightened you," he said, but she could tell he was pleased with himself.

His vanity made her temper flare. Had he thought nothing about those he would have left behind? Larthia? Tarchon? Had he not thought of her?

"Why didn't you yield?"

Grasping her by the hips, he stood and pulled her to him. "Because peril is a drug—the choice of escape or standing fast."

"It is a sickness and you should have yielded."

"Don't be so cross," he laughed, kissing the mark upon on her neck that matched the weal upon his own. "Did you see how I made Nortia fight for me? And every time I thwarted her, the blood burst within me like a current."

Conscious that he was holding her in front of others, aware also of his nakedness beneath the cloak, Caecilia knew she should break away but she couldn't bring herself to do so. Her resentment disappeared. She wanted his euphoria, his urgency, for him to keep embracing her as though he wanted only her.

"See, my heartbeat is only now beginning to slow." He placed her hands upon his chest. His skin was hot, near feverish, the sweat upon him souring. "Did you feel nothing when you saw me gasping for breath?"

"Only that you were foolish." But her voice was not scolding. She could not forget the voice that shrieked within her when she saw Amyntor crushing his windpipe, nor her relief surging at his escape.

Fingers gliding over the oil upon his skin, she stroked the ridges of muscle beneath the slickness, pressing her body along his, eyes widening as she felt him harden.

Mastarna wrapped his arms tightly around her, his mouth tasting of salt and heat as he kissed her. "Lie with me tonight," he murmured, laying his battered cheek against hers, "beneath the reed."

There was a pause as she took in his words, their meaning lagging behind for a fraction as when thunder sounds after lightning has already struck.

Thoughts of Erene flickered within her. Aware that the hetaera was observing them. Listening to them. Laughing at her for having been halfway lured into the indecency he was suggesting that night. Shame filled her. Greater than humiliation. Greater than embarrassment. How they must all be sniggering at her. At the prudish Roman who had forgotten modesty.

Forcing herself away from him, she ran, wondering if she would ever find a chamber large enough in that colossal house in which to hide forever.

• • •

"Drusus would never have dishonored me in such a way."

Cytheris shook her head as she watched her mistress pace the bedchamber. Caecilia thought she did so with a provincial girl's disapproval for immorality but she was mistaken. "Mistress, why talk about that Roman boy again? A memory doesn't keep you warm in bed as does a husband."

Caecilia glared at her, not wanting to admit the truth of the handmaid's statement. As always, she knew the Greek girl spoke sense. The thought of the red-haired youth as an avenger somehow seemed ridiculous. Drusus paled against the sheer brute force of her husband, who could snap the ankle of Amyntor, champion of Olympia.

Caecilia looked over to the wooden wall shelf where she had placed her special keepsakes, tiny souvenirs: Marcus's amulet, her mother's yellowing ivory fascinum, and her father's stylus with his teeth marks scored upon it. And, of course, her little juno. All these things were her comfort, their smoothness or roughness engendering memories as she stroked them.

There had never been a memento from Drusus upon the shelf. Their acquaintance had been fleeting; her meetings with him counted in days, not weeks. Now he could be dead. Her stomach lurched at the thought.

She'd heard the inconsolable sorrow of women wailing over the death of a husband or son, seen the cold gnawing grief of Mastarna for his dead wife and children. If Drusus were truly dead, could she grieve in the same way for a man who was made more of imagination than flesh?

Cytheris handed her mistress a fresh candle of red wax. "I think you are being too hard on the master," she said quietly. "I don't think he wished to insult you."

"How can you say that?"

"Because while Mistress Seianta was alive the master lay with no other women."

"What has Mastarna's faithfulness to his dead wife mean to me?"

Cytheris put the taper to the wick and waited for the flame to steady. "Because, mistress, they say it is a sign of love for a husband to choose a wife instead of a courtesan with which to lie beneath the reed."

• • •

The mood of the feast was subdued. The fervor and excitement of the tournament had faded. Apart from the Greeks, everyone had the air of children who had overexcited themselves and were now exhausted from their efforts.

Attention had turned from the pankration to the purple fleece. Not all the nobles were as dismissive of the omen as Mastarna.

Caecilia sat beside him as he lay upon the dining couch, determined not to meet his eye or brush against him. Once again an awkwardness had arisen between them. He looked troubled. The ecstasy of escaping death had ebbed, the familiar shadows of the everyday returning. The skin around his eye was dark as a plum and the mark on his neck livid. After his proposition she'd expected merriment and the good humor of which Erene had spoken. Instead he went grimly about drinking, swallowing each mouthful with determination to foster moroseness and short temper.

There was no apology. Cytheris's advice suggested that he probably did not think he'd caused offense. Yet Caecilia reasoned that he must know he'd contravened his promise to Aemilius.

There was sympathy, however. "Don't weep yet, Caecilia. Marcus may yet be alive. I am sure your uncle will send word of what occurred at Verrugo." Mistaking her unease for weariness, he touched her shoulder. "If you are tired, why not go to bed?"

Caecilia scanned his face, seeing only bruises and exhaustion. Surveying the other men who had gathered to discuss their concerns she understood, with relief, that no reed screens would be used that night.

As she bid her guests good night, Caecilia passed Erene. The hetaera lay beside the zilath, wearing a turban held fast by a diadem of garnets, a wreath of flowers encircling her headdress, alien and elegant. She'd been politely distant to Caecilia all evening, offering no reassurance, as if to say she'd suffered humiliation too often to be troubled by the worries of an inexperienced wife. The courtesan's indifference was disconcerting after the confidences shared during the day.

It appeared, however, that the companion did have some more advice for Caecilia. When the hetaera saw her hostess leaving, she slipped from Ulthes's couch and followed her to the door. "I watched Mastarna with you today. I saw how he was with you. Do not hasten to spurn him. You may yet displace Seianta from his bed."

• • •

The cool night air did not calm her as she walked to the outer courtyard, hoping the cold would seep within her, numb her, make her disappear.

The sound of bawdy laughter and a joyous song of prayer floated to her.

Fufluns, Fufluns, Fufluns
Oh, listen to my prayer.
May all the wine in my cellar
Prove to be strong and rare.

The Winter Feast was in progress, a celebration of the nearing of the end of the wine god's sojourn in Acheron. The villagers had built a bonfire, its smoke and sparks shooting heavenwards to the clear, crisp sky. Some noblemen and the Greek visitors had joined them. Drunk and ribald, they were rejoicing that the fruit of the vine was fermenting in casks and would soon be ready for drinking. Caecilia smiled, remembering the rustic festivals of her people.

Silhouettes were outlined against the flames as revelers capered and leaped in abandon. Drawing nearer she saw some men were wearing phalluses tied around their waists, the leather penises jiggling and bobbing as they danced. The Roman edged nearer, reminded of the harmless bawdiness she'd seen when spying peasants celebrating the Liberalia on Tata's farm.

Coming closer still, Caecilia began to feel uneasy, the comparison with plebeian celebrations fading. Some of the villagers were wearing satyr masks, others those of animals: goat or wolf or ram, grotesque and frightful. The fire's heat was like a wall around them. Some people had stripped, figures were merging, thrusting, shuddering: man with woman, man with man and, most appalling of all, unspeakable and forbidden, women entwined around each other.

Fleeing to the courtyard, Caecilia huddled amid frostbitten date palms and other exotics, shaking with shock as much as with cold.

. . .

After swallowing all the Zeri from the alabastron, Caecilia hurled it against the bedroom wall, frustrated that her supply was now empty.

Tiny glass shards spun across the tiled floor. She told herself to stop thinking, to wait until the Zeri's magic found purchase, to let the mess of emotions settle so she could make sense of them tomorrow. Yet it was not so easy.

Lying down upon the bed, she sobbed. Not with the despairing melancholy of her wedding but choking and furious, as though rage had found voice, cadence, and rhythm.

Threats had stabbed at her all day—of war and monarchy, of death and grief—but it was Mastarna's behavior that distressed her most.

Cytheris and Erene were telling her she must no longer be embarrassed and disgusted, that it was a blessing that Mastarna wanted her to act as a Veientane. The struggle of feelings was so tiring, this pull toward him that only her Romanness restrained, this pull to which another Caecilia, deep within her, wanted to yield.

Mastarna had become more than a lover. He offered solace in the utter darkness, a guarantee that, should dreams bring demons

or ghosts, flesh and blood lay within reach together with steady
breathing and the scent of sandalwood. It was hard then to understand the way in which he had finally chosen to show he cared.
Why he'd asked her to lie beneath the reed instead of drawing her
close that morning, the planes and curves of their bodies molded
together until dawn.

SIXTEEN

Saturnalia.

When the earth lay plowed, seeded, and dormant, and spring was chiding its chilly brother to surrender the world to her.

Saturnalia. When both patricians and the people feasted on suckling pig, and slaves were feted by their masters, relieved of toils and troubles for a day. All joyous for the return of light after the winter solstice.

It was Caecilia's favorite festival: where a woman could join in the rites, not just observe them, where children could sit and feast with the grown-ups, and where Tata would let her join in the parties with family friends.

After witnessing the debauchery of the Winter Feast, Caecilia was determined to show how a festival could be observed in the Roman way. And with Mastarna away helping Ulthes, the non-sense of the celebrations distracted her from her worries, giving her a chance to forget how he had hurt her.

With her efforts to share her people's customs, Caecilia's thoughts strayed to what would be happening in Rome. Not in Aemilius's stuffy household but in the countryside where, with rustic merrymaking, sacrifices would be made to the dark and brooding Saturn, god of sowing, and Juno Lucina, bringer of light.

As befitting the custom, she gave the servants their freedom for a day. Doing so for Cytheris was of little consequence compared to freeing the slave forever. The maid could have made the most of her brief power by ordering Caecilia to serve her wine or fetch her slippers, but she refused. Instead, Cytheris had resumed doling out doses of wisdom in all matters but one. She avoided warning her mistress about Seianta and the Book of Fate.

Aricia was soon sick from eating too many currants, and cake crumbs trailed from hidden morsels stashed in her pockets. Despite constraints of rank, Caecilia had begun to spoil the little girl, secretly replacing Cytheris's harsh words with kind ones. The Saturnalia custom gave her the excuse she'd been looking for to embrace her. Lifting Aricia into her arms, heavy-limbed and weary against her shoulder, Caecilia felt the child's curls brush her throat. And as she laid the little one to bed, she stole a kiss, relieved to know that, unlike Aemilia, she could love a child after all.

As she returned to the dining room, Caecilia noted Artile was absent but Tarchon was good-naturedly serving wine to a slave boy, keen to participate in her party. And, watching him, she was once again reminded of Marcus. If he were no longer alive, should she enjoy the feast?

No word had come from Aemilius since the Roman defeat. In fact, all official communication had ceased. An ominous silence.

Rumor had spread, though. A plague was raging through her city, a pox with scabrous sores and mange spread from cats and dogs. The world twelve miles from here would be a sad sight.

Yet she still wished to see it, wanted to know again how it felt to wake, every day, to a world that was honorable and pious.

• • •

When it became clear that Larthia was failing, any enjoyment in the household waned. Tarchon called Artile, who hastened to his mother's side and filled her chamber with candle scent and comfort, the air thick with soothing chants and prayers. Gone was the foreboding haruspex, and in his place stood a man who could lay hands upon the dying matron both as sorrowing son and consoling priest.

Caecilia and Tarchon would wait upon Larthia, dismissing her maids and tending to her needs, but the only solace Ati wanted, the only sustenance left to crave, was Artile's gift. Tarchon would trickle drops upon her swollen tongue, waiting for the painful swallowing to finish before administering more. Caecilia knew a dribble would never be enough to banish Larthia's pain or nourish her dreams. She knew because she, too, was finding Artile's Zeri to be lacking of late, that her dreams were growing shorter, her bliss less.

In the half-world between living and dying, Larthia would call to her Mastarna, requesting that she, like him, be buried, not burned, so that she might again hold him. Eternally faithful to this one man through life and in death—a univir. It was a Roman standard that Caecilia had not thought a Rasennan woman would desire to attain, let alone possess.

Yet Larthia's fidelity should not have surprised her, for the Veientane matron was more Roman than the girl expected. Stoic and proud and pious, the matriarch had shown how even a Veientane could choose restraint; loving feasts but not getting drunk, tolerating decadence but not partaking of it. Ati had given her a glimpse of how it might be possible to live with dignity in Veii.

And so, as she watched the matron suffer, Caecilia found herself retracing the steps of grief her father taught her to tread, wondering how she'd come to love this woman in so short a time.

Saddened to know that even if Aemilia had lived, no such love would have been forthcoming.

When the men were absent she'd curl Larthia's fingers around her own. "Winter will soon be over, Ati. Sunlight grows and the shadows begin to shorten. It is not time for you to shut off the light."

Ati. Mother.

A different word for a different mother.

A similar death but a sweeter farewell.

The Roman girl's good-bye to Aemilia had been dutiful and brief, a small girl's lips brushing a cold dead brow. This time she was no longer a child; this time she understood the desperate need to ensure last kisses were bestowed upon still-warm flesh, to have the dying whisper out her name, to be called daughter.

• • •

After the pankration, Artile had welcomed Caecilia without chastisement for her country sojourn, greeting her as a father would a favored child who's become frightened of what is out of her control.

If Caecilia expected him to be eager to discuss the message behind Tulumnes's portent, she was disappointed. Yet it did seem that her brother-in-law enjoyed watching the impact of his role in the princip's tale, like a cook who sips soup after adding salt, gauging whether his addition has made his supper tastier or not.

"Is it true what they say? Does the purple fleece truly presage fortune for its owner?"

Artile's tone was weary. "I've already told you that all miracles have been noted and recorded. A fact my brother fails to understand." There was a taint of bitterness in his voice, his animosity, as always, muted compared to Mastarna's open contempt. Of late, though, his rancor sometimes seeped through his reserve, especially after her husband's steps to exclude Tarchon. It was not easy to forget how Artile had studied his young lover at her wedding, a vigilance she now knew was a jealous need.

There was no further talk of prodigies and politics. Artile knew her needs remained the same. Caecilia, too, was relieved to resume their routine.

"My vial of Zeri is empty," she said before she had even begun her worship.

"Then show greater piety, Sister."

She listened to what was required—more blood sacrifices, more time at prayer. In return the elixir would be granted for both rituals—the first convincing Nortia to postpone her child's first breath, and the other persuading Aita to save her after she'd breathed her last. Twice the devotion, double the return.

Caecilia knelt before the haruspex, even keener that she must observe the rites, belly tightening, thirsty for the Zeri.

• • •

Mastarna was due to return at any day but had been delayed. As word spread of the astonishing fleece, superstitious tenants and clansmen gathered to discuss its import in every town square and turf shrine and market. He and Ulthes were spending much time and coin to ensure the gossip was countered, but both knew the whiff of a miracle was too alluring to be spoiled by fact.

He was urgently summoned from his business as Ati grew weaker. His mood sent the servants scurrying and set Caecilia's teeth on edge. Unlike his brother there were only sharp edges to Mastarna's worry and harshness to his queries, his resentment at the gods for taking another of his family palpable. When he first saw his mother sleeping, he grasped her hands so tightly that she woke suddenly and surprised. Although Larthia nodded at his urgings that she get better, Caecilia could see that once again Ati was humoring her adult son as though he were a child.

As Larthia lay dying, Caecilia and Mastarna spoke rarely, she tending to his mother, he attending to the threat to the zilath. Neither spoke of the pankration or the Winter Feast. He seldom slept in their bed, instead snatching rest at the palace where strategy was being devised. There he could avoid watching the anguish of Ati's last days, last hours, last rasping breaths. When he did lie in their chamber he did so after Caecilia had gone to sleep, not even waiting for dawn before he arose, choosing the oppressive darkness of the dead hours to make his escape.

Each time she woke to find him gone, emptiness filled her as she realized that her longing for Rome was being replaced with a yearning for him.

• • •

Larthia's last words were a murmur of thanks to her daughter for a small candle, some sweets, and a tiny statue of Juno Lucina. She smiled, too, although feebly, glad to be dying when people laughed and sang and prayed for the return of spring.

When Ati died Mastarna shed no tears. Nor did he seek out risk as was his usual remedy for pain. Instead he was resolutely composed as befitting the head of a clan, and Caecilia was relieved to find him acting as would a Roman.

He wanted no words of comfort or touch, rebuffing her attempts at consolation. He did not ignore her grief, though. "Know that she loved you," he said gruffly, and held her in an embrace so fleeting compared to the heated urgency of the pankration she wondered if it could be the same man. The brief caress only added to her melancholy that they could not share and soothe each other's sorrow.

A sense of loneliness filled the House of Mastarna as it retreated into mourning, making Caecilia seek out shadowy corners, feeling like she had been abandoned, needing Marcus to be there.

• • •

Snowflakes were falling, replacing the gray ash upon the mourners' hair with pure white, streaking their faces with sky-sent tears.
Caecilia did not need such artificial signs of lamentation. Her eyes
were swollen from crying and she felt numb inside without assistance from the cold. Tarchon, too, was pale-faced and weary with
grief.

Larthia's funeral procession marched slowly from the city of
the living into that of the dead. Mastarna and Artile led the mourners, walking on either side of a two-wheeled carriage upon which
the bier was borne. The two brothers avoided each other's gaze.
Mutual grief had not brought them closer and Caecilia knew that
every moment spent together at the funeral would be awkward.

Behind them acolytes guided two black bulls, victims to be
sacrificed to Aita, two souls that would be released for Larthia and
her dead husband to claim. Caecilia considered their sleekness,
the latent force of muscle and bone, the potency of their seed. To
acquire the souls of such splendid creatures would surely endow
Ati and her husband with great power in the Beyond.

A column of lamenting women followed, walking two by two
in solemn progress, the hems of their long, finely pleated chitons
trailing in the muddy slush. A fold of their heavy woolen cloaks
partly covered the diadems crowning their unbound hair. Some
raised their fingers to scratch their cheeks in despair, others held
tiny palm trees made of gold in veiled hands. Their shrieks and
wails were as jarring as the discordant notes from the aulos. It was
the first time Caecilia had heard Veientane musicians play other
than sweet harmonies. The fractious notes and gloomy drumbeats
set her nerves on edge.

Next came Ulthes and other dignitaries arrayed in vivid finery even though their mood was somber. Priests and merchants
followed, and then Larthia's artisans, hands cracked from sculpt-
ing clay all day into rough bucchero or fine red-and-black vases.

Mastarna's tenants and slaves were there, too, faces scrubbed and clothes freshly washed.

All attending a majestic funeral of a woman, mother of the richest man in Veii, matriarch of the House of Mastarna. All bringing offerings both humble and grand.

The funeral procession halted in front of the altar. Beside it, a canopy had been rigged over a monumental bed covered with costly cloth of gold. Larthia's fragile body looked almost childlike as it sank into the deep mattress. For a moment Caecilia thought she heard Ati sigh at finally being allowed to rest. How like the Rasenna to provide such comfort to the deceased. How like them to remind the grieving that all life revolved around a simple rectangle, where marriage was consummated, pleasure sought, children conceived, sleep gained, dreams welcomed, and death awaited.

Compared to the horror of Tata's pyre, the peaceful fate of Larthia reassured Caecilia that she was right to follow Artile, that she must be doubly resolute to attain divinity for her parents and herself.

• • •

When his mother died, Artile shed no tears. He, like his brother, kept his reserve. After ministering to his mother in her last days on earth with such tenderness and care, Caecilia thought he would be desolate. While Mastarna's composure thinly veiled his grief, the priest's peculiar calmness made him seem as though he was heartless, until, with the snow forming a mantle on his hat and sheepskin shawl, he commenced the funeral ceremony—and faltered.

Artile, who never erred, trembled so that wine spilled from the patera offering dish and prayers stumbled from his mouth. Over and over again he fumbled with hymns and stammered the litany so that, over and over again, the rites had to be recommenced. Not even when the oboe and drum played louder to drown out the mistakes could the crowd ignore how Artile, knuckles white, clenched the patera, desperate to right imperfection and salvage pride.

However, when it came time to sacrifice the first bull, the chief haruspex regained his calm. The consecration of the victim steadied him. He would make no mistakes when the salvation of his mother was at stake. As life bled from the beast, its soul escaped, trapped by a net woven with strands of Larthia's piety.

The Roman thought there would be some sign to herald that the gods had accepted Ati, but there was nothing. Only the shifting of the people in the cold, the ribbon of the paean's melody entwining them while the other bull moaned, straining against its halter, steam rising from its body into the chillness, knowing that it was next to be offered for Larthia's Mastarna, oblivious of the honor of being a gift for the Lord of Acheron.

• • •

Passing down between the crouching stone leopards that flanked the entrance to the tomb, Caecilia clutched nine black beans, food for ghosts. Her short nails dug into their firm skin with brief resistance. Aurelia had schooled her well to fear specters. And what better place for a ghoul to attack her than when inching her way, head stooped, down the steep wooden ramp to Larthia's tomb. She surreptitiously dropped a trail of the beans, hoping the spirits weren't greedy enough to ask for more. In truth she should have chewed and spat them out and, standing barefoot, brought pots and pans to clang and drive the evil ones away, but she did not think her husband would look kindly on Roman superstition.

Edging her way along the low-roofed hallway of the tomb she found herself laboring for breath, the dankness filling her nostrils, thick within her throat. In front of her Mastarna blocked what little light was provided by the torch. Pressing close upon his heels, she noticed there was still some unmelted snow upon his shoulders. Tarchon inched his way behind her. Artile had already gone before them to prepare the grave.

The corridor widened. Cockroaches scuttled from dark corners. When Mastarna dislodged a large vase, slaters slithered away to escape the light. Caecilia found herself walking between waist-high biers with crumbling skeletons tucked upon them as though a cook had stacked olives and fruits within a larder. She wondered if Tuchulcha had sucked the life force from them and spat out the bones to molder in the darkness.

Still numb from the winter's chill outside, her fingers blue from cold, Caecilia stepped into the warmth of a chamber of such dazzling splendor she soon found breath enough to gasp despite air heavy with clouds of incense. It was as though she stood in a small replica of Mastarna's house with its familiar wooden lintels and doorframes, tables and couches—even clothes hanging from hooks on the wall. All an illusion perfectly painted upon stone. But there was real enough treasure as well: plates and utensils and food, with a host of slave statuettes to serve Ati's spirit. Other presents, too: vases and pitchers, jewelry and coins.

Here there was no need for a family tree upon an atrium wall or the waxen heads of great men within a cupboard. True to their beliefs, the Rasenna had set up house for eternity—luxury and comfort and riches all around them, and nourishing food to eat and wine to drink, all there in the hope that this would give them succor after Vanth met them at the gate and welcomed them inside.

· · ·

Larthia's face had hardened into stone.

The sunken ravaged mouth and stumps of teeth had vanished along with thinning hair and brittle bones. Her lips were parted in desire, contoured and sensual, softened by youth.

She lay naked in effigy upon her coffin, fixed forever in her nuptial bed. Lying on her side, she faced her husband, their arms encircling each other, swathed in their transparent wedding shroud and unconcerned that their bare feet were uncovered in abandon.

Caecilia gasped at the flagrant display of affection chiseled for eternity within the bedchamber that was their tomb. Thought also of the orange veil she'd wished she'd worn for Drusus, and of the wedding mantle she had shared with Mastarna and his memories.

The poignancy of Larthia finally sharing the afterlife with her husband was also a barb. Caecilia knew that even if she had married Drusus she would be alone in death, her ashes steeped in wine and honey within an urn, relegated to a niche within her husband's tomb. In Veii there would be little hope of joining Mastarna either upon or within a casket while competing with Seianta.

On the side of the coffin was another surprise revealing how Rasennan women were valued. Carved into the stone beside her husband's name were the words "I am Larthia Atelinas." Listed below were both her parents' names, proof that she was more than a possession of her father, proof that she was considered part of two bloodlines, a privilege Aemilia Caeciliana had only received through her uncle's reluctant adoption.

Caecilia watched as Tarchon and Mastarna carefully laid Ati within the coffin. The movement stirred the dust within. When it settled, husband and wife finally lay together, the bridal mantle now their shroud, whispering their vows beneath it—again.

In the cramped confines of the inner chamber, Caecilia noticed Mastarna was intent on studying a sarcophagus other than that of his parents. It lay in a dark corner. Another husband and wife reclined upon it. Next to it was a small funerary urn decorated with a pattern of dancing children. Mastarna's children—jars brimming with a mother's loss.

Caecilia's terra-cotta enemy smiled at her from the gloom. Erene was right. Seianta was not beautiful, but there was a smooth, round contentment to her as she sat upon a dining couch with her husband, head resting against his shoulder as he embraced her. Their happiness revealed by the curve of their lips and the ease of their touch, the tenuousness of Seianta's claim upon him as concrete as it was fragile as she willed him to join her in the grave.

Immediately, Caecilia felt as though fingers were stroking the nape of her neck. As she shivered, Seianta bumped her, squeezing in beside her husband. Determined not to give in to the ghost's pushiness, Caecilia leaned against Mastarna, wanting him to put his arm around her, to show the sloe-eyed girl with the elegantly plaited hair that he was hers now, that flesh and blood, not kiln-hardened arms, could embrace him.

Yet what did it matter if Mastarna cared for her in life? It was clear that when he died he wished his ashes to sit next to Seianta's. And then where would Caecilia lie? Would her urn, as in Rome, lie forgotten in the dimness of the tomb? Would anyone in Veii sacrifice a bull to gain her salvation? And if Marcus were dead, would anyone pick roses or violets to remember her in Rome?

She felt like she was nothing. Less than nothing. Displaced among the living, unwanted amid the dead.

The incense and smoke from the lamps was making her dizzy. She thought she'd never take another breath that was not filled with the expirations of the Shades. In an effort not to fall, she clutched at Mastarna. He looked down at her in concern, encircling her shoulders as she had wished. It was a pity he did so only from compassion; she wanted him to show Seianta that she truly had a rival.

Leading Caecilia to one of the shelves carved into the wall, Mastarna directed her to rest. She perched uncomfortably beside a skeleton covered with the armor of some long-ago warrior. "Sit for a time," he said. "It's stuffy in here. We should not need to stay much longer."

A sharp pain in her bowels made her flinch and she could feel herself perspiring. It had been many weeks since she had emptied her bowels without a purgative and the discomfort nagged at her. She had lost interest in eating, the treats of the Saturnalia alone tempting her, and only Zeri easing the pain. She glanced over to Artile, cursing him for not letting her have more, resenting him for always making it a little harder to receive it. Mastarna had said this would happen, that her craving for any potion would become stronger than the draft could satisfy.

To distract her from her discomfort, Caecilia looked at the murals that lined the chamber of the sepulchre. One was of a man and woman walking in a forest of subtle greens and dappled light. Padding beside them were beasts both fearsome and tame: panther and bear, cat and hound, dancing among a tangle of ivy in Fufluns's world. At the far end of the chamber was a door. A painted entrance. The door to the Beyond. On either side of it towered demons guarding the portal to Acheron as fiercely as the stone cats protected the entrance to the tomb.

Artile stood with a patera full of wine and blood, ready to offer the family's final vows and thanks.

Mastarna covered his head with his cloak and knelt in prayer. Caecilia had watched him, as master of the house, give offerings at the family hearth, but this was the first time she'd seen him in a truly reverential pose, a supplicant, obeisant. Gone was the frantic railing against the gods or the manic celebration of Nortia. Lighting three candles wreathed with ivy, he laid a golden thyrsus staff upon the casket, the pinecone tip fashioned from amber—a sign to show Fufluns that his mother was worthy of his attention.

Tarchon offered a golden mirror and Artile presented a linen book containing holy text. When Caecilia's turn came, her hands shook slightly as she offered a delicate alabastron of lapis lazuli, glad that Larthia, finally freed from pain, would carry perfume alone to the afterlife. Zeri would no longer be needed.

Mastarna gestured to Artile to begin his liturgy, then stood back against the narrow opening into the room. Although her husband did not believe in the Calu Cult he would not deny his mother final prayers. After all, her journey to the Beyond had already started. Even as her family prayed within her tomb, she could be facing Vanth.

Artile gestured for Tarchon to kneel. And then to Caecilia.

Sweat streamed down her face knowing that Mastarna would be confronted by her worship. She wiped it away with the edge of her robe, but it still trickled across her scalp. It had not occurred to her that she would be called upon to undertake the sacraments of Aita today, thinking the burnt offering of the bulls would be devotion enough.

Artile nodded reassuringly. "Kneel, Sister."

As she knelt she heard Mastarna grunt and shift his weight. Then she felt his fingers touch her shoulder as he crouched beside her.

"Do you truly wish to do this?" he asked quietly.

The pain in Caecilia's belly sharpened. The priest was offering solace after death. To disobey him would also deprive her of what she needed most. She was burning within, her skin itchy, her throat, the back of her hands, her face.

"Your wife is a believer," said Artile, holding the offering bowl in both hands. "How does that make you feel, Brother? When a Roman can understand the desires of the gods better than you?"

Mastarna gently pulled Caecilia to standing while Tarchon scrambled to his feet beside Artile, drawing up the lines of conflict. Mastarna spoke to Caecilia only. "You should not take heed of his cant."

He stepped toward his parents' coffin and traced the lines of their carved faces. "After all these years they lie together but, if Artile is correct, my father has been tormented by demons and my mother must struggle to be saved from the same fate."

"Both feast in Acheron together now," blurted Tarchon, his voice breaking in fury as only the voices of children and youths can. "Ati made sacrifice enough to make grandfather one of the Blessed, too. You are wrong to act the heretic. You are wrong."

Artile put a finger to his lips to silence his young lover and turned to Mastarna. "Brother, perhaps you prefer Fufluns's promise of rebirth because of Seianta. Can't you feel her here, unable to gain salvation because you are not pious enough? It is you who should be on your knees seeking deliverance for your family."

Mastarna's cry filled all the space within the chamber. With a sweep of his arm, he scattered the candles, lamps, and votives, the oil flashing blue as flame briefly ignited it. Then he snatched the golden patera from Artile's hands, ready to dash it to the ground.

"You desecrate her tomb," said the priest, his voice raised, his eyes hard as his brother's. "Do not damn her before she has even knelt before Lord Aita."

Mastarna's breathing was ragged. Scanning the damage and swallowing hard, he slowly lowered the dish onto the coffin. "I did not mean to dishonor her."

Caecilia did not know what to do or say. Mastarna's sacrilege had gone beyond self-destruction. He had insulted the gods when his mother was upon their threshold. He could not have acted more rashly or more cruelly.

Face drained of color, he ran from the tomb into the narrow corridor and up the steep ramp into the day.

Caecilia felt as though the weight of the tomb above her would collapse and crush her. In a way she would welcome an end to her turmoil.

Tarchon shook as he relit the candles. Caecilia, too, found her hand was trembling as Artile commenced the rites, making sure to add prayers in placation and expiation, lengthening the time they must stay within this gravesite.

Holy Lord Aita who rules us all.
For you we bring gifts of silver and gold, flowers and incense and wine.
For you we have burned two bulls and offered their blood.
We give thanks for granting Larthia's request.
May my parents live as one divine under your protection.
May you reign gloriously forever!

The haruspex was no longer hesitating and confused. He did not waver as he gave Caecilia the cup of blood and wine to drink, confident in his purpose, guiding her thanksgiving for Larthia's deification.

The blood was warm and thick. Caecilia gagged on its taste. Artile was watching, but she could not be anything but grateful. He had not revealed to her husband that she also prayed to Nortia for a different purpose.

He stroked her hair soothingly.

He prayed.

SEVENTEEN

It stopped snowing, the clouds banished. The sky was so blue Caecilia thought it had been painted to achieve such perfection.

She sat in a stadium. Around her the Veientanes had come out in their splendor, their felt conical caps pinpoints of color across the expanse of seating. Gone was the gloominess of the funeral procession. The mourners had turned into spectators, noisy and exuberant. Larthia's journey to Acheron was to be celebrated by games dedicated to her alone. Astonishing.

How provincial the funerals of dead Roman magistrates seemed compared to the massive and sophisticated parade for Ati's funeral. And now there were to be games and a banquet, as if declaring that all in the Mastarna family were heroes, not just those who had been zilaths, announcing that a matriarch could command not only respect but be lauded through pageantry as well.

The prospect of such entertainment did little to distract Caecilia from what had happened in Larthia's tomb. Sitting beside her, Mastarna was withdrawn after his sacrilege, his stillness freezing, like ice so cold it would burn to touch.

Suddenly an explosion of cheering overwhelmed her. The crowd roared as Ulthes entered and took his seat, signaling the games to begin. Jugglers and tumblers whirled about in flashes of color and speed to the accompaniment of music. Acrobats and athletes followed, competing in footraces, jumping with weights in their hands, hurling javelin and discus.

As they left the arena, Artile entered, followed by a peculiarly clad man. At his appearance the crowd erupted into cheers: "Phersu! Phersu!" The name was familiar but Caecilia could not recall why. The man bowed to Ulthes, who acknowledged him with a nod.

The stranger wore a high stiffened conical hat. Also a short tunic, which better displayed his stocky build, broad chest, powerful arms, and massive thighs. The arrogance of his stance proclaimed he must have trained for hours to achieve such strength, but this is not why Caecilia shivered when she studied him.

The Phersu's face was covered by a mask. Vermilion with a black-pointed beard attached, the mouth frozen in a rictus, dark holes for eyes—the face of a demon, grinning and malicious.

Mastarna touched her wrist, making her jump in fright. "If you truly wish to observe the Calu Cult, don't look away and don't show distress. The people will think you are offending the heavens if you do."

"What do you mean?"

"The Phersu is an instrument of the gods. He spills blood to revitalize the dead."

Caecilia did not fully understand his warning but she did not take it lightly. The fear she'd known when she'd begged Uni for protection at the Great Temple was only ever thinly disguised.

The howls of the crowd hindered any further conversation.

The Phersu remained alone in the arena. An enormous hound was led to him. It was liver-colored with pale-yellow eyes, slivers of drool dripping from its jaws. The man held the hound by its leash firmly, giving it no slack. It was clear the beast knew its master. A nail protruded from its collar into its flesh.

A prisoner, hands bound behind his back and tethered around the neck, was dragged before the crowd. To Caecilia's horror, the Phersu placed a leather bag over the man's head, then freed his hands to give him a wooden club. Yanking the dog's lead so that the nail bit into its neck, the cur howled, barking and snapping with pain, lunging at the hooded man fruitlessly until the Phersu let the leash go slack.

On hearing the animal's snarling the blinded prisoner lurched back in terror, urine trickling down his legs as he tried to run. The Phersu reined him in even as he let the hound have its way.

Suddenly Caecilia was in a cocoon created by the mob as they stood up, sound and passion surrounding her. It was as though the crowd had become a great beast, one that could be good-natured but now was maddened with fever, ready to spring. It reminded her of the contagion of emotion at the pankration, only this was greater, this was overpowering. One had become many—all had one thought, one feeling.

Behind her Tarchon was, as usual, shouting as loudly as the rest. She stared at this creature of Veii, beautiful but flawed, thinking his ecstatic spirit would explode from him at any moment as pulp bursts from a tight-skinned fruit.

Blood spurted from the man's thigh and flank. The dog was hanging from him, its fangs sunk deep into his flesh. The victim vainly tried to strike the beast with his cudgel, staggering under the attack.

Mastarna sat stiffly, saying nothing, expressionless.

Caecilia was sweating. A cold clamminess. Bile rose in her throat.

Mastarna glanced at her, his sternness easing. "Stay calm, it's nearly over."

The savagery continued until the Phersu finally let the cur leap at the man's throat. Gouts of blood soaked into the slush.

Caecilia had no more courage left to watch as she heard the hound's barking turn to the territorial growling of a house dog as it worried at a bone. She turned to find Arruns focused upon her instead of the human sacrifice within the arena. At that moment she remembered why the title of the executioner was familiar. Arruns had once been the Phersu. The masked one. Mastarna had called him that after the raid.

Caecilia stared at the tattoo of the serpent coiling around Arruns's neck, its blue-inked fangs devouring half his face, needing no mask to strike terror. And yet she had come to trust the servant, felt his menace was directed at her enemies, not against her. "You were the Phersu?"

He nodded, his gaze unwavering, no sign of shame or pride or arrogance that he could have killed in such a manner.

"But it is not my people's way."

Mastarna pulled her around to face him. "Don't judge Arruns. The acts of the Phersu are consecrated."

Shaking her head, tears pricked her eyes. "Sacrificing another human? Your people are barbaric!"

"It's you who seeks the salvation of Ati's religion. Did Artile not tell you of all the sacraments? Today that criminal's death was a duty paid to Larthia and our ancestors to revitalize them. You are the matriarch of our House now. You want to follow the Calu Cult, then respect Ati and honor all her beliefs."

Caecilia thought of the goats and lambs whose throats were slit so silently by Artile's acolytes after they had been made docile with potions and elixirs. The condemned man had died loudly, desperate to summon courage, goaded by the crowd.

She thought she had found a way to dance upon the shifting earth without faltering. To forget that a chasm lay beneath her into which she could plunge whenever another piece of Veii's corruption was exposed. Here was wickedness to which even Larthia had been party.

Unable to obey Mastarna any longer, she put her face in her hands and wept, not caring if the people of Veii were offended by her weakness, knowing only that she was too far from home.

• • •

Glimpses of stars and silver birds sparkled upon the indigo cloaks of the dancers. Ribbons streaming from long curling tresses, heads thrown back, arms outstretched to the heavens, their slender limbs apparent through the sheerness of their elegant chitons. Their stamping shook the earth. Their song stirred the dead.

Caecilia studied them from the side of the banquet hall. They were dancing to reanimate Ati and her forebears. The Veientanes were taking no chances with Larthia's soul. Sacrifice was not enough. After the terror of the Phersu came this whirling exultation of life.

So beautiful. So beautiful.

If Caecilia had not lived through the horror of the day she would have clapped her hands in joy. Clapped her hands and called for more.

• • •

Around her Mastarna's guests enjoyed the feast. The women, hair crowned with wreaths, had laid aside the silver eggs they carried— symbols of life, symbols of protection—as they reclined next to their ever-attentive partners.

Tarchon was unsympathetic with her distress at witnessing the Phersu earlier in the day. "What he does is holy, Caecilia. You are too squeamish."

It was difficult to hide her loathing, but she remembered Mastarna's rebuke. She was the matriarch and must show her tolerance even as she strived to disguise her disgust.

Being busy helped. She'd ordered double the usual number of casks, and the tantalizing aroma of roasted pork insinuated itself along the corridors and courtyard. Crowded inside from the winter's cold, Caecilia could feel her cheeks burning without aid of fire or wine as she coughed from the smoke that stung her eyes.

Being busy, though, did not stop her wanting to slip away to escape with a draft of Zeri.

She needed to talk to Mastarna, but he had been occupied all night hosting the banquet, once again donning pensive armor. There had been few opportunities to speak, and when they did their conversation was coolly polite and peppered with practical matters and interruptions. She needed to ask him if Fufluns's Pacha Cult also expected human sacrifice. Dreaded, too, that he would say yes. She wanted to speak to Artile, also, to ask him why a man's blood needed to be spilled.

• • •

Twilight was upon them. In Rome it meant the end of the day, going to bed and being ready for dawn and a new workday ahead. In Veii it was a signal for couples to extend the day with lamplight and lust.

In summer, smoke from lamps could billow into the night sky as couples lay behind the reed screens, but in winter, when darkness held sway over most of the day, both Romans and Etruscans dined with charcoal braziers blazing and palls of acrid, oily fumes hanging pregnant over the dining room.

As the hostess, it was Caecilia's task to signal for the reeds to be erected. The air was fetid, crowded with the sweat and scents of diners, the fragrances of wilted flowers, and the fat and odors of discarded food. And so, when she gave the order, the Roman wondered if she was suffocating because of the fug within the room or from humiliation at presiding over dissipation.

Caecilia scanned the banquet hall. Ulthes was occupied with Erene. Artile remained upon his dining couch, talking to Apercu.

Mastarna was nowhere in sight.

• • •

Outside, the night was clear and crisp and cold. Escaping the banquet for some fresh air, Caecilia admired how the spreading branches of the shrubs were covered with slow-melting whiteness. Ice had formed in the fountain; even the birdbaths denied sparrows a drink and dip.

The grapevines were denuded of foliage but clung with writhing strength to the columns flanking the arcade, some thick as saplings, as old as grandfathers. Enjoying the quiet, Caecilia entered the walkway and was startled to find Mastarna sitting on one of the benches.

Gone was the determined head of the House. Gone was the angry and shaken man of Ati's tomb. In the dimness, shoulders slumped, an accumulation of grief pulled him earthward. He stared into nothingness, perhaps toting up the numbers of his family, those left living and those dead: father, mother, wife, and children—a dynasty lost.

Noticing her, he asked her quietly to join him, then leaned his back against the wall, staring ahead to the columns and the threaded vines.

Caecilia had worn no cloak, thinking she would only stay outside for a moment. "It's cold here. Don't you want to go inside?"

Mastarna unwound his heavy winter tebenna and placed it around her shoulders. "How frightened you must be to follow Artile so devoutly. I have neglected you."

"That's not true, but you dismissed my fears while Artile offered me salvation."

"Don't you believe that I'd never let Tulumnes harm you?"

"You make a pledge only a god can fulfill."

"Then I am no different than Artile."

Caecilia pulled the cloak tight around her, her voice low and weary. "Don't you understand? I am always afraid. I have felt fear or worry of some kind almost every day since I came here. I am a foreigner in a foreign land, cut off from my people and unable to give succor to my dead parents. But Larthia showed me that there could be hope if I believed in Aita."

Mastarna turned and hooked loose strands of hair behind her ear. "Then I have failed you. I thought you believed I called you Bellatrix for a reason. I thought I'd convinced you that you were brave."

"I will never have courage enough to stomach what I saw today." She pointed along the passageway to where Arruns stood sentinel. "How can you bear him to be your servant?"

Frowning, Mastarna glanced at his guard. "Don't you realize that Arruns would die for you?"

The girl shuddered even as she remembered that the man had once saved her.

"Do not judge him too harshly. He came to Veii after being enslaved as a prisoner of war. I saw him as a warrior and so gave him the choice of wearing the hood of a condemned criminal or gaining freedom by donning the sacred mask. What would you have chosen?"

The thought of Mastarna dispensing mercy among the merciless gave her pause. "How was it that you could let Arruns choose?"

"I was the zilath."

"But you do not believe in the Calu Cult."

"I did then. As did Seianta."

Hearing him speak the name was both a shock and a relief. At last Mastarna might shade in the outline of a woman consisting of splinters of other people's memories, small mosaic tiles that had yet to form a picture.

Hunching his shoulders, he slouched back against the wall. "After she died I wanted to believe in the promise of rebirth. But no amount of expiation could appease the gods for what I did."

Caecilia was stunned. "Why? What did you do?"

He remained silent for a time, making her doubt he saw anything around him. "She loved the sea," he said presently, almost as though talking to himself. "She was a child when I met her, precocious, spoiled. Her father, Aule Porsenna, sought our services to protect his cargoes. He would let his daughter walk along the wharves among the fishermen or climb the coiled ropes and amphorae, which stood, as tall as men, crowding the docks.

"For years I sailed with Porsenna's fleet, for I would have grown fat and lazy in Veii, learning the theory of war but never practicing it. As a mercenary I was schooled and hardened into a man, by Ulthes and by the pirates whom I killed.

"When Seianta turned fourteen she gained my attention for other than her childish pranks. Barefoot, she'd walk along the shore and bathe naked in the sea so that soon she collected both shells and my admiration.

"All here liked her for her easy manner and wit, although Ati would sometimes frown at the wicked way her new daughter used a sharp tongue to deride others. I did not think her spiteful, though, only young and thoughtless. She made me laugh." He bent forward, his hands on both knees, staring at the ground. "I loved her."

Sitting motionless beside him, a part of Caecilia wanted to flee, to close her ears and eyes and ignore that what he said was hurtful. Wishing he would look at her as he had at Seianta when the girl danced upon the gray sand before the glassy Tyrrhenian Sea.

"I saw her today upon her coffin. Isn't it a comfort that you at least hold her there?"

He shook his head. "It merely reminds me that she was once my bride, radiant and content before grief turned her pliant curves to bony angles."

His bitter tone surprised her after the sweet story of their courtship.

"Her hair was brittle when she died, smelling of myrrh and stale smoke. Two grooves had formed on either side of her mouth from repeating the same words over and over, ruts of ritual and tiredness and sorrow. Laughter had been chased from her eyes, first by fervor and then by the burden of keeping the gods satisfied."

He leaned back again, sighing. "I was not blameless. I wanted an heir. And it was prophesied that I would beget a son who would beget a son." He paused, turning to her. "But only after great anguish."

This time his hesitation filled her with relief but she didn't touch him in case she distracted him from his story. She nodded slightly. "Tell me."

"Seianta, too, was predicted to be a mother. But only the second part of my prophecy came true. Time after time our babies died." Mastarna closed his eyes briefly as though in pain. "But we never gave up hope that one day our promised son would be born."

Caecilia shivered. Artile's vision of her future was nearly the same as Mastarna's. Seianta thought her prophecy matched her husband's as well. Her mistake was believing she'd be the mother of living children.

Thinking she was growing too cold, Mastarna paused to draw the tebenna close around her, the thick woolen weave soft against her face.

"We thought we were blessed when Seianta's belly grew smooth and taut and heavy with Velia. And beneath a mere layer of skin and flesh and muscle I felt our baby brush against my fingers, like the tiny wings of a fledgling.

"But our daughter was not like other children. Born one moon too early, she always lagged behind. By one year, when others were pulling themselves up to totter on unsteady feet, she was no bigger than a babe, her breath labored and her heartbeat frenetic.

"Seianta fretted, constantly comparing Velia with other infants, believing it was she who was to blame for such imperfection. Tormented, always tormented by the thoughts of her failure to bear a healthy child."

Caecilia listened, not knowing what to say. She wished she could reach inside herself and draw a mantle of comfort about him. Instead she sat silent, her hands in her lap, realizing that Seianta possessed more fortitude than she did.

"All suspected our little girl would die before the priest hammered the nail into Nortia's temple. All suspected but none would speak of it to Seianta. All except Artile." Mastarna's tone was harsh. "He fed upon her weakness, persuading her to observe the rituals of the Book of Fate, telling her that if she were devout enough she could defer our daughter's death for seven years."

A spasm gripped Caecilia's bowels that hurt so much she clenched her teeth until it passed. So far Uni had not thrown her lighting bolt. Every day the goddess denied her a sign of success, the danger of conceiving a disfigured child remained. And every day she woke with guilt as she found herself loving Mastarna, wishing that there were a guarantee that no monsters would be born.

"What happened to Velia?"

Mastarna massaged his brow, struggling to speak of it after all this time. "As she grew older she did little other than cry, a thin piercing whine that broke you asunder. Listless, struggling to breathe, she was unable to suckle so that she, who was tiny, grew even smaller. I could tell that Nortia meant her to die young. And so, when after months no miracle occurred, when no lightning struck from the correct sector, when no sign was given that my wife's prayers had been answered, I forbade her to perform the rituals, thinking them futile."

Mastarna twisted the gold and onyx ring around his finger, head bowed, a catch in his voice. "I told her I did it because I loved her, but she would not believe me. She beat and scratched me, claiming I was condemning our daughter to an early death." His body sagged with grief. "And perhaps she was right because Nortia claimed Velia a few days later."

Again words failed Caecilia. Again she wished she could truly understand the nature of his sorrow—what it was like to lose a child—praying also that she would never experience the anguish of Seianta.

Their babies had been cherished enough to be kept in a funeral urn decorated with dancing children. In Rome they would have been burned, their ashes scattered across the family hearth, lost forever after the fireplace was scraped clean and then stoked with wood to cook meals and warm the family. At least Caecilia knew now that she would not have to give any baby such a Roman ending, that any child of theirs would be more than a forgotten unformed soul.

Mastarna rose and moved to a column, gripping one vine with his hand as he stared at the wintry garden. "Seianta keened when Velia died. She would not stop, could not stop. Rocking the little body in her arms, not letting her go. I tried to stroke her hair, to hold her near, but it was as if my touch was acid. Only Zeri gave her respite."

Caecilia's heart beat faster. She struggled to keep her voice level. "Zeri?"

"It let her escape from pain, but in the end it made her sick."

"She grew ill?"

"Yes. I discovered that Artile had been wrongly giving it to her for a long time as a sacrament. By the time our little girl died, she was enslaved by the elixir."

The stone bench had suddenly grown harder and colder. Caecilia sat upon her hands to hide how they were shaking. She had grown uncomfortable, too, with awareness. Did Artile wish to own her, own her thoughts? Had she been wrong all along to believe the priest was not serving up malice when he doled out the elixir? There were only so many times she could deny that her story and Seianta's were overlapping: their hungers, their fears, their wants, their weaknesses. Only so many times she could disregard Mastarna's suspicions about his brother.

Mastarna pushed his fingers through his short-cropped hair. "And so Artile was able to console Seianta while she would not let me near her. I had neglected her, you see. Preoccupied with treasuring the office of the zilath, I was blinded to her plight. And, to be honest, I was not about to be drawn into her grief lest it force me to examine my own. I told myself it must be sorrow alone that was burdening her rather than Zeri sickness. It was only when I caught her licking the lid of the vial rather than lose one drop of euphoria that I fully understood."

A stab of pain crossed Caecilia's belly again, recognizing that she, too, was treading more than the edges of addiction. Her insides were already hardening and her hunger was satisfied by the smallest portions of food. Soon she would be as thin as when she first arrived in Veii. She had thought her symptoms only fatigue, had never imagined there was evil to bliss. How could she be so naïve when Veii always balanced up goodness with vice, any pleasure with pain?

"I begged her to stop drinking it," continued Mastarna, "but she refused to cease bowing to Artile as he placed a yoke around her neck. In the end it did not matter what I said because she had already begun to hate me. For certain she had not forgiven me. I grieved for the touch of her hands upon me in love or passion, but she tolerated me in bed for only one reason. She wanted another child.

"And with her obsession came a terrible urgency to conceive and carry and bear a baby. An anxiety for a son to greet daylight and be blessed quickly by the gods lest they change their minds. And so she lay beneath me with closed eyes and mouth pressed into a thin line waiting for me to finish."

He crouched before her. "As you did on our wedding night."

Caecilia stared at him. That night had been left behind them long ago. How strange to find it was Seianta's hatred for Mastarna that she had envied. Little wonder the Tarchnan girl still haunted her husband.

Sitting down beside her, Mastarna stroked her cheek with his calloused thumb. "And that is why I couldn't bear that it would always be like that between us. That's why I gave you the Alpan. So that your worry would dissolve and you would not hate lying with me in our bed."

Alpan. The need for the mild love potion seemed a distant memory.

Shame flooded through her. The secrets he revealed were of past hurts. Those she kept were only of betrayal. Still she kept silent, too frightened to confess what she knew could not be forgiven. Too frightened to lose him.

Perspiration pricked her hairline. The thought of being denied the Zeri was as agonizing as any of the pains that gripped her insides. She did not think she was strong enough to forgo it.

When she did not reply, Mastarna began pacing. "While I neglected her, Artile bound Seianta to him, taunting her that Velia was still not one of the Blessed, urging her to be faithful only to him. It was a bitter thing to watch her gaze at him with gratitude and trust.

"To our relief she fell with child quickly. Planting a seed was never a difficult task for us. Being able to nurture one was our burden. But as the child grew steadily within her, Seianta reclined most of the day under the elixir's spell, vomiting and sweating, wetting our bed when she had no energy to rise. Craving the Zeri more and more.

"I could not bear to watch her self-destruction. I repeated my mistake. I forbade her to drink her brew. She told me she hated me. I told her I felt the same. She cursed me."

His voice was flat and hard and empty. "But stopping the potion only made it worse. As the Zeri seeped from her pores, she'd stumble, unable to clearly see walls and furniture. Doubled up with pain, she screamed that the god of the forest was watching her, an evil omen before labor. The crying and moaning and writhing were ceaseless. As was the pleading. I was weak. I could not bear it. I let her have the Zeri. Thirsty for its peace, she nearly choked as she hastened to swallow it."

Mastarna sat down beside Caecilia, avoiding her gaze. "Vel was born two moons early. One hour only, and then his mere quiver of a heartbeat ceased. I knew then that we were damned."

His voice was a monotone, the spaces between his words quiet gaps that sorrow filled. "My son was so small I could hold him in my palm, the promise of a dynasty with which Nortia had taken from me." He cradled his head between his hands. "Vel had no eyes and his mouth was cleaved in two. It was a blessing that Seianta died before she saw him."

Caecilia took his hand. It was cold, colder than a winter's night should have painted it.

Mastarna still could not face her. "I adorned her body with a necklace of seashells and pearls together with a bouquet of blue wildflowers which grow beside the road to her home city.

"Artile was remorseless. 'Bow before me, Brother. Succeed where your wife failed. Take the sacraments of the Calu Cult. Save

Seianta and your children. Save yourself.'" But my pride and hatred would not let me. Not wanting Aita's blood-filled salvation I turned instead to Fufluns and prayed my family would be reborn."

Raising his head to look at her, he squeezed her hand so tightly it hurt. "But doubt lingers, doesn't it—like smoke that stays in the weave of cloth long after you've left the fireside. What if Artile was right? I began taunting Fate so that I might die and share their torment. But Nortia mocked me by keeping me alive."

Suddenly the silence that fell between them was interrupted by drunken revelers spilling out from the heat and smoke of the banquet hall into the fresh cold air. Their laughter and carousing was somehow shocking after listening to his tragic story. Some stumbled into the arcade but Arruns soon chased them back into the garden.

Caecilia took off the tebenna and wrapped it around both of them. "After today I only believe in the afterlife of my people. Your family are with the Shades, Mastarna. They are at peace."

He shook his head. "I don't know what to believe anymore. All I know is that I no longer wish to tease Fate. I saw how Artile looked at you today, how you sought his counsel in the sepulchre. I do not accuse my brother lightly, Bellatrix. He is like a lover, possessive as he is greedy. Greedy for the pain he can inflict on me by absconding with your soul. When you knelt before him in the tomb I felt as if I were dying."

Caecilia laced her fingers through his. "Artile doesn't possess my soul. You do."

Mastarna smiled before growing serious again. He cupped her chin with his fingers. "Now do you understand why I didn't tell you about Vel? I didn't want you to be afraid. But I believe that our child will not be born from despair, Caecilia. That was Seianta's and my curse alone."

Finally believing that she could be as strong as the Tarchnan girl, Caecilia kissed him gently. "I know we will have a son."

Mastarna smiled again. "I thought I would be safe if I married an Aemilian. I did not think I could fall in love with a Roman."

In the wintry night, their words were punctuated by a frosty hush. Touching his mouth with her fingers Caecilia traced the chill thread of his breath. "See, you are far from dying."

He kissed the inside of her wrist. "And do you no longer love your Drusus?"

Caecilia blinked in surprise, suddenly aware that he'd been jealous of a memory while she had envied a ghost.

She shook her head, then, taking a deep breath, lay back upon the bench, untying the sash around her waist and drawing up the sides of her chiton—wanting to prove to him that she could be Veientane after all. Mastarna raised his eyebrows as she tugged at his robes, too. As he slid his cool hands, brown upon pale flesh, under the warmth of her clothes, caressing the curves of inner thigh, belly, and breasts, she shivered as the cool air brushed her skin. His body was smooth and hard against hers as he eased within her, rocking slowly, her moans low and deep, then urgent, louder as their rhythm grew faster.

The cursing of a servant bustling along the passageway startled her, making her remember the risk, realizing that the guests were watching. Panicking, she tried to stifle Mastarna's groans, placing her hand across his mouth, but he merely kissed her fingers.

Arruns was watching, too, his face impassive as his eyes traversed their union, taking in every detail. The scrutiny of the loathsome man heightened her anxiety and she fought to free herself from Mastarna's arms.

"Forget them," he said softly, but loosened his embrace so she could break free. She glanced toward Arruns again but he had turned his back to them, gesturing the servants and onlookers away. As ever, standing guard.

"See only me," Mastarna urged.

Caecilia was not sure if she could. She could not bear to gaze once again upon a ghost, but in the dimness his eyes beheld only her.

Behind the vines.

Beneath the reed.

SPRING 405 BC

EIGHTEEN

Caecilia peeled back her deceit as one peels the layers of an onion, not cleanly as with a knife but messily as when fingers are used and tears are ensured.

An acolyte was sweeping the workroom when she arrived at the family sanctuary. It was cold, drafty, the brazier fire making little difference. On the threshold of spring, the novelty of fresh snow had passed; Caecilia was impatient to scrape the ice from the doorstep and the mud from her boots.

In the days following the funeral she had avoided Artile, knowing he would be tallying each day she'd not attended the sanctuary, recording her infractions.

To her surprise, she found him untidy, the black paint on his fingernails chipped and his hair uncombed, evidence of the toll his mother's death had taken on him. She expected harsh words when she told him she'd renounced the Calu Cult; instead, the haruspex responded with the coldness that Mastarna so fostered and which made the two brothers more alike than they would ever admit.

"Are you so easily convinced by your husband that I am wrong? A man who must cling to the Pacha Cult to salve his conscience when it suits him?"

"It is my choice to return to the ways of my own father. I am content to join the Shades."

Caecilia drew her palla about her and shifted closer to the brazier, still confused as to the priest's part in Seianta's story. "Why did you give her so much Zeri?"

Instead of replying, the haruspex called for the incense to be lit, the scent and light stirring a response within her, the comfort of routine.

He rubbed one eye, smearing the kohl around it. "What has he said, Sister? That I caused her death?" His tone was weary. "Do you believe that Seianta had no choice but to guzzle the elixir as a child slurps milk? My brother was the one who caused Seianta hurt. She was a believer and he denied her worship. It was misery that made her take too much Zeri, but it was Mastarna who killed her."

He was spinning a spiderweb between them, expecting her to be ensnared.

"After Velia's birth, Seianta's womb was slack from delivering both dead and living babies," he continued. "They were counseled that she would die if she gave birth to another infant."

The priest moved closer. She could smell the familiar bay leaves on his breath.

"Mastarna was desperate for an heir, knowing Seianta's longing would overcome prudence. He betrayed her in continuing to lie with her. In the gamble to have a son, he risked his wife's life."

Caecilia turned to the fire, the acrid smoke making her cough. In that moment she hated the priest for picking at her feelings for her husband.

"He is still desperate for a child, Sister. So don't believe him when he talks of love. It is the children you will bear that he desires."

He took Caecilia's hand; his own was cool, soft, soothing against the heat of her skin. "Children who could be disfigured and cursed until you bear a healthy son."

The girl took a deep breath, determined not to heed him. "Mastarna and I share the same prophecy. We are destined to have living heirs."

He sighed. "Time will only tell. Do you want to take that risk?"

Caecilia met his gaze defiantly, showing him the doubts he'd seeded were gone. Her husband was laying claim over the territory where his brother previously reigned, asking her to accept fate instead of deferring it. Making her believe she could, at last, accept living in Veii forever. Encouraging her that it was time to worship at his hearth alone. It was time for fear to be banished. It was time to conceive their son. Mastarna had convinced her that, together, they could love every child that was born to them and face either sorrow or elation.

"I am prepared to accept my fate," she said, aware that her hands were shaking slightly, the pull of the Zeri hard to shift.

Artile stared at the tremor in her hands. "Ah, Sister, what about my gift? Do you think you would be stronger than Seianta if you cease your worship?"

The sticky thread of his web clung to her. Her supply of Zeri was nearly empty. Even with the tale of Seianta's torment, the elixir called to her. "Why did you give it to me and not to other believers?"

Artile held out a tiny vial. "Because I only give it to those who are in need. I do not like to see anyone in pain, Sister. Not Ati, not Seianta, not you."

Caecilia's hand hovered over the alabastron knowing it would fit snugly in her palm.

Hating him for his power, telling herself to be strong.

• • •

Standing on the arx, Caecilia leaned against the fine squared masonry of its wall. Beside her, Tarchon craned over the side, but the girl could not bring herself to peer down the vertical plunge to the ravine. The wind blew fiercely up the sweep of the citadel, chilling her cheeks and reddening her nose. She licked her lips to fend off dryness as her silver earrings burned her earlobes with cold.

"I am freezing," she said, regretting her suggestion of climbing up there, but she needed a place away from prying eyes and ears. She needed to ask Tarchon a favor.

"I need some Zeri," she said, taking a deep breath of cold, crisp air.

Tarchon stopped rubbing his hands together to keep warm. "Why would you need such a potion?"

"Because I can no longer ask Artile for it." The wind whisked away half of her words, but she knew Tarchon's hesitation was not because he'd failed to hear her.

"What happened to the Roman who would not sip wine?" His voice was soft with disappointment.

"Don't lecture me. Your teeth are always stained with Catha. You spend your nights in thrall to one elixir or another."

"Yes, but I don't sup on Zeri behind Mastarna's back. The drug that killed his first wife."

"Artile said it was a sacrament."

The youth frowned, pushing away from the wall. "Nevertheless, you should not have taken it."

Caecilia stiffened, galled that a mollis should tell a Roman her duty. It was not easy to admit her failing, but ceasing to kneel before Artile did not cure her craving. She wanted to stop but she could only do so slowly. A little less each time.

Tarchon's tone was angry. "Do you know Seianta's story?"

She nodded.

"Then forget the Zeri. Artile should never have given it to you."

Here was another confusion. Wasn't he Artile's lover? "You speak against him?"

"No matter what you may think, the haruspex doesn't own me. He is a man like any other, and feels jealousy and pain just as you do. The trouble is that in hating Mastarna so fiercely he forgets that he hurts others, too."

"So he preached to me only to injure my husband?"

"Don't misunderstand me. He is no fraud—and, no matter what Mastarna says, he is kind. And so, if he dispensed the Zeri then he did it because he saw your need. But understand that he requires complete devotion and does not brook disobedience. He is angry that you ceased worshipping the Calu Cult. Just as he was disappointed with Seianta. He thinks you have betrayed him."

"And yet he has not revealed my addiction to Mastarna."

Tarchon sighed. "You're so naïve. If Mastarna finds Artile is feeding Zeri to another of his wives he would kill him."

His words were like the wormwood tonic Aurelia used to dole out, given for her benefit but having a nasty taste. She had seen Artile's discretion as a sign of allegiance; instead, it was for self-preservation. His deception scalded her just as her aunt's noxious medicine burned her throat.

"What should I do?"

"I do not want to see you damned. You must follow the Calu Cult but not drink the Zeri."

Caecilia shivered, her feet turning blue within her red leather boots, nausea rising within her. He was frightening her, drawing her back to dread and endless prayers under the guidance of a priest who saw her only as a pawn. "I can't kneel to Aita. Not when such worship means the taking of a life. Please give me the Zeri."

"No." His vehemence was unnerving. "I won't watch you die as Seianta did."

"I heard that she suffered most when she stopped the drug."

"You will suffer just as much if you take it for too long."

Caecilia surveyed the horizon where gray sky pressed upon bruised purple hills. Many sights in Veii had sickened her—the Phersu's dog and his prey, the rutting wine-sodden guests—but this was different. He was forcing her to admit that this vice was hers alone.

"He would never forgive me if he found out."

The youth shook his head. "You are wrong. I have seen how it is between you. He would be angry but he'd still love you. Besides, I will help you give it up. Mastarna need never know you were possessed by its spell."

Unable to find courage, Caecilia crouched beside him, her fingers digging into his arm. "Please. Give me just a little. It helps me see visions of my home."

The youth scrabbled to his feet, roughly pulling her to stand, then swept his arm in an arc across the landscape, shafts of sun piercing the curtains of cloud. "There is your home."

"I can't see Rome from here."

"It is not of Rome I speak. All roads circle our city. All roads lead here. This is your home."

"I only want to see my family."

Grasping both her arms, Tarchon shook her. "Who is your family? You hanker for Marcus, but in all your time here you've received no letters from him."

"How can you say that? He could be dead!"

"Perhaps, but even before the fall of Verrugo you heard nothing from him. No, I think your cousin spoke of his affection, but in truth he forgot you as soon as you left."

"Please, Tarchon, don't say such things."

"Did anyone truly love you there, Caecilia? Love you as Mastarna does? Love you as Larthia did? As I do? You are so quick to condemn us and yet we have done nothing but accept and care for you." He released her. "We are your family now."

Caecilia wanted to dispute him but could not. She'd always thought her cousin to be her best friend, her only friend. Now she realized she was wrong.

In the distance, the sky was darkening. The wind was edged with ice, slicing through their clothes.

"Come. The storm is nearly here."

Caecilia ignored him, studying the approaching shrouds of rain, wanting to endure the cold, to blot out her need for the soft, warm reverie of the Zeri's peace.

Thunder grumbled as clouds thickened upon the horizon. The lightning that followed was no flicker, no long streak with frayed edges; instead a curtain of light that lit a distant expanse of forest twisted with bare branches of muted green and brown.

High on the citadel, Caecilia did not miss its flare. The lightning had come from the northeast.

The sector of greatest good fortune—Uni's realm.

As she watched, Caecilia thought she should be giddy with excitement, knowing that, after all these months, after all the sacrifice and prayers and blood, Uni had at last granted a sign. Instead, it was as though she had taken a false step and, tripping and stumbling, landed facedown upon the ground.

The lightning declared she would have no child with Mastarna for seven years. She turned and slid down the stonework to sit upon the ground.

Tarchon tugged at her to rise as rain started to slash across them. "Come on," he said, but she shook her head, refusing to move. He knelt beside her. "What's the matter?"

She stared at the raindrops bouncing off his cheeks and hair. She was a child again, badgering her father for new shoes only to find they pinched her feet, knowing she'd made the wrong choice but must wear them and be grateful.

When she told him about her worship of the Book of Fate, he sat down next to her, oblivious of the pelting rain, his silence lasting only the time between claps of thunder. "For this, he will never forgive you."

For a time they stayed quietly, water streaming off them, cloaks drenched, rain dripping from their chins, their fingers, their hair. Her tears were warm compared to the freezing rain.

"You may be lucky. Only a fulgurator can tell us if the lightning is proroguing or that indeed it was Uni who sent her bolt. Many gods reside in the northeast sector."

Caecilia scanned the horizon where lightning still flashed intermittently across the valley, as always amazed that the brilliant flashes were like words of a celestial language expressing divine moods.

She would not dare approach Artile to find the meaning, though. She did not want to know now. Perversely, she only hoped that her prayers had not been answered.

Tarchon was watching her, his fair face dark with disgust. "Why did you do it?"

Caecilia found she could only whisper. "Artile told me I would give birth to Mastarna's monsters. I was frightened, Tarchon, so very frightened. Please understand."

"Monsters?"

"Like Seianta's."

He frowned, a look of confusion passing across his features, a hint of doubt about his lover. "It was she who was cursed, Caecilia. The gods had forsaken her, not Mastarna."

"Please, please do not tell him."

Tarchon's tone was somber and severe. "Trust me, I will keep your secret. Mastarna must never know."

Slipping on the cobblestones, they skidded to where Cytheris was waiting. Draping her mistress in a dry cloak, she glared at the youth for his neglect, disturbed to see the girl's distress.

Tarchon leaned into the carriage as Caecilia settled inside, his contempt building into anger, his voice scathing. "You think us vile and corrupt, but ask yourself this question. If you could return to Rome tomorrow what would make you stay?"

. . .

It had been raining steadily when she arrived at the country villa. Climbing down from the carriage she sank into knee-high mud and struggled to the front door.

After a few days, though, the smell of the rich mud was pleasant compared to the stink of her room: vomit and pee, sweat and ordure, rising in a miasma, saturating sheets and robes.

They bound her hands in bandages. She joked at first but afterward cursed them. Her fingernails were short but they could scratch, scratch the insects that crawled beneath her skin.

At first she thought they were small and few enough to squash. In the end she felt as though spiders were hatching eggs within her and ants marching through her veins. Tarchon could not see them nor Cytheris feel them, but they believed her cries and bathed her grazes when bandages were rubbed hard enough to grate skin.

She lay in a room with a dancer painted upon its ceiling. Stepping and stamping in celebration of life he mocked her from above, laughing at her anguish. She wished she could catch the click of his castanets or hear the swish of his parti-colored kilt but there were no sounds other than her own.

Sometimes the dancer would play cruel pranks, mimicking the contortions of her muscles or playing hide and seek with her as vision glided from near to far, blurred and sharp, in turns.

Only Tarchon and Cytheris were allowed within the room, discreet in their knowledge of her malady, telling the servants that the mistress suffered from a contagious fever.

Caecilia grew used to being naked in front of Tarchon. Modesty fell away. Her body ceased to be her own. After her failings no dignity remained that could be lost.

They made her eat broth, which she could not keep down, drawing her knees to her belly with cramps. Whereas before she had strained above the privy, her bowels now voided in a steady stream. Cytheris would bathe her face and neck and arms, but rose water was soon usurped by sweat, malodorous and fulsome, while the air smelled faintly of feces even when they had scraped and wiped her clean.

She could sleep only briefly, living in Tuchulcha's world even when awake. She begged for the Zeri. Just a little taste. She thought she would die without it. Wished she could.

• • •

Mastarna's bewilderment was amiss on a face that rarely registered confusion. His silence was short-lived. His roar made even the dancer miss a step. Cytheris scuttled from the room at his command, and Caecilia could hear him shouting at his son and Tarchon shouting back.

He did not raise his voice to her, though. Instead his arms encircled her as she shook. Stroking her sodden hair, he drew the sheet gently over her and pressed his cheek against hers. It was cool, retaining a slice of winter. "When I heard you were ill, I could not stay away. You should have told me."

"I was afraid."

His sigh was full of hurt. A spasm shivered through her. Mastarna took her hand and inspected the bandage, specks of blood upon it, carefully caressing the sore broken skin of her arm.

His touch made the insects start their exploration. They swarmed over her feet, burrowing in deep. Frantically, she reached down to scrape them from between her toes. When he tried to stop her, she pushed him away. He had seen this all before. He was patient. When the insects slithered away, he held her.

When he finally took her home, chamomile laced the fields, and posies of verbena and forget-me-nots adorned the crossroad shrines. Flowers on the edge of spring. Floral scents that reminded her evermore that she had one more secret to hide—one that he would not forgive.

. . .

Mastarna had returned early from a meeting with the zilath, his mood buoyant, unable to restrain excitement. "Good news! Vipinas will support Ulthes!" He was shouting, sweeping Caecilia off her feet in a bear hug.

Her eyes opened wide in surprise as he twirled her around. It seemed so easy to be happy. To have a future. To imagine living in peace.

Suddenly, Caecilia was filled with gratitude for the lean man with the gold-and-ivory teeth who'd finally been persuaded to Ulthes's cause. For with Vipinas's tribal influence and with Apercu already an ally, Tulumnes could only rely on Pesna's votes. Victory was guaranteed.

Setting his wife down on the floor again, Mastarna called for some wine. "We have more than this news to celebrate," he said, handing her a small leather pouch. "It's for your birthday. Although I'm always careful to say that a woman grows a year wiser. Saying they are a year older tends to make them frown."

Caecilia laughed, pulling open the drawstring.

"It's the same design as the wolf fibula I gave you when you first came here," he said, not waiting for her to remove the gift. "You seem to have lost it."

Caecilia kissed him a thank you. "It's even more beautiful than the first one." Fingering the engraving of the mother wolf suckling her cubs, Caecilia remembered how she'd sacrificed the other clasp to Uni on the day the lightning struck the palace. Mastarna had given it to her to ward off homesickness. She no longer needed such a keepsake.

"And when the election is over I will give you another present. We will visit Rome."

Goose bumps formed on her skin. "Rome?"

He nodded.

She covered his face with kisses, glad that she would see the seven hills again and walk around Tata's farm. "But you said I couldn't return unless the treaty failed."

"True, but now that Tulumnes will be defeated I feel differently."

"And if I am with child?"

His face—his battered, scarred, ugly face—transformed with delight. Caecilia realized he'd mistaken her question for a confession, that she had already conceived, that she was not barren after all and that his unspoken fears could be discarded.

It was cruel to watch him wilt as she shook her head at his silent query. "But I pray I will carry our son soon," she said, encircling his neck with her arms, touching her forehead to his.

Mastarna smiled. "Then I will take you back to show him to your family."

"But that is not what you said before!"

"Because now I don't think you'd take our son away." He held her hands. "Nor do I think you would leave me."

It was strange to hear him say the words. To achieve the goal that she'd knelt and prayed and begged for only to find that it was hers after all just by loving him.

As she hugged him, he grinned. "We must give him brothers, too," she said.

"You only want boys then?"

"No, of course not."

As he spoke she inwardly entreated Nortia not to spitefully make her wait and wait and wait in punishment for her foolishness. And she prayed that Uni had not already sent her sign.

. . .

Caecilia could not tell if she was perspiring from the heat of the bath or from their lovemaking. She slid beneath the water then emerged, sweeping water from her hair and cheek and brow, enjoying the warmth of the sunlight streaming into the chamber. Mastarna lay beside her, eyes closed, his breathing returning to normal. As she began to rise he stopped her, his hand lazily resting on her thigh. "Stay."

She smiled and laid her head upon his shoulder, his flesh warm against hers, pleased that it was different now, that he wished to prolong touch, to hold her in the ebbing.

Mastarna trailed his fingers, knuckles scarred, through her hair as it floated in the water like seaweed.

She smoothed her hand across his chest. To her amusement there was an imprint of the figure of Atlenta pressed into his skin. "Look. We held each other too tightly."

Mastarna looked down, then touched the space between Caecilia's breasts where the reverse side of the pendant's engraving also appeared. "It seems Atlenta has made her mark on both of us."

He kissed the top of her shoulder, then rose and helped her to stand. "It's time to get out, the water is cooling."

Water streaming from him as he stepped from the bath, Mastarna dragged his fingers through his sleek, wet hair. His legs and arms were dark from the sun, his body the color of honey, the livid cicatrice no longer alarming, all the scars upon his skin explored and charted.

Cytheris wrapped Caecilia in a linen sheet, rubbing her dry. Mastarna checked her, claiming the right. The handmaid grinned and bustled about waiting for her mistress to be released so that she could attend to her dressing.

Leaning her head to one side, Caecilia twisted her hair into a rope, wringing it dry. Mastarna stroked her birthmark. "I told you this was the sign of a fortuitous marriage."

She pointed to the painting of the warrioress on the chamber's ceiling. "Let's pray our marriage is more fortunate than Atlenta's. I hope we don't end up being eaten by lions."

Mastarna frowned. "Atlenta and her husband weren't eaten. Turan transformed them into lions when they trespassed into a sacred garden. So our fate may not be so bad."

His words lifted her spirits.

"Although I hope your mistress isn't as cruel as the huntress," Mastarna said over his shoulder to Cytheris.

"No, master." The Greek girl giggled, her smile revealing her missing dogtooth.

Caecilia wondered how much more of the tale she did not know. "How so?"

Mastarna kissed her again. "Because she plunged a lance into the breast of those she defeated. You won't do that to me, will you, Bellatrix? Now that you have conquered me?"

• • •

Smiling, the Roman fingered the sheer cloth of her chiton, threaded with gold, the wedding dress she'd never worn. A world away from the white woolen tunic and orange veil. A lifetime away from either the Roman or Veientane bride she had been.

She stretched, enjoying the fragrance of lilies and the tightness of the soft linen upon her shaven skin. No longer ashamed of how the garment clung to her body and breasts. Her hair was bound loosely and crowned with a shining beaded diadem. The vanity of knowing kohl emphasized the roundness and color of her eyes made her painted lips curve in a smile.

She was sitting under a canopy in one of the enormous wooden stands erected on the plain outside the city to celebrate the Spring Festival of Fufluns. Nearby lay the dark, sloped hill where the initiation ceremonies into the god's cult would take place that night.

In the woods, birdsong vied with trilling flutes, while the sweet-scented narcissus bordering the roadside were trampled as more and more people lined up to gain entry to the games.

Around her, the crowd was waiting for the commencement of the drama competition where playwrights vied for honors just as Olympians strove to win the olive wreath. The air rattled with their talk and laughter as loudly as the bees hummed and buzzed in the white hawthorn blossom outside. The world had shrugged its heavy winter cloak from its shoulders and emerged as spring with as much aplomb as an actor entering from the doors to a stage.

Yesterday prayers and praise had been given to Fufluns, the god of theater, god of wine, and god of resurrection. Today the Drama Games would begin and Caecilia was not about to miss one moment of the fifteen plays that would be performed over the next three days.

Dew had to be wiped from the benches when Caecilia made her way to her seat. The morning was chill, the dampness coating the grass and trees ready to be burned away. The light was crisp and bright. No clouds. She took a deep breath to inhale the blueness, contentment filling her.

As she waited for the official procession, she prayed she would not be disappointed, that this time enchantment would not be spoiled by cruelty. She wanted to believe Mastarna's assurances that there would be no violence except that exacted through artifice.

She had never seen a play before. Lurid mime shows were sometimes performed in Rome but not before an audience of women—plebeian perhaps, but not patrician. Caecilia hoped what she saw today would be more than clumsy theater. She wanted to be moved to either mirth or tears, seeing no shame in commoner or noble doing the same.

After spreading cushions and soft rugs, Cytheris opened a hamper to serve goat's cheese and olives. A heavy-lidded Tarchon stretched out along the row, one leg bent and one arm flung across his face, once again deprived of sleep from his nightly carousing. No doubt sated from enjoying himself with some lover.

After a time, a servant dressed in the livery of Apercu's House approached and tapped Tarchon on the shoulder, slipping some Catha into his palm. For an instant, Caecilia felt a twinge of envy, traces of longing for the Zeri emerging like water seeping to the surface when a hole is dug in sand.

Tarchon closed his hand around the messenger's and kissed it quickly. The Roman glanced away, embarrassed as always to witness the youth's display of affection, also understanding how Tarchon could survive wakefulness for days and nights on end.

"Don't look so stern. He's a freedman. Carthaginian."

"Yes, from the House of Apercu, not ours. You should be careful."

The youth sniffed. "How you Romans do love rules."

Caecilia watched how the Etruscans were scrambling to gain the best position, setting up their pillows, food, and wine for the long exciting day ahead either on the grass verge or in the stands. They were as colorful as ever. She now understood such hues distinguished the classes. The rich were dressed in ornate kilts, their women in elegant chitons, while those in nettle green and elderberry blue took their places in the better seats, relegating the poorer in patches of brown and black to areas that cost the least and afforded the worst view.

Vendors were selling refreshments, the chatter of their business exchanges irritating but the aroma of oily sweetness awaking homesickness in her. At home the Liberalia would be celebrated now. Liber's priestesses would be setting up small-handled altars in the streets for the offering of honey cakes, while fourteen-year-old boys would untie bullas from around their necks, remove their purple-bordered togas, and don the plain robes of a man.

"Look," said Cytheris. "They're setting up the skene. A palace. See the columns and statues, mistress? That means it will be a tragedy."

The maidservant was as excited as her mistress. That morning Cytheris had taken great care in plaiting and pinning her long, bushy hair, the powder and rouge upon her cheeks lessening the ugliness of her pockmarks. Caecilia had given her a fine new chiton: pleated, blue and white. The servant had adjusted it to expose as much cleavage as possible. It was clear the Greek girl saw an opportunity to enjoy the feast tonight. She would call to her Greek god Dionysus, but would be satisfied if a man rather than a god embraced her.

Caecilia's own apprehension about the celebrations that night had been allayed. Mastarna promised her that he did not expect her to join in revelry similar to that which she'd witnessed at the Winter Feast.

Discordant snatches of musicians practicing double pipe, timbrels, and drums drifted to Caecilia as she surveyed the orchestra. In the center stood an altar, an ever-present reminder that these plays were dedicated to Fufluns.

"The first play will be performed by the troupe visiting from Greece. They have come all the way from Athens where the Great Dionysia is even now being held," said the maid.

"Do you know what it is about?"

"It tells how Dionysus rescued his mother, the mortal Semele, from the Underworld. He convinced Thanatos to release her so that she could live on Mount Olympus."

"Thanatos is Death," explained Tarchon. "Personally, I'd prefer to watch a satyr play."

"Oh, yes," agreed Cytheris. "Sad and funny all at once."

"A satyr play?"

His eyes were bright with the drug. "Yes, where a chorus of fat-assed satyrs stand in a grotto and sing about their plans to abduct the heroine."

Cytheris was giggling.

"I'd prefer something more serious," sighed Caecilia.

"Ah, there'll be plenty of pathos." Tarchon searched in the basket for a flask of wine, eager to begin worshipping. "Three tragedies today alone. Too many, if you ask me."

"They say the Greek play is touted to win the games," said Cytheris.

"I hope so. I've wagered a fortune on it."

Caecilia laughed. It would not be Veii if there was no gambling. No doubt the betting was already progressing in earnest among the crowd. And knowing Tarchon, he had placed wagers on more than which playwright might win. It could be an expensive week for him if he gambled every day on anything that amused him.

• • •

The councillors' wives arrived before the parade. The noblewomen bustled into their seats, fans fluttering and jewelry glinting. After enjoying the luxury of observing the theater preparations in peace, Caecilia felt as though she had been invaded. As usual they greeted her with strained voice and conceited gaze, but today it was not just Caecilia they insulted. They ignored Tarchon as if he were a servant, invisible and unimportant.

Her tutor's astonishment was deeper than his blush. No one had ever failed to acknowledge the heir of the House of Mastarna.

Caecilia stared at the youth, willing him to stand firm and to challenge them.

Instead, dropping the flask, he shoved his way along the bench, stumbling over the bottle as it clinked at his feet. The wives savored his departure with mean little smiles and knowing glances.

Caecilia wanted to go after him but knew it would serve no purpose. Tarchon understood that this would eventually happen. The youth was growing too old for a blind eye to be shown to his behavior. The time had come for Mastarna to disown his son or suffer disgrace himself.

Lady Apercu, dewlap and bosom quivering, positioned herself as far away from Caecilia as she could while Pesna's haughty young wife turned so that to converse would mean nudging her on the back with voice if not fingers. Only Lady Vipinas nodded briefly, her face marked with its ugly liver spots and wrinkles. It was unexpected. Startling. Of the three women, Caecilia thought Vipinas's wife would never acknowledge her. Understood, too, why that would be so. Her only son had died at Roman hands. A mother was not expected to forgive such a thing.

It was midmorning when the principes finally filed into the theater. The crowd had grown restless at the delay, but their impatience was quelled when Ulthes appeared in his ceremonial dress, face painted with vermilion dye as befitting his office.

As the zilath entered Caecilia noticed he was swaying slightly and that two of his twelve lictors flanked him as if ready to catch him lest he miss a step. When he reached his chair, he sank into it as though he'd ended an odyssey.

Apercu also sat at the edge of the orchestra beside the zilath. The princip held special eminence at the festival. As the Maru, head of the college of the Pacha Cult, he was entitled to also sit upon a throne. Apart from the god himself, both men were to be the principal spectators and judges.

The retinue took their seats, chatting and laughing. Servants darted among them, ensuring cups were filled, cushions plumped, parasols tilted, and tidbits offered. All were observed by the crowd who had settled themselves hours before without such flair or fuss. The councillors and their wives were as interesting a distraction as the drama to be performed.

Tulumnes and Pesna were seated close together, schoolboys gossiping in class. Vipinas conversed freely with them, but Caecilia knew her husband would not be concerned at the older man's friendliness with the other candidate. The numbers had been toted up. At the end of the three days of the Drama Festival the election would be held and Ulthes would be returned.

As he approached, Mastarna grinned at Caecilia's golden gown. "Does this mean we are to be wed again?"

Smiling, words tumbled from her about her morning. Listening to her chatter, Mastarna sat with his thigh pressed along hers, casual and proprietary, but Caecilia was soon aware that she did not hold all his attention. Instead, Mastarna's glances were troubled as he studied the zilath.

Ulthes did not look well. The vermilion paint on his face seemed to have spread to his neck. The midmorning heat was not intense enough to cause his dripping sweat.

Caecilia touched the back of Mastarna's hand. "What's wrong with Ulthes?"

"I don't know. He was unsteady on his feet when we began the procession. He is stubborn, though, and would not say what ailed him." As he spoke, Mastarna turned in his seat as if looking for someone.

Erene was seated several tiers behind them with the lesser members of the entourage, eyes fixed on her patron. The hetaera's face was pale. Her sheer chiton with its border of fine red spirals was that of a courtesan, but her expression was that of a devoted wife. Mastarna signaled Arruns to fetch her.

"He was fatigued last night but too restless to sleep," said Erene in response to Mastarna's questioning. "No drink will satisfy his thirst. This morning his head throbbed so that his vision was blurred. I begged him not to come." The Cretan continued to observe Ulthes, agitated that she could not be by his side. "I have never seen him like this."

Caecilia tried to reassure them. "Perhaps it is just something he has eaten and will be purged in time."

"Let's hope so." Mastarna made room for the hetaera to sit down.

A trumpet sounded and the crowd grew quiet. A chorus of twelve filed from the parados at the side of the stage into the orchestra, causing Caecilia to gasp in awe. The actors were dressed as priestesses, strange wild creatures, their masks fixed into expressions of elation, leopard skins draped across their shoulders and snakes coiled through wigs of tangled hair. As the musicians played a forlorn and haunting tune, the choir's chanting stirred the air, the soaring voices creating an emptiness within her. Caecilia put a finger to the base of her throat, letting the music fill her. It mattered not that they sang in Greek. The beauty of their sound and dance transcended meaning.

An actor appeared, also wearing a mask, mouth agape, eye-holes dark. Under his tunic and goatskin cloak he wore leggings and long sleeves decorated with bright whorls. His boots were strangely pointed. The young man was beautiful, even more beautiful than Tarchon, with golden hair curling down his back. A young god—Dionysus. Divine but present among mortals, not in heaven but upon a wooden stage on a sunny day in spring.

Another actor entered—a woman with a diadem in her hair. Her linen mask was drawn with exaggerated arched eyebrows and a fine straight nose. Caecilia guessed she was the woman Semele, abandoned in the Underworld and waiting for her son to save her. Her form was slender, and when she spoke her voice was dulcet and mellow. The only sign that she was a man was her hands as the long white sleeves did not cover them. Broad and masculine, they were out of place with her slimness.

Then a character strode onto the stage with a mask more dreadful than the Phersu's, hard and black as ebony, features grim, mouth leering, eyes blank. Thanatos stood before them guarding the entrance to the Underworld. Separating Dionysus from Semele.

Caecilia shuddered and glanced at Mastarna. He sat with jaw clenched, preoccupied with Ulthes. The zilath was learning forward, head cradled between his palms, rocking and moaning. Apercu crouched beside him, a hand on his shoulder.

Tulumnes, too, was surveying his rival. Droplets of perspiration were breaking through the normal clammy sheen upon his skin. He tugged at the neck of his robes and called for the wine jug repeatedly, looking as though something was lodged in his thoughts in the same way gravel hides in a shoe and cannot be budged.

Erene's scream rose in solo above the chorus when Ulthes slumped to the ground. She clambered down, trying to reach him, but the lictors warded her off. Mastarna followed, vaulting the row of seats and pushing Apercu aside, commanding the bodyguards to let Erene through.

The crowd had been quiet while watching the drama, rapt in wonder at the spectacle and songs and speeches, but their hush had a constant undertone of gasps and gestures. At the collapse of the zilath, a weird silence descended as everyone realized Thanatos might not just be present as an actor on the stage.

The zilath's ragged breath, horrible, desperate, helpless, wheezed into the air. As Erene held him, his head lolled back and his eyes went blank. He moaned and muttered. He rasped out the names of demons and of his sons. He clutched at Mastarna with his three-fingered hand.

Erene kissed his face so that she was also covered in dye. Wiping his face clean they saw his skin was deeper scarlet than the paint. She called for water, begging Ulthes to drink but he could not swallow. And then he sank back in her arms, eyes rolling back into his head, mouth ajar showing his cracked, chipped teeth. Not dead. Not yet.

Prizing Erene away, Mastarna lifted his friend and carried him to the pavilion outside the theater. The shade of the tent was a relief after the brightness of the sun. Calmer, Erene sat beside Ulthes on the divan, stroking his brow, his spiky hair. Outside the eerie quiet began to splinter into murmurings.

Inside the tent, no one spoke.

After a time, Ulthes's laboring breath ceased. Sobbing, Erene pressed her cheek against his chest while Mastarna closed the dead man's eyes. Caecilia watched her husband bend and place his lips upon Arnth Ulthes's mouth.

No one heard the intake of her breath as Mastarna breathed in the zilath's soul. No one seemed to notice but Caecilia that his kiss was more like a lover's than a friend's.

NINETEEN

Mastarna was staring at Ulthes, seemingly unaware of the many eyes focused upon him. Unable to shift her gaze from her husband, Caecilia thought she must have been mistaken, that his farewell was nothing more than what was expected, that her imagination had become caught up with the drama unfolding both on and off the stage. Or perhaps it had been a trick of sight? The pavilion was dim after the brightness of the day and it had taken some time for her eyes to focus in the gloom, to blink away silhouettes and swirls of red and green before normal vision restored. Nevertheless, her heartbeat competed with the pulse in her head. She struggled to concentrate on one thing at a time, to put in order what she'd seen: death and humiliation.

"Mandragora." Artile spoke the word with a voice used on the wide, windy steps of temple and portico. It rose clearly above the swelling lament of the crowd pressing upon the thin walls of the tent. The murmurs of the principes inside were spreading also, their whispers edged with fright. "I have seen others die this way when they have been too greedy or are given it without knowing."

Caecilia took some time to comprehend his words as they echoed within her as though bouncing off a stone corridor, meaning and sound lagging, syllables magnified, understanding jumbled. Mandragora. She knew it could be either potion or poison. Hadn't Mastarna given her the Alpan because it contained a small dose of the love plant? And also warned of its potency? A hint of malice was in its taste as well as euphoria. The zilath must have taken much to die so horribly.

Erene lay with her head on Ulthes's chest, waiting for the rise and fall of breath that would not come. The vermilion dye upon her face had mingled with her tears as though she were weeping blood.

Tulumnes was staring at the courtesan. Caecilia had thought him pensive at the play, but he'd since lost the look of one pondering upon a problem. Instead arrogance had returned. "Mandragora is a love philter," he said. "Perhaps this hetaera has lost some of her skills. Perhaps she poured too much into his cup last night."

Mastarna broke away from his dead friend and strode over to the princip, his face only inches from the other's. "Don't pretend this was not your doing!"

A fresh sheen of sweat oozed from Tulumnes's pores, trickling down the sides of his face. "You must be mad."

Vipinas put his hand upon Mastarna's forearm. "Calm yourself. He's right. It's a grave thing to accuse him of murder."

"Listen to him," said Tulumnes, his voice assuming the tone of the aggrieved. "The whore is the one to question."

Mastarna moved back to Erene, squeezing her shoulder gently when she did not respond. Caecilia could tell from his expression that he was remembering the Alpan, too. Tulumnes had thrown doubt onto the matter.

The companion raised her head, pushing tangled hair from her face. Her pale skin was smeared with kohl and crimson, but when she met the stares of the nobles and their wives her voice was defiant. "I have not gained fame because I cannot please a man."

Caecilia looked at her in awe. The courtesan may have come from the slums of Heraklion but Erene was not cowed by the aristocracy, even if the bangles on one wrist jangled softly, fueled by the trembling of her hand.

"You know he was not one to partake of philters, either for dreams or love," she said to Mastarna.

It was true. Ulthes always liked to keep control, taking neither drugs nor too much drink so as to better keep an eye on his enemies. Caecilia glanced at his corpse. He had not been wary enough.

"There were many people at the banquet last night," continued Erene, "all celebrating the start of the festival. Anyone could have given him the Mandragora."

Mastarna would be thinking the same. He'd been gambling late, joining Caecilia in bed for only a few short hours before meeting with the tribal leaders prior to the procession. Now he would be worrying that he could've prevented such treachery, that if he'd been at his friend's side he might have stayed the hand of the assassin, even if the poison had been deposited in a blink of an eye—in as short a time as it had taken him to kiss Ulthes so tenderly.

She should have gone to him, taken the few steps that would bridge her doubt and bring him comfort, but she could not.

She sensed his frustration. There was no evidence as to who the murderer was, but all knew that Tulumnes had the most to gain. Like the destroyed purple fleece, proof was absent.

"The question of how the zilath died will have to wait," said Vipinas. "There is a more pressing need. What is to happen about the election?"

"That's simple," said Mastarna. "Postpone it. Ulthes must be buried with due honors first."

The old aristocrat shook his head. "We can't defer the vote, Mastarna. The League of the Twelve is due to meet. Veii is the wealthiest city. Either a zilath or king must be in attendance."

Vipinas's words seemed to encourage Tulumnes. Although keeping a wary eye upon Mastarna, the tall noble straightened his shoulders, puffing out his chest. Pesna, too, had taken note of his colleague. The normally hunched and anxious toady was surveying Mastarna haughtily.

"There is no need for an election," said Tulumnes. "The gods have spoken three times to signal that a monarch be crowned: first the thunderbolt that struck the palace, then the purple fleece, and now the zilath dead on the eve of the election."

Mastarna lunged at him, clutching his robes with both fists. "Ulthes did not die as a sign to prove your victory!"

Vipinas again took control. "Both of you stand back!" There was no denying the old man commanded respect. Bony limbs and a humorless demeanor could not disguise his reputation as a war hero.

Mastarna released Tulumnes but was not ready to be calm. "There will be an election and you will lose," he shouted. "A candidate will be nominated and then the four tribes loyal to Ulthes will vote in favor of a zilath. The clans of Ulthes, Mastarna, Vipinas, and Apercu."

Tulumnes smiled. "Don't be so certain that all will vote as you expect, Mastarna." He paused, turning to Apercu. "There are those who can no longer brook sacrilege by remaining in your camp."

The fat princip stood as though caught in the act of thieving, hoping that to keep still would curtain him from view. His bullfrog throat puffed in and out in agitation, his face beet red.

Last night he had been affable and charming, flattering Caecilia as he always did, the only aristocrat other than Ulthes who treated her with any warmth. He and Vipinas had spent much time with the zilath. It had not seemed strange to her. These three had become a tight ring of conspirators with her husband. It was their custom to drink and plot and plan.

Last night, though, Caecilia remembered that the portly man had drunk much but did not become drunk. Odd for a person who took pride in cramming his ample belly too full and spilling over with merriment. There had been an irritability about him, too, that was unusual and that she now clearly understood.

The aristocrats within the tent shifted and whispered in a dance of unease and surprise. All must be thinking the same thing. All must be wondering if a man as perfidious as Apercu could also be a murderer. Their attention gradually turned to Mastarna, waiting.

A muscle in Mastarna's cheek twitched as he realized how deeply he'd been betrayed. His best friend had died and now the man he thought a staunch ally was a traitor.

Apercu averted his gaze. Perhaps he would have welcomed rage instead of reproach. But when Mastarna did not speak, he gained confidence to pour out his spite.

"I despise you for marrying this Roman bitch. This descendant of the Aemilian who killed your father. I lost my two brothers at Fidenae! How could you bear her in your bed?"

The councillor had always been kind to her. Always the avuncular hand at her elbow or worldly piece of advice in her ear. She had overheard others at court whispering their hatred but she'd never imagined that Apercu was one of them. His betrayal of the zilath and Mastarna was of state proportion, but this private betrayal was no less devastating. She'd been drawn into trust and friendship only to find herself loathed and ridiculed behind her back.

"I am a devout man, the Maru of Fufluns," he continued. "I can no longer ignore the warnings of the gods. It is clear to me that Tulumnes should rule."

He gestured toward the opening of the tent where the crowd's wailing had slurred into a syrup of maudlin grief, pierced by the keening and ululating of women. Prayers could be heard threaded through the crying. "The people will demand the three omens be heeded. The zilath's death was a sign. The chief haruspex will confirm the gods wish a king to rule."

Artile showed no emotion at the sound of his name other than the merest narrowing of his eyes, and Caecilia realized how sweet it must be to have the power to determine the destiny of a city and destroy his brother.

It was a calmly spoken sentence. "Ulthes's death is a powerful portent."

Caecilia gasped. His words condemned the zilath to eternal torment. As a prodigy, Ulthes's body would be cut up, burned, and buried. Just like the lightning's scar on the palace. Just like the purple fleece. The evidence of the gods' intentions scoured from the world.

Mastarna's cry whipped the room, loud and sudden and sharp, making Caecilia's already racing heart jump. Artile stepped back in fright.

Immediately Tulumnes roared at Ulthes's bodyguards to seize her husband. In the cramped space, the lictors stepped forward, the area bristling with the raised axes and stout rods of men as hard and cruel as Arruns.

A murmur spread through the room at seeing the twelve black-clad men, once the servants of the zilath, showing no hesitation in obeying.

Vipinas was enraged. "What's this? Release him!"

"Don't waste your breath," said Mastarna. "Gold has more meaning than allegiance to a dead man."

"The zilath was a believer in Aita," insisted Vipinas to Artile. "Don't deprive him of the chance to join the Blessed."

"I only interpret the signs," said the priest, smoothing one eyebrow. "I did not make the sacred law."

Vipinas appealed to Tulumnes instead. "You can't deny him a funeral. The people will despise you."

The princip shoved the old nobleman aside. It was the first time Caecilia had seen the lean, pale-skinned man blush, a pink tinge like candlelight through wax.

"The people will do as I tell them." Safe between two bodyguards, Tulumnes pointed to her, infuriating in his smugness now that his opponent was truly dead, truly gone. And in that moment Caecilia knew without doubt that this man had committed murder with sneaking sureness and cowardice.

"This whore is a reminder of how we lick Rome's ass instead of thrashing it. The treaty should never have been continued." He prodded Mastarna's chest, making him struggle against his captors.

"Forget Rome," Mastarna said coldly. "Neither my tribe nor Ulthes's will let you take power."

Tulumnes called for a chair, enjoying his prisoner's discomfort. "You don't seem to fully understand. There will be no election. My allies and I have already called our clans to arms. Our men are ready to fight, but I would prefer you pledged support instead. After all, you have often said that civil war is a boon to one's enemies. They avidly watch the cockfight and then cut off the head of the victor in its exhaustion. Gaul would relish the chance. So, too, Rome. Do you want to endanger our city out of stubbornness?"

Mastarna grimaced. "You are even more feeble-minded than I suspected if you think I'll help you become king."

The gleam of sweat returned to the princip's face. "Again, I think you fail to comprehend. I do not wish to kill the man with the ability to raise Veii's largest army. Nor do I wish to lose the support of one as venerable as Vipinas. So let me give you an incentive to convince you to support me."

The lictors were men hired to harm: broken teeth, windburned faces, coarse hands, and dirty fingernails. Their black robes did not hide their rankness or the stains from their last meal. But when one of them seized Caecilia's arm, she was surprised she felt no terror; instead the same current of alarm ran through her as when the bandit held her, giving her courage to try and wrench herself free.

"It is time for your wife to serve her purpose. Not only will she be held as surety for your allegiance but as a hostage to Rome. The time has come to conquer her city."

As Mastarna struggled against the men who restrained him, Caecilia was reminded how the Phersu had held back the hound, goading and kicking while it strained to attack its prey. Tulumnes's threat was the cruel nail in the cur's collar that dug into its flesh.

To Caecilia, though, the threat was an old one. Danger had dogged her steps on her wedding day and fed her fear as she knelt at the altar before Artile. She had lived with it for so long that it had come to be like a dull ache in her side that could be tolerated or even forgotten only to flare into sharp pain when she was fool-ish enough to stretch too high. Today her foolishness had been at its greatest. Today, basking in sunshine, she'd beheld a spectacle believing that the ache was healed.

Tulumnes studied her, anticipating her terror, but Caecilia did not flinch or raise hands to mouth or utter a cry. Remembering Erene's composure, the girl was determined to show how a Roman, just like a Cretan, could despise him.

The nobles stood within the pavilion as though in a tableau, dressed and draped for spring with bright clothes, smooth skin, dark hair, sloe eyes. They should have been beautiful. Instead their faces were strained either in complicity or with the shock of betrayal. Already there was a slow drift to take sides, those for and against, the dread of brothers fighting brothers and fathers fighting sons the only thing they now had in common.

Vipinas protested again but Tulumnes placed one finger to his lips for silence. For the second time that day, the aristocrat reddened, back stiffening with the insult. Compared to the army

Mastarna could muster, the influence Vipinas wielded over his small tribe was little threat. Tulumnes spoke of respect, but in truth the self-proclaimed king would easily crush Vipinas's tribe. Ulthes's clan would also need to reorganize themselves after the death of their leader. The tall princip must have factored this into his plan.

Mastarna smiled at her. A grim, hopeless smile. It made her cringe to see him so. A powerful man rendered powerless. It would seem that the thunderbolt that speared the palace was not just a warning for Ulthes.

And then she remembered her husband's promise to his friend. Would the zilath expect such a vow to be kept now that he'd been murdered and betrayed?

"You're a fool," said Mastarna, finally turning his gaze back to Tulumnes. "Do not think that famine and plague will hinder Rome. The hungriest wolves are the fiercest."

There was a stubbornness that resided in Tulumnes's jaw-line, a furrow between his eyebrows that signaled implacability. Mastarna's words may as well have been shouted into a well that would be drained and never used again. Boarded up and then forgotten.

Tulumnes turned to his peers. "The Romans have lost men at Verrugo and are still besieging the Volscian town of Anxur. Diplomatic communications have ceased between our cities while Rome struggles with that foe. If we gain the assistance of the broth-erhood of cities we will have all the Rasenna behind us. We will be invincible. Then, once again, a king will rule over Rome as god-head, judge, and general."

"The Twelve will never support you," said Vipinas. "The north-ern cities see Gaul as a greater menace, and the brotherhood is always slow to unite against another city's foe."

Tulumnes glared at Mastarna. "That's why you must accom-pany me to the council meeting at Velzna. Aule Porsenna is head zilath this year. You must use the influence you still have with your former father-in-law to convince him to support our cause. And if you are successful, I will return your bitch to Rome before war is declared."

The tall man signaled the lictors to release both husband and wife. When Mastarna stepped closer to Caecilia she noticed his sweat smelled of fear, frightening her.

"I am not afraid to die," she declared, glaring at Tulumnes. But it was a lie spoken without thinking. A wish more than a fact.

The would-be king smiled. It was a smile that said he was half-way to righting the wrongs of Rome against his father. It was a smile that rejoiced in defeating his Veientane enemies. "Aemilia Caeciliana, I am not threatening you with death. Dishonor and humiliation is the vengeance I seek. A shame similar to that which my father endured. I wish you to despair so deeply that taking your own life will be the only choice. And so, if your husband does not assist me to gain support of the Twelve, I will cut off your hands and send them to Rome with a demand for surrender. It will then be up to your people to decide if you are worth saving. And to ensure both of you fully understand that I am serious, each of these twelve lictors will take turns with you before they wield the axe."

· · ·

Time stretched, slowed down, stopped. Without imploring Fate to make it so.

Through it all, Erene sobbed quietly at Ulthes's side, her cries quiet and anguished.

When she was dragged away, a frail scapegoat between brutes, her sobbing neither rose to a wail nor dimmed to weeping but remained constant, endless, inconsolable.

Tulumnes took the crown of high office from Ulthes's head and placed it slowly upon his own. It was slightly askew, hindered by his lopsided ears. It was harder for him to remove the purple cloak, which lay bunched beneath the body. Two lictors lifted the deadweight so that it could be retrieved. Each ministration making Caecilia cringe.

All of them watched him don the trappings of office. His handsome face was painted with the vermilion of king or zilath. In the dimness of the tent he looked like some demon. All he needed was wings to rival Tuchulcha.

The principes spilled from the pavilion into a day that had slyly changed to afternoon. The people's mourning altered pitch as the news of Ulthes's death exploded from the pavilion into the weeping, grieving throng.

"I go to greet my people," said Tulumnes.

Gone was the discontent that had chained his soul for so long, gone was the young boy tormented by his father's disgrace. "Stay and say farewell to your dead lover and wife," he said to Mastarna. "After that, I expect you to be faithful to me."

. . .

Mastarna knelt beside the body of his friend and wept. It was the first time Caecilia had seen her husband cry.

Two lictors guarded them, but it was as if they were invisible so great was her misery.

The horror of Tulumnes's warning seemed unreal, too enormous to digest, too terrible to consider. Instead she concentrated on a hurt that was more personal and just as cruel. For the meaning of the kiss had not been imagined. All this time she'd been foolishly envying a ghost when a rival of flesh and blood existed. She sank to her knees, sobbing.

Hearing her cries, Mastarna quickly knelt beside her, only to recoil as she shrank from his touch.

"You were lovers! Were all those nights of politics merely feeding your need for each other? Did you steal from the warmth of his bed into mine?"

Mastarna stared at her, his expression as confused as when he'd found her ridding herself of the Zeri. "What are you talking about? Ulthes was my mentor. I was only his beloved when I was a youth."

Mastarna tried to hold her again but she shied away. "Don't touch me! Don't touch me!"

She struggled to her feet. "You were his bride. Freeborn lovers! Am I to know nothing but shame?"

Mastarna flinched at her insult. Then without taking his eyes from hers, he barked at the lictors to stand sentry outside. They dithered, unsure of obeying a nobleman who was now prisoner to the king. Finally they left, no doubt satisfied to eavesdrop through the tent cloth. All Veii would know of the drama by nightfall.

Over her time with him, Caecilia had learned that Mastarna was quick to temper but reserved his rage for cowards and fools. She'd grown used to the rhythm of his moods, from melancholy and recklessness to tenderness and devotion. He'd only been angry with her once—when she'd used the pomegranates that night. It was a cold wrath that had led her to the rituals of the Book of Fate, a deceit she still held close.

"What is this nonsense?" He remained motionless, his broad shoulders and chest emphasizing his potential to harm. One blow from him would fell her. "Don't you understand there is going to be a war, Caecilia? Both our cities will be imperiled. Many people will die. So tell me, with all your Roman logic, why my being Ulthes's beloved when I was young should be so important?"

His voice was chill, making her wish she could stop herself, curb her tongue, concentrate on the threat that faced them. Instead all she could think of was Ulthes and him together—and that he had lied to her before.

"A Roman warrior could be killed for what you've done. A blood taint is upon you. A stain that has spread to me."

Patience returned to his voice. Just as there always was when dealing with her prejudices. "You are not in Rome anymore, Bellatrix. Ulthes and I were not like Artile and my son. I was only beloved to him from the age of fifteen until I grew a beard. It is the way here. I thought you understood. I thought you had learned to see Veii through other than Roman eyes."

"No, you blinded me but now I see. You have made me another Lucretia."

Reaching over to play with one of her pendant earrings, he ran his hand down the sleeve of her wedding gown, the thin cloth a sheer skin between his fingers and her arm. He smiled, making her feel like a child exaggerating the pain of a minor scrape. "Don't be foolish. I love you, Caecilia. You are a Veientane wife. My Veientane wife."

Feeling the familiar ridge of callus upon his palm, smelling traces of sandalwood still lingering beneath the sweat, she knew it was happening again. He was making her believe there was no shame in accepting corruption, that it was she who was deluded, that it was Rome that was wrong to expect her to be faithful to its ways.

Yet her disgrace was not what was most painful. She felt an anguish within her so agonizing that no sound would be deep or loud enough to expel it if she opened her mouth to scream. For the image of Mastarna bending to kiss Ulthes would not leave her. She had seen him weep, his misery embedding doubt—doubt as to whether he'd ceased to love his friend after he'd reached manhood, after he'd married Seianta, after he'd married her.

Erene had said the three of them comforted each other after Seianta died. Caecilia had thought the courtesan to be the only one to give succor. Her imagination had not stretched too far. But having watched the revelers at the Winter Feast, her education had been furthered. The thought of Ulthes and her husband together hurt and sickened her, sullying her memory of the zilath and disgusting her that Mastarna had been his bride, the lesser of the two.

"I am glad that Artile's prediction must have been wrong. That there was no need to try and defer my fate after all."

Again he looked bewildered. "What are you talking about?"

"He told me I would give birth to your son and so I prayed to Nortia to postpone bearing him for seven years."

His almond-shaped eyes looked bruised. She lowered her eyes, unable to watch a strong man's face lapse into that of a stricken child's.

"Why? Why would you do such a thing?"

"You kept the truth about little Vel secret. Then Artile told me you were prepared to let me have your monsters in your lust to sire an heir. Just as you did with Seianta."

This time his touch was not gentle or inveigling. He dragged her to him effortlessly with one hand. "Seianta and I both knew our marriage was cursed. We both wanted a son, no matter the cost."

His fingers gripped her arms so fiercely she thought he would break them as easily as he'd snapped Amyntor's bones. They sank into her flesh, deep enough to mark the soft whiteness for days. "So my brother led you in these rites?"

Caecilia nodded, defiant.

He'd never lifted a finger to her, his restraint almost a weakness for a husband. This time she did not expect mercy. She closed her eyes, not wishing to see him strike, but there was no blow, instead harsh breathing, ragged and hectic.

"And have you continued kneeling in such prayer? Even as you whispered your love to me?"

Caecilia wavered, the scent of chamomile and verbena filling her. "No, I stopped the rites after Larthia's funeral because I loved you. I was prepared to take a risk, but now I know the lightning I called down was not from Uni. My destiny is to return to Rome—mutilated, dead or alive."

She pushed her hands against his chest, each movement painful because he was still grasping her arms. "I wanted your son, Mastarna, but not any longer."

He began to shake her, her limbs knocked and flung around as easily as one of her old wood-and-rag dolls. Terrified, she began to cry.

Hearing her he quickly released her. She sank to the ground, chest heaving. He reached out to her hesitantly, guiltily, but he was still angry. "You knew I longed for a child. You knew!"

Caecilia struggled for breath, her distress peaking in crests and troughs as he paced beside her.

"You are no Lucretia! You were seduced by me, not raped," he growled. "And a seduction only succeeds when there is desire to be tempted. You chose to be a Veientane on the day you took the vial of Alpan from my hand, Caecilia. You chose it, too, on the day you sat in audience beside me as my wife."

She kept her head lowered, unable to speak. The bitterness in his voice was scalding.

"I promised Ulthes not to start a war, but that pledge is over. And if not for you, I'd have tried to kill Tulumnes today and let my death be a spur to rebellion. For you see, wife, even if you think me base, I have honor enough not to let him harm you."

Mastarna returned to Ulthes's side, grasping the three-fingered hand of his friend, his face collapsing into the grimness reserved for any talk of Artile. "Go to your priest and see if he will take you back as his disciple. Pray to Uni also, but let this be your prayer—that I can convince the Twelve to help us and that Tulumnes keeps his word and sends you home."

Turning his back on her, Mastarna stooped to bathe his friend's face and hands. The knowledge that his lover's body would be desecrated must have been intolerable above all the unbearable things that had happened that day. Unable to watch him, Caecilia lay on her side upon the rug's dirtied weave and, exhausted, closed her eyes.

After a while the lictors appeared, seemingly unperturbed by the quarrel they'd overheard. After all, a man beating his wife was only fitting, especially a Roman one who'd caused such trouble.

Escorted from the tent, Mastarna went to play his new role, that of the king's loyal supporter. He said nothing as he left.

• • •

Hours passed. Caecilia lay with knees huddled against her chest, limbs cramping, not caring that they did. Her only companions were the two guards, sullen at missing the feast.

Two lictors and a dead man.

The stuffy air within the pavilion had dissipated into evening cool. Dimness surrounded her, the gray between awareness and sleep. No one had come for her. She'd expected to be bound and dragged away but instead she had been left alone.

Until he came. Until Artile stared down upon her in silence.

When she stood up she hobbled for a few steps like an old woman, resenting that her aches reminded her she was still alive.

"I did not know you hated Ulthes and Mastarna so much. I did not think you hated me."

The haruspex sighed. "Sister, it is not a question of hatred. The gods send their miracles and I am charged with reading them."

She found courage to glance at the dead zilath and resisted the urge to weep. His face was no longer suffused with color, sweat no longer covered his brow, his craggy face no longer was contorted.

Leading her outside, Artile held out a double-handled chalice. "I see you are in need." His voice was mellow, lulling. She remembered how she once found comfort with him. "I have missed you," he continued, stroking her hair with soft hands. "I have missed your devotion."

She should have pushed him away but it was easier to follow, to fall back into the role of priest and follower, and to believe he could help.

Outside, dusk stained stone and wood in orange and pink. Such showiness nudged at Caecilia's grief, and she wished darkness would soon blanket the garishness. On the hillside, fires were flickering, mischievous compared to the languor of failing light. The keening and wailing had transformed into a hubbub of joy. The Rasenna were ready to celebrate that they were alive even as Ulthes lay dead.

"The king is wise. He has delayed telling the people that the zilath's body is to be destroyed," he said. "The Festival of Fufluns and its mysteries will dull the pain of their grief. At the end of it they will be better able to cope with change."

Caecilia knew there would still be an undercurrent of anxiety. A lucumo had been appointed without an election and Vel Mastarna, who had so opposed a monarchy, now strangely stood at Tulumnes's side, assuring them that a civil war had been avoided.

The drinking had already started as large wooden vats were filled with strong unwatered wine. Caecilia knew what scenes would follow. The Winter Feast had been a rehearsal.

Panic rippled through her. Mastarna had said she need not stay for the revels. She could not escape to her room tonight. She would need another exit. Artile offered her the cup again.

"Drink it and it will ease the pain. It will speed you to pleasure faster than Zeri. It is Divine Milk, the milk of the gods."

The Zeri had taken worry away before. It was still hard to forget its power or ignore its call. It was difficult to imagine that this elixir was stronger.

The image of the mocking dancer in the villa shimmered before her; how she'd lain vomiting each drop of the potion from her veins, writhing and moaning and scratching to rid herself of its thrall. One sip and she would be enslaved again.

It tasted like goat's milk. Sour with a hint of earth in it. She thought drinking from the breast of the Divine would have been sweeter.

She drank deeply, used to bitterness.

· · ·

Tarchon had fled to Artile's side for protection after his humiliation. Her weakening did not cause him to frown. He'd already shared the Milk, his pupils eating the browns of his eyes. "Call to Fufluns and he will answer."

A familiar sense of ease coursed through her, so strong she knew she couldn't stop or slow it, rushing her into a current of elation. Then Cytheris was beside her, shoving Tarchon away. Admonishing and then pleading, her brow creased and her mouth pursed, she tugged at her mistress' hand. Caecilia did not respond, pushing the handmaid from her. Happiness was bursting within her, chasing concern away, making her giggle at the servant.

A rough stone altar wreathed in ivy had been built at the base of the hill. Sacred staves marked the ritual space and a bloodied double axe still lay upon the table. Candles dripped wax upon its surface. Candles upon candles. Flaring in competition with the firelight. A goat, sacred animal of the god, had been sacrificed, the aroma of its roasting meat pungent upon the breeze. Cepens were filling bulls' horns with Divine Milk to give to people eagerly lining up to receive communion.

Apercu stood in front of the killing table beside a stone phallus, high as a man, symbol of Fufluns's resurrection, power, and fertility. The Maru's face was hidden by a bull's mask, his chest and paunch bare, a goatskin cloak around his shoulders, and shod with leather hunting boots. Two young women knelt before him. One was unknown to her. The other was Pesna's comely wife. Heads covered with filmy veils, they were dressed in gossamer shifts so sheer it was if they were robed in candlelight. Wedding gowns, Fufluns's brides, initiates of the Mysteries.

Sensing she was being watched, Caecilia focused beyond the flickering play of shadow and light. An enormous mask crowned with a wreath of vine leaves and grapes loomed above her. Bliss filled her as she stared into the blank eyeholes and gaping mouth of Fufluns, longing for a glimpse of the Divine, wanting her soul to merge with his.

Her heart throbbed. Loud and soft. Fast and slow. Keeping time with cymbals and drums, timbrels and castanets. Long straight trumpets blasted notes into the darkness, the air solid with sound.

• • •

There were six of them. Priestesses dressed like the actors in the play's chorus.

If Caecilia had not drunk the Divine Milk she would have quaked at the sight of them. Over their long pleated chitons they wore leopard skins, the fur sleek with its dark patches. One caressed a snake that slid around her arm, a scaly ornament, a slithering bracelet. They carried thyrsus staffs with ivy trailing from them. When they touched the tips to the lips of those around them, Caecilia swore honey flowed from them. They were dancing with the same intensity and jerkiness as did a flame, whirling and stamping and leaping from one foot to the other, making themselves instruments of beat and rhythm and melody. Their song swept over Caecilia, infecting all, expelling the cool from the spring evening, spreading heat. Welcoming ecstasy.

The revelers began climbing the hillside, their torches a mass of wavering pinpoints in the darkness. They wore leering satyr masks. Anonymous in their fervor, fantastic in their worship. They screamed to the god to reveal himself: "Bacchoi, Bacchoi!"

Following them, the maenad priestesses arched their backs then whipped forward, necks almost snapping with the force. Over and over again. The initiates, eyes vacant, mimicked them, falling into the same frantic trance, cries floating up with spirals of smoke as they climbed to the peak of the hill. The crowd followed.

Beneath hawthorn and beech, Veientanes rutted, celebrating death and resurrection in shuddering moments of climax, their souls reaching out to Almighty Fufluns, euphoric.

Watching them, Caecilia was stirred, wet. Hands tugged at her, inviting her to lie with them, but there was no time, the priestesses beckoned. And the Roman girl, color and music twisting within her, called to Fufluns, too. Joining in the dance of the maenads, she threw her head backward and forward until, with each crack of her neck, a surge of pleasure exploded through her. Forgetting all care. Forgetting Mastarna.

• • •

Hours passed. Caecilia did not tire. The Divine Milk was strong and long lasting, but when her limbs at last flagged and melancholy crept into her laughter she refilled her cup. This time there was no rush of pleasure. Instead it was as if fingers were creeping along her spine, making her skin tingle and goose bumps form.

This time the revelers' screams and laughter were frightening, their masks macabre. Nearby a priest swung a bullroarer. As its revolutions increased in speed, the sound progressed from a moan to a scream to a roar. Deafening and horrifying.

In the clearing at the top of the hill there was another altar. A wicker basket lay upon it. Hidden inside was the sacred phallus. The brides knelt, eagerly waiting for it to be revealed. Tethered to the table were two fawns. They bleated persistently, their cries discordant with the rhythm of pipe and drum.

The night had grown darker, the stars erased. The fires were burning low, white ash and charcoal forming drifts around their bases. Suddenly Caecilia felt surrounded, hemmed in, crushed by the mass of followers. A beat throbbed within her loudly, but she did not know if it was her heart or the drums. Her skin was clammy and nausea filled her. Everything she looked at twisted and shifted, magnified. The ground was unsteady beneath her feet.

A man wearing a bull's headdress staggered toward her. He wore a goatskin cloak and leaned on his thyrsus staff. Streaks of purple wine mottled his breasts. It was the Maru.

Grasping her arm and pushing her to her knees, he hitched up his kirtle with his other hand. Caecilia could see his soot-ringed eyes through the eyeholes, the coarse-haired mask grotesque in the shadow and light. He stank of wine fumes. Terrified, the world spinning around her, Caecilia was not sure if he were a man or Fufluns himself.

Hot stinking bile erupted from her, pouring over his chest, spattering her chiton. Apercu released her, stepping back as she convulsed and heaved. He studied her for a while, then, grunting, wiped her vomit from his skin and walked away. Caecilia lay there puking up the last remnants of the potion, her tongue and mouth and throat burning with the taste of acrid sick.

Time stretched.

Quivering, she curled into a ball, pulling her hem over her feet in case the maenad's serpent slithered beneath her skirts and bit her.

Then from the darkness someone lifted her onto their lap. Solace and comfort enfolded her. Sure that it was Mastarna, she leaned her head back upon his chest. But it was not a man who held her. She was cradled against the soft breasts of a woman.

A woman who held her as a mother would. A curtain of wings cocooned her. Caecilia looked up into the face of a guardian angel.

The arms around her tightened, the pinions no longer white but black, shimmering with iridescence. Scales, not feathers; membrane of skin, not down. The fetid breath of her comforter assailed her, a breath that stank of bile. Caecilia twisted around to see who held her. Pale and soulless eyes glared at her, a slit of black bisecting them. And Tuchulcha, sharp vulture's beak poised above her, tilted her chin to him as would a lover.

TWENTY

Cytheris was cradling her and stroking her hair. "Hush," she said. "Hush."

It was dawn. Bleak. The sun begrudging an appearance. The ground's chillness seized her limbs. Cytheris had draped a cloak over Caecilia but the girl still shivered in her torn golden gown. The ache in her head was agonizing. Just moving her eyes hurt. She searched for Mastarna and then remembered.

Bodies lay jumbled around her, masks askew, mottled and streaked with wine stains. For a moment she thought them dead until she saw that some were twitching. Nudity had lost its allure in the half-light. Fire and candlelight were forgiving, but in daylight there was nothing appealing about blotchy skin and veined legs or bodies resembling congealed fat.

Flies buzzed around scraps of roasted goat and half-eaten figs. The air, hopeful of a breeze, smelled of pee and wine, hazy with smoke, lethargic with the cold. Extinguished torches smoldered where they had been carelessly dropped. Scattered around her were shreds of flesh and hide. Dappled and pale. A fawn's.

All but one of the maenads had disappeared. She lay flat on her back snoring loudly, her mouth ajar, her robes fanned out about her. Her snake curled up in a tight ball in one fold of her leopard-skin cloak. Dried blood smeared around her mouth. Upon her teeth and gums. A strip of lightly spotted fur dangling from one hand.

Caecilia retched, her stomach empty.

"Hush," murmured Cytheris. "Hush."

On the altar, amid paterae and stumps of tallow, one young bride lay sleeping. Her veil was gone, dress torn. Her face stained with tears, the lap of her gown with blood.

Pesna's wife sat propped against the side of the sacred table, head drooping, a thin thread of saliva trailing from her lips. Her shift was also ripped, stripes of red upon her back. The soles of her feet and her knees were filthy as were the palms of her hands. Her husband stooped beside her, face pinched and anxious. Swaying, Pesna strained to raise his wife but she was too drugged to stand. He was weeping.

Caecilia nervously scanned the scene for Apercu, her heartbeat painfully tapping at her throat. To her relief the Maru was sprawled asleep, still wearing the bull's head, his muffled snorts and whistles far from godlike.

Weariness overcame her. Too tired to weep she laid her head on Cytheris's shoulder as she watched the revelers wake. Priests were moving among them with bulls' horns of milk. Wineskins were passed from hand to hand. A panpipe was trilling from lower down the hillside along with the hiccup of drums and bells. The sound of laughing drifted to her. The carousing of the night was continuing into the new day.

She closed her eyes, only to sense someone was observing her.

Artile—steady and sober.

Fufluns was not his god. This feast was not his celebration. And yet he'd given her the Milk. He'd let her see and do shameful things.

"I have given you the chance to see Mastarna's god, Mastarna's resurrection. Return to the Calu Cult, Sister. Return to me."

• • •

In the end it was Tarchon who carried her home. After Cytheris found him lying between his green-eyed lover and one of the many sloe-eyed boys he'd had that night.

Dark circles of exhaustion ringed his eyes. "The Divine Milk was too strong. You should have flown, circled the earth, and lain with a god, Caecilia. You were not meant to suffer so." Wearily, he bore her in his arms. He would not let another touch her. He lay beside her on the bed in her dirtied wedding gown and soothed her to sleep.

He did so because Mastarna was not there.

• • •

She slept fitfully for three days. In the fuzziness of first waking she heard shrill keening, eerie and heartbreaking, desolate and pan-icked. The people had been told of Ulthes's fate.

The zilath's corpse, dismembered and quartered, was being burned and buried beyond consecrated ground, destroyed to pro-tect Veii from any trace of divine intrusion. There should have been a procession that swayed and wound along the wide symmetrical avenues of the citadel to the City of the Dead. Blood should have been spilled in the great man's honor and for his salvation. Instead the insulting way in which Ulthes was buried would be remem-bered long after by more than his family and his tribe.

With Ulthes gone, Tulumnes's ordination was held with indecent haste. The day after the desecration of the zilath's body, the College of Principes confirmed his appointment as lucumo. But although the chief haruspex placed his right hand upon Tulumnes's head to transfer power to him, Tulumnes was not crowned, wishing his coronation to be glorious and splendid. A date was set upon his return from Velzna, when games and festivals and tournaments would be held. In the meantime, but for a golden coronet upon his head, Laris Tulumnes was priest king, and the task of surviving his reign had begun.

Caecilia called for Cytheris to draw aside the heavy bedroom curtain so she could look into the garden. The sky was streaked with smoke, plumes of black against palest blue from the Veientanes lighting small fires in the street in memory of the zilath. The air brimmed with their grieving, the lament aching within her, too. And lying alone in the big tall bed with its coverlet woven of plaited red, blue, and green, Caecilia wept. Wept for Arnth Ulthes. Wept for Mastarna. Wept for herself.

Cytheris bathed Caecilia's grazes and bruises. There was a sharp cut upon the girl's cheek where she'd danced too close to a maenad's whip.

"Who were those women? They were not at the Winter Feast."

"They arrived here with the Greek actors. I have not seen maenads act like that. Their god is Dionysus in his guise of the Wanderer. Unlike Fufluns, who is gentle, he calls upon them to spread his message through wildness and violence. It is the first time I have seen an animal torn apart in sacrifice or the brides scourged to gain divine acceptance."

Caecilia remembered how the Veientanes had abandoned themselves readily to the ecstasies of the Wanderer last night, sensing that in the future they would be all too willing to re-create their rustic Fufluns in a darker form.

Watching her handmaid bustle around the room, Caecilia realized how much she owed the maid for protecting her from the drunk and drugged followers for hours. She knew she should've listened to her at the beginning of the night. Now a flood of salty tears would not be enough to cleanse her, nor a river of lustral water.

Sitting on the edge of the high bed, feet dangling above the tiled floor, Caecilia wondered if she was expected to be dutiful to Mastarna or to Rome.

His panoply hung on the wall with its crested helmet and bull's head shield. Its presence proof of his vulnerability to Tulumnes.

When Caecilia tried to pull the curved iron sword from its hook, she staggered under its weight. It clanked to the floor, lethal and lifeless. How had Lucretia lifted such a weapon to plunge it into her breast? Caecilia could barely raise Mastarna's three inches from the floor.

Sitting down, she turned the point toward her, her finger nudging the sharp tip tentatively. The merest touch drew blood. She wanted to draw the blade across her wrist, to open a vein, to let life seep from her slowly, a different kind of ebbing.

She did not have that type of courage. She was no Lucretia.

· · ·

Routine saved her. The mechanics of existing.

Life descended into small efforts. Washing her face each morning and night, combing and pinning her hair, dressing herself. Taking an infinite amount of time with her ministrations. Laboring upon decisions: What to eat? Which prayer to say? Which book to read?

But routine also led to memories of him. How he would pause at the bedroom curtain to adjust his tebenna, ensuring the folds hung neatly, unable to hide this small vanity despite his ugliness.

Or how he'd consult her as they listened to the concerns of their tenants in the reception hall lined with boxes of scrolls and linen books.

But other memories tormented her, arousing jealousy again and again. Those of Arruns shaving his master's half-beard in the afternoons, making her wonder if Mastarna had been ensuring Ulthes's cheeks were not scratched in lovemaking instead of hers.

It was not simple to discard all that connected her to him. She wore Marcus's bracelet. No other ornament. The Atlenta pendant had been dropped into a pouch and stored with her clothes. Before that awful day she used to stroke the embossed figure upon it absently, a habit, a comfort.

There was the empty bed, too, and the smile reserved for her upon waking. She wanted to be rid of him but, like a phantom limb, he'd become part of her. And so, when she heard he'd left the city, unwillingly traveling with Tulumnes's court, she retrieved the locket from its hiding place and laid her head upon his pillow, eventually falling asleep upon his side of the bed when she could cry no more.

• • •

Caecilia once again stood on the high citadel, gazing at square fields of varied shades of green. Soon it would be harvest time, a year since she was wed.

The breeze tickled her face but no stray tendrils of hair slid across her cheeks. She wore woolen fillets in her hair befitting a Roman matron, and had covered her head with a palla, plain and unfringed. Her clothes were no longer of fine thread and pleasing hues. Rings and necklaces lay tangled, earrings and fibulas in disarray, chains broken, links scattered, gems dropped and lost.

The stola and tunic scratched her unshaven skin until she grew familiar again with the homespun bulk. The earthen color was restful to the eye after busy threads of silver and blue. When the humble sandals pinched her feet and blistered her heels, she welcomed the pain as a penance.

No more cosmetics added blush to cheeks and rose to her mouth. Without lotions, her skin was soon dry and hangnails snagged her clothes. The luxury of daily baths was forfeited. Cracked lips and dirty hair reminded her that salves were close and perfumes nearby but would not be used.

Donning Roman robes and eschewing Veientane ways did not bring her peace, though, nor lessen her guilt. Like fleece spun to a tenuous thread, virtue had been stretched thin, snapping at the smallest pressure, the tiniest temptation.

She wanted none of Rasennan religion. All she wanted was the boundaries of her people, their codes and customs. For nearly a year she'd prayed to the gods of Mastarna's household but it was the protection of her family's spirits she needed. Would they ever forgive her for her neglect?

The brutality of the Phersu's blood sacrifice haunted her and the whip mark suffered in the revels of Fufluns had only just healed. Both Artile and Mastarna had played a tug-of-war with her mind and soul, tempting her to abandon her people's beliefs. She would not heed either of them any longer, rejecting Aita's gruesome salvation as well as Fufluns's depraved resurrection.

An eagle appeared, gliding on the breeze before her, wings spread in perfect symmetry. Caecilia stood parallel to it, although the raptor was oblivious to its witness, intent on the prey scurrying in the scrub below. Plummeting, cruel as an arrow, it swooped upon its quarry and flew, effortlessly, from her.

A few yards away two lictors lounged or strutted in her wake wherever she went. She knew little about them other than one liked beer and pickles too much, and the other picked his nose. Her world was limited to the house and the Great Temple, even though she chanced seeing Artile there. The guards did not begrudge her the freedom of standing at the arx wall either, to relish brief moments of escape in sun or wind or rain.

Tarchon stood beside her. Since the Festival of Fufluns, the youth had made excuses for Artile, saying that Divine Milk was offered to everybody, that the priest had thought she wished to see Fufluns, too.

"The elixir's power comes from those red-spotted mushrooms. Reindeers eat them and their milk dilutes the magic so that mortals may safely drink it."

Caecilia was not so quick to believe the priest's innocence. Resentment now tinged all her dealings with him. She steadfastly refused to return to his control, swearing she would not drink another potion—ever. "You shouldn't trust Artile. His predictions are false and cruel. Believing in his powers has only led me to heartache."

"You judge him too harshly. After all, he is a mere man and not infallible. You are wrong to question his practices and beliefs. There are only two things that Artile lives for—serving the gods and loving me."

Caecilia grimaced. "Then if he cares for you so much he should let you take a wife and avoid being shunned."

The youth grunted. "You think it is so easy? How can I sire children when I do not desire women? Growing stubble on my chin won't stop me being his."

"Maybe so, but you should still renounce him. After all, you have other lovers. Ones who are not freeborn. There is the slave boy with the green eyes and now the Carthaginian freedman." Caecilia reached over to touch yet another bruise that shadowed his face. Punishment, no doubt, for infidelity beneath the Divine Milk's spell. "Why swear allegiance to the priest when it can only do you harm?"

Tarchon shook his head. "I can't leave him, Caecilia, even though there have been bruises and squabbles over time.

Sometimes I want to be free of him, to be what Mastarna wants me to be, to shout at him that I am not a child. I flaunt slave boys in front of him because I want him to understand he doesn't own me, but in the end I still love him."

Once again Caecilia thought it a strange word for a man to use for another man. Had her husband felt the same emotion for his mentor?

The girl took a deep breath. "Just like Ulthes and Mastarna."

Tarchon frowned, his voice becoming sharp, his defense of his father surprising. "Ulthes broke no rules. Don't ever compare him to Artile or Mastarna to me."

"Why not? You're all freeborn."

His irritation was deepening. "It's the way of our people. Larthia had lost her husband and needed to raise her son to be a man. To be chosen as a mentor is not easy. Ulthes had to follow the rules of courtship. The first offer must be rejected while the parents judge whether the nobleman is prestigious. After that there is capitulation, the settling of terms, the confirmation of rules."

Caecilia swallowed her distaste, disappointed that Larthia could play such a role. All had failed her here—everyone.

"Tarchon sighed in disgust. "How can you deny that Vel Mastarna is a great man, Caecilia? He married you, a Roman half-caste, to cement a treaty with an enemy who killed his father. He was decried for such rashness and condemned by many of his clan. He sought peace. He fought tyranny until betrayed. He is a valiant warrior. The youngest zilath to hold office. A just master to his slaves and tenants. A good son to Larthia and father to me."

Caecilia was quiet, the silence becoming heavier and more uncomfortable.

Tarchon refused to be ignored. "He was a loving husband also to Seianta. Is a loving husband to you. He has chosen to bow his head to Tulumnes rather than see you harmed. Would he be considered worthy to be a Roman, do you think, under your customs and laws?"

This time her silence was from inability to find words, hating him for twisting what she believed in.

"And if you think that honorable enough, consider this. Who taught Mastarna to be such a man—after his father died and before he grew a beard?"

Caecilia turned to the horizon again, hoping to catch sight of the eagle. To admire its beauty, to have a reason to be distracted so she did not have to acknowledge the truth in Tarchon's words. But the great bird had gone, it alone knowing where the hidden thermals lay, where it could spread its wings and hover, as though standing still.

Tarchon was studying the sky, too, brooding. "I don't understand you," he said. "You have accepted me for being Artile's beloved. Why can't you do so for Mastarna?"

"Because he is my husband! Because he is a great leader! Don't you see that I must condemn him for the very reasons you praise him? In Rome, despite his achievements, he would always be seen as Ulthes's bride. At worst, as a soldier, he would face execution. As a politician, he would be ridiculed and despised. And under the eyes of my people I am now stained because I have lain with him and loved him."

"Still love him," Tarchon said, quietly. "Besides, this is Veii. No one believes what you do. No one will care."

Caecilia clenched her fingers and tapped her breast. "But I will. I care."

"This is only Roman stubbornness," he said in exasperation.

Caecilia turned on him, tired of his criticisms. "Have you ever thought what it would be like to step into my shoes?" She spoke in Latin, greeting her own language like an old friend, a language that held no ambiguity for her and in which she still dreamed. "To be sniggered at for your beliefs and snubbed by Veientane women? If you were taken from here and forced to live in Rome, would you be any less Rasennan even though you bowed to Roman customs? Would you embrace all their ways and be content to forsake the Calu Cult and so lose your chance of salvation?"

Her anger was swelling, frustrated that she was misunderstood, that he did not want to understand. She took his hand and placed it on her birthmark. "I was born a Roman. Until this year I had lived there all my life. The customs and laws and beliefs of my father's people are ingrained in me as permanently as this blemish. In my city the innocent is the one who is blood tainted. Like Lucretia, who was raped by an Etruscan. Like Verginia, whose father slew her rather than let her become a patrician's mistress. It is not a question of love. It is a question of honor."

Tarchon's hand slipped from her throat. "Listen to yourself, Caecilia! This is Mastarna you are talking about. Mastarna! The man who loves you."

She gazed out again to a day that was hot and blue and perfect. It should have been dark and oppressive to match the grimness of her mood. "Did he truly? Or have I always been a pale third behind Seianta and Ulthes?"

"What are you talking about?" His patience had been stretched too far.

"I saw how it was between them. Ulthes was Mastarna's lover until the day he died."

Tarchon's beautiful eyes hardened. "I didn't think even a Roman could be so stupid," he said, as he strode away.

Abandoned, Caecilia listened to the wind whistling through chinks in the masonry, filling in the silence, a hollow sound to accompany the emptiness inside her.

• • •

In her isolation, Tulumnes's lictors became surrogate Aurelias, watching her spinning and weaving or directing slaves to cook and clean. Strangely enough, Caecilia found a perverse enjoyment in enduring what she disliked most about being a Roman woman, telling herself that if she'd been content all along to spin wool and thread it across a loom she'd not have been tempted by Mastarna and his city.

Attempting to weave virtues of honesty and modesty once again into her soul did not help her loneliness. Tarchon's exclusion of her trapped her in misery, doubts still perversely assailing her, unable to accept his assurance about Mastarna, choosing to pick at any scabs that could heal the wound.

There were others in the city who were trapped also.

One day at the Great Temple, she knelt praying before the statue of Uni. Nearby an artisan was repairing the terra-cotta cladding on some of the columns. Caecilia recognized him as one of the craftsmen who worked in Larthia's workshop.

The lictors were outside. Their malice distracted by ogling the townswomen who'd gathered around the citadel well. Their absence gave her a chance to ask for news.

When she first sat in audience, Mastarna's tenants had greeted her warily. But as she'd slowly charmed them, learning their names and those of their wives and children, their respect for her had grown. Now that they were denied Mastarna's protection, it worried her that she could do nothing for them.

"Are you and your family well? What of the other potters at the workshop?"

The man scanned the temple chamber before speaking.

"Times are not good for anyone under the patronage of the House of Mastarna, my lady. But it is worse for those tenants in the country. Pesna has begun a campaign of violence against the tribes of Mastarna, Vipinas, and Ulthes."

Caecilia murmured a prayer. Tarchon had told her that Tulumnes's crony had been left behind to rule while the court was at the sanctuary at Velzna. And the princip savored this power, straightening his thin shoulders and puffing out his chest in the lucumo's wake.

The man swallowed nervously. "Pesna has sent the king's bailiffs to collect taxes. Not just for the city treasury but for his own private levy as well. Farms have been stripped of most crops so that the people struggle to feed their families with what remains. Those who resist are killed and their fields set afire. Wives and children are raped and beaten."

Suddenly a cepen walked across the temple portico, causing the potter to cut short his tale. The man hastily moved out of range of further conversation. Caecilia wished she had some words of comfort to give him, some way of making things right.

Sitting back on her haunches she wiped away a tear, grappling with images of a countryside resounding with the wailing of women as they stood upon charred ground, smoke drifting around them as they mourned their dead and wept over their own rapine.

• • •

Deprived of visitors, it was a surprise when the lictors allowed one in particular to call. The hetaera, Erene, had survived after all. Caecilia never thought to see her again.

The courtesan's golden locks had been drowned in black dye, making her skin sallow. There was a fragile web of lines at the corners of her eyes and a crease between her brows. And the lines between mouth and nose had deepened as though she'd borrowed the somber mask of a tragedian.

Caecilia realized the woman was older than she'd thought. Closer to her thirtieth summer than her twentieth. How Erene must weep when she saw herself in the mirror. Paint and powder no longer hid time and worry upon her face. There could be gray, too, creeping into that cropped hair, but the dye would disguise it. What would become of one such as Erene as beauty faded?

The courtesan's lips curled upward briefly when she saw Caecilia's tunic and stola, but her tone was tired rather than patronizing. "You have regressed, I see, into a Roman."

Caecilia frowned, noticing that the hem of the hetaera's chiton was grubby and her shoes mismatched, making the Cretan blush at the Roman's scrutiny. "I have not slept much since he died," she said.

Caecilia understood. Sleep had been reluctant to tarry more than a couple of hours with her as well. The night demon appeared most nights.

"How is it you have been released?"

"Tulumnes was prepared to be merciful."

Caecilia knew it was unlikely the lucumo would be compassionate without demanding something in return. "What was his price?"

Erene's eyes narrowed in disgust. "Before he left for Velzna he held a symposium with all his court there. I was made to perform: to sing and recite and play the lyre just as I would have done for Ulthes and his friends. Only this time I was expected to grant favors to every nobleman and servant present as if I were a common flute girl."

Caecilia was stunned. How often had she thought this woman to be an expensive whore? She felt ashamed to have done so. Tulumnes's humiliation of Erene sullied Ulthes's memory, too. And reminded her of what her fate could be if the lucumo made good his threat of letting his lictors take her. "I am sorry you have suffered."

The companion smoothed her palms along the sides of her gown as though wiping away Caecilia's sympathy. "I am returning to Crete, although I wish it were Athens. But the Spartans hold sway over that city and they are as sanctimonious as Romans. Besides, there is too much competition there for one as old as I am. In a backwater like Heraklion a fat official would be grateful for a hetaera of my class."

Watching the courtesan pull her robes down to hide her odd shoes, Caecilia knew that Erene's future was gloomy. She would be leaving behind all she knew and had come to love. Without a patron, the promise of destitution and prostitution beckoned.

Theirs had never been a friendship, more a strange acquaintance. And it struck Caecilia that it was unusual for a wife to feel concern for such a woman. Yet Erene had wept bitterly that day in the pavilion, unlike Ulthes's wife who remained captured in her own misery, adding the death of her husband to the tally of the sons she'd already lost.

"You must wonder why I am here," she said. "My house has been confiscated as well as my jewelry and artwork and furniture." Erene paused, her hesitancy unfamiliar. "But Mastarna vowed to me that, should Ulthes die, he would ensure my protection."

Caecilia tensed. How could he expect her to honor such a promise! Charity was granted to kin and clients, tribe and clan, certainly not to a Cretan companion. What was Mastarna thinking when he made such a pact?

Or was it agreed when he met the courtesan in Ulthes's house? When his friend had been generous enough to let him lie with his mistress, when all three comforted each other? The thought made Caecilia catch her breath. Tarchon had dismissed such suspicions. Erene could tell her the truth. "Tell me," she said, hesitant of hearing a painful answer, "were Ulthes and my husband always lovers?"

The hetaera raised her eyebrows, and then the condescending look of the Erene of old returned. "Do you ask out of jealousy or merely to define the degrees of your humiliation?"

Caecilia stiffened, retreating behind a barrier of virtue. "They have transgressed both Roman and Greek law."

Erene laughed, leaning forward to put her hand on the girl's knee, making it clear that, although she had begged for aid, she was not prepared to temper her contempt. "Have you learned nothing here? All around you there are indiscretions that would not be brooked in Rome—men lying with wives at banquets, men keeping courtesans, men mentoring freeborn boys—and yet you refuse to accept that, in Veii, they are not sins."

Caecilia pushed the woman's hand away. "You haven't answered my question."

Leaning back, the hetaera sighed. "Men like Ulthes and your husband would court disaster if they forgot their duty. They are statesmen, leaders, and have many enemies. Have you ever known them to do anything to shame their families? Ulthes may have sometimes enjoyed slave boys, but Mastarna only loves women. So rest easy. Your husband was never Ulthes's beloved once he'd become a man."

Caecilia fell silent, relief almost crippling her. Turning away to regain her composure, she rose and walked to the atrium safe. The strange Rasennan coins were heavy enough to give weight to the purse. Gold and silver. Ships imprinted upon them. Forever after such currency would remind her of Erene and their odd acquaintance.

The companion pulled the purse strings tight and murmured her thanks. "I heard what you did. How you invoked the gods to delay giving him a son."

Caecilia met her gaze, prepared to weather a rebuke.

"He was so happy on the day of the play," the courtesan continued. "And so were you. You looked as though you'd at last become a Veientane."

The lictors moved to the hetaera's side, ready to escort her from the room.

"So tell me, Aemilia Caeciliana, why would you want to hurt a man who loved you so?"

• • •

Tarchon came to her, breathless. "A messenger has arrived from Velzna with news. The king has been ejected from the League of the Twelve."

As he spoke, Caecilia imagined Tulumnes, draped in hubris and folly, striding into the vast congress of the cities, which stretched from the far northern mountains to those hugging the western coast. Insisting arms be pledged for war against Rome. Demanding to be made head of the council.

"It seems the brotherhood was not brotherly enough to embrace either the only king among them or Veii's ambitions. And, in petulance, our great lucumo refused to provide the mummers and actors he'd promised for the festival. An insult not only to the League but to the gods. And so the council ejected him like a drunk into the street."

Caecilia found herself trembling. The prospect of death was real and very near. It would arrive in the time it took for Tulumnes's entourage to journey home. During Mastarna's absence she'd tried to believe the threat was distant like a storm that rolls along the far horizon. Now if she heard the thunder and looked overhead, the bolt could cleave her in two.

Six weeks.

A mere six weeks for the lucumo to bring discredit to his name and that of his city.

Forgetting their argument, knowing she needed his forgiveness, Caecilia wrapped her arms around Tarchon's waist, pressing her face against his chest, glad that he was there—that she was not utterly alone.

She thought of Mastarna. How she'd wasted her last moments with him. Longing to see him. Although it would be better that they did not meet again if it meant he must watch Tulumnes's lictors taking turns with her. Or perhaps he would not care after all that she had said and done.

Still, there was hope. With the monarch's disgrace, rumor would surge through the city. Slippery as an eel and as difficult to kill. Rumor that Artile's prophecy might be flawed. That Tulumnes should not be crowned. And the monarchy might yet fall if her husband were free to rise up against him.

Caecilia hugged Tarchon tighter. "You were right. I was wrong about Mastarna. Help me repay him for putting his life in danger for me."

Frowning, the youth pulled her gently away from him. "How could you do that?"

"Rome is only twelve miles distant. If I wear stout boots, a traveling cloak, and carry water I would reach it in a day. Don't you see? If I escape, Tulumnes could no longer threaten Mastarna. Your clan could rise up against the king."

"But you are held captive."

"Not if you help me. Not if you show Artile what type of man Mastarna wants you to be."

The youth smoothed his hand through his oiled hair, fiddling with his turquoise earring. "I can't, Caecilia. Artile would be very angry."

She squeezed his forearm hard enough to make him pay attention, knowing how difficult it was for him to take the first step to defy his lover. "Yes, you can," she urged. "Artile would be pleased to see me go."

"Not if it means I might be executed for assisting you. Besides, Mastarna would be furious."

"No," she said, not expecting her husband to ever love or forgive her. "He would be grateful to be rid of me after what I did."

Tarchon wound one of his many gold neck chains around and around his fingers. "You do not know that for sure," he murmured.

Caecilia squeezed his arm again. "Think about it! I would no longer be a hostage. Tulumnes would not be able to use me against Mastarna or my people."

As he stood biting his lip, white-faced and silent, Caecilia's own fear revived. Voice hoarse and plaintive, she hugged him again. "Please, Tarchon! I don't want to be raped. I don't want to lose my hands. I don't want to die."

So near to him she could smell perspiration bleed through the scent of rose water.

The youth breathed deeply, summoning courage. Deciding.

SUMMER 405 BC

TWENTY-ONE

On the kalends of each month Cytheris would wash her hair.

As the new moon eased its way into the night sky, pale and skinny as a newborn, Caecilia hesitated at the entrance to the kitchen as she sought out her servant, aware of the snicker and snorting of horses from the stables next door. She watched Cytheris fill a pail and remove the stopper from a flask of sweet-smelling oil she'd given her. It was late in the evening. The cook and kitchen maids had gone to sleep ready to wake up at dawn.

Ducks dangled from hooks, their gamey smell causing Caecilia to crinkle her nose. Massive iron pots hung from the fireplace, a giant stone mortar and pestle beside it. Tongs, shears, and knives were stacked upon a table. These were no humble tools. They were ornate, decorated with figures of nymphs and animals, the pots' lids molded into faces with leering grins.

Aricia unraveled her mother's long braid so that a blanket of wiry tresses spilled across the floor like grain tips from an amphora. The little girl helped her mother brush the mane, tackling the task in segments because of its length and thickness. Once Caecilia had suggested that Cytheris cut it shorter, but the Greek

maid was resolute. In Magna Graecia, shorn hair was the sign of
a slave, and so Cytheris gave thanks to the Rasenna for every inch
because it made her appear like a freedwoman.

With her hair heavy and dripping after its washing, the slave
dragged it out of the water and snapped at Aricia to rub it dry.
Then she sat, allowing herself the luxury of doing nothing but gaze
into the flames. Her daughter sat at her feet twining the locks of
wet hair around her fingers or pretending it was her own, covering
her own black curls with the ends of her mother's.

When Tarchon had finally agreed to help her, Caecilia had
been determined to hide her plans from the maidservant so
Cytheris would not be punished for abetting her escape. And so,
the maid's routine proved fortunate as it gave her mistress time to
prepare for her departure.

Pausing at the kitchen door to watch the girl and her daughter, a lump formed in Caecilia's throat. If she had found it odd for
Mastarna to have given her a handmaid it was even stranger to discover Cytheris was a friend, even though affection was tempered
with subtle degrees of authority, invisible lines of rank.

Caecilia could not leave either without mending a rift that
had grown between them of late. The servant did not approve of
Caecilia's reversion to Roman ways despite all that had happened
at the Festival of Fufluns.

At first Cytheris had tried to be patient, perhaps thinking her
mistress' righteousness was a way of coping with heartache, but
when Caecilia continued to condemn the master over his bond
with Ulthes her patience faltered. She saw nothing wrong with it,
accepting that among Greeks like the Athenians it was the way
destined for boys of noble birth.

Aricia hid behind her mother when her mistress entered the
room dressed in a long hooded cloak and carrying a small silver
casket inlaid with ivory.

Cytheris's pockmarked cheeks were slashed with color when Caecilia told her she was leaving forever. The slave who always found it hard to curb her tongue fell silent, making Caecilia wish she could hear her gossiping instead.

Earlier, Caecilia had packed the belongings she wished to take with her. There were not many: the contents of her little shrine and the mirror Larthia had given her. It was a treasured keepsake. For despite the knowledge of her mother-in-law's dark faith, Caecilia prayed that Ati's soul hovered above her.

In her bedchamber Caecilia's Veientane possessions remained: chests of rainbow gowns and baskets of expensive shoes, pots of carmine and albumen, flasks of perfumes, ivory hairpins and amber clasps. All left behind, as though offerings within in a tomb. Only she did not seek to return hereafter to a Rasennan life, nor did she think the Mastarna family would want to remember her once she'd gone.

Caecilia crouched beside Aricia, kissing her head. Then she bade the tiny slave hold out her arms as she gently pushed two silver bracelets over each hand. The little girl smiled as the bangles slid up and down her wrists, clicking and rattling.

Cytheris rapped her daughter's hands and ordered her to remove them.

"They are a gift," said Caecilia, checking her. She drew the Atlenta pendant from the casket. "And this is for you."

"No, mistress, I don't want it."

Ignoring her, Caecilia placed the box of jewelry in the hand-maid's lap. "Listen. There is enough in here to compensate Aricia's purchaser. Enough to pay for your freedom also. There's a letter to the master inside, too. Give him the casket and you will both be freed. You know well what necklaces and bracelets are within, together with some gold coins and jewels I won at gaming." She paused. "You are valuable slaves and so are costly. I do not want to cheat him."

The irony had not escaped Caecilia that the vice of gambling could be converted to good, that Mastarna had taught her a sin that could be useful. "I also directed him that you are to keep the pendant and the golden earrings and diadem."

"But I don't want you to leave," said Cytheris. "Don't forget the haruspex predicted you are to bear the master's child."

Caecilia was silent. Since Tulumnes's expulsion she'd often thought about Artile and his prediction. On that autumnal day when the priest astounded her with his skills she hadn't questioned his art or expertise. Now she knew that Artile's promises were no more valid than Aurelia's superstitions. He had bewitched her, convincing her that the Etruscans conversed with the Divine when instead they babbled like children before them.

Caecilia shook her head. "The priest was wrong. Fortuna must have determined a different course for me."

"Then all that worship of the Book of Fate was in vain."

It was not surprising that the maidservant had read her thoughts. Cytheris often knew what she was thinking. This time the servant's observation was sly and clever. Caecilia would not have followed the Book of Fate if not for Artile. His false portent had begun the downward spiral to losing Mastarna.

"You could have told the master about the elixir, about my deception. He is, after all, the head of the house."

"I owe my allegiance to you."

"Then you must despise me for failing as a wife."

The Greek girl shook her head. In the firelight the ends of her frizzy hair were lit up, a layer of light over the dark tresses. She knelt before Caecilia, pressing her face into the folds of her chiton.

"How could I hate you? You who asked the master to free my child? What other mistress would have done that? Don't leave me. Please take us with you."

Caecilia stroked Cytheris's head, then, kneeling, put her arms around the maid. "Don't you see I can't? If I do I would be stealing my husband's property. I can't do that when I've already sought to deprive him of a child."

Seeing her mistress would not heed her, Cytheris called to Aricia. On her mother's order the girl fetched a razor so that Cytheris could cut a lock from the vast spread of her own hair, then from her daughter's. Opening the Atlenta pendant, she furled the black and brown tresses into the locket and returned it to Caecilia. "Don't lose it, mistress. Don't forget us."

Before she could reply, Tarchon appeared. There was a seriousness about him that Caecilia had never seen before. An air of authority which danger can sometimes make in a man. Impatient, he frowned at the familiarity of a mistress with her slave, but Caecilia took her time in her farewells. Breathing in Cytheris's aniseed scent for the last time, she kissed both servants. Then, amid a kitchen where metal lions and griffins glared from the sides of pots and pans, Caecilia slid Marcus's iron amulet upon Cytheris's wrist and bade her good-bye.

• • •

Tarchon led her to the Great Temple in darkness. The bodyguards, her perpetual shadows, lay sleeping in Mastarna's garden, dregs of valerian drying in their wine cups, their snores surprisingly soothing for two such large and ugly men.

Although a mere slice, the moon shed enough light upon the backstreets and the sides of buildings as they crept along. When they reached the sanctuary's forecourt, they sped across the flagstones.

Caecilia's escape route lay within the temple's portico and ornate pillars at the very feet of Uni herself. One of the secret shafts of which Tarchon had spoken months before lay beneath the skirts of the goddess, gouged from the rock to enable her priests to escape into the drains should ever the arx be sacked.

In the dimness, the great goddess loomed above Caecilia, the hard surfaces of her terra-cotta frame and face softened by the half-light. The girl stood before the statue and gently laid one hand upon a giant toe, thanking the deity for her protection.

On the day the lightning bolt struck the palace, she'd begged Uni to save her. She had tried to be devout. She hoped the goddess would not think she was abandoning her because she was returning home, assuring her that she would still be worshipped under the name Juno when she did.

• • •

"Who's there?"

The darkness rimming the portico braziers was dense with mystery. A door to the far cell opened, a shard of light piercing the gloom. Artile stepped forward with a lamp, causing Caecilia to shiver and tug at Tarchon's sleeve. Both had thought the haruspex would be absent from the temple. When there was no reply, Artile strode toward them, forcing the two interlopers to immediately retreat.

"Who's there?" There was no fear in his voice. What had been an inquiry was now a demand.

Tarchon stepped into the radius of lamplight. Caecilia saw how the priest smiled, thinking the youth had come to him unexpectedly as he used to do, not as they had become—complacent and treading the same pattern of recrimination and forgiveness.

But when Tarchon drew Caecilia forward, Artile's tender glance was replaced with surprise and then anger when the youth explained his intention to help her escape. "Don't be foolish. You'll be punished."

"I cannot stand by and let Tulumnes hurt her."

Caecilia felt proud of Tarchon's defiance. He was combative, almost eager to confront the priest. Earlier he'd assured her that he could deal with him, arrogant in his power over his aging lover. Yet Caecilia knew that the youth could easily accede to the man who had once acted as a parent.

Artile's voice took on the familiar rhythms of persuasion as he reached for Tarchon's hand. "Come, my love, why risk your life for this Roman? I don't want to see you come to harm."

The youth gestured him away. "She is my friend. I won't desert her."

The priest's eyes narrowed, fists clenched at his side. It was the first time Caecilia had seen fury rise in him. Until then she'd only witnessed the evidence of the depth of his anger in the marks on Tarchon's face and arms. "Do you think I've protected you all this time from the threat of Mastarna's wives only to see you executed for helping this Roman?"

"Protected me?"

"They would have deprived you of your inheritance."

"You aren't making sense. I only inherit if there is no child of Mastarna's flesh."

"You are the rightful heir to this House. No one else!"

Caecilia turned to Tarchon for an explanation, but he shook his head.

"I did nothing that those women did not want themselves," said the haruspex. "Driven to control their destinies. Both of them knelt before me willingly."

He turned to Caecilia. "Both of them did not deserve to bear a living child."

The hairs on the back of her neck stood on end. For a moment she wavered in meeting Artile's gaze, a gaze that had led to trance and then submission before. The priest's face had finally gained a warrior's harshness. All this time he'd been waging a war she'd not even known had been declared.

"Seianta was persistent in her quest to bear a child. And it amused me that you wished the opposite. Both of you drank the Zeri thirstily."

"The elixir," whispered Tarchon. "What was in the Zeri?"

"A guarantee. The pulp of pomegranates and a touch of silphion."

It took a moment to understand, but when she did Caecilia felt a hurt that was more than betrayal. It was a cruel pain meted out by one who gained pleasure from inflicting it. It was different, too, from Artile's callous neglect at the feast. Even then she'd believed that he still cared for her. Instead he must have always hated her, his loathing polished and tended carefully ever since she'd arrived in Veii.

How gullible she'd been to think the chief priest would respect a Roman, remembering how he'd steered her fingers too close to the flame upon her wedding day. How many times had she poured a libation of blood and prayed under his guidance? How many times had Seianta done the same? Both vulnerable. Both trusting. Both, in a way, loving.

And in return he'd given them a special sacrament.

Pomegranate that could stop a woman falling with child.

Silphion that might scour a child from a mother's womb.

Zeri that might create a monster.

Small monsters. Mastarna's dead children.

"You're mad," said Tarchon, grabbing hold of the priest and shaking him. "I can't inherit. My father is about to disown me because you won't give me up!"

The priest reached up to touch the youth's cheek but Tarchon shied away.

"Don't you see? That is why I hate Mastarna most of all," said Artile, dropping his hand to his side. "He's forcing me to surrender you to him. Stopping his wives bearing children was the only way both of us could rule this House together."

He grasped at Tarchon's robes. "If you leave with her I will not be able to protect you. Tulumnes will know you helped her."

The youth shook off the priest as he would a leper, the need to escape urgent, to be freed from the possessive sickness within the room. "If all goes well I will return," he said coldly. "But not to you. Never again to you."

Artile turned to Caecilia. It made her skin crawl to hear his desperation. "Please don't take him from me. Please, I beg you."

"There is no use seeking her help," said Tarchon. "I am my own man now."

Crestfallen, the haruspex watched the youth strain to lift a trapdoor behind the statue. Lifting the lantern, he beckoned Caecilia to follow.

"If Tulumnes's men seek me while I am gone, you must lie. You will say I've been with you in this chamber. Do not add being an informer to your sins."

Caecilia paused, realizing this was another permanent farewell, but, unlike Cytheris, she would be glad never to see Artile again. "Did you always hate me?"

His eyes remained hard. "Do you really think I could let a descendant of Mamercus Aemilius bear my family's heir? The grandniece of the man who killed my father?"

"You're not the great seer you profess to be."

His smug, knowing smile made her hate him afresh. "Ah, you think my prediction false? Not so. It was you who misunderstood, just as Seianta did. The gods revealed you would bear a son who would beget a son. It seems we were both wrong to believe it would be Mastarna's."

"And the lightning from the northeast? What did the goddess say?"

"Nothing, Sister. The bolt I saw thrown that night was not from Uni. Your quest to defer your child's birth failed."

• • •

Anyone else would think they were descending into the lair of demons, but Caecilia knew better. She was climbing down a slippery wooden ladder into freedom, heading away from vice.

The rough walls of the rock shaft were dry, the air heavy with the fusty smell of stone. She clutched each rung tightly, petrified of slipping, of hurtling into the darkness, thumping and bouncing off the sides.

Tarchon was below her, holding a lantern above his head with one hand as he edged downward. The pathetic circle of yellow light did little other than to illuminate the hem of her tunic and the leather of her sandals. She was descending by touch alone, concentrating on the rhythm of her descent, forgetting everything but the pattern of movement. One foot, one hand, one foot, one hand. Over and over again inside the belly of the citadel of Veii.

A dank smell assaulted her when she stepped from the shaft into a shallow rock gallery at the foot of the cliff. Dankness so thick she felt she could peel it from the walls as she would the rind of a ripe cheese. But a short time later, as she crouched and shuffled her way under the overhang in the dark, Caecilia suddenly saw a different blackness overhead, one of stars and space.

Two horsemen stood waiting for them, holding a gelding by its reins, hired guards for the ride ahead.

Clouds now blotted out the sliver of moon. The journey would be in darkness, the hills and flats, plateaus and ridges, of the Etruscan countryside hidden. Trees of laurel and oak would be gloomy shapes, only their scent and the sound of the breeze through leaves would mark their presence. Caecilia felt disappointed that she would not pass through such scenes in daylight, that she could not enjoy Veii's countryside one last time.

Tarchon leaned down from his horse, offering her his hand.

"I don't know how to ride," she said, remembering how Tata had stubbornly denied her the chance.

"There is no need. Sit behind me and hold on."

When she had mounted, the horse stepped forward, frightening her. The strangeness of having a beast beneath her, muscle and hide and heat shifting out of her control, distracted her from her worries briefly as she clung to her tutor. For the first time in hours Tarchon laughed and gently placed her hands upon his sides.

By dawn she would be at Fidenae, if no brigands waylaid them and if Artile did not raise the alarm.

And by midmorning she would be in Rome.

How would she see her city after the splendor and depravity of Veii? As a country cousin with crooked teeth, large feet, and ungainly walk? Would she look down upon it as she had once looked down on Veii? She knew it was right that she was leaving, so why did her heart stutter and stammer in its beat? Why did she feel as though she was traveling into the unknown?

The pace was relentless, but as distance was put between them and Veii, the riders slowed from a gallop to a trot and then to a walk as they passed through the straggly end hours of the night. At first terrified she would fall off, Caecilia soon relaxed into the gait of the horse, although after a time the bones of her backside were jarred and jolted. Her hands did not leave Tarchon's sides either, but after a time she relaxed her grip on his tunic.

Her tutor rode the fine long-legged horse with a skilled ease that surprised her, his aptitude for horsemanship belying the effete manner he fostered. The fact that the youth had continued to help her was also a revelation. He could have left her with the bodyguards and hoped they escorted her to safety. Suddenly Caecilia found herself wondering what type of man he could have been had his mentor been one such as Ulthes rather than Artile.

She laid her head against his back in tiredness wishing her mind was clear, that her thoughts could disappear. Perhaps in Rome they would stop cluttering her head. It was thinking that was a torment. It was thinking that made her weary.

Soon the song of the larks accompanied the sound of clip-clopping hooves. The birds were disembodied heralds of daybreak. Sunrise mimicked sunset, only the colors were fresh, unused. In the distance Caecilia spied Fidenae, its citadel perched upon the horizon. Seeing it made her think of the journey to Veii. Soon they would be passing the clearing where the bandits had attacked her. Then boundary stones on either side of the road would appear, marking Fidenate territory. Halfway to Rome, halfway from Veii.

Tarchon reined the horse to halt abruptly. Soldiers were blocking the road, challenging them. Roman soldiers. The sound of their Latin seemed ponderous after being deprived of hearing the speech of her countrymen for a year.

Signaling the bodyguards to stay back, Tarchon spoke to the Romans calmly, but his Rasennan accent was as thick as the soldiers' was rustic and they did not understand him.

Caecilia awkwardly slid off the horse, her legs cramping a little as she stood. The two sentries fell silent when they saw her, confused as to why a Roman matron should be with three barbarians.

She smiled a welcome, although it should have been them doing the greeting. "Do not harm us," she said slowly, proudly. "I am Aemilia Caeciliana, citizen of Rome."

• • •

A camp had been built a short distance along the road. It was impressive with a full-scale ditch surrounding it at least twelve feet wide and almost as deep. A high mound had been raised behind it and on top of that was a fence of timber stakes, the wounds of its freshly cut wood still raw. Pennants were flying and the Standard of the Wolf Legion adorned the gate. What seemed to be a small town of leather tents was set out in rows within. Everywhere soldiers were training, running, jumping, or throwing javelins. Alongside them arrow-smiths filed tips for spears and arrows, sword cutlers hammered iron, and bow-makers carved weapons from wood and bone. And above this bustle and the babble of cursing and joking wafted the aroma of turnip and onion soup, plain and simple, making her mouth water.

The last Roman soldiers she'd seen were those patrolling the ferry, dressed in shoddy gear and stiff with boredom. The warriors before her wore brightly polished armor and were performing drills that suggested action rather than precaution. The camp had an air of permanence, too, and the sight of such preparations made her uneasy. Why was such a force here? Had the Fidenates rebelled again? It seemed unlikely since Fidenae was Veii's ally, and news would have spread if such a conflict had occurred.

As they walked through the camp the noise of barked orders, scraping metal, and conversation ceased. Instead there was only silent scrutiny of a tall girl in Roman garb and a Rasennan peacock parading as a man.

Tarchon stood close by her. She was proud of him. The hirelings had refused to follow them into a Roman encampment, not prepared to trust the soldiers even with Caecilia vouchsafing their safety.

As they neared the command tent its flap was flung back and a young soldier appeared. Caecilia thought it was a vision because the man was known to her amid all these strangers.

It was her cousin, Marcus, very much alive.

· · ·

Seeing him made her realize how imperfect memory was, and that an iron amulet was a poor substitute compared to being near him with the cowlick in his hair, acne scars upon his cheeks, and his patchy beard. His face was tanned and gaunt, and there was a gash across the bridge of his nose. So many times she'd wondered if he were alive, questioning why, within such a short time of being enlisted, he could have been killed.

She wished he wore no armor as she hugged him tightly, his cuirass denying her the chance to press herself against warmth and flesh. But she quickly found it was not metal and leather that were the only barriers because Marcus immediately pulled away from her, embarrassed by her public display.

Disconcerted, she instinctively bowed her head. It was the first of many things she must remember. There were so many differences between her people and Mastarna's. Differences that she'd adopted as her own. For a moment she wondered how often she would reveal that she'd forgotten what was correct and what was pious.

Marcus's words were warm, though. And his face revealed his delight and relief. "Cilla, I thought never to see you again."

"Nor I you! I heard all were killed at Verrugo."

"Luckily I was transferred to the siege at Anxur before Verrugo fell."

"And what of my letters? I thought Aurelia would send them to you."

Her cousin frowned. "But I didn't receive any letters! And when you didn't reply to mine I thought you no longer cared."

Marcus sighed. The girl shook her head also, but was prepared to forget the pettiness of her aunt when she noticed the cut upon his forearm, scabby and puckered. "You're injured!"

"It's nothing. Drusus suffered greater wounds."

"He is alive?"

"Of course. He'll be very pleased to see you."

Drusus. In all her planning and plotting to return she'd not thought of her admirer, too busy to find time to consider what she would do should she succeed. Hearing that he'd survived made her glad but not with the heartfelt relief of a lover seeking to be reunited. She no longer ached to see him, did not know what she would say when she did.

Marcus was studying Tarchon with the same curiosity as had all the other men. The deep moss green of the Veientane's tebenna and his painted eyes, his earring and gold chains, must have made the Roman wonder how his cousin came to be in the charge of such a man.

Compared to Tarchon, the Romans were shaggy and crude. Where once the shaven and short-cropped Etruscans seemed vain, Caecilia now saw the beards and shoulder-length hair of her people as unkempt, and their hairy forearms and chest hair protruding from their tunics as coarse.

She glanced at Tarchon, who was returning the blatant scrutiny of the men. And it was clear from his expression that, while he had learned their language, it had not prepared him for how they appeared.

Marcus broke from examining the Etruscan. "Where is your husband?"

Caecilia knew it wouldn't be the last time she would be faced with this question. No one would expect her to travel without Mastarna's permission. "He is returning from Velzna. Laris Tulumnes proclaimed himself king but has now been ejected from the League of the Twelve." She took his hand. "Tulumnes is crazy enough to declare war even without the support of all the Rasenna."

Marcus did not seem surprised at such news, making her conscious again of the activity of the camp around her. It looked like the Romans were mustering an army, not a delegation. "Cilla, one of our allies has already informed us about Tulumnes. Camillus has been sent to meet him to renegotiate the treaty."

"Has he been elected one of the consular generals?"

"Unfortunately not. Father was successful, though."

Even though her cousin's face registered disappointment at his hero's failure to gain office, Caecilia was heartened. Aemilius had always favored peace with Veii. Tulumnes may yet be convinced to keep the truce.

Marcus lifted the flap of the command tent. "Perhaps it's best you come inside."

She motioned Tarchon to follow. He hesitated. Until then he had not spoken, but as they were ushered in he whispered quickly, "Do you know what you are going to say?"

Caecilia shook her head. Questions. There would be many.

And they would not like her answers.

. . .

Camillus rose to greet her and she remembered how he alone among the politicians had shown sympathy on her wedding day. The bronze pectorals on his breastplate were burnished and bright, the folds of his military cloak falling with precision and elegance. Of all Roman men, Caecilia thought him to be the most like a Veientane in his vanity. The unusual gold ring flashed upon his hand, and his beard and hair were trimmed. Surrounded by his officers, he was an imposing figure, a commander and now an ambassador. She immediately felt safe in his presence until she saw a fetial priest standing behind him dressed in a curved white cloak and white boots and wearing a small bowl of a helmet. Caecilia knew such a holy man would be present for only one of two reasons—to either broker a treaty or declare war.

"Where is your husband?"

Caecilia was irritated at the question, more so because Marcus answered for her.

Camillus glared at her. "So you are here with neither Tulumnes's nor Vel Mastarna's permission?"

"Yes, I escaped with the help of Mastarna's son, Tarchon. I sought to relieve my husband of the burden of having a Roman wife, and I no longer wished to be held hostage to the disadvantage of Rome."

The silence in the tent was such that she could hear the subtle squeak and creak of leather against metal, and the shuffling of booted feet. The commander stroked his beard as he sat upon his chair. "While such bravery is commendable, Caecilia, it is also misguided. Your unsanctioned return will give Tulumnes an excuse to seek compensation. You have broken the treaty. You have given the Veientanes a reason to invade."

Caecilia was dumbstruck, a prickle of heat spreading across her chest and rising to her face as she realized her escape had not helped the negotiations but endangered all.

Beside her, Tarchon made a noise of disapproval and cleared his throat. "Would you rather send her back to be raped and mutilated at the hands of the lucumo?"

The effect of hearing Tarchon speaking Latin was startling. Camillus's eyebrows shot skyward. While the uncouth guards had struggled to understand him, these officers heard exactly what Tarchon said despite his Etruscan accent. The silence was broken by indignant shouts.

As Camillus signaled for calm she saw how the men glared at her tutor in the same way as the principes—a contempt for one who should be ridiculed and forgotten, offended that he'd entered the world of Roman men and dared to question them. Today, though, Tarchon's reaction was not of quiet deference to such men. Instead, amid all the bravado of shining bronze and aristocratic robes, he faced them confidently, his weakness no longer defining him.

But Camillus chose to ignore him, causing Tarchon to be insulted even more. "I think it's time for this Etruscan to return to Veii where he must face the consequence of absconding with his father's wife."

Caecilia was astounded. Did Camillus believe Tarchon was exaggerating? Didn't he understand she'd been in danger? She glanced across to Marcus for assistance, but he, too, showed his disdain for the Veientane.

If there had been amazement at Tarchon speaking Latin, it doubled when she spoke in Rasennan to him. The Romans tensed as they listened but could not comprehend. Some glared at her, confronted to see how she had become like their foe, how she spoke their tongue easily and could keep secrets from them.

Tarchon did not shy from touching her as Marcus had. But this time Caecilia remembered it would be imprudent to show she welcomed such a display. Already the Roman men around them were tensing, ready to apprehend Tarchon for showing her affection. She wanted to embrace him, to forget the constraints she had chosen to renew, but she did not want him harmed. And so, even though she wished him to remain, she nodded for him to go as he stood hesitating over whether to leave her.

And in that moment she saw that it was ended, that once she had taken leave of Tarchon there would be no connection to Veii. Laughter and learning would be lost. Friendship and love. "It's best you go. If you are away too long, not even Artile will be able to vouch for you."

"I can't leave you like this. I don't trust this man."

"Don't worry, Camillus is honorable," she said, although she was already confused by the commander's behavior. "Please, you must go."

Tarchon smiled faintly. "Then I bow to the counsel of my stepmother who I will never forget." Then to add scandal to Roman indignation, he reached over and kissed her on both cheeks. "No matter what they say, Caecilia, these men are as hungry for war as Tulumnes. You mark my words."

Unable to tolerate Tarchon's familiarity with a Roman woman any further, Camillus ordered the Veientane be escorted from the tent. Caecilia anxiously prayed the purse of silver she'd given to the bodyguards would make them wait for him as promised and that the Roman guards would not treat him badly as they sent him on his way. Hoped most of all that he would be safe upon his return to his city.

A chair was brought for her and she was handed a beaker of water. For a moment she wished the contents would transform into wine but was too nervous to smile at such a thought. The cup was of finely turned wood, even and smooth, unpainted, plain. She rolled it between finger and thumb. The tent was also unadorned except for the insignia of the wolf—the symbol of Mars, the Roman god of war. The austerity of the surroundings was unsettling. She thought a return to sober Roman ways would soothe her, washing away all the vile things she'd endured. She thought transition would be immediate, that she would step from their world back to hers with the ease of changing from street shoes to indoor sandals, but it was not so.

When she'd arrived in Veii, her homesickness had been tangible, present with all five senses from waking until bedtime. Now she felt homesick and yet was home. She had wished everything to be black and white again, for there to be rules, for the world to be simple, and yet as invisible boundaries once again erected themselves around her, what was once familiar seemed strange. It was a comforting oddness, though, which she would grow used to. It gave a sense of what it was to have once been safe and where the customs and law of her people formed a shield.

"You have changed, Aemilia Caeciliana," said Camillus. "I think perhaps you have forgotten modesty and how a woman should act."

Caecilia clenched the goblet a little too tightly, water spilling from it as she remembered how sanguine the commander had been when Tarchon told him what Tulumnes had planned for her.

"What did you expect," she said, including Marcus in her gaze, "when you sent a bride to live with lions?"

At her words Camillus leaned forward, eyes grave and unexpectedly sincere. Persuasive and charismatic, she glimpsed again why Marcus and Drusus followed him; that, although sitting amid many, he made her feel as though she were the only one present. "Caecilia, as I watched you wed Vel Mastarna last year, charming in your orange veil, I saw you had courage and that you understood you were not merely a bride. I saw that the possibility of sacrifice made you both terrified and proud. So don't say you were unaware of what your fate could be. Rome made no promises to you other than to attempt to keep you safe without imperiling our city. And that is why we agreed to meet with Tulumnes's delegation. Rome wished to negotiate your release before the king called for war."

Studying the statesman Caecilia suspected he was lying, not due to any telling sign upon his face but by the way Marcus froze for a fraction at his leader's words. "I don't believe you," she said, hurt he was trying to gull her as if she were a child who could swallow lies with a posset of milk. "I do not think you came here to save a Roman daughter but to forsake her."

Camillus's voice was steely. "Very well, Caecilia, let me be candid. I know it is hard to discover that Rome would choose its welfare over your own, but you were to be the rallying cry, a reason why soldiers should fight even as they lauded you as a daughter of both the people and patricians."

Caecilia stared at him. He'd assured her that he would pray for her as would a father. How foolish she'd been. All Camillus had ever wanted was to attack Veii no matter the cost. And she should have remembered how he'd told Tata that he was as impatient to march against the Etruscans as he was eager to see Rome's veterans paid.

"And when Rome refused to surrender and Tulumnes returned my body, ravaged and mutilated, would the cause have been all the fiercer?"

Camillus flinched this time. "We would have wept, Caecilia, and your death would have been avenged."

She stood and moved over to stand before him. "Peace may still be possible now that the lucumo has been expelled by the League. Vel Mastarna will no longer be constrained to protect me. His tribe can rise up against the king."

Camillus tapped the arms of the chair and roared at her. "Sit down! Think about what you have done. Your flight may have already caused Tulumnes to kill your husband."

Legs shaking, feeling like she was a stranger in her own body, Caecilia put her hand on the back of the chair for balance before slumping into the seat.

Mastarna dead? Like a child believing their parents will live forever or a young man thinking he is invincible, she'd always thought he would somehow survive. How foolish she'd been. If Tulumnes could not coerce Mastarna any longer, he would kill him, especially since Pesna had already begun weakening the strength of the Mastarna tribe.

Seeing her distress, Marcus requested permission to go to her. "We'll find out his fate tomorrow, Cilla," he said, crouching beside her. "Tulumnes may not have stomach enough to harm your husband. And without the support of the League he may choose to continue the treaty."

"Marcus is right. Tomorrow's meeting will answer all our fears," said Camillus, his encouraging voice revealing how he must be in the Curia or Forum, lulling and luring all to his cause. "But no matter the result you'll be revered for facing depravity and eluding your captors."

Resentful that he should think her stupid, she glared at him. "So whereas before I was to be honored for dying defiled and defiant, now I am to be lauded for withstanding evil and maintaining virtue? Or will I simply be shunned for having been wed to a foe?"

His eyes flickered, irritation swelling. "I fear you've learned bad habits, Caecilia. Did your husband always indulge you in talking to men in such a way?"

She wanted to shout that she'd given audience to tenants and clients, that she'd banqueted on a dining couch with men and discussed philosophy and politics and poetry, but she bit her tongue knowing that these men could not cope with such a revelation— that it would confirm to them how a woman could become disobedient and disrespectful.

The commander stood, causing all around him to stand to attention. "You must be tired," he continued, not allowing her to speak. "Your cousin will take you to your quarters."

He slapped Marcus on the back. "Did you know he was awarded a crown of oak leaves for saving a fellow citizen and standing his ground until the battle was over? It's a time for celebration among the Aemilians with such a valiant son and courageous daughter."

Her cousin wore the same look as when he'd shown prowess at training. There was modesty and satisfaction, relief also that he had pleased his father. This time, though, his half smile hinted at something extra. More than pride—a touch of arrogance, a hint of ambition. She wondered what feat he'd performed to gain such honors.

As they turned to leave, another soldier entered the tent and saluted the commander. He gave his message as quickly as he could, all the while staring at Caecilia.

She could not take her eyes from him either. Tall and angular, Drusus wore a corselet that looked slightly too small for his long torso. One of his calves was bandaged and his shoulder was strapped. His arms, legs, and face were covered in half-healed grazes, and he stooped slightly beneath the low-roofed tent, his hesitant stance reminding her of his usual awkwardness.

His gaze was not uncertain, though, his intensity making her bow her head for the second time that day.

"Ah, here is Claudius Drusus," said Camillus, "who owes his friend his life."

Caecilia noticed that the expression Drusus normally reserved for Marcus had altered. Where there had been adulation, instead there was resentment. The richly dressed and eloquent Camillus was indeed unusual if he could command their allegiance and yet drive a wedge into their friendship.

Relieved to escape Drusus, she nervously followed Marcus out into the encampment, unable to shrug the young soldier's stare from her thoughts.

The destiny glimpsed through an orange veil had turned out to be hers after all. She could never avoid being owned by Roman men. And yet she had to concede that what had been asked of her was no more than what was expected of all Romans, of Rome itself: to embody the virtues of faithfulness and fortitude, to preserve family honor, and to put her city above friendship, even above love.

Whether returning upon bier or horseback, whether martyr or survivor, she was to be a symbol. Once again she was Aemilia Caeciliana, daughter of Lucius, niece of Aemilius, wife of Mastarna. Caecilia had disappeared.

TWENTY-TWO

Bellatrix was hiding, swallowed by scudding clouds, the moon shining only dimly.

It had been raining all afternoon, the steady soak turning the dusty grounds to quagmire, but the overall mood was joyful at the thought that perhaps the drought would end, that crops would grow from shriveled seeds, and animals would once again be able to drink from rivers instead of lying down to die.

Better yet, it might be an omen heralding that it was time for Rome to prosper through war.

The supply tent was stuffy, crowded with entrenchment tools: shovels, wicker baskets, ladders, hoses, and buckets. Caecilia shared it with amphorae of olive oil and grain together with barrels of salt. They had not anticipated needing quarters for a woman.

All afternoon she'd sat upon an upturned tub and watched the downpour as the soldiers continued with their drills. Tall stakes were planted in the ground and the warriors practiced their sword skills against them, lunging with wooden staves at imaginary enemies—Volscians and Aequians. Or Veientanes. In all her time in

Veii, Caecilia had never seen such activity. Mastarna commanded a sleeping force, only formed when he made the call.

She sat in the tent by herself because she had been dismissed. Having been treated like a man for more time than was seemly, she'd been sent to her room like a chastened child.

When the rain stopped she ventured a few yards into the encampment to study the late-evening sky. The soldiers sat before an enormous bonfire, stripped of their armor, tunics sodden. They sharpened swords and spears or oiled their shields, the weapons all of varying quality and quantity, yet she noted even the poorest veteran was tending to his helmet with the same vigor as the officer's servant left to care for his master's panoply.

Their laughter was deep and manly, lacking the descant of women to soften their bass. Loud, too, and raucous. A gathering of men and maleness. Dismissive of all but warriors. No place for a woman.

After a time some of them noticed her and their laughter made her blush as much as their words. She remembered how she had been encouraged to sit before another fire just one year ago. Mastarna and the three principes had not banished her nor treated her like a child. Tonight, dressed in a humble stola, she felt more naked than she ever had when wearing clinging robes. Many Veientane men had studied her but theirs was more appraisal than ogling, a signal of their desire to seduce rather than crudely satisfy their lust. It was odd, then, that having returned to the morality of her city she felt even more ill at ease among Rome's men than she had been amid the decadents of Veii.

"You should not be out here, Cilla." Marcus stood between her and the soldiers.

"Why is that, Cousin?"

"The men are to be given a ration of wine tonight in celebration of your flight."

"So the more they drink to my honor the more they are likely to threaten it."

Shaking his head, Marcus touched her elbow and led her to the tent. "You have changed, Cilla," he said softly.

"Yes, I have changed," she sighed.

"What did he do to make you so?"

Tears pricked her eyes. She wiped them away abruptly, unable to cope with kindness, not wanting sympathy. No one in Veii thought her husband dishonorable for being Ulthes's beloved. No one there understood her reaction, but all Romans would understand and agree if they knew. Yet she did not want Marcus thinking that Mastarna forced her to succumb to vice.

It was disturbing to find also that, although she had strived to return to Roman virtue, she had in fact become what she had tried so hard to resist. The transformation was complete. She could not escape it. In Rome she was and always would be a Veientane wife.

Safe from others' scrutiny, her cousin took her hand and squeezed it like the old Marcus. His fingers were scraped and calloused. "Did he hurt you?"

"No, I was weak and tempted by Veientane ways. And in my desperation to see Rome I did terrible things."

"I don't believe you. If you did anything wrong it was because he forced you."

The girl reflected on what she'd endured. Marcus may have sampled vice in brothels and taverns this year but not wickedness, not sacrilege. She was not about to tell him what he could not imagine, the temptations she'd given into, or what she'd seen, of how she'd worshipped. If she did so he would not be able to ignore such confessions. And she already knew she did not have courage enough to face dying for her blood taint.

Instead she concentrated upon him. How many battles had he fought? How many men had he killed? Unlike her, who had been sacrificed, Marcus was prepared to surrender his life for Rome.

"It's not just I who have changed," she said, staring at his newly healed scars. "How valiant you must have been to gain an oak leaf crown."

The youth reddened. "I was no braver than any other man that day. I did what was needed and expected."

His words were humble but, despite his blush, she once again saw a difference in him. Before he'd been doubtful of heroics and his ability to excel. The burden of being expected to step onto the Honored Way had been great and his resentment heavy. His father, his family, and his friends always wanting more of him—more courage, more shrewdness—and all for one goal. To hold imperium. Now she sensed that, having been awarded for his valor, he hungered to do so again and again, not only to satisfy Aemilius but to outdo him.

"Your father must be pleased."

"Yes, he basks in my renown as though he himself raised the lance and struck the blow instead of being encumbered with age and high office."

The edge of sarcasm was also new.

"He's been elected consular general. Doesn't that make you proud?"

"Of course, but I would be happier if Camillus had also been chosen. My father and his allies have sought peace for too long, letting our enemies grow strong."

"Tell me how you saved Drusus."

He smiled, eager to tell his tale in a way that would be handed down in the Aemilian family for generations: the glory of battle, its gore, its terror. "After Anxur had been blockaded for many, many months, Drusus and I were ordered to leave Verrugo and prevent Volscian forces bringing relief to the besieged city. The transfer was timely because shortly afterward the garrison at Verrugo was overrun and all our soldiers were slaughtered there. It was good to be able to avenge our dead."

Marcus turned to her, a glimpse of the uncertain youth returning. "On the day of my first battle I studied the enemy's crested
helmets as they held the line and wondered whether their hands
were shaking as much as mine."

"How frightened you must have been."

His expression changed to one of bravado. "I had no time to
be afraid, Cilla, I only saw the Volscians as one monster wanting to
slay me." He was absorbed in his story now. "After a time I did not
think about killing. Blood streamed down my face, running into
my eyes, my helmet digging into my flesh. Then I saw Drusus. His
horse had been felled. He was vainly trying to continue fighting
even though the tendon of his calf was cut and his shoulder torn.
I managed to fend off three Volscians trying to attack him, then
raised him onto my horse and carried him to safety before returning to fight."

Caecilia's eyes widened to hear of such an impressive feat.
She covered both of his hands with hers, feeling the rough crusts
of scabs upon his fingers. The cold manner in which he spoke of
killing surprised her. She wanted the softhearted boy who'd once
confided in her to express some regret. "Did you truly feel nothing
when you slew a man?"

"That's a strange thing to ask."

"You would have told me had I asked you the same question
a year ago."

"I don't know what you want me to say, Cilla. I will never forget the eyes of the first one I killed. It was the look of a man dying
for his land—land that has now become Rome's."

His answer told her that Camillus had stolen his heart and
stirred him more than his father ever could. She shivered, realizing
that Veii would be shown no mercy should it fall.

Until now she'd lived in trepidation that her Roman family was
in danger, imagining the wall of her city crumbling, the temple of
the Great and Mighty Jupiter being burned. She'd seen her city as

the weakling, starved and sick. Deprived of the view of the Forum and Curia, she'd forgotten what it was like to be among the men of Rome: lean, cruel, and always hungry.

The Veientanes were overconfident, believing their citadel impregnable, believing in their invincibility and yet unused to battle. For the first time Caecilia wondered if their defenses could be breached after all. Rome was inexorable and Camillus was too lean a wolf, the leanest she had seen.

Did she want brutal sharp-edged justice to be meted out? It was too awful to imagine tenants, craftsmen, and slaves slaughtered, their wives and daughters raped, their babies skewered, their houses destroyed. And how could she bear to see the city razed? Its gaudily decorated houses, bustling marketplaces and inns, and the wall of the citadel itself, upon which she'd surveyed the world at the level of an eagle. And what of Tarchon? Cytheris? Aricia?

What of Mastarna?

Her world might have become muddy, crowded and distorted, but one thing was clear—she did not want Veii to be destroyed, she did not want loved ones to die.

"I don't understand why Rome is now able to fight. Before I left, plebeian soldiers had been refused a salary and another war front needed to be avoided. Why are the reasons for extending peace last summer forgotten?"

His expression reminded her of the day she'd tried to talk of politics with him and Drusus, cautioning her that she'd trespassed onto male territory.

"Please. Surely I'm entitled to know."

Marcus hesitated but then relented. "The people's tribunes poisoned the plebeians against fighting, claiming the patricians only wanted war to stop the people having time to rebel against them, warning them that the League of the Twelve would join forces against us. But when Anxur finally fell everyone rushed to the city wall to watch our victorious army martial in the Campus

Martius. Campfires burned bright that night and songs of triumph were heard; hunger pangs and fevers were forgotten. Plunder was stacked high, higher than the funeral pyres: bronze and silver and gold. And for the first time it was given to the common soldiers, not just the nobles.

"Then, when the patricians also sent wagons stacked high with bronze into the Forum as their contribution to a salary tax, the people's tribunes knew they were beaten. They could no longer grumble that the plebeians alone would bear the burden. After that, men from all classes came forward to add what they could to the pile so our warriors could be paid to march upon any enemy that rose against us."

Caecilia rubbed her fingers along the leather edge of the tent flap, wondering what Tata would have thought. Remembering how he had spoken often of the spirit of their people. Whether cavalry or infantry, slingers or archers, all Romans wanted to fight, all wanted land, all wanted glory.

"You seem very sure of our strength."

"Two thousand soldiers have volunteered to serve in the legions. And there are two extra consular generals to lead them."

The Roman girl sighed, tired of the boasting of men and their desire for conflict. "I just want peace. I don't want the treaty to fail."

The youth put his hand on her shoulder, his expression earnest. "Then pray Tulumnes will not try to fight now that the Twelve doesn't support him."

As he spoke, he bumped the tent flap, sending a shower of water splashing onto him. Surveying his dripping tunic, Caecilia no longer saw the soldier but the boy, and just as she would have done a year before, she giggled, forgetting all the somber talk.

Marcus was cross but, hearing her laughter, he smiled, wiping himself with his cloak. "I've missed you, Cilla. As have my father and mother."

"Aurelia has missed me?"

He nodded. "Of course. She had no one left to bully."

Caecilia laughed as she helped to dry him. Suddenly she felt safe because, for all his seriousness and fervor, this youth was still her Marcus. He would love her always.

• • •

The candle was nearing the end of its life, a stub of pig's fat producing more smoke than light. Caecilia was loath to snuff it out, though, fearing utter darkness. It stood on an upended bucket, her little juno beside it. In Veii, Caecilia had neglected the tiny guardian and relied instead on angels both divine and mortal. Now she would have to call upon inner strength and hold the talisman close.

Sitting on the lumpy straw pallet that was to be her bed, Caecilia pulled the pins from her hair, forming a pile of the plain bone clasps. With her hair plaited loosely and still fully dressed, she lay down to sleep. Outside, the soldiers were still carousing, and she did not relish being unclad should any defy orders and approach her tent.

When she heard someone at the opening, she drew her shawl tightly around her, hoping it was only Marcus. But it was not her cousin who urged her to let him enter.

It was his friend.

She scrambled to her feet, aware that her hair was loose and that she was barefoot. Aware, too, that she was alone with a Roman man who was not from her family and who had wanted her to be his wife.

A year ago she would have run to him, joyful to finally feel his arms around her, but all she saw before her was a besotted youth whose innocence had been beaten away by enemy shield and sword. Instead they stood awkwardly apart as she remembered how he came to be wounded. Yet although his struggle must have been real enough he was but freshly scarred compared to a grizzled warrior such as Mastarna. His cuts reminded her of a child with grazed knees and scraped knuckles. Mastarna's bruises were as much a part of him as his stubble or his scars, a constant reminder of his tug-of-war with risk.

"My father has died. I have no uncles. I am the master of my House."

She nodded, wondering if she should applaud one so young bearing such an onus, then remembered the type of master Mastarna had become after Ulthes taught him to shoulder such responsibility from the age of fifteen. "Then you have a heavy duty."

"I am no longer a boy," he persisted, "being told what I can and cannot do."

She lowered her voice. "And what is it that you want to do?"

A year ago he'd been circumspect, nervous of offending a virgin and venturing only to steal a kiss. Now his eyes roamed over her. "You have changed, Caecilia."

The girl remained silent at the refrain.

"You wear a stola and palla, but not like any other wife I've seen."

"How, then, do I wear them?"

"Like bonds restraining you."

The boldness of his statement surprised her. Would he dare to speak such words to any other woman? Caecilia didn't know whether he'd enjoyed the favors of a slave girl or a whore, but it was clear the humble ardor that had made him stammer her name last spring had formed into something other than calf-love.

She slowly straightened the sides of her tunic, wondering what would interest him more—an admission that she'd transgressed or a virtuous denial. "You risk a whipping in visiting me. Or do you think I am so stained no one would defend my honor?"

Drusus stepped back, knocking over a stack of shovels, his face losing its lust.

With clumsy fingers he pulled some colored cloth from beneath his breastplate. It was the patch of veil she'd asked Marcus to give him on her wedding day. It was stained, frayed around the edges. A few threads had run so there were gaps within the gauze and bright spots of color where the weld dye had been retained. "I have kept it since that night. It has been my link to you."

Reaching out to touch it, Caecilia found it greasy with grime and sweat, perhaps even blood. It had lain securely in the heat of battle between his tunic and corselet, and then fingered and caressed at night when the world paused in conflict and men thought of home.

Drusus had been with her when she journeyed to Veii. For a time he'd lain in her bed between her and her husband. And she, it transpired, must have lain within his, too. But after a time she'd struggled to recall anything other than fragments: the color of his eyes, the russet of his hair, or the timbre of his voice, its hesitancy and lightness. The image of the youth before her was still fractured, his face and form instantly familiar but not the man within, a man who must have held her chastely in his heart as keenly as he lusted for her.

"You know I would have married you but Father wouldn't let me."

Fumbling, he reached for her hand, making clear he'd learned the mechanics of desire but not its artistry. And at that moment she knew that, should he ever hold her in his stilted embrace, he would plunge her into marital propriety under the cover of darkness, just as Cytheris had warned.

"I've always honored you, always loved you," he continued. "On your wedding night all I wanted to do was kill Aemilius for betraying you, kill my father for refusing to let me marry you and, most of all, kill Mastarna. And each night you were in his land I prayed for the time when he and his entire House and all his people would be destroyed."

She disentangled her fingers, stunned at the fury of his emotion and at the thought that such hatred and pain existed because of her. How could there be such bitterness when Drusus did not even know Mastarna? How could there be such love for her when they were little more than strangers?

"Why did you want to marry me, Drusus?"

"Because you never mocked me. Never condemned my reckless tongue or impetuous ways. I did not care that you were half a noble. You were an Aemilian. Cousin to my best friend. I wanted to be part of your family."

"We hardly knew each other."

"More than most who are betrothed." He moved nearer but did not try to touch her. "I will marry you when you are free of that Veientane."

Caecilia sat down upon the barrel, rubbing her temples to make her headache go away, half wishing that when she looked up the youth would have disappeared. If there were any doubts before it was now certain she couldn't love Drusus, just as she shouldn't love Mastarna.

"You do not know what I've become other than to sense I'm more an Etruscan than a Roman wife," she said quietly. "The matrons of Rome will not let their daughters sit beside a woman who was once wedded to a heathen. You might think I'll be hailed in the Forum but the chatter of gossip in atriums will be deafening. Remember that you are now head of your House; in time you will want to be a senator and even a consul. To do that you need a wife who is untainted."

"I welcome being the husband of a woman as famous as Lucretia. And when I slay Mastarna on the battlefield, we will both be lauded."

Caecilia scanned the earnest youth as would a mother humoring her child for boasting he'd slain an imaginary rival. How could she have been impressed with his bragging before? Neither of them knew what dangers really existed.

But she could not mock his fervor, no longer confused as to the shape and sound of the inner man. Drusus may be a callow youth infected by Camillus's zeal, but she also recalled how his face had been bruised from his father's blows, a hurt he had suffered for her.

There was amazement, too, in discovering that, like Lucretia's husband, he was prepared to forgive her for being ruined by an Etruscan.

If these Roman men were prepared to forgive a blood taint, then shouldn't she do the same for Mastarna?

And listening to him, she glimpsed hope that she could gain some shelter, perhaps salvage honor, by marrying him. For what other choices had she? To remain a univir, faithful to Mastarna after death even though he was a foe? Becoming a wife who was not a wife and, in time, a widow who was not a widow, all the while living cloistered within Aemilius's domain, her inheritance administered by him and doled out in meager parcels?

Life with Drusus would be predictable and secure. He was serious but at least he was kind. And his wealth and family influence in the city could not be ignored. She'd surrendered independence when she'd left the wall of Veii. Now it would have to suffice to carry the keys to all rooms except the wine cellar, be hostess to her husband's colleagues but not share his dining couch, and attend to the duties of the atrium instead of receiving his clients.

And there would be a blustering sort of passion, a one-sided devotion, as she shared his bed while remembering how she'd lain in Mastarna's. In either case there would be no temptations, no dark worship, no chance of wickedness anymore.

She thought of Artile and his prediction of a son who would beget a son. Tried to reconcile that it must be this Roman's and not Mastarna's. Realized she would bear an unchosen child after all.

Smiled ruefully at how the blind but all-seeing Fortuna must be laughing.

• • •

Lying on her pallet after Drusus had gone, Caecilia noticed the patch of orange, which had floated to the floor. Back in Veii, in a large linen chest, her wedding shroud lay folded, fine weaved with golden thread.

For an instant the memory of standing beneath the double veil with Mastarna returned. He'd been preoccupied with a ghost as he whispered his vows to his new bride. Now he was free to be reconciled with Seianta, and lie in death beside her.

Caecilia had felt smothered by the orange veil. Under the Veientane bridal mantle there had been room enough to see Mastarna's face, smell his scent, feel his breath gently upon her cheeks, freedom as well to peer out through the netting to the strange new world beyond. And so she did not know which was sadder, the Roman bride who left her uni-colored world or the Rasennan wife who chose to return to it.

• • •

It took a few heartbeats to remember where she was when she woke among the other items of inventory. The frenzied barking of the camp dogs pierced the gloom, rising above the noise of soldiers at their drills. In the early morning mist the hounds harried the horses drawing the carriage of a consular general through the gates.

Aemilius had hastened to the camp as soon as he'd heard of her arrival. Strangely, the sight of his plain but handsome senatorial toga made Caecilia want to cry in relief that she might finally see her home.

"I am thankful to find you safe, Daughter."

The brief sense of a welcome homecoming vanished. Aemilius knew, or at least suspected, what awaited her in Veii. Had she meant so little to him?

"Are you, Uncle? Are you truly glad to face one you had already made a ghost?"

His usual look of annoyance when conversing with her returned. Caecilia did not care. She'd been angry with this man for too long.

The display of animosity between father and adopted daughter was interrupted when Camillus appeared. The atmosphere between the commander and the consular general was tense. Camillus clearly resented Aemilius being elected instead of him. Worse still, he'd now arrived to oversee a meeting the commander considered should have been under his control.

Aemilius was also prickly. Although Camillus's ambition had been thwarted, the consular general could not ignore that the war hero enjoyed the adoration of his men and would no doubt ultimately gain office. Camillus was renowned for his valor, and valor brought fame, and fame brought power. All the commander needed to achieve his aims was a war.

Both men ceased their show of ill feeling when a messenger arrived. Both looked troubled at his news, their reaction unsettling.

The Veientanes had sent word that Tulumnes would not be meeting with them that day. Instead, Vel Mastarna would be ambassador for Veii.

• • •

The wind was sharp and hot. The type of wind that badgers tempers and tugs at trees and flags and cloaks. It whipped the large unwieldy banners of the Romans so strongly that one flag-bearer struggled not to tip over. It had twice reefed the sacred flints and oak leaves from the fetial altar.

An open pavilion had been erected beside the Cremera, the river's surface buffeted and ruffled. On either side of the clearing the walls of the ravine loomed over the men gathered on the boundary between the lands of Rome and Veii.

Caecilia sat between Aemilius and Camillus, wedged between them like a child guarded by her parents, conscious of how the men smelled of leather and stale sweat. Marcus and Drusus stood to attention behind them, proud to be chosen to be among the sentries that guarded such dignitaries. Nearby the fetial priest prepared for the rites quietly, almost meekly, for a man who was heeded by the god of war.

The enclosure was crowded with emblems. Aside from the Wolf insignia, there were badges of individual courage also. Two centurions stood next to dozens of the silver standards and spears that had been won by the officers, while they themselves wore armbands and torques, their corselets studded with phalerae discs, decorations to warn the enemy of the type of men that both led and fought for Rome.

Aemilius had exchanged toga for armor, the breastplate a little tarnished compared to Camillus's polished and embossed corselet. Her uncle must have been jealously aware that his head was bare while the commander, like Marcus, wore an oak leaf crown.

Soon a troop of fine-legged Etruscan horses approached with plaited beribboned manes and trappings of bright-blue cloth. The elegant Veientane flags alternatively snapped or streamed out upon the contrary wind. The contingent marched to the strains of trumpet, timbrel, and cymbals, both melodic and martial compared to the raw flat notes of Roman horns.

And leading the delegation, imposing despite wearing no armor, rode Vel Mastarna. Caecilia's heart beat painfully at the sight of him. He was accompanied by those principes who had shown fickle loyalty to Tulumnes only weeks before. She itched with curiosity as to what had happened to the king, remembering how she'd last seen most of these noblemen at the Festival of Fufluns, their grotesque masks disguising little. She shuddered at the memory. Just behind Mastarna rode Arruns, his hooded eyes impassive.

Her husband looked weary. Not the tiredness that is salved by sleeping soundly or being relieved of worry, but a fatigue that seeps into bones making limbs ache. Exhaustion was etched into the creases around his eyes and the grooves from nose to mouth as permanently as his scars.

He scanned those within the pavilion, especially the fetial priest, greeting the Roman officers formally. Finally he turned to Caecilia and nodded curtly as if they'd never lain in each other's arms or whispered endearments. She looked away, wondering why she would expect him to act in any other way.

"So, Mastarna," said Aemilius when all were seated, "how is it that you and not your king attend this council?"

"Because the lords of Veii no longer support Tulumnes after the brotherhood cast him out for his hubris. Our brave lucumo has fled in fear of his life."

"And have you now claimed the crown?"

"I am no king," said Mastarna, stiffening. "I return to call elections to choose a zilath. Veii does not need an enemy on its doorstep. As Tulumnes has been deposed I wish the truce to continue."

Relieved, Caecilia smiled. There was no need to defend Rome after all. No need to risk Roman lives or for Veientanes to die.

Camillus stood and moved closer to the Etruscan. "I am afraid it is not quite that simple. There is still the matter of compensation."

At first Caecilia was unsure she'd heard correctly. Turning to Aemilius, she waited for him to counter the commander, but her uncle avoided her gaze.

Mastarna was equally confused. "What compensation?"

"Your city breached a prior treaty on commencement of the last Fidenate war. The penalty is a payment of five wagons full of gold." The commander leaned forward. "Veii broke the pact by fighting at Fidenae."

Mastarna laughed in disbelief. "That debt was erased upon signing our current treaty. You must be mad to think my people would pay such an amount after more than twenty years. I could never agree to such terms."

"Then you give Rome no choice."

"Uncle, stop this!" Caecilia grabbed Aemilius's forearm, but he shrugged her away.

All three men were standing. Caecilia wanted to join them but felt sure Camillus, if not her uncle, would physically restrain her. Mastarna addressed Aemilius alone, snubbing the commander. "Tell me this is not true."

When the consular general glanced at Camillus before he spoke, Caecilia understood that, above all else, her uncle was a politician and a hunter, weighing up benefit and disadvantage, not prepared to be bested by his subordinate. The time had passed when he could remain a dove.

"Circumstances have changed, Mastarna. I'm afraid it is no longer a question of trade tolls and corn. Rome is strong again and the plebeians are impatient. They are citizen-soldiers, not tenants."

"You mean they want land. Veientane land."

Her husband reached into his robes. Caecilia could hear his gold and onyx ring click against the tesserae box as he studied Aemilius. "Then you've already decided that a war will be waged no matter who rules Veii." His tone was icy. "You are unwise to think Rome can defeat us when it has never done so. Rasennan kings ruled you, remember."

Aemilius bridled. "And we sent the last one scuttling back to his Etruscan home."

Mastarna raised his hand. "Then from either viewpoint, it seems there is no hope of peace."

His gaze moved to Caecilia. It took her breath away to once again meet his eyes.

"Since we are talking of compensation. There is the matter of reparation owed to my city. When my wife fled from Veii the existing truce was breached. Accordingly, I demand your city pay a penalty or return her."

Startled, Caecilia half rose in her seat as Mastarna spoke to her in Rasennan.

"You were not to know what would happen, Bellatrix. But I wish you could have stayed."

"I thought escaping would help you," she stammered.

The lapse into the Etruscan language infuriated Camillus. He placed his hand upon Caecilia's shoulder, restraining her from standing. "Speak only when you are granted permission," he snapped at her. "And do so in our language."

Caecilia was deciding whether to struggle from his grip when she heard Drusus cry out in fury behind her. "You Etruscan turd! She'll be my wife," he shouted, striding across the tent and spitting in Mastarna's face, "after I kill you!"

Before the youth could take another step, Aemilius exploded in anger, barking an order for him to be removed, unable to hide surprise at the young patrician's declaration.

Two guards grappled with Drusus as they escorted him from the tent. As she watched, Caecilia felt uncomfortable for his rashness rather than flattered. He would be punished for his lack of discipline and excessive emotion—for disgracing the officers around him in front of the enemy.

Mastarna calmly wiped away the spittle with the edge of his cloak, ignoring the youth's interruption as though Drusus was no more troublesome than the buzzing of a gnat. Instead he concentrated upon Caecilia, addressing her again in Rasennan. "Come back to me, Bellatrix. Tell them you wish to come back."

Caecilia was speechless, wondering why he'd granted her forgiveness.

Aemilius raised his hand. "The matter is closed. No compensation will be paid. We will never surrender her."

"Then I repeat my request as a husband, not an ambassador."

Aemilius registered surprise, but his voice softened. "Don't you understand, Mastarna? Caecilia can no longer remain as your wife. The time has come to sever nuptial ties. You agreed to divorce her if the treaty was broken."

The wind had found its way inside her head, making it impossible to think. She heard Aemilius's words, but they were whipped up into the thoughts spinning in her head like a leaf swept from the ground and disappearing into a whirlwind. Time had sped up and she was struggling to catch up with it.

"Please let me stand," she calmly asked Camillus. She was determined to face Mastarna. She had done so on the day she wed him and was not about to be divorced without doing the same.

The commander hesitated, then relented, but Aemilius hovered close beside her.

"Under Roman law my daughter has remained under my authority even though she lived in your house," he said. "Now she has returned to reside under my roof. Caecilia has chosen Rome and so, in the presence of ten good Romans, I declare this union to be ended."

This time Mastarna's gaze was not distracted by Seianta as it had been on their Roman and Veientane wedding days. His attention was held only by Caecilia as they were divorced.

After two ceremonies and consummation upon a nuptial bed, after a year of living with this man and loving his family, their marriage was ended. Without her involvement.

Quickly and easily, with no ceremony or the taking of the auspices. Simply by a declaration spoken before ten witnesses. Just as she thought she wanted.

Yet her husband, who was no longer her husband, did not wish to let her go. "I wish I hadn't been so angry with you."

Aemilius took Caecilia's wrist, holding it down against his side painfully, his stare baleful as though guarding her from an assassin.

Stunned, Caecilia remained silent, biting her lip as her uncle's fingers dug into her flesh.

Mastarna stood with open palms. "Then if she is to remain, release her and allow us to make our farewells."

Her uncle hesitated, glancing at Camillus. The commander shrugged his shoulders, looking bemused as to how negotiations had been reduced to marital affairs.

• • •

Surrounded by the delegations of two cities, they faced each other under a canopy buffeted by a spiteful whistling wind. They spoke in Rasennan so that they could hide while in full sight.

Near him, seeing his scarred ugliness, the dark almond-shaped eyes, and short hair, smelling his scent, hearing his beautiful voice, she wished there were no Rome or Veii. That there were only Mastarna and Caecilia.

"You've taken to wearing homespun again and chewing your nails, I see," he said, smiling briefly. When he reached out to smooth his hand along her shawl, she could hear the Roman men behind her mutter, could almost feel their bodies stiffen. Conscious that their time would be cut short if they touched again, she stood inches from him, an agony of nearness.

"I don't understand why you want me."

"Because when we fought that day I forgot how young you were. How frightened you had been, a fear I fostered without knowing. Even so it was hard to believe you were in the thrall to the man I hated the most. That you'd tried to take from me what I yearned for."

"And yet you have forgiven me."

He nodded. "At the sacred spring at Velzna, with its green coolness and the aura of the divine, I remembered how you'd spoken of wanting our child in the time before we argued. And so I sought guidance as to what to do and Nortia showed me the way. Tulumnes was deposed, Apercu fled, and Vipinas raised an army against Pesna. Veii was freed from a king's madness and I stopped hating you. All I wanted was to be home. To be in our house. To be in our bed." He paused. "And then word was sent that you had gone."

A pulse started throbbing in her temple. Relieved that her uncle and Camillus could not understand what was being said, she recalled all the times Mastarna had not been angry when he could have been, how he had forgiven Artile's seduction of her into the Calu Cult, how he hadn't berated her when he'd found her spewing forth the Zeri as winter ice melted into mud and slush.

"I'm so sorry I deceived you. I'm sorry, too, that I was so hateful, but I couldn't stop thinking of you and Ulthes."

"We did nothing that needs pardon by either you or the gods."

"Yes, I understand that now, but I thought you still loved him more than me."

Mastarna touched her arm again. "How could you think that?"

Aemilius shifted closer, but Mastarna's glare stopped him interrupting further.

"I wish you could return to me," he said, reverting his attention to Caecilia. "You are no more Roman than I am."

Memories of the night with the maenads returned. "You say that, but you know it's not true. Don't you see it is better this way? I am out of place in your world—the world of the Phersu." Her voice was breaking. "And I saw what Fufluns expects of his worshippers. Knowing you follow such a god scares me."

Mastarna frowned. "I don't know what happened at the feast," he said, "but there is good and bad in everything—people, cities, even the Divine. I never made you kneel before any of our gods, Bellatrix. In Veii you always had a choice, and you chose what you thought was beautiful and comforting and thrilling. You could have remained devoted to your Roman spirits if you wished. I would not have forced you to follow my people's religion."

Caecilia's head ached. All around her were things of utility or ceremony. All angles and uniformity, solid, unadorned. In the sharp, concrete Roman world, Mastarna stood as though some mythical beast, strange as a hippocampus, mysterious as a chimera.

He spoke of choice but there had only been temptation. He spoke of love but it was corrupt. And standing there, she felt the distance between them was like a gulf even though he stood only inches away.

"But how long would it have been before you resented me for not joining in your worship? It would have been unbearable to watch you drinking Divine Milk and lying in the arms of others."

Mastarna leaned over and cupped her chin in his hand, his fingers exerting the slightest pressure. "Only Nortia could know of such a future. All that is certain is that if you'd stayed with me you would have borne our child, you would have been loved."

At the caress Aemilius seized Caecilia's elbow and yanked her back, pushing her behind Camillus and signaling the two centurions to advance toward the Etruscan.

Arruns and the other Veientane guards stepped forward, but Mastarna put up his hand to calm them, the dignity in his voice warding off the two Roman soldiers.

Caecilia tried to push her way to the front, but Marcus placed his hand upon her wrist, making her wince from the traces of his father's roughness. His palm was sweaty but his fingers were firm. "Stay here, Cilla."

"It seems I was wrong to believe you are men of honor," she heard Mastarna say. "Instead you are true Romans—bleating of virtue while you smite your foe." His tone was bitter, wounding.

"Let us dispense with these marital matters," said Camillus to the consular general.

Aemilius nodded. "It is time to keep your promise to divorce my daughter under Etruscan law."

Mastarna laughed. "You talk of promises? You talk of keeping good faith?"

Trapped behind the red cloaks and bronze armor of the two Roman leaders, Caecilia felt helpless. Time had overtaken her.

Finding strength to wrench away from Marcus, she squeezed between the general and commander so she could speak to her husband. "I love you, Mastarna. I will never forget you."

He smiled and nodded, and it was as though it was their Roman wedding day and he was squeezing her fingers in comfort.

Then, bowing deeply, he spoke in her tongue, the invisible shelter provided by his language wrenched from around them as the last link was severed. "Hear me, Aemilia Caeciliana. Your father has spoken. You are no longer my wife. I shall return your dowry. You can take your things and go."

• • •

The fetial priest covered his head with a woolen shawl, raising aloft a red dogwood spear with a charred iron tip and invoking the gods to bless his city's cause. "O Jupiter and Mars. Give us your ear! I call you to witness that Veii is unjust."

Mastarna and his men had retreated into their territory, faces solemn and hostile.

The holy man held a salver over the spear tip, but before he could consecrate the blade with pig's blood, Drusus surprised all by limping over to him and seizing the lance from his hand. Then, still with one shoulder strapped, the young soldier awkwardly tore the bandage from his calf and thrust the blade into his wound, smearing it with his own blood. He glared at Mastarna as he did so, his curses stolen by the wind.

The priest impatiently reclaimed the weapon, pointing the javelin toward enemy soil. "I, priest of the Fetial College, acting for the Roman people and the Senate, declare war upon your nation."

As he hurled the lance, the wind snatched it, causing it to waver then skitter to a stop in front of Mastarna. For a moment there was only the sound of horses snorting and pawing the ground.

Finally, the Etruscan slipped from his stallion. Picking up the spear, he lofted it high into the air where it landed, deeply embedding in the ground at Camillus's feet.

The two cities, those unrequited lovers, were at last at war.

EPILOGUE

The wind had blown itself out, leaving a humid haze rising above the road to Rome. Caecilia sat upon the rocking cart, swatting at the flies that lazily landed upon her lips and eyes until, immersed in misery, she let them crawl, sticky-footed, upon her. She was exhausted, numb, feeling that, although she had set events in motion, the result was not as she'd expected. It was as though she'd opened a door to shoo out a wasp only to have a hundred more fly in and bite her.

With war declared, Camillus and her uncle had dismissed her, her presence superfluous and shameful, her life as a Roman woman to resume without delay. Aemilius did not speak before dispatching her; instead he turned his back, pretended to adjust his breastplate, hair untidy from the wind. It was the angriest she'd ever seen him, but this did not frighten her. He had forsaken her. Self-righteousness was a shield.

There was no sign of Drusus when she returned to the encampment. He'd been confined to quarters awaiting suitable punishment for his infractions. No doubt Camillus would try to convince him not to wed a woman who might be hailed as a hero as well as a harlot.

The men who'd marched him away had been embarrassed—uncertain how to cope with a soldier whose fervor was spoken aloud for a woman instead of the state.

She thought of Mastarna, of his recklessness, his passion, his calculated wooing of death so different to the bluster and drama of the red-haired youth. What would Mastarna do now that she'd left him forever? Would he taunt Nortia to take him or would he patiently succumb to divine will, accepting that his Roman bride had gone? She could not stop remembering his look when he'd divorced her. Like the Romans had knocked off a scab upon already wounded flesh.

Marcus was allowed to say good-bye to her, at last breaking the restrained silence between them. As he checked that she was comfortable upon an uncomfortable seat, he noticed her arm was bare of adornment. "Where is my amulet?"

"I gave it to a friend. But now that you are near I no longer need such protection."

He smiled a little sadly and touched the red marks on her wrist that replaced the bracelet. It was Aemilius who had caused them but she could not forget how Marcus had gripped her wrist harshly. Just like his father. Just as Drusus would if required. The iron grasp beneath their gentleness differing only by a few degrees.

"I am sorry if I held you too tightly," he said.

"It was the fact you chose to restrain me that was painful."

His face assumed serious lines. "I will always love you, Cilla, but I cannot give you my support if you don't learn to be a Roman woman again. I listened to how you spoke to Aemilius and the commander, and I am afraid for you. Here a wife must always owe loyalty to her family above her husband. You must heed the counsel of my father again."

Caecilia brushed the flies from her face. For a moment pin-pricks of black swam before her eyes. The world was closing in on her. She braced herself, waiting for the dizziness to pass. "Don't worry, Cousin. I know our customs and rules. I know our laws and religion. They will comfort me and I will not disappoint you. I know my place."

She could tell he was checking her words for sarcasm but he need not have worried. What she said was true. To hanker after the freedom of Veii would destroy her just as returning to that city and its vices would be her ruin.

Marcus steadied the ox as it shifted in its traces. "Cilla, I didn't understand what you said to your husband but I did see how you looked at each other. You won't tell me what passed between you while you were in Veii, but it is clear to me and to all who watched that Mastarna loves you."

The young soldier glanced to where his friend was being held. "Drusus has waited for you all this time. He is hasty and rash and should not have acted as he did, but he's been faithful to you and will honor you."

He touched her arm lightly. "I also saw how you trembled at Mastarna's touch, and I don't think it was from fear. So be kind to Drusus. Let him believe you never went willingly to your husband's bed, for it would kill him to know you still love the Etruscan."

· · ·

A stalwart veteran rode beside her with a warty chin and rotten teeth. Despite his gruff demeanor, he was keen to chatter about past battles. The redness of his nose, though, suggested his appetite for ale was greater than his prowess at fighting.

Each plodding step of the ox reminded her that in a very short time she would reach the Tiber and the old weathered ferry. By nightfall she would stand on hallowed Roman ground, her life changed forever.

Covering her head with her shawl against the sun, she wished the soldier would be silent and let her stew in her own quietness as she rode upon the swaying, jolting cart.

Suddenly the soldier's mount whinnied in fear. Alarmed, Caecilia lifted her head and saw Arruns leap upon the hindquarters of the horse as does a leopard bringing down a deer.

An image flashed before her of the protector piercing the body of the bandit boy. As Arruns squeezed the man's throat until the veteran's face grew red then scarlet then purple, Caecilia screamed at him to spare the soldier who'd had the ill luck to be her escort. "In the name of Juno, please don't kill him."

The Phoenician looked doubtful but obeyed by striking the man on the side of the head, thereby granting him deep slumber and what would be a painful awakening. "Come, mistress, we must be quick," he said, lifting her from the wagon.

"Let me go. I am no longer your mistress."

Arruns grunted, sweat breaking upon his brow. It was clear there was no time to talk even if he'd wanted to. "Please, my lady!" He extended his arm to her as if he were offering to accompany her, a gentleman with a snake tattooed upon his face.

Once she had been afraid of him, thought him the strangest man in the world, the symbol of what she most loathed in Veii, and yet she knew he was faithful to her, that he would never harm her.

"Why have you come here?"

"Master sent me. He wishes you to have a chance to choose Rome or him."

Caecilia sank to the ground, not knowing what to think or feel. Heat coursed through her chest, through to her throat. Mastarna's persistence was overwhelming. Once again the tight center of safety Rome offered had been surrounded by him, leaving her suspended between the two. Compelling her to give him an answer after all, to sift through the shallows and depths of what her life had been before and decide whether it could be again. Making her decide if she loved him enough.

Freedom was terrifying. Ahead of her lay Rome, where she would find rectitude and safety. And behind her was his city—danger and love.

Arruns helped her to her feet, anxious to leave. "I will make sure you are guided to wherever you choose."

Fumbling inside his tunic he drew out Mastarna's golden tesserae box, shaking the dice onto his palm and offering them to her. "From the master. He also said to tell you, where you are Gaia, he is Gaius."

The dice were worn on the corners, so worn that the peculiar symbols were hard to decipher on some of the surfaces. Mastarna no longer used them at the tables; his opponents would not allow it. But he never went anywhere without them. They were his luck.

She thought of how many times she'd knelt before Uni's altar and begged and prayed and cried for Fortuna to listen to her pleas; remembered, too, Artile's soft hands upon her soul and Mastarna's tender ones upon her heart. One man urging her to postpone destiny, the other showing her that Fate could not be controlled.

The Phoenician stretched out his palm to her, willing her to take the tesserae.

To go with him meant she would be cut off from her people. And, no matter what Mastarna may promise, most in Veii would not see her as other than the daughter of a foe.

She had no doubt, either, that if the Romans breached the wall of Veii they would kill her—vengeance for humiliation. And she thought briefly of Marcus and Drusus, wondering if they, too, would come to believe she should die in such a way.

Caecilia studied the baubles in the calloused, grimy hand. They were hers now to either use or not. Should she keep them as a reminder of what they'd lost? Or perhaps she should let Nortia show her hand? After all, she'd gambled with them before and they had changed her life. Or should she, once again, stand before Mastarna to renew her vows, offering the tesserae as a humble dowry?

Arruns was impatiently scouting the clearing. Caecilia stared at him, afraid to look either ahead or behind her. Her legs unsteady, her pulse too fast.

She smiled, curling her fingers around the dice.

They were smooth to the touch.

GLOSSARY

Acheron: In Greek mythology, the river of sorrow in the Underworld; in Etruscan religion, the Afterworld or the Beyond, a place to which the dead journeyed over land and sea.

Alabastron: A small flask for perfume or fragrant oils originally fashioned from alabaster but later made from pottery, metal, or glass.

Arx: Citadel or fortified high ground within a city.

Auspices: Before any decision of state was made, omens were observed and interpreted. This involved watching the flight of birds. To do this one needed *patrician* blood. Only certain magistrates such as a *consul* or *censor* could take the public auspices, i.e., as opposed to the head of the household observing omens for private purposes.

Bondsman: A debtor who forfeited his liberty to his creditor to satisfy his debts. He was enslaved until he paid back what he owed.

Bulla: A locket of metal or leather worn to ward off evil spirits. It was removed when a Roman boy reached manhood at fourteen. A Roman girl wore a similar amulet, which was removed

on the eve of her wedding. Etruscans wore bullas throughout
their lives.

Cantharus: A two-handled drinking cup sacred to the god
Dionysus (Greek), Bacchus (Roman) and Fufluns (Etruscan).

Censor: One of two magistrates who were ex-*consuls*. This magistrate, among other duties, supervised public morals and con-
ducted the census. A censor was entitled to take the public
auspices that preceded every major action taken on the state's
behalf.

Cepen: Common word for an Etruscan priest.

Chimera: A mythical beast that was comprised of the parts of a
lion, goat, and snake. It was defeated by the hero, Bellerophon.

Chiton: A long robe worn by both men and women alike in Etruria
and Greece. It was similar to the Roman tunic. During the
classical period, Etruscan ladies wore linen chitons that clung
so tightly to the body that the breasts and nipples showed
through the material. It was usually worn with a mantle of
heavier cloth.

Cista: A small casket, usually cylindrical in shape, used for keeping
cosmetics, perfumes, or jewelry.

Comitium: The open-air area in Rome where the *plebeian* and
tribal assemblies met. The speakers' platform was located here.
The Comitium stood opposite the *Curia* or *Senate House*.

Consul: One of two magistrates with *imperium* who held the
highest position in the Roman Republic. Both consuls had
the right of veto over each other and were entitled to take the
public *auspices* that preceded every major action taken on the
state's behalf.

Consular General: A military tribune with consular powers. For
many years in the early Roman Republic, military tribunes
were elected instead of *consuls* because generals were needed
on so many war fronts. As *imperium* was not granted, *plebeians* could hold the office. *Censors* took the public *auspices* on

behalf of the military tribunes to enable decisions of state to be made.

Cuirass/Corselet: Body armor consisting of a breastplate and backplate made from metal, leather, or stiffened linen.

Curia (Curia Hostilia): The Senate House in the Roman Forum.

Fascinum: A phallic-shaped amulet worn around the neck. The regenerative power of the phallus was seen as a powerful force against the evil eye.

Fibula: A clasp or brooch used to secure a cloak or worn as an ornament. Simple ones were the shape of a large safety pin.

Fillet: Bands of wool that a Roman matron would plait into her hair. They were a symbol of a female married Roman citizen, as was the *stola.*

Flammeum: The "flame"-colored veil worn by Roman brides. There is dispute as to its actual color. Some sources refer to it as the yellow of a candle flame, others as orange. Weld (*resida lutea*) or expensive saffron was used to dye the cloth.

Forum, the: A rectangular plaza in the valley between the Capitoline and Palatine Hills. It was the political and social center of Rome.

Fulgurator: An Etruscan priest skilled in interpreting the will of the gods through analysis of different types of lightning and thunder.

Greaves: Armor that could protect either the shins only or the entire leg to the thigh depending on the wealth of the soldier.

Haruspex: An Etruscan priest skilled in the art of haruspicy, i.e., dissecting a sacrificial animal's liver for the purpose of divination. A haruspex wore a distinctive hat that twisted to a point. He also wore a sheepskin cloak fastened by a *fibula* at the throat and carried a *lituus* staff.

Hetaera: Literally meaning a "companion" in ancient Greek, a hetaera was an educated courtesan kept by a patron and who entertained men in symposiums or in their own salons.

Hippocampus: A mythical beast that was half horse and half fish.

Honored Way (Cursus Honorum): The method by which a man rose to the supreme office of *consul*; a political ladder whereby a man was elected to certain magistracies in prescribed order and only after reaching a particular age.

Hoplite: A citizen soldier in the heavy infantry who fought in a phalanx formation and was recognizable by his round "hoplon" shield.

Imperium: Supreme authority in Rome including command in war, interpretation and execution of the law, and the right to inflict punishment. The ability to take the public *auspices*, which preceded every major action taken on the state's behalf, was granted along with imperium.

Juno: A divine essence that acted as a protecting spirit or the "guardian angel" of a woman. It could be represented in effigy or by cameo. Men called such a spirit their "genius." Juno was also the Roman Mother Goddess and the wife of Jupiter, king of the gods.

Kottabos: Drinking game where wine dregs were thrown at a small disc on a stand with the aim of filling it to the extent that it was knocked onto a larger disc suspended below to make a sound like a bell.

Laws of the Twelve Tables: The legislation that formed the basis of the constitution and customary law (*mos maiorum*) of the Roman Republic. The laws were inscribed on twelve bronze (or ivory) tablets that were displayed in the Forum.

League of the Twelve: Economic and religious confederation of major Etruscan cities. There is conjecture as to exactly which cities were included in the League, but I have included those considered most likely on the map using their Etruscan names.

Lictor: In Rome, one of twelve civil servants who protected the kings, and later those magistrates holding *imperium*. They carried a bundle of rods called the fasces, the symbol of power and authority. *Consuls* were entitled to twelve lictors. The tradition of the lictor and fasces was believed to derive from the Etruscan kings.

Lituus: Crooked staff used by augurs to mark out a ritual space for the purpose of divination.

Lucumo: An Etruscan king who was elected by aristocratic colleges rather than all citizens. He remained in office until his death. However, the exact nature of the Etruscan political power structure and its mechanisms has not yet been determined.

Maenad: A priestess who followed the god Dionysus (Greek), Bacchus (Roman), and Fufluns (Etruscan), was reputed to dance in an ecstatic trance during Dionysian rites, and who wore distinctive clothing such as leopard-skin cloaks.

Maru: The name used for an Etruscan magistrate who may have headed a college of a religious cult. However, the exact nature of the Etruscan political and religious power structures and their mechanisms has not yet been determined.

Mollis/molles: The pejorative Latin name given to men who were exclusively homosexual rather than bisexual.

Palla: A long, rectangular-shaped cloak worn by Roman women that could be wrapped around the body and thrown over one shoulder or drawn over the head. It was associated with Roman matrons.

Patera/ae: A shallow dish used to make libations to the gods.

Patrician/s: Wealthy landowners of noble birth who traced their ancestry to the original founders of Rome and claimed to have "divine" blood. They held the highest positions of power during the time of the early Roman Republic.

People's Tribune/s (Tribune of the Plebs): Ten officials elected to protect the rights of *plebeians* as they held the power to veto decrees of the *Senate*, and actions of magistrates. As such they could hinder the levy and funding of troops. It was the only political position a *plebeian* could hold in the early Roman

Republic. Their person was sacrosanct and inviolate and as such, the death penalty could be inflicted on those who interfered with the exercise of their power.

Phalerae: Gold, silver, or bronze discs awarded for valor and worn on a breastplate during parades.

Phersu: A masked man who performed blood sacrifices during Etruscan funeral games. He was the precursor to a Roman gladiator.

Plebeian/s: Roman citizens that were not *patricians*. They were denied the right to hold magistracies during the time of the early Roman Republic.

Porne/Pornai: Greek word for common prostitutes. In contrast, flute girls entertained men with music at *symposiums* and also granted sexual favors.

Princip/Principes: Etruscan aristocrats who held power to elect leaders and participate in government. However, the exact nature of the Etruscan political power structure and its mechanisms has not yet been determined.

Rhyton: A bowl used for mixing wine and water.

Saeculum/Saecula: Time period of variable length, the end of which was determined by omens.

Satyr: A male companion of the wine god Dionysus (Greek) or Fufluns (Etruscan) depicted with horse's ears and tail, and sometimes a horse's phallus.

Senate: An advisory council consisting of ex-magistrates but in effect the most powerful governing body in Rome. A senatorial decree (*senatus consultum*) had no formal authority but was generally always made into law.

Senator: A member of the Roman Senate. Senators only qualified to be elected if they had previously held office as a magistrate and were wealthy. Senators were entitled to wear a toga bordered in purple and a tunic with a broad purple stripe.

Silphion: A plant believed to be of the Ferula genus. It was used in antiquity as a seasoning (laserpicium) but was more famously known for its contraceptive qualities. It was the primary export of the North African city of Cyrene. Due to its efficacy, the plant was so much in demand that it was farmed out and is now extinct.

Skene: In ancient Greek drama, a building where costumes and props were kept and upon which background scenes were painted. It was located behind the stage platform.

Stola: A long, sleeveless, pleated dress worn over a tunic. It was fastened at the shoulders with *fibulae* and worn with two belts, one beneath the breasts, and the other around the waist. The stola and woolen hair *fillets* were the symbols of a married female Roman citizen.

Strigil: A metal instrument used to scrape off dirt and sweat from the skin.

Symposium: A drinking party in ancient Greece where men met to discuss politics, philosophy, and culture and were entertained by musicians, poetry, flute girls, games, athletic displays, etc.

Tebenna: A rounded length of cloth worn by Etruscan men over a chiton as a cloak. It was similar in appearance to a toga but shorter.

Tesserae: A game that was usually played with two dice shaken in a cup and then tossed onto a gaming table. Dice were also referred to as tesserae.

Thyrsus: A staff of giant fennel tipped with a pinecone and entwined with ivy which was associated with the god Dionysus (Greek), Bacchus (Roman), and Fufluns (Etruscan).

Toga: A rounded length of cloth derived from the Etruscan *tebenna* that was draped as a cloak over a tunic. It was the distinctive garment of a male Roman citizen. Magistrates and senators were entitled to wear a purple border on their tunics and togas.

Torque: A necklace of twisted metal open at the front.

Tufa: A form of limestone. The Italian regions of Tuscany and Lazio where the Etruscan cities were located were famous for the tunnels that could be carved out of this soft stone. Tufa could be red, gray, or yellow in color.

Univir: A married Roman woman who did not remarry after she was widowed. Literally meaning "one man"; highly esteemed in the Republican Rome.

Zilath: Chief magistrate of an Etruscan city with similar authority to a Roman *consul.* He was elected each year by aristocratic colleges rather than all citizens. However, the exact nature of the Etruscan political power structure and its mechanisms has not yet been determined.

AUTHOR'S NOTE

More than ten years ago I found a photo of a sixth-century BC sarcophagus upon which a husband and wife were sculpted in a pose of affection. The image of the lovers intrigued me. What ancient culture acknowledged women as equals to their husbands? Or exalted marital fidelity with such open sensuality? Discovering the answer led me to the decadent and mystical Etruria and the war between early Rome and Veii.

When ancient Italy is mentioned, most think of Rome as the dominant culture. Yet the Etruscans had built a sophisticated and extensive civilization well before the Romans were fighting turf wars with other Latin tribes such as the Sabini, Volscii, and Aequi. At one stage Etruscan kings ruled Rome, the third and last of which was expelled after the tragic rape of Lucretia. In fact, at its height, Etruria and its settlements extended throughout the modern regions of Umbria, Emilia-Romagna, Tuscany, Lazio, and part of Campania, and also dominated trade routes stretching from the Black Sea to northern Africa.

The Etruscans were called Tusci or Etrusci by the Romans, and the Tyrrhenoi by the Greeks, while referring to themselves as the Rasenna. Over the years there has been much conjecture as to whether they migrated from Asia Minor (first mentioned in the accounts of the Greek historian Herodotus, who wrote of the legendary journey of the wily Prince Tyrrhenus); however, it is now accepted that the Etruscans were indigenous to Italy.

Learning the two rival cities of Rome and Veii were situated only twelve miles apart across the Tiber gave me the idea of exploring the prejudices between the society of the hedonistic Etruscans and that of the austere emergent Rome. And so, the story of a marriage of a Roman girl to an Etruscan man was born.

Although recent archaeological digs are revealing more about the Etruscans, their civilization has often been dubbed "mysterious" because no literature has survived other than remnants of ritual texts. Instead, their world is revealed through their fantastic art. Engraved mirrors, funerary sculpture, and paintings, as well as votives, furniture, and utensils give us a glimpse into their world and, in turn, serve as a rich vein of inspiration for episodes within the book. As for the authenticity of the scenes I describe, I have attempted to be consistent with current historians' views, but ultimately I present my own interpretation of how Etruscans might have lived.

In contrasting the two societies it was important to portray early Rome as opposed to the more familiar eras of the later Republic and Empire. Unfortunately, most of the history of both the nascent Rome and its Etruscan enemy comes from accounts recorded by historians many centuries later through the prism of their times. In effect, the conquerors of Etruria wrote about Etruscan history with all the prejudices of the victor over the vanquished.

Another source of knowledge about Etruscan culture is fragments of texts from contemporary travelers to their cities, which were quoted by later historians. These Greek commentators (who came from a society that repressed women) often described the licentiousness and opulence of the Etruscans and the wickedness of their wives. The validity of these fragments is often criticized by modern historians because of their authors' prejudices. One notorious example is Theopompus of Chios, a fourth-century BC Greek historian, who expressed his shock at the profligacy of the Etruscans.

Theopompus wrote, among other scurrilous observations, that his hosts had open intercourse with prostitutes, courtesans, boys, and even wives at their banquets. Furthermore, "They make love and disport themselves, occasionally within view of each other, but more often they surround their beds with screens, made of interwoven branches over which they spread their mantles" (fragment from *Histories*, Book 43 of Theopompus of Chios, as quoted by Athenaeus in *The Learned Banquet*, sourced from Sybille Haynes, *Etruscan Civilization*, The J. Paul Getty Trust, 2000, pp. 256–57).

From studying Etruscan tomb art, it is clear these people celebrated life: dancing in what appears to be ecstasy, and with wives dining in tight sheer robes as they sat drinking wine next to their husbands. Many worshipped Fufluns, the Greek Dionysus and Roman Bacchus, whose later cult adherents were famous for indulging in debauchery. Yet Theopompus's views seemed at odds with the commitment that is also depicted between Etruscan couples in funerary art. So which version was correct? In the end I concluded that his account couldn't be completely discounted because the concept of a society that condones female promiscuity while also honoring wives and mothers is not necessarily contradictory. For while it can be erroneous to compare modern societies with ancient ones, it could be argued that this attitude to females occurs in many present-day Western cultures. With this in mind, I devised the concept of melding fidelity with sexual abandon through the act of "lying beneath the reed."

To demonstrate why it was so extraordinary for the Etruscans to afford high status and independence to their women, I compared the equivalent attitudes of the Greeks and Romans to females

in daily life. In doing so I described the lives of slave and courtesan, maid and matron, through the Grecian Cytheris and Erene
and the Roman Caecilia and Aemilia together with the Etruscan
Larthia and Seianta.

An understanding of the attitude to female sexuality was also
needed. This research was fascinating to say the least. It soon
became evident that Roman and Greek sexual morals involved
a complex construct that makes our modern-day gender politics pale in comparison. Sex was seen from a frame of reference
of male bisexuality rather than the polarities of heterosexual or
homosexual love. Power and status was all-important. There was
an emphasis on class distinction and the dominance or passiv-
ity of participants rather than gender—that is, the concept of the
lover and beloved. Women, freedmen, and slaves were all considered on a lower level to freeborn men. Lesbianism was completely
taboo, as the idea of a woman preferring another woman over a
man was unthinkable. Accordingly, whether a woman might enjoy
sex was irrelevant. The conception of children, preferably male,
was the primary purpose. In the case of the Etruscans, however, I
concluded that their men might vary from Greeks and Romans in
their attitude to women's sexual gratification as it's established that
they afforded women equal status. Certainly, the visible expressions of undying love, as depicted in funerary art, would seem to
support this.

There is ample evidence to confirm that male sex was practiced in Etruria as well as in Greece and Rome. Ancient historians
speak of the Etruscans' inordinate love for youths and boys, and
Etruscan tomb art displays it. I doubt, however, that their men's
concern over status would have differed from the Greeks' and
Romans'; that is, aristocratic freeborn warriors could not be seen
to be subservient to a male slave or freedman or, indeed, another
freeborn man. Again, bisexuality was the defining force with sex
between males, and it was not necessarily considered in the same

way as we view gay sex today. In fact, homophobia was just as prevalent then as it is now. In Rome homosexuals were called "molles," meaning soft. As for pederasty, as far as I am aware, there is no evidence either way as to whether this was observed in Etruria. Its culture, though, was heavily influenced by the Greeks, and in city-states like Athens, Sparta, and Thebes noblemen were known to teach young freeborn boys of their civic and military obligations through this practice. Accordingly, in also portraying men's sexuality in the book, I explored the ancient world's rationale for pederasty, and the psychology and hypocrisy behind that custom.

Drugs such as qat (Catha Edulis) and opium (Papaver Somniferum) were used in the ancient world, together with aphrodisiacs containing poisonous ingredients like mandrake, or "mandragora." Nevertheless, the names "Catha," (after the Etruscan sun goddess, Catha, and the plant genus) "Zeri" (meaning "serene" or "free" in Etruscan) and the love potion "Alpan" (after Venus/Turan's handmaiden) are my own suggestions. "Magic" toadstools were also used during religious ecstatic ritual, with their toxicity diluted via what I called "Divine Milk"—that is, the milk or urine of reindeers that had eaten the fungi.

Pomegranates were used for contraceptive purposes, but I was unable to find any conclusive evidence as to their efficacy. Silphion, however, may have been effective because it is now extinct, presumably because demand outstripped supply. It was the main commodity for Cyrene, with that city's coins bearing an image of the plant.

The Etruscans followed the tenets of the Etrusca Disciplina, with its complex branches of haruspicy, divination, and interpretation of lightning. Their belief in prophecy and the proroguing of fate was raised to a science. In fact, the prediction of their civilization's demise after ten sacred saecula appears to have come true. Unfortunately, as the Syracusans seized control of Etruria's trade routes and the Romans slowly dominated its cities, the more life-affirming cult of Fufluns was overtaken by a death cult preoccupied with the torments of the journey to the afterlife.

The characters that appear in the novel are fictitious, except for those referred to in ancient history and legend. The fame of Marcus Furius Camillus, who is mentioned by the Roman historian Livy and named the second founder of Rome by the Greek biographer Plutarch, is still recognized by modern Romans—Furio Camillo is an underground metro station in Rome. However, any character-istics I may have attributed to him are purely my own invention. Livy also wrote of the valiant Mamercus Aemilius who led Rome to victory in two Fidenate wars (for simplicity, I chose to compress these two conflicts into one). The stories of Lars Tolumnius (Laris Tulumnes), Lucretia, and Verginia all featured in the histories of Rome. A consular general named Manlius Aemilius Mamercus (upon which I modeled Caecilia's Uncle Aemilius) is also men-tioned by Livy, but no details of his life are provided.

When I finally made a pilgrimage to Veii I found very little remains other than a few archaeological sites in the beautiful Parco di Veio national park. It was pleasing, though, to think that the old city, once considered the most splendid in Etruria, may still lie buried among wooded ravines and open spaces rather than under asphalt and concrete.

As for the sixth-century BC married couple, I finally saw them in the Louvre in 2003. The memory of our meeting still makes me smile.

A bibliography is available on my website (www.elisabeth-storrs.com/research.html), but sources I found of particular value in my research included: Sybille Haynes's *Etruscan Civilization* (The J. Paul Getty Trust, 2000); Eva Cantarella's *Bisexuality in the Ancient World* (Yale University Press, 1992); editors Nancy De Grummond and Erika Simon's *The Religion of the Etruscans*

(University of Texas Press, 2006); Jean-René Jannot's *Religion of Ancient Etruria* (University of Wisconsin, 2005); and Livy's *The Early History of Rome* (translated by A. de Selincourt, Penguin Books, 1971).

THE GOLDEN DICE

If you enjoyed reading *The Wedding Shroud* and would like to see what happens next, here is an extract from *The Golden Dice*, the second book in the Tales of Ancient Rome series.

"Skilfully plotted and with vividly drawn characters, *The Golden Dice* is a suspenseful, romantic, exciting drama . . ."
Sherry Jones, author of *Four Sisters, All Queens*

During a bitter siege between Rome and the Etruscan city of Veii, three women follow different paths to survive.

Caecilia, Roman born but Etruscan wed, forsakes Rome to return to her husband, Vel Mastarna, exposing herself to the enmity of his people while knowing the Romans will give her a traitor's death if Veii falls. Semni, a reckless Etruscan servant in the House of Mastarna, embroils herself in schemes that threaten Caecilia's son and Semni's own chance for love. Pinna, a destitute Roman prostitute, uses coercion to gain the attention of Rome's greatest general at the risk of betraying Caecilia's cousin.

Each woman struggles to protect herself and those whom she loves in the dark cycle of war. What must they do to challenge Fate? And will they ever live in peace again?

The Golden Dice, the sequel to *The Wedding Shroud*, is the second book in the Tales of Ancient Rome series. The third book, *Call to Juno*, will be published in 2016.

The Golden Dice was judged runner-up in the 2013 international Sharp Writ Book Awards in general fiction, and was named as one of the top memorable reads of 2013 by Sarah Johnson, the reviews editor of the *Historical Novels Review*.

THE
GOLDEN
DICE

— A Tale of Ancient Rome —

ELISABETH STORRS

THE GOLDEN DICE

VEII, WINTER 399 BC

He smelled of leather, horse, and beeswax polish, the bronze of his armor cold against her despite her heavy woolen cloak. When he kissed her, though, hard and hungrily, his mouth and tongue were warm despite chill lips and cheeks.

"You need to take this off," she said, as she always did, pressing against the corselet, needing the feel of his body.

"Don't worry, I plan to," he replied, as he always did, then laughed and kissed her.

She could not move away from him, arms tightening around his waist, not trusting that he had returned, that another year had passed and he had not been killed.

For there were only two seasons now: war and winter.

Before this, it had been summer that made Caecilia smile with its lazy heat and languid evenings. But after seven years of conflict, she welcomed the hint of ice in the north wind and the bare stripped branches of trees ready to bear the burden of snow. Short days and long darkness no longer seemed oppressive because, in winter, her husband would come home.

Another long, clear note of the war trumpets sounded. Still holding Mastarna close, Caecilia turned her head to scan the tumult around her, glad the horns did not herald a charge but instead a return, as line after line of soldiers entered through the massive Menerva Gates of the Etruscan city of Veii.

The vast town square and wide avenues seethed with the color of the massed crowd, and timber- and terra-cotta-clad houses and temples were gaudy with garlands and ribbons. As the army marched into the forum a surge of people breached its formation, military discipline forgotten as wives and children hastened to kiss husbands and fathers while mothers and older men embraced sons.

Amid the throng, fine, long-legged warhorses shifted and whinnied as they were held fast, steam rising from their hides in the coldness of the afternoon, hot breath snorting from their nostrils. Adding to the clamor were laughter and merry tunes from double pipe, castanet, and timbrel, interrupted by snatches of sobbing, the lament of women whose men had not returned: a tragic counterpoint to celebration.

Caecilia could not ignore their sorrow. Even in her happiness a tight knot of apprehension remained, the voice that told her this reunion was due to respite in conflict, not its resolution. She chided herself not to sour the sweetness of Mastarna's return with the anticipation of his inevitable departure.

There was a rhythm to the fighting.

When the war season began with the lengthening of days and the greening of fields, the Veientanes would ride out to meet the Romans, who were assaulting Veii with a dogged vengeance. A vengeance sought in the name of Aemilia Caeciliana. A vengeance sought against her.

For seven years Caecilia had watched the Romans, who were once her people, hew pickets and planks and stakes from Veientane woodland to build stockades and siege engines to surround her adopted city, hindering trade, blocking supplies, and raiding farmlands until, by bright autumn and the falling of leaves, Veii's patience would falter as it waited for winter and the enemy to retreat. Each city pausing. Licking its wounds. For Roman bellies needed to be fed, too. Roman crops needed to be sown: barley and pulses and wheat. Roman families needed to embrace their men, and Roman generals needed to be elected.

Mastarna's cheek, heavy with bristle, brushed against hers, his own apprehension hinted in his deep, low voice, a voice whose timbre always stirred her. "And the baby?"

Smiling, she broke from him and searched for two women who stood jostled by those celebrating around them. Both were grinning as they observed husband and wife. The stout, wiry-haired maid called Cytheris gripped one hand each of two small boys while the nursemaid, Aricia, stepped forward on command and handed a swaddled bundle to her mistress.

"Another son," Caecilia said proudly.

Mastarna took the babe with the confidence of a man practiced in such a task. Even so, the mother wondered at the sight of a warrior cradling soft tininess against the hard contours of his corselet.

Exchanging his nurse's warmth for the cold comfort of his father's armor didn't please the child. His protests were loud and strident. Unperturbed, Mastarna chuckled, planting a kiss upon the baby's head as he hugged Caecilia once again. "Thank you. I could have no better wife."

"Nor I a better husband." She reclaimed the bawling baby who settled immediately at her touch.

"Now where are those other sons of mine?" Mastarna turned to face his older children. Wide-eyed and wary of the scarred, metal-clad giant who had returned into their lives, the boys were speechless.

Mastarna's thigh-high greaves grated as he crouched down beside them. "Don't tell me you've forgotten me?"

The older boy was solemn, bowing in greeting. "Of course I know who you are, Apa. Hail, General Vel Mastarna!"

"Hail, my son," said his father with equal seriousness before placing his leather-lined bronze helmet upon the boy, engulfing him. The child pulled it back, tilting his head so he could spy the world through the slits between nose and cheek pieces, both hands held firmly on either side to bear the weight.

Seeing his brother gaining such favor, the two-year-old forgot his awe of the warrior. He hastened from behind Cytheris's skirts, bounding over to wrest the trophy from the other. "Give me, Tas, give me!"

The five-year-old turned away, raising the bright-blue crested helmet firmly out of reach, not prepared to surrender his prize. "Go away, Larce. Apa gave it to me."

Mastarna laughed and lifted his younger son onto his hip. The boy's startled expression changed to one of glee as he caught sight of the curved sword strapped to his father's side. "Look, Ati," he shrieked at his mother, gripping the hilt. "Sword! Sword!" Despite struggling to remove the weapon from its sheath it remained secure.

"Hello, Caecilia."

A soldier stood beside her with open arms. It took a moment to recognize the bearded man as Tarchon. Mastarna's other son. Adopted. Little older than she was. The thought was sobering. In spring she would be twenty-six.

There was no sign of the effeminate youth she once knew. He was a man now, boasting battle scars. What warrior did not, after so many years of war? Nevertheless, his fine face was unscathed, its beautiful symmetry incongruous against the blatant masculinity of bronze.

"Thank the gods you have been spared." She hugged him.

Tarchon returned the embrace, cautious of the bundle of boy squeezed between them.

"Thank the gods also that you bore my brother safely." He touched the baby's cheek gently with one finger and was rewarded with a smile. It was no surprise. Tarchon pleased everyone—everyone except his father.

"He has your big, round Roman eyes, but I won't hold that against him."

Caecilia frowned, glancing at the sloe-eyed Etruscans around her. She doubted they'd ever forgive her for being a daughter of Rome. "Yes, but others might."

Tarchon kissed her cheek. "I'm only teasing. Besides, all here respect you now."

Before she could reply, Mastarna interrupted. "Isn't it time I named my new son?" He swung Larce to the ground. The boy immediately grasped his leg, demanding to be returned to the heights. Cytheris quickly drew him away.

Caecilia nodded. Ever since her son was born she'd been anxious to perform the ceremony. After all, the child was two months old and rightly should have been claimed within nine days of his birth. There was always an undercurrent of concern within her. What if Mastarna did not return? Would the right of this boy to take his father's name be questioned? What would become of her, no longer Roman but never Etruscan, if her husband should die?

"What name have you chosen?"

"Arnth. After Arnth Ulthes, our great friend."

Mastarna searched her face. "Are you sure?"

"Very sure. It is a strong name, given in honor of a noble man."

"He would be pleased that you wish to remember him." He stroked her hair. "Now let me claim him."

Despite her desire for the rite to be performed, Caecilia hesitated at the thought of placing the child at his father's feet. The crowd around them was unruly and she was afraid that the horses could trample the baby.

Then she noticed Arruns, Mastarna's guard—head shaven, the snake tattoo upon his face adding, as always, a rugged menace to him. Without needing an order he cleared a space around the family, holding the reins of his master's horse tight.

Laying the baby on the cobblestones, Caecilia anxiously watched as Mastarna lifted him above his head.

"All present here bear witness that this boy is my son. His name shall be Arnth of the House of Mastarna. Child of my loins and that of Aemilia Caeciliana's—known to all as Caecilia."

Unlike Larce, the infant did not enjoy being raised in the air, screaming with a fierceness at odds with his size. Mastarna hastily lowered him, holding him close, before taking a gold amulet necklace from Caecilia and placing it around the little boy's neck.

"May this bulla protect you forever from the evil eye. May all the great and almighty gods watch over you!"

Caecilia took the sobbing baby from his father, soothing him once again. As she did so, she noticed that the crowd around them had quieted. She tensed, holding her breath, aware their stares were reserved for her, their silence signaling resentment of her as much as respect for Mastarna.

And she knew why that must be.

Seven years ago, in a glade beside a river between two cities, she had made a choice to forsake her home. A choice Rome claimed provoked a war. And she had questioned that decision many times. Not because she did not love her husband but because his people did not love her.

She knew what to do today, though. Had done it before. She slowly held Arnth out to the crowd. "I give my son to this city. Another man-child to bear arms for Veii. Another warrior for you who have become my people."

There was no response at first, their gaze wavering from her to the baby and then to the warrior.

Then cheering erupted. "Hail, Arnth of the House of Mastarna! Hail, General Vel Mastarna!"

Relief filled her, reassured in that moment to know that, even if the Veientanes hated her, she was safe as long as they revered her husband.

ACKNOWLEDGMENTS

Special thanks to my husband, David Storrs, without whom I would never have completed this book, and who overcame his ambivalence to historical fiction to read it and make valuable suggestions. To my sons, Andrew and Lucas, who have only ever known a mother who forgot sometimes to return from Etruria and start cooking dinner, and to their grandma, Jacqui Storrs. To my father, John Drane, who first gave me a love of ancient history, and my mother, Beth, who encouraged me to use my imagination—I am sad they did not live to read the novel.

Many thanks also to Natalie Scott, who has been a wonderful mentor for as long as I have been writing, together with patient members of my writing group who listened to all my versions over ten years—particularly Cecilia Rice, who continued to encourage me after each rejection. Thanks to Joyce Kornblatt, my other mentor, who convinced me to think of myself as a writer and helped me find a new voice to tell the story; my agent, Gaby Naher, who championed the book, and my Australian copyeditor, Catherine Taylor, who has always supported my vision of the stubborn, vulnerable, and courageous Caecilia.

Enormous thanks to the Lake Union team, and to the delightful Jodi Warshaw in particular, who was prepared to offer an opportunity to an Aussie author to reach a wider readership, and to Michelle Hope Anderson, my American copyeditor, who has ensured the book is the best it could be. Special thanks to the generous Ursula Le Guin who was prepared to endorse an unknown author's novel together with kind reviews from Isolde Martyn, Judith Fox, and Ben Kane. Thanks also to the wonderful group of authors at HFeBooks, particularly M. Louisa Locke and Rebecca Lochlann. A big hug for Lisi Schappi for designing my website (www.elisabethstorrs.com) and blog, Triclinium (www.elisabeth-storrs.com/category/blog/triclinium), and to Rod Crundwell for composing some "Etruscan music" to accompany the images. I'm also grateful to Kate Duigan for producing the map. Thanks to Mumtaz Mustafa for designing the beautiful cover, and to Tom Greenwood from Greenwood Studios for doing such a professional job in producing the photo of the lovely Marcella Wilkinson who generously offered to model for the cover.

Finally, many thanks as well to all those not mentioned who have supported, encouraged, and given valuable advice over the course of the writing of this book.

ABOUT THE AUTHOR

Elisabeth Storrs has long held an interest in the history, myths, and legends of the ancient world. She is an Australian author and graduated from the University of Sydney in Arts Law, having studied Classics. She lives with her husband and two sons in Sydney, Australia, and over the years has worked as a solicitor, corporate lawyer, and governance consultant. She is a director of the NSW Writers' Centre and one of the founders of the Historical Novel Society Australasia.

The Wedding Shroud is the first book in the Tales of Ancient Rome series. The sequel, *The Golden Dice*, is now available. The third volume, *Call To Juno*, is currently being written.

The Wedding Shroud and its sequel, *The Golden Dice*, were judged runners-up in the international Sharp Writ Book Awards for general fiction in 2012 and 2013, respectively. *The Golden Dice* was also named as one of the top memorable reads of 2013 by Sarah Johnson, the reviews editor for the *Historical Novels Review.*

Recently, Elisabeth has written "Dying for Rome: Lucretia's Tale," the first short story in her collection *Short Tales of Ancient Rome*, in which she retells the history and legends of Rome from a fresh perspective.

Elisabeth would love you to connect with her on Facebook (www.facebook.com/pages/Elisabeth-Storrs), Twitter (www .twitter.com/elisabethstorrs), or via her blog, Triclinium (www .elisabethstorrs.com/category/blog/triclinium). And you are welcome to visit her website (www.elisabethstorrs.com) for more information on her books and to sign up for her newsletter.

Please consider leaving a review of *The Wedding Shroud* with your thoughts at the point of purchase. A line or two can make a big difference and is much appreciated.